SIREN

A TWISTED HEROES NOVEL

R.J. LEWIS   A.R. ROSE

Authors Note

A Siren is a fantasy romance reimagining created for adults. Reader discretion is advised. A Siren contains content that may be triggering for some, as well as sexually explicit content.

Your mental health matters. For a full list of content warnings, please visit www.authorarrose.com/content-warnings.

A MERMAID HAS NOT AN IMMORTAL SOUL,
NOR CAN SHE OBTAIN ONE UNLESS SHE WINS
THE LOVE OF A HUMAN BEING. ON THE
POWER OF ANOTHER HANGS HER DESTINY.
HANS CHRISTIAN ANDERSON

To all the girls who loved playing mermaids as a child, who now wouldn't mind being on their knees for a pirate.

This book is for you.

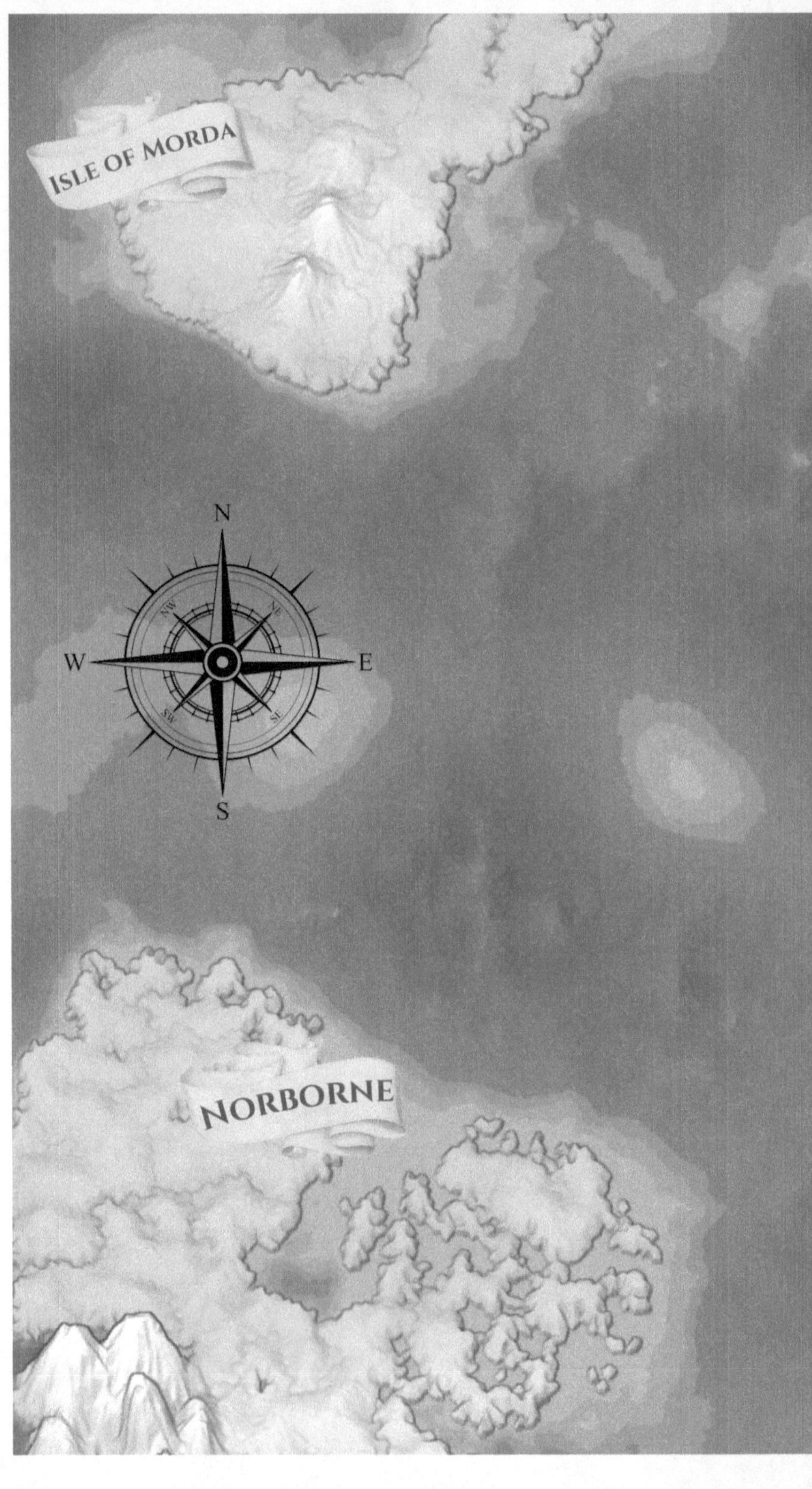

ISLE OF MORDA
N
NW NE
W E
SW SE
S
NORBORNE

CALLA
CALAMITY ISLE

You were a prince of pride and power

But you abused your throne

and hour

You made the people cry and cower

And now you face your final dower

You shall be banished to the sea

Where waves and storms

will torture thee

You shall not die but live in pain

And never live on land again

You shall have magic in your veins

But only use it for your chains

You can preserve two souls

from death

But share with them your

endless breath

This is the curse that you must bear

Until you learn to love and care

C haos. Screams of agony in the Black Sea. The long strands of colorful hair and sparkling eyes that speak of purity and sin. A heart beating raucously, desire like liquid heat in my veins as she swims gracefully to me, her bare breasts teasingly visible above the waterline.

Tick-tock.

Tick-tock.

Cock thickening, lust clouding my thoughts as she draws near to me, her skin glimmering even in the darkness.

She's so beautiful, it physically puts an ache in my center. And I know it's not real—she's an illusion. A murderous little fish, hardly human. I know I must kill her—she knows she must kill me. Yet she stops right before me, those innocent eyes growing blacker, her skin greyer, her teeth sharpening as she bares them to me.

She's playing with me.

Taking her time.

Her instincts ache to rip my heart out.

As her beauty fades into the sea, the monstrous-looking

siren swims before me, omnipotent. My body instantly grows rigid, the lust dissipating from my body. But before I can fight, an enchanting sound falls from her lips. It's so riveting, my being softens, though my mind is screaming—screaming so loud, I feel like a trapped prey in my own body!

She nears, drawing so close, I feel the ripples in the water surrounding her. Surrounding us.

A sudden burn radiates from my chest as she carves into it with her long claws, and then I hear it—a piercing of flesh and bone, followed by a pain so great, I lose complete mobility.

I stare wide-eyed into the black eyes of this demonic woman as she holds my heart in her tight grip.

And crushes it.

STIRRING FROM MY DREAM, I hear him before he's even entered my quarters. His stench—cigar smoke and misery—permeates the air the moment the door opens. His quiet footsteps are so light—that of a frail old man— even my fucking dog, Rex, doesn't stir at my side.

My eyes open, but I remain still. His silhouette disturbs the darkness as he approaches my side. On reflex, my hand curls around my switchblade beneath the pillow. Years of engrained training to be ready at any unexpected threat, you'd think I wouldn't be set off so quickly, being in the comfort of my own fucking ship.

But, alas, that is not the case.

Bloodshed is like water to me now. It's *everywhere*. I need it to live, to survive, to *rule*. And just like water, I might drown in it one day. Because all it takes is for one enemy to outsmart me, and as I've learned with a dead family behind me, an enemy will *always* find a way to get to you.

It's why I clench my blade tight; it's why I stare up at Grimy and know that, despite his loyal servitude, he might be the one to plunge a dagger into my chest when I least expect it.

Even the one I trust the most, I question.

I'm crazy. Those dreams are getting inside my head...

He doesn't reach out to touch me. Instead, his voice wafts to me in a hesitant whisper. "We are fogged, your —Captain."

Not a rarity. I flare my nose, growling, "If all you've come here to do is tell me we've been fogged, I swear to fucking God, you'll be walking the plank within the hour, Grimy."

He pauses in his response, and I stare at his face intently, waiting for more. "We should be nearing the Isle of Morda—"

"If it's reefs you're concerned with, have Martin at the bow of the ship with a sounding line—"

"Already done—"

"You should detect how shallow the waters are—"

"That's the thing, *Captain*, we have." Grimy sounded uneasy now, shuffling from foot to foot. "We've been treading at six fathoms for *hours* now. It's as though...it's as though we haven't even moved."

IT'S three in the morning and quiet as death when I step out onto the deck to judge the situation for myself. Lanterns hang every few feet above my head, their light illuminating barely enough to navigate through the dark. When I shoot Grimy a questionable look, he tells me, "The electric coils keep shutting off. Even the torches don't stay on." To prove it to me, several crewmates produce their flashlights and switch them on and off repeatedly, to no avail. I say nothing as I pace past them and to the bow of the ship. It's a long walk—my three-decked black ship is 150 feet long and 43 feet tall. My ancient companion Rex huffs by my side, his body struggling to keep up. I drop my hand in front of his snout to ease him, and he licks it.

I can hardly see in front of me. The white fog is so thick it's like a curtain, obscuring all visibility.

Young and carefree Martin is standing over the depth sound line. When he hears my footsteps along the creaky wooden deck, he shoots a wide-eyed look over his shoulder. "Still the same, Captain! Six fathoms!"

Six fathoms is too shallow for comfort. We're close to land—possibly the Isle of Morda, which is riddled with jagged cliffs and reefs. And what a fucking hole that island is. I truly hope we aren't anywhere near it.

We can't fuck about.

I shout out, "Slow us right down! Send the longboats!"

It's protocol to deploy the smaller boats and have them lead in front of the ship. Within minutes, the deck has come alive with crewmates, some scraggly, others polished, some old, some far too young to be on here. All loyal to me—loyal to the man who has allowed them steady work and passage despite their crimes and shadowy pasts. Most of my men on the Tempest are convicted felons who have either escaped prison or are searching for their next spree of wicked crime.

And me?

Fuck, I'm running, but not for the same reasons.

I should be living in the light, not raiding islands in the dark like some treasure obsessed pirate.

My ship should gleam in gold, not filled to the brim with questionable currency and prohibited liquids that sell for an exorbitant price on the black market.

Yet here we fucking are.

My clothes are covered in grit, my dark palms creased in grease and calloused from work. My black hair is cropped short like a true gentleman should have it, though it's been a long time since anyone's called me a gentleman. I should behave with principle, my mind the valuable source of power. Instead, I'm rippling with muscle because the sea demands payment for surviving on it, let alone thriving.

It's a grand fucking existence if you couldn't tell.

It's not long before we drop the long boats into the waters filled with several of my men, holding tightly onto lit lanterns. They deploy in front of the ship. We're moving at a snail's pace now, still navigating blindly through the fog that will not let up. A crewmate is shivering not far from me as he peers out over the deck rail, staring into the invisible abyss.

A steady flow of cold air passes through us. It doesn't

have the same force as the wind; it feels like we're being fanned with wet ice.

My head snaps in the direction it's coming from, and for a moment, the stillness feels like another entity altogether. My body straightens, my stance suddenly defensive. I slowly pull the switchblade from my pocket, my fingers curling around it tightly.

Grimy comes to a stand beside me. I feel his stare as he looks up at me anxiously, whispering, "James."

I don't look at him, much less acknowledge that familiar tone. "I don't want to hear it," I grit out.

"We've tempted fate too long on these waters—"

"Would you rather I have stayed on land, with my tail between my legs, stuck with that ridiculous, stale girl you tried to arrange—"

"All girls from Barrhaven are a little... rigid."

I shoot him a dry look. "She refused to even shake my hand."

"Have you seen the state of them?" He tsks, adding, "You make a fuss wherever you go, searching for an impossible woman. And this Barrhaven girl wanted nothing to do with you because you were spotted at the brothel—"

"Doing business with the Madame that looks after those whores."

Grimy looks disturbed, shaking his head at me. "You keep trying to explain yourself. You sold them drugs!" To make a point of it, he grabs a stray needle on the nearest water barrel and thrusts it up to my face. "This thing here, loaded with that disgusting green liquid that would tarnish your family name if they were still alive and knew what you've been up to. Your own crew take it, one's left it right here, for Goddess' sake, still loaded and ready for use."

I snatch the needle out of his hand and cast him a dark look. "You forget your fucking place, Grimy."

Grimy purses his lips, aware now of the eyes of my crew falling to us from every direction. He's made a grave mistake fucking about with me in front of my men, never mind during a fucked-up situation as this. A situation he will insist is siren-related. As if I haven't heard it enough already, even my own crew is tired of his ramblings.

In the Black Sea, we've dealt with demonic presences far too often, and while this is strange as fuck, it would have to get a whole lot worse for it to be siren-related.

There are no sirens left.

But my past gnaws at me, reminding me that isn't entirely true.

Suddenly, a crewmate from one of the longships bellows in the distance. "We're being pushed back!"

"By what?" Briggs, my second-in-command, shouts back from the bow of the ship.

There's no response, and now there's tension and fear rippling through my men. I sense their unease, and I fight to contain my own, but then the ship comes to a jerking stop. It's so sudden, several of us falter in our step.

"We've stopped dead still!" shrieks Martin.

I look at Grimy just as the Tempest begins to quake beneath our feet, the wood groaning like it's in pain.

This is all too similar.

It's happening all over again.

Grimy's eyes are shining with fear and loathing, but then he grabs at my wrist, making sure the bronzed bracelet is still there. Of course it's there. Where the fuck else could it be? He doesn't have one of his own, and we communicate the realization through our looks. He gives me a faint smile. "It'll be alright, Captain, so long as you find me—"

Suddenly, the Tempest jerks forward, moving quickly along the waters. Screams erupt from all directions as crewmates seek refuge or attempt to take command of the ship.

But there's no point.

Because, for once, I suspect Grimy is right.

A siren has found us.

CHAPTER 2

James

It's exactly like it was before. The boat jerking beneath my feet, the sudden onslaught of waves as they come crashing over the Tempest, soaking us to the bone. The fog is still heavy around us as I pace around the ship, ordering the men to batten down the hatches.

"Be ready!" I keep demanding. "Arm yourselves!"

We clear off the deck, rolling the water barrels to the deck below, all the while enduring wave after wave of ice-cold seawater. I know this is just the beginning. This sick fish cunt is playing with us, and all I can think about in that moment is my father's words as he wrapped me up in blankets, removed the bracelet from a lockbox and slid it around my wrist, muttering words in witch tongue. I watched it glow as it grew smaller to fit around my wrist. He shoved me in a nook behind a chest of clothes and told me as the ship shook as if enraged, "Don't come out, no matter what!"

I remembered thinking then that the ship had come alive. And it feels that way. A sense of tugging despair washes over me as I spin around, soaked to the bone already, about to watch the people I've sailed with for years face their demise.

Fuck her, I won't let it happen.

Not again.

"Cover your ears!" I shout now, a sense of urgency in my movements. "COVER YOUR EARS!"

I carry Rex and shove Grimy, Martin, and Briggs below deck, forcing them into one of the small prisoner's quarters.

"Why no one else?" Martin cries, wrapping his fingers around the bars.

"Because there's no one else worth saving," I growl as I lock the cell door.

Grimy is pale, looking frailer than I've ever seen him. "What are you going to do, James?"

In one pocket I have my blade, in the other the needle I ripped from his hand earlier. Determination rushes through me as I grit out, "I'm going hunting."

By the time I surface, the waves are half the size of the mast. We still don't have control of the ship, yet my men—cut from the same cloth—refuse to let up. They change the direction of the black sails, moving along with the waves now to ride through them. Determined for the ship not to turn on its side, to not be confetti at the mercy of the waves as they pummel us from one direction and then come at us from another.

The Tempest lurches sideways, and screams tear through the air, more commands to hold on. Thunder roars above and then rain falls in buckets, turning to fist-sized hail within moments. They come in sideways, cutting through the sails like a knife through butter. Skidding along the deck, punching through the pilot-house windows.

"Below deck!" I demand. "No more—"

A sound cuts through the air, so loud, so distinct. My spine stiffens, and the blood roars in my ears now. Such a familiar sound. Such a familiar *song*. My head feels light, but I still have control of my body, though it hurts to move now, like my limbs are fighting against weight.

"Cover your ears!" I bellow out.

But it's too late.

I see the immediate change in my crew. One by one, they go completely still, their heads twisting in the direction the enchanting voice is coming from. Their faces look up to the dark skies, their eyes rolling to the back of their heads like they're possessed.

And then it happens.

One beelines over the edge of the ship and disappears into the fog.

The Tempest rises on a wave and falls into the sea, crashing into the water in the most disorientating way. I fall to the floor of the deck and slide to the other side. My shoulder crashes into the side of the Tempest. The world spins as I look up, attempting to get up—

Another crewmate practically walks over my body to jump off the ship.

"Kuerick!" I shout. "Don't—"

But he's gone into the night just as the Tempest jerks to another stop. Thunder roars and a flash of lightning strikes, cutting straight through the sails and the ship, searing a blackened hole into it. My ears are ringing, I can taste blood on my tongue, and there it is still, that song floating in the air around me. The voice of an angel, making my heart beat harder, my body grow hotter. Even with this damned, witch-cursed bracelet, I can still feel the effects of the siren's song.

But my body is still intact, and I have to know where she's coming from.

The ship quakes again before jerking forward quickly. *Here we go again.*

The waves are higher, the unrelenting force of the ship moving faster in the water now, but instead of before, the song grows louder, and more of my men are jumping off the same side of the ship, moving in the siren's direction. I attempt to stop them. To grab them by the arms, the legs, even the waist, but it's futile. The siren's power is too great. I'm forced to watch them fuck off my ship like rats scattering from a crash.

I feel angry at first.

Then hotter.

My cock swells, my mouth fills with saliva, the fervor to suck at a piece of pussy, to rut into a woman like a horny, possessed fool. My heart pounds the way it would if I loved a woman.

I feel enraptured, but still I don't feel the same level of possessed as my men as they one-by-one sail into the ocean.

Now I'm horny, but I'm also filled with rage.

Rage because finding these vile men took—

"FOREVER!" I shout out into the vicious night.

Years and years.

This fucking fish cunt.

You still have your loot.

Yes, I do, but if this fish continues to fuck with my ship, it won't survive another hour. And she's already put a lightning sized hole in it—

Another bolt of lightning strikes, the deafening sound cutting through the starboard side of my ship.

Fucking *two* holes now.

I crawl to the mast and wrap my legs around it, holding on tight as the ship rises and falls. The waves aren't as abhorrent as before because this siren cunt is growing bored.

"Don't, Rue," I warn in vain as another crewmate walks possessed to that damned side of my ship. "She's gonna tear your fucking heart out!"

"It's love!" Rue cries out before plunging himself off the ship.

"Fuck love," I growl. "It's worse than a siren's song."

I mentally count how many heads I have to replace. Expensive. It will be very expensive. I wonder how much this finned bitch will get me if I saw her tail off and put it up for auction. *One siren tail up for grabs, fellas.*

Gotta put her out of her misery soon before that can happen.

Quickly, I get up and throw a line overboard. Time is running out. As the waves begin to die down, and the fog begins to clear, I settle the needle between my teeth and climb down the line and into the water. One final clap of thunder rumbles overhead when I surface. I hear the cries of my crew as they swim toward the glowing figure in the water, her melody even more immobilizing from down here. I get ready to swim to her, my cock so hard it's going to burst through my fucking slacks.

There's blood in the choppy waters. I taste it every time the seawater washes over me. The familiar coppery taste. The pained screams allow me to swim faster, to circle around her glowing, gorgeous form. I stop a moment as she crushes a fist into the chest of sick Olgan—a disgusting fellow with a closet of skeletons I know all too much of. She pulls his heart out, and as she does, the blood splatters all over her glowing form. I can see the curve of her tits from where I am, and I wonder for a fleeting moment what fish-cunt nipples taste like.

I'll have to find out when I cut her up.

They deserve it.

Every single one of them.

I knew when I stalked this dangerous strait that I would come across filthy marauders. No sane person would risk these waters. Only pirates and smugglers and fucked-up fugitives who have pillaged harbor towns, committed atrocities, and took off running would be so desperate. These fools deserve to be gutted in some capacity for all the ways they've wronged not just the innocent, but *us*—sirens who've been at their mercy, who've had their songs ripped from their throats and tails sold on the black market to hang in some trophy room of a wealthy buyer.

My plan was already in motion to fully destroy their ship when I saw it approach from a distance. The giant black sails were a dead giveaway that this was no ordinary ship.

Nothing could have changed their fate. Had they strayed off course, I would have followed. Not a ship was safe from a siren during the shift. When our instincts kick in, nothing can stop our bloodlust.

Watching the fragments sink to the ocean floor is incredibly satisfying—but first I relished in ripping their hearts out and watching *them* sink.

It was my favorite part of the shift. I make a little game out of it as I pluck the slimy beating organ from their bodies and pretend I'm picking off the men I know: shitty bosses, crappy dates, guys with douchey motives and smooth lines.

This one's for you, Nico. No means fucking no.

Plunk. Heart in the ocean.

Keep it in your pants next time, Jace!

Splash. The murky depths of the water swallow it whole.

Satisfied, I dive beneath the surface and take pleasure in the way the frigid water envelops my body like an old friend's embrace. Silver glints from a school of fish sparkle through the darkness and I follow their movement, allowing myself to glide along with them before back flipping further down.

I love to swim. Ever since I was a child, the water called to me—beckoning to me like I belonged in it. Entering it, however, was a different story. Father strictly forbade it. Swimming is a privilege I ache to behold, but the other three hundred and sixty-two days in the year I am to stay out of it.

Breaching the surface, I open my mouth and release another wave of enchantment, ready to play with the men again. The seductive melody drifts through the air, cutting through the harsh sounds of the storm.

My siren song lures a few more into the fog-locked sea. Unbeknownst to them, they're about to be greeted by the kiss of death rather than the tender kiss of a lover as my song has lured them to believe.

A deafening clap of thunder blasts overhead, obeying my command, my hand twisting as I guide my magic to control the storm. A harsh wave sweeps over their deck, flooding the old ship. Two more men swan dive off the deck and into the frigid darkness to meet me. Having fun as the maestro, I impulsively send a second wave to follow with a flick of my opposite wrist and knock another crewmate overboard.

Their gargled screams fill the air, half terror and half sound of drowning. I let them struggle, their flounder driving my adrenaline.

Diving beneath the whitecaps, I swim deep, swirling around until a small whirlpool surrounds me. My hair whips around in a blanket of platinum, pink, and purple as a surge of euphoria rushes through me. At this very moment, I feel at one with the ocean. I continue to spin, creating a monstrous whirlpool, until I grow dizzy.

Satisfied that my vortex is strong enough to swallow their ship, I return to the surface and inhale a breath of the crisp ocean air. My hands run along the wet strands of my now slicked back hair as I scan my surroundings, taking in the whimpered screams of the men who still struggle to tread the intense waves.

The breeze is quieter now; the storm is calming. Men have drowned, nature reducing my workload.

Everything around me is eerily calm as I am jostled from my thoughts. I swim to the human closest to me.

Clutching my hand around the front of the white shirt that clings to his body, I pull him close. He struggles, his terror breaking through the effect of my enchantment. His eyes search mine as he begs for mercy. For a chance to live.

He thrashes against my grasp and attempts to peel my fingers off his shirt, but my strength is no match for his anguish. While my enchantment takes a toll mentally, the ocean takes it physically. I roll my eyes. "You dim-witted assholes are all the same," I tell him as I begin my nautical lullaby. My song floats through the air above us, instantly relaxing him in my grasp. Wasting no time, I use my nail to score the shape of an X on his chest, directly over his heart. My sharp talon-like nails slice easily through the fabric and his skin. He lets out a guttural cry, his eyes rolling back into the depth of his skull. The man is not fully coherent thanks to my song, and blood seeps from the wound of my own creation. I lean back to admire my handiwork.

"Beautiful," I mutter to myself before I finish clawing through his marred skin and yank his heart from his chest.

Instantly, I release his body and let it sink below me before turning my attention to the heart held in my right hand. *Disgusting.* You'd think something that symbolizes a notion as beautiful as love would be a little more attractive in its own right. Shaking my head, I open my hand and let the lifeless organ plop into the sea.

With another roll of my wrist, the storm rages harder above me, and I smile.

I love the control the shift gives me. For the rest of

the year, I'm useless as far as my magic is concerned. I can't make a ripple appear in a puddle, let alone a powerful ocean storm.

I've missed this.

There's something so exhilarating about adding a bit of theatrics when you kill an evil man.

Not that I kill a lot of them. But, if they deserve it, I have no problems getting my hands dirty. Though my father strictly forbids it.

"As long as you live under my roof, you'll obey my rules."

Yeah, yeah. But on the days of the shift, all bets are off.

The feeling of power is too consuming to pass up—an addictive rush I look forward to. The power is so intense, my father used to say it was a weakness itself.

Many sirens refuse to give up the mindset once the shift is over, choosing to live a villainous lifestyle instead of returning to a human form and going about their lives for another year. Personally, I choose to live a double life, enjoying the rush of the power and harboring it throughout the year, while still maintaining my soul.

My soul is why, no matter how much I push reality from my mind and turn my humanity off, I knew I'd mourn the destruction I caused come the end of the shift. It was only night one, and I'd already caused so much of it.

But for just three days a year, I force myself to let the ruthless beast within me unapologetically terrorize the ocean as I seek ships and destroy, as our species was created to do in order to protect our home.

For the remainder of the year, we live among

humans—an enchantment bestowed upon our kind to ensure our survival. We are no longer safe in the ocean.

A seagull soars overhead, giving me an approving *caw* before I dip below the surface again. Using my fin to propel me to the next buffoon, I pull him under by his legs, giving him an award-winning smile when his eyes land on mine through the dark waters. He seems to melt into my grasp further and I blow out an exasperated breath that becomes bubbles. So early into the first night of the shift and already the stupid, lustful way these men look at me grows tiresome. The false sense of love and adoration that coats their vision and fills them with so much hope is irritating.

But then I kill them. So there's the silver lining.

Before I fall too deep inside my head, I quickly slice the skin of the man I hold, carving an X above his heart, and shove a hand into his chest. My fingers curl around it, and I pull it free from his chest cavity.

I repeat this process with the remaining men until I am sure I have accounted for all of those in the water. My chest heaves as I push to the surface once more, twirling my wrist to send another tidal wave to sweep the deck of the ship. Patiently, I watch to see if any more crewmates fall.

A mixture of irritation and relief bears down on my chest when the water stills, showing that my work with this ship is done. The air is silent from screams, the water free of the very thing I hunt.

For a moment, I allow myself to enjoy the simple pleasures of the cool caress of the ocean.

Leaning back slightly, my body relaxes and I take in

the sight of myself in my shifted form. I feel the most beautiful beneath the moonlight, embraced by the ocean. My long hair is incredibly vibrant, covering my naked breasts. My tail sparkles from the light of the moon, perfectly encompassed by the reflection of the light-ring as I allow my fin to breach the surface. It's truly a pity that sirens cannot shift of their own free will anymore and must lead a life on land instead.

If I could, I'd live my life surrounded by the sea.

I don't feel alone out here.

A rush of endorphins flows through me as I admire myself in my shifted form, the effects of my siren magic seeping into my skin, pushing a wave of sensuality through my body, leaving a tingling pang in its wake. I enjoy the moonlight for a few more seconds before allowing the fog to obscure it. Just as I'm allowing my guard to drop and fully relax in the water, the treacherous white caps calm and a glint of light catches my attention from my peripheral. My heart spikes. As I turn, I see that I have made a grave mistake in assuming everyone is dead.

Oh, no.

Immediately, I dive under—

I'm fast, but not fast enough.

A muscular arm wraps around my middle while the other firmly presses a cool steel blade against my carotid artery.

"Don't move, you demon cunt," his deep voice growls from behind. My body grows rigid in response. "One move and your voice is mine. Don't test me. I'll slit your throat without batting an eye."

"So do it," I taunt, sliding my hand to wrap around the wrist that holds the blade to my throat. "By the time you move your weapon, my song will have you enchanted, and your heart will be mine."

"Says the siren slut with the switchblade to her neck." He laughs, and it's a deep, throaty sound. My stomach dips, and I force myself to not try to turn to see him. A pull in my chest aches to know what he looks like. A strange heat floods me, spreading across my body. *What is that?* The arm wrapped around my middle presses me back into him further. "No, I think I'll keep you for a while."

"Why would you want to keep me?" I grunt against his hold, testing his strength.

His hold is tight, not enough to bruise, and the pressure against my neck is just enough to strain my voice. *Smart man.* He's smart enough to know how to keep a siren from using their abilities, which means he's done his own research into our kind. Surprising, since most believe we're extinct and no longer a worry.

I can feel his legs kicking beneath us as he pulls me further into his chest, treading water to keep us afloat.

"Well, for starters, you just killed my entire crew," he answers without a hint of strain in his voice, despite working hard to keep us both above water. "Who's going to help me on deck? Or in the kitchens? Who will keep me company for the journey back, now that my men are gone?"

"Sounds like someone else's problem."

"No, it very much sounds like *yours*," he hisses directly into my ear, his head pressed against mine.

A small sting on the side of my neck takes me off guard and I suck in a breath from the impact. The asshole injected me with something.

It takes seconds before my vision becomes clouded and my head fogged.

"Sleep, Little Mermaid. You're my prisoner now."

Before I can fight the weight of my eyelids, everything goes black.

CHAPTER 4

Aria

A throbbing ache pulses through my head while I replay the vague memories of a pinch, followed by icy darkness taking over my being. Paralysis plagues my body, my limbs heavy and unmoving.

I try to pry my eyes open again, but it's no use. Whatever the repulsive human injected me with is strong. Too strong. A siren in shifted form is powerful, with the magic freely flowing through our veins. It pushes us to maintain dominance over the human men, yet one dose of whatever he injected me with knocked me out cold.

Gala Green.

It had to be.

Gala Green is the most potent drug on the market and sold by the most sordid people. It's known for being a mesmerizing glowing green substance that, if injected with the right dose, can radiate you sky high into a blissful state you'll never want to come down from. It's why so many get hooked. What the drug dealers don't warn you—*because why would they*—is that Gala Green is paralyzing if taken in large doses. Fatal with just the wrong amount—or the right amount, depending on your end goal.

This human knew that. He knew exactly the dose to give to knock someone into full paralysis. Fucker got lucky that it happened to work on a siren.

My head continues to throb as I will my eyes to open, but they're still too heavy. I'm so tired, my head rolls forward on my shoulders, heavy and immobile as my neck no longer wants to hold it up. A groan pushes past my lips, and just when I think I may fully come to, I'm pulled under yet again.

THE WEIGHT of my head rolling forward pulls me back into the present and I test to see if my eyes will open. They do, although only enough for a sliver of darkness to pull through. My vision is blurred completely and it burns.

Fuck, do my eyes burn.

I snap them shut, the feel of them too much of an effort to endure. A groan vibrates through my chest thanks to the ache in my body, but the noise hardly escapes my newly gagged mouth. I trace my tongue over the thick binding, trying hard to will my gag reflex to stay strong.

Rope.

Of course. It's why the corners of my mouth already feel raw.

My skin feels hot and damp with a layer of sweat, as

if it's been doused with kerosene and ignited. The effects of the drug exiting my system are excruciating.

I shake my wrists, testing the strength of the restraints I'm shackled in, unsurprised to find they are tight and unmoving. The chains attached to the handcuffs rattle against the metal pipe along the wall, and my wrists burn from the bite of them. It won't be long before my arms become sore from being elevated. I breathe calmly through the discomfort.

How long have I been like this? I move my fin to test its operativeness, relieved to find that I have movement back, although my tail now aches from the lack of moisture.

Contrary to the stories of the sirens, being away from water won't kill us. However, the longer we're out of water in our shifted form, the more unbearable the pain becomes. *This is not good.*

Once again, I test my eyes, cracking them slightly.

When I open them completely, I'm relieved to find my vision clearer, though still blurred. Lifting my head feels like a chore, but I slowly look around, taking in my surroundings and trying to gather any bearings I can.

The room is dark but the surrounding shapes appear to be crates ranging in size; some of them have fallen on their sides, perishables and cans scattered along the floor. A large painting is fixed to the wall and covered with a sheet—

I see a cell on the other side, its door open. Next to it is a table with instruments I can't see from here.

Judging by the chains I'm in, I think it's safe to assume I'm in the prisoners' quarters. If not prisoners' quarters, certainly a room meant for someone lesser than, if the stench has anything to say about it. The space reeks of stale cigarettes, bodily odor, and must, as though the room has been unused for some time.

I fight against my eyelids that beg to close, forcing them to remain open. The lack of water is affecting more than just the dryness in my skin—even the lack of moisture in my eyes makes every blink feel like sandpaper. I allow myself time to readjust to the room, attempting to distract myself from the pounding in my head by taking in the space.

My breath catches when I land on a dark silhouette in the corner, crouched by the door.

The slight movement catches my eye and puts me on edge as my heart sinks to the bottom of my stomach. *Shit.* My pulse quickens as the person moves to stand, prowling toward me with slow, deliberate steps.

My eyes trail every step; I hold my breath, unsure of who, or *what*, is holding me captive.

The Black Sea holds great secrets, and there is no shortage of creatures that live amongst the humans, hidden in plain sight.

And those who lurk in the darkness and depths...

I'm not easily frightened, but knowing the secrets I keep has me questioning what other secrets are out there.

The being grows bigger the closer he gets.

Until he's finally here.

It must be the man that caught me.

Crouching beside me, his lips draw so close to my ear I can feel the warmth of his breath on my skin. Goosebumps layer my upper body. I'm exposed and acutely aware of his proximity.

Unprovoked, a sudden rush of heat floods my body, and I can feel the telltale warmth of desire pool in my lower belly. My breathing hitches with intensity as that warmth expands in my chest again, confusing me.

Traitorous body, he's the enemy.

The air in my lungs constricts as he skims his calloused fingertips against my arm. The rhythmic motion calms my nerves and temporarily disarms me. It feels like a comfort rather than the touch of an enemy. My teeth sink into my bottom lip as his fingers dust my collarbone, tracing his way upward before his hand wraps around my neck, constricting my airway.

A moan climbs up my throat, a strangled cry mixed with pain and lust. I swallow it down, but it's too late..

He feels the movement beneath his hand. His eyes drift down to look at his grip around my throat before he snaps them back to mine. The warmth in my chest turns to burning, followed by a strange tugging sensation I can't explain. I abruptly feel the urge to close the distance between us.

What the hell is happening?

"Not so fucking enchanting now, are you, Little Mermaid?" he taunts, applying more pressure to his grasp. His thumb pushes on a pressure point beneath my jaw.

I shouldn't like it as much as I do.

The corners of my lips turn up in a slight smile, causing darkness to swirl in his already inky eyes.

He shifts his footing, moving closer to me. With our

bodies almost touching, I wonder if he can feel the intensity of my heartbeat through the pulse point his thumb still presses against. The way his tongue darts out to wet his lips tells me he can. I roll my head, my eyes never leaving his as I rise to meet his challenge, silently letting him know he doesn't scare me, and taking note of the way his chest rises and falls.

Steadily breathing.

He's in complete control of himself, save for the slight twitch in his hand, the only giveaway he's not totally immune.

His expression is indifferent as he gazes at me. "Tell me, did you plan to come after my ship and kill my crew specifically, or were their deaths a wrong place, wrong time situation?"

My eyes volley between the tragic shadows in his. A part of me is hopeful to find even just a shred of humanity in his remarkably handsome features, but all that stares back at me is hatred. He's masking his arousal well—I *know* he feels just as lustful as I do.

He also knows I can't speak to answer, and he smirks at me before saying, "You know what, don't answer that. It's a moot point, anyway."

The sudden pinch of another needle at the column of my neck makes my stomach fall. *He's drugging me again?* I thrash against his grasp, but my consciousness immediately begins to wane. The drug is such a hit; I feel a high come over me.

The soft feel of his nose nuzzles against my cheek as he whispers, "Sweet dreams, filthy fish."

And I'm pulled back into the darkness.

I watch as the light drifts from her eyes, right before they shut completely. Her pillowy lips part as she slips unconscious, though the rope in her mouth doesn't allow much room to open.

As I stare down at my now sleeping prisoner, my mind fills with lustful thoughts. It would be so easy to untie the rope from her mouth and fill it with my aching cock. I reach down and adjust myself, anger curdling through my veins yet again. My bracelet should be keeping the arousal at bay, yet the amount of blood that's filled my cock tells a different story. How easy it would be to fuck her mouth until I empty my heavy balls, my seed overflowing from her mouth, dripping down her luscious ti—

No.

See, this is what these sirens do. Provoke your lust until you're unlike yourself.

I'm just unused to the buzz in my body.

How long has it been since I've felt aroused?

I push the intrusive thoughts from my mind. I may not be a good man, but I prefer my women willing and fucking conscious.

The drugs in her system will keep her knocked out for a while, and though tempting as it is to stand over her until she wakes again, I pry my eyes away from her, ignoring her beauty as I back away.

I'd have put her in the cell, but she doesn't fit it. Her fin is too long, and I prefer to keep her where I can see her the second I enter the room.

It's hard to believe something so fucking beautiful can be so cruel. She ripped out the hearts of my men, and I can't wait to rip out *hers*.

Slamming the door behind me, I lock it, not wanting to take any chances. The Black Sea harbors vile creatures and while I'm confident I know most of a siren's abilities, I'm not willing to take any chances. My heart thunders behind my rib cage, adrenaline thick as I let my thoughts about this evening's shitfuck events simmer.

Back in the captain's quarters, I sit on the edge of my bed. With my elbows propped on my thighs, my head hangs cradled in my hands with my fingers threaded through my hair. I have a raging headache that throbs, making me want to act on the fury within and go kill the demon shackled to the pipes.

Fucking fish killed my crew, wrecked my ship, and somehow has managed to rattle me, all within a few hours' time.

Fuck.

CHAPTER 6

Aria

I wake with a startle, my eyes snapping wide as anxious palpitations drive my heart into overdrive. My chest rises and falls in rapid succession as I struggle to even breathe. My body trembles, and a thick sweat coats my face and upper body. The damp tendrils of my hair matte together and stick to my forehead and the back of my neck.

Frantically, I look around the space as my vision swims with flashbacks of dark eyes, a devious smirk, and the pinch of a needle.

Blowing out another deep breath, I'm relieved to find I am temporarily alone in the space I'm shackled in.

Moonlight streams in through the open porthole and illuminates the room, granting me enough light to see better once my vision adjusts. It's nighttime, and I was right. I'm definitely being kept in some sort of prisoners' quarters. Next to me is a single door, and to the left of it a chair sits in the corner, positioned to face where I am held captive. That chair wasn't there before.

Shackled here and helpless, I can't help but wonder what I'll have to endure.

Back in Norborne, we aren't bathed in riches, but we're comfortable. I lived a sheltered life and the home I share with my father and two sisters is quaint and humble but bustling with life. Briony, Celeste and I share a bedroom, while our father has another. Our rooms aren't suites designed for royalty, but they certainly are more hospitable than my current...*lodgings*.

I wonder how my sisters are faring. Only Briony reached the age to allow a shift, but even then, she has favored being in her human form and Celeste is shy and uncertain; I can't see her causing the same sort of havoc I did. I'm suddenly grateful I don't have to worry about them at a time like this, that their quirkiness has saved them from what could have been a similar fate.

I swallow through the dryness in my mouth, peering around me to see if my captor has set out any water for me. Wishful thinking, I know, and a bit of a ridiculous hope considering I'm cuffed to a steel pipe against the wall with rope gagging me. Still, I drag my eyes along every inch of the room in hopes of *something*. My head rolls along my shoulders, stiff from the position I've been stuck in for what feels like days. But I haven't shifted back to my *human* form, which tells me I've been here for mere hours.

That'll be a real treat for him—to learn that sirens shift. Unless he already knows, but I can't imagine he does, judging by the look on his face when he captured me. It was as if the pieces of the puzzle were falling into place with the reality of my existence.

Most humans believe sirens are nothing more than folklore by this point—an extinct creature whose stories they've passed through the generations. There hasn't been a sighting in decades. If one is lucky enough to find even the remains of a siren, they can fetch a hefty price for their tails on the black market. We've had to learn to protect ourselves at all costs. It's the reason why we shift. Why we *walk* among them. Live among them.

We just don't get to love them.

We can fuck them, though, and that's half the fun.

A smile curls at my lips. What would it be like to fuck *this* beautiful man? With his sharp facial features and taut muscles hidden beneath that white linen that clung to his chiseled—

Goddess, what am I thinking?

I push away the thoughts as rapidly as they come and remind myself that he is my *literal* kidnapper. He drugged me. Chained me to a pipe.

As though he can hear my thoughts, I catch the sound of footsteps approaching, and my spine straightens. Moments later, shadows dance through the gap at the bottom. My mind goes into fight or flight and I focus on my breathing, slowing it while I shut my eyes, pretending to be asleep.

The door creaks open and I hear him step into the room. The air around me changes—electrifies and thickens.

My pulse quickens and I find it harder to breathe, fighting the urge to open my eyes and look at him. My body reacts to his presence in a way I'm not accustomed to. The door quietly clicks behind him, almost silently, but the thump of his boots against the floor gives away his movements as he stomps toward me.

"I know you're awake," he announces, his voice much closer than expected. I drop the act and open my eyes to glare at him with a look I hope reads of disgust rather than curiosity.

He studies me, his head tilting as he assesses me silently. "I'm going to take the rope out of your mouth so you can answer my questions, but make no mistake, if I even get a slight intuition that you're about to use your song, I'll slit your throat and rip out your vocal cords with my bare hands."

I swallow a combination of a laugh and a grunt, my natural born snark wanting to come out to play.

Don't threaten me with a good time, buddy.

His fingers brush against my cheek when he reaches around to the back of my head to untie the knot that's kept the rope firmly in place. As he leans forward to ease the knot apart, his scent envelops me and I unintentionally inhale. His intoxicating mixture of sandalwood, leather, and saltwater floods my senses. Goddess, I've never been one to care much about the scent of a man. Why is this one catching my attention?

The ropes fall away, and I waste no time moving my jaw to ease the discomfort. I wish I could massage my sore cheeks, but he's left my hands bound.

"So tell me, siren," he spits with malice. "My ship. Did you intentionally attack us, or did we just get lucky?"

Amused, I bite my tongue, schooling my features to a look of impassiveness. My gaze falls to the floor, staring at a plank with scratches disfiguring the otherwise smooth wood.

There are two ways I can play this.

Weighing my options, I decide on feigning innocence.

Did I know that was his ship? Well, no, considering I don't even know who *he* is. He seems to think I do, though. "I have no idea what you mean," I tell him honestly, although I sugarcoat my voice into a sweetness that feels unnatural to me. "I don't even know who you are."

"Do not lie to me," he gruffly retorts, voice deathly calm. His irises ignite with malevolence. If I didn't have full confidence in my abilities to enchant him completely within a few seconds flat, I would be a little nervous.

But I can, and I *will*, when the timing is right.

But my song didn't work on him in the ocean.

The recollection makes me hesitate, and as I allow myself to contemplate *why,* I let my eyes slowly rake over his body. My chest is doing that tug thing again, an unwelcome feeling that leaves behind a dull ache. I exhale a deep breath, my heart skipping a beat as my eyes land on the bracelet on his left wrist.

Why do I recognize that bracelet?

Realizing my silence is stretching too long, I throw back at him, "Why does it matter? Dead is dead. How did you evade my song?"

My eyes slip back to the bracelet, and I notice an inscription scrawled along its metal—though my vision isn't fully back to normal, so I can't make out what it says.

"Eyes on mine, you demon whore. Answer my question."

"I answered your question," I state, my eyes narrowing with irritation.

"No, you—"

"Yes, I did. Dead is dead." I'd cross my arms over my chest if I could to drive my attitude home, but I'm still shackled, and my arms are growing more numb as time passes.

He surprises me by remaining silent. Coming to a stand, he strolls the room with languid steps, back and forth, before settling on the wall opposite of me. He presses his back against it, then crosses his arms and watches me. The attention is a little disconcerting because he isn't speaking.

Deciding to seize the moment, and desperate to ease the desert dryness inside my mouth, I break the silence. "I'm dehydrated. If you're going to hold me as your prisoner, could you at least give me the basic necessities and get me some water?"

"You're dehydrated," he repeats, vacantly.

Something about his tone unnerves me, but I steady my voice. "I am."

In a blink, he's on me, his hand gripping my cheeks and jaw and squeezing tight. His fingers dig into my skin, forcing my cheeks to hollow. His movements are so sudden, his eyes blazing, looking like a complete barbarian. The strength of his hold pries my mouth open. My eyes flare wide as he leans over and spits in it.

"Drink up, Little Mermaid. This is all the generosity you'll get from me." He releases my face, pushing it backward as he does.

Without missing a beat, I close my mouth and swallow, raising my chin to him. His Adam's apple bobs down his throat and satisfaction permeates through me, appreciating the shocked reaction he wasn't fast enough at hiding. And frankly, I'm impressed with my response despite my heart battering inside my chest, fearful of that crazed look in him.

There's also another reaction he isn't able to hide, and as my eyes drift lower, I take note of the swell of his cock that threatens to burst from the fabric of his pants.

The bastard liked that.

Nose flaring, he grabs the rope and silences me, tugging it tighter around my mouth than before.

"Inha bin sheen," he breathes down at me, that wrathful expression sending chills down my spine.

I school my shock, looking emptily back at him as he leaves. It's only when he's gone that my eyes drop to the floor in disbelief.

He spoke Sinwa–the tongue of the sirens. His words run through my mind: *"Inha bin sheen."*

Death by beauty.

I was right.

He is no ordinary human.

CHAPTER 7

James

"I say we scale her fin, flesh out the bones, and make her into Siren Soup."

Head still pounding, I don't speak for a moment, but all I'm thinking is, *"Of all the men she killed, how the fuck did she miss Luca?"* She kept alive the one crewmate I wouldn't have thought twice about losing. Turns out, while she was on her murderous spree, enchanting everyone's cocks into her orbit, good old Luca had drunk enough booze to put an army to sleep.

We're on the deck, surveying the damage. With the large hole through the boat, I'm painfully aware we're taking on water in the bilges. Luckily, it's slow going, so we're not sinking anytime soon. The sails need to be patched up, though, and every electric coil is busted. We're still depending on the few lanterns that survived the siren-induced storm and feeling pretty fucking primitive right now. Still obscured in darkness, bobbing around the ocean like a paper in rocky seas, visibility is dangerously low.

That heart-snatching fish is still using her powers to fuck us up.

"You're not going to kill her, are you?" Martin says in a high-pitched voice, eyes wide as he looks at me. "Can't we just let her go, Captain?"

"So she can come back around and kill the last of us off?" retorts Luca.

"Don't be stupid," Briggs says, combing through the knots in his long, blond locks. He's fuming because his hair is fucked up, and I want to shave that fucking hair off just to give this pretty boy some fucking perspective on our situation.

"She's protecting her home," Martin argues. "We don't hate sharks for doing what's natural to them—"

"She hunted us down, you fucking idiot," roars Luca.

"Nothing that beautiful means to hurt!"

We stare at Martin for a moment as his eyes well up with... tears.

I can't fucking even right now.

I cast a *what the fuck* look at Grimy, and he sighs heavily, saying, "She is interfering with us as we speak. Martin thinks he's in love with her. It's just lust, boy. She's tainted your feelings—"

"And is making us all walk around with a stiff one!" Luca growls, clutching at his cock through his trousers. Briggs shoots him a grotesque look, like his pretty sensibilities have been offended. "I can split a pussy in half with this boner. I wonder if that fish has a cunt on her."

Now Briggs is dry heaving as Martin takes a step toward Luca and shouts, "Don't you dare!"

Luca doesn't step back because I suspect he knows

how big he is in comparison to Martin, who is barely eighteen—or maybe he's fifteen, or maybe he's fucking thirty—it's hard to tell with these malnourished late-bloomers. Instead, the broad-shouldered marauder goads him with a smile. "I'm only saying if we're gonna keep her alive like you want to, we can make better use of that mouth—"

As Martin's wispy body lunges for him, I intercept him and swing an arm out, wrapping his neck before kicking his legs out. I bring him down, pressing my knee against his back as he shakes through his rage. "You will ease it," I demand.

There's so much vehemence in Martin. I can feel his change. He's not himself anymore. Not the pussy hungry tool he usually is. This little shit fled from town because he was a little too forceful with the girls.

Love is certainly not in his vocabulary.

"You're weak, Martin," Grimy huffs from above us. "Too vulnerable. Perfect prey for a siren. You're lusting after an illusion. One that would turn your stomach inside out if you were to see her in her true form. They shift before our eyes into a beautiful creature, but they are darkness incarnated. A monster that, in its clutches, will plant nothing but unadulterated fear inside you. She will feast on your heart after she tears it from your chest, and it won't end from there. There are stories that these sea beasts harvest souls; that they will scour the ocean floor and beyond, feeding on hearts and enslaving the souls of men for eternity."

Martin's strength gives out, his rage leeching from his body as Grimy's words sink in. Meanwhile Briggs is rubbing at his chest, looking disturbed. I let Martin go, sensing his defeat and fear. I glance at Luca who stands mutely now, that goading smile all gone. Grimy's words have startled them. I might have felt the same way once upon a time, but I've heard it all before too many times to care. Except now I'm repeating those words to myself as my body quakes to be back in her presence.

There's something about her.

Something inside me clicks into place when I draw closer to her.

My chest tugs as an inexplicable warmth fills it—

I don't like it.

Not one fucking bit.

"Check the bilges," I order Luca. He nods stiffly and races off to do just that while I look at Briggs. "Keep an eye on the seas, and on Martin." Briggs nods, running his fingers through those unmanageable knots. I sigh. "And enough with the fucking hair-combing, Briggs." He nods once more, then follows after Martin.

"You're going to visit her again," Grimy remarks with disapproval. "Even with that bracelet on, you're still at risk."

I grunt indifferently. "I'm stronger than all of you combined thanks to this bracelet fused to my fucking wrist. Unless you have a better plan of attack, Grimy, I've no choice but to go down there and find out why she chose to attack us."

"You still think it was targeted."

It wasn't a question. I just look at him, saying nothing, but he can read me well. I don't *think* it was targeted, I'm positive she attacked my ship for a reason. And it might have something to do with the very bracelet that is keeping me from falling into her trap.

Something I see within Grimy's eyes reminds me of colorful hair and darkness.

After fetching a bucket of water, I leave them, returning below deck feeling all kinds of fucked-up. The closer I get to the prisoner's quarters, the cloudier I feel. This mermaid is lust personified. My cock has been hard for hours now, and as I approach the door, I'm pretty sure I'm going to come in my fucking pants because her aura is thicker here, more so than last time.

She's working me.

She can't get into my head, so she's trying to get into my body. Like the way she swallowed my saliva when I spat into her mouth. She appeared delighted, eyes sparkling, like she enjoyed the taste of my spit.

I stand still for a moment, imagining my cum in her mouth instead. I'd shoot my load so far down her throat, I'd make her milk my cock with it.

I want to punch my fucking head in.

The burn in my chest grows stronger, and from what I've gathered by the others, I'm the only one feeling it.

I remove the key to the door from my pocket. I'm the only one carrying it because if I feel this fucked up by her, I can't imagine how unbearable it must feel without my bracelet on. My men would have been down here in a second, freeing that wicked sea beast in a heartbeat.

Opening the door, I walk in and shut it behind me swiftly. I lock it, perfectly aware she's watching me just feet away, shackled to the steel pipe that runs along the wall. I can feel her in the air around me, passing over my body like a sweet caress.

I don't dare shudder. I refuse to let her know she's getting under my skin, making my heart pump, making my blood burn. *It's not real.*

I try to tell my dick that.

Placing the bucket down, I turn around and stride over to where she sits. Moonlight streams in and illuminates her shackled figure. I hold my breath like I can't bear to breathe her stench in. It's an act, of course, because if there's a scent that smells like lust, this is it.

Without looking at her, I mechanically unwind the rope around her mouth. Once it's off, I leave her. I walk away, purposely ignoring her. Let her think she's just a passing fancy. A fleeting thing under my control. A meaningless problem that I will get to when I want to.

"So nice to see you in the flesh," she coos as I stand by the steel table on the other side of the room. I look over the torture instruments, raising a particularly sharp one in my hand as she continues. "I was just beginning to fawn all over your painting. Almost came just from staring at it, thinking of all the *slutty* things I could do to the man it depicts." She lets out a short moan, and it makes my skin prickle with awareness. That sound quickly dies, and a breathless laugh escapes her. "Unless you wanted to look like a fuckboy, I hope you cut the hands off the man that made it."

She's referring to the three-foot tall acrylic painting of me I hauled into the darkest wall of this prisoner's quarter so many years ago. I've only just managed to forget its existence. It was covered by a sheet, but with the jostling the boat endured, it's now in the corner on the floor, *not one fucking scratch on it.*

The Tempest gets sea-fucked, and my painting lives on. The Goddess is cruel.

I can't even look at it without feeling my insides churn. I look nothing like the preen egomaniac of my past. If it were up to me, it would be at the bottom of the ocean, but Grimy refuses to part with it. Says it brings him back to a time in the past he was most happy. Probably because he was more useful back then. And now... well now he's trapped on a ship he hates on an ocean he believes is cursed.

If this Siren thinks this portrait is bad, she should see the other two I have—the other two that look untouched and still have the sheet over them. *Unbelievable.*

Sounding bored, I answer, "I did cut his hands off. I dried them out like jerky, too. They're hanging from the ceiling. Pity it's too dark for you to see them."

"Why is it such a pity?"

"Because I want you to see where I'll be hanging your tail after I've sawed it off your body." I turn to look at her now, my cruel smile spreading across my face. Picking up the lantern from the table, I step toward her and hang it off a hook in the ceiling beam. It casts a dim glow over her, but it's enough I can look her over with more clarity than before.

There's no scowl on her face. She doesn't look the least bit frightened of my words. In fact, she returns my cruel smile, and for a moment, I commend her strength. She is a tough fucking siren because I can tell she's in agony. There's a sheen of sweat on her forehead. Her plump lips are dry—even her colorful hair looks brittle and dull. Her skin is paler than before, taking on a ghostly white. And her delicious looking tits are full behind her long hair as it covers them. Her chest moves rapidly, her breathing labored.

Only that's not the worst of it. Her tail—curved awkwardly in the space she's confined to—is dry and flaking. Lines split down the thick meat of it, and every shuffle she makes is an attempt to reposition the tail, to get it off the ground and remove the pressure.

"Not looking your Sunday Best, Siren," I note dryly as I take a stool nearby and position it in front of her. I play with the Heretic's Fork in my hand, and her eyes follow the motion. "My crew's still deciding whether to torture you to death slowly, or eat that fucking fin in front of you."

Her eyes cool. "I'm not so sure about that, *Captain.*" My cock twitches at the way she says that word. A slow smile spreads across her face like she knows exactly how hard I suddenly am. "Even imprisoned down here away from the last of your men, I think I still hold quite the sway on them, wouldn't you say?"

She can feel our arousal even from down here.

And she's so fucking arrogant about it.

I wonder how much she can hear, too, to know to call me Captain.

Damn fish.

"Are we hard?" I return on a shrug. "Yeah, we're hard, Little Fish. But we're fucking marauders. We're used to being split down the middle with the urge to fuck. You think this is something new? That what you're doing is some sort of punishment we're not used to?" My smile is all teeth as I clutch my hard cock through my trousers, causing her eyes to flare. "When I feel an itch, I fucking get it scratched, and it doesn't bother me how I get it, either. Even if it's from the mouth of a murderous sea beast that put it there." I lean forward, resting my elbows on my knees, delighting in her suddenly guarded expression. "And when I fuck that mouth solely for my pleasure, you better learn that riling up a bad man like me comes with very serious implications."

Silence hangs in the air now. I expect her to look away, to understand the weight of my words. She is at my fucking mercy, and she knows it, but her eyes run over me slowly, like she's suddenly looking at me for the first time. A tongue darts from her mouth, and she runs it along her bottom lip to wet it, but she's so dehydrated, it barely moistens.

"Are you done flirting with me, Captain?" she finally asks.

"Depends," I retort. "Are you done using your powers?"

She blinks innocently at me. "I have no control over the way I make you feel. This is what I am. As a matter-of-fact, now that I think about it, we're the same."

"Explain, fish."

"You're a pirate; you pillage the land, and I pillage the ocean. You can't tell me you haven't murdered a bad man or two along the way." Now her lips curve into a soft smile. "I happen to make you hard, and you happen to intrigue me."

"What about me intrigues you?"

"You're all man. I like that."

"Don't try to bewitch me."

She pouts. "Now, why would I do that when I know it won't work?"

Fuck me, the way she speaks. Her voice is so fucking beautiful, it hurts. I grind my teeth, staring at her evenly. "That's right. It won't work on me. I see past your illusions."

She raises her brows in question. "And what is it you think you see?"

"The beast you truly are."

She suddenly blows a kiss my way, and I swear to fucking Goddess, I can feel it press against my lips. "If you truly knew, Captain..." she tells me, shaking her head.

If I truly knew what?

I wait for her to finish, but she doesn't.

I feel uneasy with myself. My body is charged, so fucking tight with desire, it's slowly beginning to fuck with my head. I've been down here too long. I was supposed to interrogate her. To hurt her. And yet I'm running my eyes over every inch of her, my gaze trapped on her lips, then her tits—

My cock pulses, and I grit my teeth.

Standing up, I grab the bucket of ice-cold water and throw it aimlessly over her. I'm rough, my movements brisk. Her moans swiftly fill the air the second I've doused her in water. Standing over her, I peer at her now. Her eyes are closed, her lips parted as she moans in pleasure. The water immediately seeps into her skin, tail, and hair. A subtle glow erupts from her. It's a temporary salve to the pain. But now that she knows the relief I can offer her, the more torturous it will feel when I withhold it from her.

"I'm not trying to ease you," I say darkly. "I'm simply buying more time to destroy you, Siren. I'm a thorough man—"

"You've got art that doesn't show you in the same likeness anymore," she suddenly interrupts, her eyes opening to look at me. Even her blue eyes are glowing. Her voice is stronger, the sheen of sweat gone from her skin. "In fact, it's been a long time since paintings like that have been made. You've got a bracelet on your wrist inscribed in witch tongue. Do you want me to tell you what it says?"

"How can you be sure I don't already know?"

She tilts her head to the side. "Because if you knew, you wouldn't be in the ocean."

Remaining guarded, I don't speak.

We stare at each other for several moments.

The blood curdling screams of my past haunt me. Even now. Standing before this temptress.

Her lips, now smooth, spread into a charming, breathless smile. "Oh, Captain. One second you want to torture me, the next you want to fuck me, and now you want answers. Come back to me when you decide what it truly is that you want, and maybe I'll obey." She lets out a light moan, pushing her full tits out, drawing my attention to them. "Do whatever you want, and it'll be our little secret."

Still goading me.

Still trying to fuck me up.

She must think I'm all talk.

That the artwork of me is still an indication of who I am.

But that's not the man I am anymore.

I move to her in three swift strides. Grabbing her chin, I force her face up to look at me. I peer down at her at the same time I throw the torture device on the ground. Growling, I bite out, "What did I say about being careful?"

I keep her mouth clenched shut tightly as I undo my slacks and remove my cock. She can't move her head, but her eyes dart down to look at my swollen head. Her eyes come alive, and her body shudders. I run my thick cock along her siren lips, my teeth clenched as I rasp, "You think I'm still sensible? That I abide by a gentleman's code even out here?" I pump my cock, slapping it against her face harshly. A pleasurable quake rocks my body. A feeling I haven't felt in eons. "I'm not that fucking man anymore, Siren."

It's starting to dawn on her. I can see it in her fierce gaze. There's so much rebellion and curiosity, but now she's staring at me like, yeah, I fucking will deliver on my threats. That despite the pulsing in my balls, the need to fuck and worship her like a goddess, she does not own me fully.

She's finally understanding who is truly in control.

And my hard cock at her lips? It's a demonstration of how powerless I can make her feel.

Gritting my teeth, I let go of her mouth and tuck myself back into my slacks. Grabbing the rope, I'm rough when I begin to wrap it around her. This time, I wrap it around her throat in a tight grip. Her eyes widen in surprise, but I don't give a fuck if she can hardly breathe.

I've had it with her fucking with my body.

"If you won't entertain me with the truth, I'll find other ways you can entertain me," I threaten, tugging at the rope around her throat.

She stares back at me, eyes so wide and unblinking they start to glisten.

Before I'm about to bring the rope around her mouth, a *BOOM* slams into the side of the ship, knocking me forward. I use the wall to steady myself just as a loud screeching fills the air. It doesn't sound human, either. At once, shouts erupts, racing footsteps along the deck above, a cry for, "Captain!"

I look down at my prisoner, and she's smiling up at me. "Seems you boys aren't the only ones fighting for my love, *Captain.*"

The shouts from the deck carry through the open porthole as the captain's men scurry frantically, rattled from whatever has slammed into the boat. I strain my ears to hear what's happening above, my mind still reeling over the captain's struggle to fight off his lust, and the forceful way he held my face and rubbed his tip across my lips.

I'm mildly ashamed to admit that I didn't hate it.

"Captain! It felt like it came from the starboard!"

"Well, don't just fucking stand there!" my captor bellows to the few that remain of his crew. "Get armed and eyes out. We're doing a full walk from stern to stem! I want to know what we hit, or what the fuck hit *us*!"

His tone is rough as he barks orders to the men, and something about his tone has me squirming. He's angry, filled with so much vehemence, but there's an underlying reason for that. He may think he's the one in control, but I've made him tick, and now he's taking it out on the last of his crew.

The water he doused me with is a temporary reprieve from the pain I'd been feeling, and I'm grateful for it, even if he only showed me a small charity as a way to threaten me more. It was enough to give me the strength to rebuild the burn within. To remember to fight against him. To meet his challenge and not back down against his threats.

Because that's exactly what he's doing. Threatening me. Proving that I am his prisoner and at his mercy. But while I may physically be at his mercy, mentally he is at mine. The way his eyes hood and his length thickens each time he enters the room he keeps me locked away in, I can practically taste the lust that rolls off him in waves. He's not subtle about the way he looks at me, but I know he's not trying to be either. He *wants* me to see that I'm affecting him, because he wants to prove that he can resist me, too.

I'm inside his head, living rent free as the star of his dirtiest fantasies.

What I'm not sure of, though, is *why*?

It didn't take me long to realize why I recognized the bracelet he wore. In fact, I should have realized it much sooner than I did. Father would be angry that his years of drilling history and stories into the minds of my sisters and I didn't sink in enough to have me know it the moment I saw it.

An immortality bracelet. One created by the darkest of witches. Only the royalty could afford the price of her powers, which poses the question: is he an Erickson?

Word had spread countless years ago that King Erickson died at sea after fleeing his kingdom, but the prince was never found. Whether he was alive or dead still remains unknown.

He has to be Prince Erickson. Or else how would he have come to pay such a hefty price?

And, inscription on the bracelet—*Protect. Resist. Revenge.*—meant to allow whoever wore it to be invincible against their enemies.

We are enemies.

Sirens.

Humans.

Except, the humans do not know we shift. If they knew, they'd stay out of the ocean. *Our* ocean.

We may rip the hearts from the men whose ships we pillage and burn, but an eye for a fucking eye.

What's baffling to me is how *Captain Erickson* isn't fully resistant to the enchantment of my song. I'd never been told of the bracelet failing or allowing magic to sneak through. For all intents and purposes, this man should have full protection.

Yet, in my presence, he exudes sexual tension.

It completely disproves my knowledge of the witch's spell, and frankly, his lustful desires are rubbing off on me, which also disproves the potency of my powers with the shift. In my siren form, I'm able to combat the arousal that's slowly building inside me from the enchantment I expel, but this time, it lacks its typical protection.

And once the shift is over, the lust I feel will be harder to resist.

I'll be desperate to ride him and seek pleasure from his body.

I'm fucked.

Something about the word *forbidden* makes the taste so much sweeter.

"What do you think it was, Captain?" The question floats on the breeze and I shift my head in its direction, straining my neck to hear more of what's going on. The sun peeks over the horizon now, and I blow out a breath of relief, knowing I'm that much closer to the shift being over. Though I'm not sure how long I've been down here—the Gala Green warping all sense of time—I know that with every passing moment I get closer to no longer needing water for relief.

I can make it through one day or two, no matter how excruciating the pain may get.

"I see nothing, Grimy, but that doesn't mean we're not being stalked."

"Another siren?"

"This is the Black Sea. Could be fucking anything." He lets out a harsh breath. "We're taking on water by the second, and if we don't patch the hole by sunset, we're in deep shit."

"I'll send Luca and Briggs down with me."

"Martin will be on a lookout."

"And you, Captain?"

"I'm going to look over the longboat we have, then pay that siren another visit."

Their footsteps scatter.

My heart flips in my chest, and I close my eyes, letting out a breath as I lean my head back against the pole I'm tethered to. It's only then do I realize he never finished retying the rope. It's constricted around my neck, but not my mouth.

I'm temporarily conflicted on whether to use my song or to stay silent like a good little prisoner. I strategically plan my next move, but Father didn't raise a quitter and I've always been quick to jump.

I open my mouth and control a light, sweet, lustful lullaby to float into the empty room.

With a subtle song, the captain shouldn't visibly notice the extra subtle effects it has on his men, but if they're still as enchanted as I think they are, one or more should come to my side shortly.

Once I end my song, I turn my head to watch the sun fully rise, hoping that its warmth will soon seep into the room.

I wonder briefly if they figured out what hit the boat, curious if one of my sisters had come across us after all. But I don't sense a siren nearby, and even if I did, they wouldn't know I'm being held captive.

It isn't unlike me to wander away for some time, especially during the shift when I'm free to explore the ocean without the scrutiny of my father. In the water, we expect sirens to be swift, undetected, and efficient. We can scale the ocean in a matter of hours. We're not barred to one area in the sea, but are expected to steer clear of where other sirens are already stationed. Father had strict instructions to stay together—close enough where we could gather each other's assistance if needed, but far enough to not invade each other's territory. He hated when we ventured on our own, sick with worry about losing one of us like he lost our mother.

No wonder Briony prefers her human form—the stress of the shift would be too much for her.

Plus, she loves her humans.

My thoughts wander away to memories of my mother, but I'm quickly pulled back to the present by the sound of footfall beyond the door. I hold my breath, wondering if it's *him* or if one of the lust-filled idiots has snuck down in an attempt to save me.

I hope for the latter.

I need to get my sorry self back in the water before I deteriorate even more.

"*Pssst*...milady...are you in there?" a whisper-shout calls from behind the door. The thick wood separating us muffles the sound, but his words still come through clearly.

A shameless grin spreads across my face, ecstatic that one fell into my clutches so quickly.

I pull myself into a dramatic headspace, thinking up the saddest possible thing I can think of—spotted puppies being used as sacrifices for financial gain—and bite my tongue to further guide the tears to fall.

"I'm in here!" I cry out, releasing the sound of a sob. "Please, oh please, help me!"

"Stand back, milady. I'll break the door down."

I can't stop my eyes as they roll. Dimwit thinks I'm standing by the door? Has he never seen someone held as a prisoner before? Surely he knows the captain wouldn't leave me to wander around the room as I pleased?

The first loud *THUMP* hits the door, followed by a pained groan. I roll my eyes again, and when another large *THUMP* followed by another groan sounds, I force myself to stifle a laugh.

Where did the captain pick this crew up?

Worthless.

All of them.

"This isn't going to work, milady. I'll be right back," my "savior" calls through the door, his shuffling foot-steps growing distant. Fuck me, if this is the man that's here to save me, I may as well wave a white flag in surrender.

He returns within minutes, and I begin to hear what sounds like metal upon metal scraping at something.

Is he picking the lock? Potentially less worthless, then.

As he continues, I look up at my hands, studying my nails and the dried, prickled skin. When I get back to Norborne, I'm going to get a manicure to end all fucking manicures.

It takes my savior several minutes, but when I hear the telltale *click* and see the door crack open, I'm filled with relief. If he can pick that lock, he can pick the one that holds me shackled and free me.

I quickly hide my smile, remembering that I have to be sad and shit.

The tears continue streaming down my face as he enters the room, and I feign a look of terror as he approaches. I can be a damn good actress when I want to be and from the look of horror etched across this young man's face, I'd say I'm pretty believable in my show.

"I'm not here to hurt you, milady," he assures me, slowing his movement.

"You won't?" I sniffle.

"The opposite, in fact," he explains, smiling widely at me as he declares, "I want to claim you as mine."

If not for his height, I'd ask if he has even hit puberty. Instead, I raise a brow and ask, "How old are you?"

"Eighteen," he answers proudly, like that makes him a full-fledged man or something.

The boy has the body stature of an even younger teenager. Lean and tall, but gangly and awkward. His cheeks are full and round, still hanging onto the baby fat that he hasn't lost. A bit of acne is scattered across his forehead and chin. I watch his chest inflate with more pride under my attention.

And he wants to *claim* me?

Inwardly, I shudder. *Gross, no thank you.*

"Can you free me?" I ask him before biting down on my tongue, producing a new wave of tears. It hurts to cry. To lose more moisture, but this is necessary.

"Of course I can, beautiful. I wouldn't dream of leaving you here any longer." His eyes rake along my body, starting from my fin and up my tail, before lingering on my breasts, then finally up to my face. "Exquisite," he whispers before scurrying over in a rush and straddling me to remove the rope around my neck.

He takes a large whiff of me, and I watch his eyes roll back into his head. I'm not sure I hide the look of disgust that sweeps across my face, but he doesn't take notice. "Can I... Can I..." he stutters, leaving his sentence unfinished, leaning forward and licking my neck from my collarbone to my jaw. His tongue is rough and wet, and I gag a little.

He moans and presses further into me, and his erection fights against the fabric of his pants as he presses against my stomach. Regret roots deep within me for using my song to try to get free.

His breaths come out ragged as he groans, "Oh, Goddess, you taste delicious."

"Did you come down here to rescue me or assault me?" I ask through gritted teeth, hating the vulnerability that creeps up inside me. I know I can't physically remove him, though I do still have my song. I can easily open my mouth and stun him further...

His hand comes up and moves my hair to the side, exposing my right breast. He stares down at it with a gleam in his eye, his hand hovering, ready to touch me.

I do my best to bide my time, hoping if I distract him, he'll remember this is a rescue mission. "What's your name?"

His eyes snap up to mine as a smile curves up his lips, exposing his teeth, which glimmer in the morning sun that's cast a ray across where I'm shackled. "Martin, but you'll be moaning Master, soon enough," he tells me, pulling his smile wider with triumph. "And what is the name of my future bride?"

What the fuck?

He doesn't give me time to answer before he leans forward, hovering a little closer to my breast than I'd fucking like.

"MARTIN!" calls a voice.

Martin immediately stills, and he doesn't move for a few seconds. Like a statue, he's situated over me, the bony weight of him crushing my tail.

"You should, uh, go answer that," I say.

His eyes look into mine, and he looks ridiculously territorial. "They'll have to pry me away from you."

I want to curse at him to fuck off my tail, but I remember I'm the victim here. My eyes water. "If they find you, my sweet Martin, they'll take you away from me forever. You have to set me free the right way."

His lips purse to one side as he considers this. "I hate that you're chained, milady."

What is up with this *milady* shit?

I nod. "I know, *Master*, but I can be strong knowing you'll come back to me."

He nods adamantly. "I wouldn't dream of being away from you!"

I swallow a dry heave. "I believe you."

Now his face is thunderous. "You know I wouldn't blink twice about facing them all up there. I can crush them with my bare hands. I swear it, milady!"

The only way I can roll my eyes is to shut them as I feign sadness. "I know you could."

"MARTIN!"

He huffs a sigh, looking enraged but defeated.

"Go," I say, breathlessly. "But come back to me... when you're absolutely certain you can free me, that is."

He pouts as he wraps the rope around my mouth. Back to being muzzled. He climbs off me, and I let out a sigh of relief when he comes to a stand. "I promise to return, and we will leave, my sweet crab pie."

Ew, what the fuck?

I attempt to give him a hopeful smile through the rope and nod.

My pathetic smile slides off my face the second he leaves.

I am so fucked.

CHAPTER 9

James

"Martin is acting funny," Briggs tells me as I haul another bucket of water out of the bilges.

Briggs steps back, all disgusted by my filth. Shirtless, in my dirtiest trousers, I'm covered in grease head to toe, smelling like seawater and rust. My chest is moving quickly as I wipe the sweat off my forehead, leaving another coating of grease behind, judging by Briggs' extra look of disgust.

"What's he doing?" I ask, voice curt because I don't have the fucking patience now to talk about Martin.

"He keeps singing," Briggs explains.

I sense Grimy's movements slowing behind me.

"Okay," I draw out slowly. "What's the issue, Briggs?"

"He's singing about our captive. Says he's going to marry her and put his seed in her belly." Briggs nearly gags. How the fuck did I recruit this man into my crew when he can barely stomach a fucking song?

Luca cackles from the pilothouse, and even Grimy is

coughing to hide his laugh. I simply shoot Briggs an empty stare. "What would you like me to do about it, Briggs?"

"Can you ask him to stop?" He runs a hand through his gorgeous blond locks. "And to also stop taking so many damn bathroom breaks?"

My movements slow as I narrow my eyes at him. "I've not seen that man-boy going past for toilet breaks. Is he not pissing off the side of the ship?"

"No, he's been using the other side—"

"That toilet has been backed up since the storm," Grimy cuts in. "He'd have to cross us to go to the toilet."

"Well then, I've got no fucking clue—"

I climb out of the bilges a second later, pushing past him and to the crews' quarters.

That burning in my chest grows stronger as I close in on it. I rub at my chest, confused with the feeling.

I stop at the door. The lock is in place, but it's facing the opposite direction. Frowning, I pull out the key and unlock it. I swing the door open, gripping the switchblade in one hand as I look directly into the room.

Everything looks as it should.

My captive is still in the same place I left her, head down, her hair swaying around her. For a moment, I take pity at the sight of her. My chest tugs once more, and with it, a feeling of loneliness channels through me. Which is strange. Because I'm not feeling lonely. Not like this, anyway.

I take a step, and the floor beneath my foot creaks.

She doesn't move at the sound.

Unease runs through me.

Looking at her, you'd think she was lifeless. I take another step, studying the room once again, checking for anything out of the ordinary. I come to a stop before her, and like before, she's not looking too good. Her tail's duller, the shimmering effect absent even with the sunlight streaming through the room.

I crouch down and raise a hand. I wipe away the strands of hair from her face to look at her. My fingers tingle, the urge to be gentle with her causing me to slow my movements. I stare at her closed mouth, at her plump lips, and layers deep, I feel something within me stir. Her eyes are closed, and weakly, she moves her head away from my touch as she weakly asks, "Are you back then?" Her voice is barely audible through the rope gagged in her mouth.

My brows come together. "Were you waiting on me, fish?"

At the sound of my voice, her eyes whip open. There's a bit more life in that expression. Alarm runs through my chest—but I'm not feeling alarmed, not at all.

Where are these emotions coming from?

I study her, the way her gaze flicks to the door and then back at me.

Now a different feeling spreads across my chest. *Confusion.*

I turn my head, following her line of sight to see an empty doorway. *Huh.*

Cold realization hits me.

"Expecting me or someone else?" I suddenly wonder

aloud as my eyes harden back on hers. Untying the rope, I continue asking my questions. "You lonely, Siren?"

"Lonely?" she repeats with a dramatic gasp as the rope falls. "It's always a party on this ship. What with all the screaming and the thumping about. I used to think men aboard ships just drank and fucked around, but to hear all this hard labor? I feel quite glad I put you men to work with my craftsmanship."

"Your destruction of my ship is craftsmanship to you?"

She smiles, charmingly. "It was like art to me, Captain. Now, don't tell me you didn't enjoy what I did to this place."

Trying to provoke a reaction out of me yet again. My expression remains flat. "Terrific job, sea whore."

"Back to flirting so soon?"

"I enjoy foreplay before a good fuck."

She lets out a playful moan, sarcasm thick in her voice as she says, "Please, tell me more."

I inch closer, face wavering close to hers as my hand glides up her arm. I feel her skin pebble beneath my touch. Arousal spreads across my chest—and again, I didn't put it there, nor am I feeling it anywhere outside of my cock. "I like it pretty rough, Siren," I explain, voice low. "I like a good fight, too." My touch runs along her collarbone to wrap around her throat. "And I like to squeeze right here, hard enough to mark what's mine."

"Yours?" she repeats, those eyes burning into mine.

I squeeze her throat just a little bit, and her breath lightens. "Yes, Little Fish. I only fuck what's mine."

"Such a romantic, Captain," she forces out, but her pulse quickens just the same.

Letting go of her throat, I pick up the rope again and lightly brush it along her mouth. "Romantic would be gagging you all over again, but tighter this time." I run my tongue along my bottom lip, aware her eyes are tracing the movement as I add, "On that note, I'm curious why it was in your mouth when I came down here, considering I forgot to tie you back up."

Horror shoots through my chest—which is interesting. Because I'm fucking positive this Little Mermaid is feeling horrified by my discovery. I tilt my head to the side, studying her reaction, but she's good. Her face remains playful.

"Would you look at that?" she simply responds, giving nothing away.

"Are you playing around with Martin?" I query, bored, though I can't deny the rage that bubbles in my blood at the thought. *Territorial?* That would be primitive of me to be because she is not mine, and yet...

"Who's Martin?" she innocently asks.

"Did he promise to release you? Is that why he keeps singing about putting his seed in your belly?"

Now her face twists with disgust. "You can't blame me for the way I make your men feel."

"So, it's not your fault that he's singing tales of a happily ever after with you?"

She coolly shrugs. "I've been right here. How is it my fault?" Now she smiles as a strange look crosses her face. "My, my. Are you jealous, Captain? That your men want to shoot their seed in me? Because...I can almost *feel* something..."

My jaw locks as we stare at each other.

But I can sense the questions behind her gaze because she's sensing mine just the same.

She felt my rage, didn't she?

Just as I felt her horror.

She's playing with my head.

"What spell are you using on me, Siren?" I quietly demand.

For the first time, her face clears, and she shakes her head seriously. "No spell, Captain."

"Then why...?"

I don't have it in me to vocalize the question because I can't be certain it's not just me growing insane.

"I'm not doing anything," she says slowly now, irritation flaring in her gaze.

I don't believe her.

I continue to study her for some time, trying my hardest to ease any feelings inside me. She may not be in my head, but she's in my emotions. It must be some siren spell I don't know about, but Goddess' sake, my bracelet should be keeping that shit at bay. I touch my bracelet, conflicted, uncertain of what to do with this fish.

I could kill her—

I should kill her.

Yet there's that burning again in my chest that lurches at the mere thought of it.

Gritting my teeth, I growl, "Be careful trying to get into the hearts of my men. Kill another one, and I won't be so merciful."

"You call *this* mercy?" she retorts, shaking at her bound arms as she glowers at me. "How about just letting me go? I'll leave you be—"

"Not a chance."

"If I can't kill you with my song, what use are you to me?" she argues.

I ignore her question, deciding to disengage as I come to a stand. "I'll free you when you start talking. Are you willing to talk, beast?"

She flinches, like calling her a beast was a serious insult. But not sea whore, no, because that makes fucking sense. I take her silence as an answer and turn back to the door.

"How do you know Sinwa?"

I pause in my step and take a moment to gather my response. "Why did you attack my ship?"

"You said, 'death by beauty.' Do you know what that meant to our old society?"

I twist my head, letting her see my profile as I say, "It was an offense. You weren't allowed to use your song to kill. 'Death by beauty.' A curt reminder that you're going against the values of your old kind."

"How do you know Sinwa?" she tries once more, voice harder, sounding rattled now.

And again, I simply respond, "Why did you attack my ship?"

If she won't answer, neither will I.

She huffs a breath, dissatisfied.

I leave a moment later, and this time the burn in my chest grows cooler the further away I am from her.

The strange tug in my chest doesn't like it.

Separate from my desire is a flicker of a visceral impulse to make sure *nothing* and *no one* touches her without my fucking permission.

This is madness, and this is havoc—

This is a fucking problem.

CHAPTER 10

Aria

The ocean air filters through the porthole and sends a shiver down my torso, pebbling my already cold skin. I want nothing more than to pull my arms tight across my chest and hug myself for warmth, but the bastard Erickson—or, at least, that's what I'm referring to him as, though I still don't know his given name—still hasn't unchained me.

I'm in desperate need of water.

Everything about me is cracked and chapped. My lips. The skin on my hands. My poor, beautiful tail. Even my hair is incredibly brittle and dull. If I could run my fingers through it, I would bet it'd break off between my fingers.

My tail is suffering the worst disfigurement. Thick cracks curve through the once glimmering scales, some so deep and open you can see raw flesh. Dehydration plagues the rest of it. My scales are flaking off and turning an ashen gray. *Dying.*

I won't die, though, not from lack of water.

What I do feel like I will die from is hunger. I would give anything for a piping hot bowl of capellini noodles doused in butter, garlic, and parmesan.

Admittedly, I've spent far too much of my time shackled thinking about food.

Food. My second favorite F word.

How long have I been down here?

I resent the time I was incapacitated, my system filled with Gala Green. Losing perception of time may be the worst thing thus far. I have no idea how long I have until the shift ends, and if I don't make it back to the ocean in my siren form, I have no chance of getting off this ship. No chance of escaping *him*. At least not until we make it to land.

My stomach rumbles, a deep ache sitting dead center in the middle of my gut, begging to be filled with warm breads, hot entrees, and decadent desserts.

I miss my sisters. They love to cook, and I love to be their taste tester. I picture them cozy in their beds, snuggled into the warmth of their linens. If it's morning, like I think it might be, Celeste likely has stolen one of Briony's romance novels and is reading it under the blanket, while her soft snores fill the bedroom I once shared with her.

The bedroom that I *share* with her.

I'd break free from this mess soon. No need to think in past tense.

Jutting my tongue between my lips, I rub it over the broken skin. It feels like sandpaper against the already sore divots, and as I attempt to swallow, the dryness catches in my throat.

Unfortunately, a groan vocalizes at the very moment the door harshly swings open.

"Uncomfortable, Little Mermaid?"

The Erickson is standing in the doorway, looming, as his dark eyes sweep over the room. Reaching up, he rests his hands against the top of the doorframe, as though he has not a care in the world nor a practically lifeless siren chained up.

His gaze is heavy on me and a rush of curiosity pangs through my chest. I slightly raise an eyebrow at the sudden feeling. *How odd.*

Rather than answer him, I push my tongue between my lips again, attempting to relieve the ache.

He gives away nothing as he continues to stand in the doorway, not entering, yet not leaving. "You must be," he muses, voice thick with arrogance. "Being chained up in that position must be quite uncomfortable. You must also be thirsty. And *hungry.*"

I raise my head at the mention of food, giving him my full attention.

"Ah. So the beast is hungry, then. Didn't get enough hearts when you pillaged my ship?"

"I didn't *eat* them, you sicko," I retort, sickened by the mere thought. "I'm not a barbarian."

"Just a heart snatcher, then. *Much* better."

"Are you going to feed me?" I snap.

His eyes darken and he shifts his stance, no longer holding the door frame but now leaning against it casually. "No."

"No?"

"No. You can go much longer without food. Believe me, I know. And until I decide what to do with you, I won't waste our already scarce rations on you. I have mouths to feed on deck. Yours is the least of my concern."

The venom on his tongue radiates through his words, and my chest burns with fury. So much hatred spews from him, practically tangible in the room.

The feeling is mutual.

"I hate you," I hiss, though my voice lacks the oomph behind it. My body is weakening—deteriorating further as this repulsive man stands before me...*what*? Taunting me?

His lips curl upward into a cruel smile. One he wears quite frequently. "And I, you, fish."

"Then why are you here?"

He crosses his arms in front of his chest, looking very cozy against the wooden frame he rests against. I wish I could cross my arms. Shit, I wish I could just move my arms. I can't even feel them at this point.

Erickson studies me for what feels like eternity before pushing off the doorframe and moving just beyond it, to where I can only see a sliver of him from behind. He bends at the waist and picks up something.

When he turns into my full view, I see it's a bucket. Water sloshes over the top and I can't help but squeeze my eyes together, feeling hopeful he's about to douse me with it as he did before.

Instead, he sets it down just inside of the room.

"Behave," he cautions. "And when I come back, I

might sprinkle a few drops on you. Watch the glow on your skin come back momentarily before it fades again. See how long it takes. We could play that game for hours, Siren. Doesn't it sound like fun?"

The smooth, smug way he delivers that question forms another knot in my already hollow stomach. *No, it doesn't sound like fun, you stupid fucking jerk.*

I'm seething mad, gritting my teeth to fight off all the things I want to shout at him. But my words may be the reason he withholds the water later. So, I swallow down the string of curses, and watch as he leaves again.

THERE'S a lot of commotion right after he leaves.

I hear Martin's screams, then pleas. My noble knight in shining armor is begging for my captor's mercy. I roll my eyes. So much for a grand escape.

Straining my ears, I listen as threats are being made. Martin is told he'll be under Briggs' strict supervision. The captain is too busy patching something important up and can't do it himself. I can feel his aggravation at that all the way down here.

That man—

What is it with him?

It doesn't feel natural. I've easily loathed attractive men—so it's not his damned beauty that's fucking with my head.

I swallow, mouth dry, throat aching. Everything aches, and is slightly worse than earlier. Including this

Goddess-damned ache in my chest. It hurts something fierce, and I'm suddenly aware it has to do with that man. He feels something too and seems to think *I* put it there.

But I'm weak.

Even opening my mouth and attempting a song is beyond me. Not that I want to even try. I'm not keen on driving Martin insane, especially when he's still my only fucking hope out of this place. As shitty as that hope is turning out to be.

Time is just a figment of my imagination at this rate. Every minute is stretching on, disappearing into some limitless abyss. I yearned for this power—for this shift— and now I just want it to be over. I'm in too much physical agony. Sirens are not made to be out of water for this long, and though it won't kill me completely, it fucking feels like it will.

As I close my eyes, I fall into that place between sleep and consciousness.

My entire body begs to let go. My limbs are heavy and unmoving, body stiff from being kept in the same position for so long. Blood now seeps from my tail, small rivers of red sliding down it and pooling on the wooden planks of the floor. The fire inside of me is mere embers and though I keep telling myself to find the spark—to push through, to *survive*—my eyes feel incredibly heavy.

Later, when the door slams open, I barely turn my head. My chest tugs, that warmth growing with intensity, and a contented sigh floats past my lips.

Water rushes over me like a sudden wave. I gasp,

opening my eyes as my captor tosses the bucket of water over my tail. I moan unabashedly, watching as my tail greedily intakes the water. The cracks begin to heal as soon as the final drop soaks in, and I don't bother hiding the first genuine smile in what feels like days as I watch my scales regain a slight shimmer.

The captain sets down the empty bucket and picks up another. This time he starts at my head and pours a small amount over it. The water cascades through my hair and over the swell of my breasts. Some even pool in my belly button from the way my body's still slumped against the wall. Slowly, he continues to pour water over my body, making sure it touches every inch of me.

I want to cry from relief.

Against my better judgment, I whisper, "Thank you," as he sets the bucket down.

He doesn't answer, but he stands for a moment, his eyes catching onto mine. We look at each other, saying nothing, and even though the silence sits between us, there's an ocean of emotions I can't describe.

I can't put a finger on it, but there is a sense of familiarity, like I've felt this feeling before, like...like I've *sensed* his presence before. The past comes flitting through my memory, and I *know* I'd have seen this man in the flesh... but there's a reminder in the darkness, of falling into a dream, of waking and wondering—

I close my eyes for a moment, stunned.

Impossible.

When I finally open my eyes, he's already leaving. He walks out of the room without a second glance. His footsteps sound curt, and a feeling swarms my chest that I know must come from him: *irritation.*

Whether it's at me or himself, I can't tell.

The door snaps shut and I hear the lock engage, but this time I can hardly care, too enamored by the way my body glows and glitters again, and my strength begins to return.

CHAPTER 11

Aria

The room is dark when the sound of the lock being picked wakes me. Numb and exhausted, I allowed myself to close my eyes earlier, if not for rest, then for a simple way to pass the time.

I assume tonight is my last night in my siren form. *It has to be.* And that means I only have a handful of hours to make my escape before they discover me in my human form.

But then what?

If I'm discovered, what will come of me then?

I really don't want to find out. Staying on this ship isn't an option. I have to think fast.

Act fast.

And pray to the Gods and Goddesses that the noise on the other end of the door is dear fucking Martin 'Master'.

The kid is a fucking joke.

"Pssssttt... *milady*," he whisper-shouts, popping the door open a crack. Through the dim lighting—the only illumination from the cloud-covered moonlight—I can see Martin's mouth pushed through the crack as he speaks to me. The crack *he* produces, like he can't open it further.

A pair of lips and the tip of a nose pushes into the room, and that's it.

Why he doesn't just fully open the door is beyond me.

But he's here now, so I guess it's showtime.

Clamping down on my tongue hard enough to draw blood, I squeeze out the tears that form from the pain and let them roll down my cheeks. "Oh Martin! You came back for me!" I singsong sweetly. "Please! Please help me."

Finally pushing open the door, Martin strides into the room like he's the king in new robes. His long, skinny hands even roll down the front of his dirty dress shirt as though he's smoothing out new digs.

Crouching down beside me, he skims his calloused finger down the bridge of my nose.

What a fucking weirdo.

"I managed to sneak away from Briggs as he combed through his hair. I'm going to get you out of here, milady. I have a plan," he tells me. "Once the captain is in his quarters, and Grimy has retired, I'll make sure Briggs is good and out with a hearty dose of Gala Green, then I'll sneak back here and pick your locks. We'll run. Together, milady. The ship has one last longboat, still in decent shape even after that doozy of a storm. I'll pack it with supplies, then we'll be free and away from the Tempest before sunrise."

Away from that Erickson, too.

I shake my head adamantly. "Oh, Martin, you have a plan!"

Not sure it's a good one, but it's a plan. All I need is for the man-child to break my locks free and get me to the deck. I'd take it from there, but he certainly doesn't need to be clued in on that slight change in his plans.

His smile is wide as he casts his eyes down my body, licking his lips as he takes in the sight of me. My skin still glows slightly, though it's dimmed as hours have passed since the captain tossed water on me. My hair has dried and the strands of pink and purple blend, matted together with the tendrils of platinum mixed in.

Martin exhales, pushing the air roughly from between the O he's created with his lips.

I'm suddenly on high alert as I watch his body language, unapologetically glancing down at his crotch, unsurprised yet really, *really* unhappy to see there is a rigid bulge straining the fabric.

Fuck.

If I ever get off this fucking ship, I'm going to have to drink a pub dry to get that image out of my head.

Focus, Aria.

I have to avert his attention and get him ready to put his plan into place. My eyes connect with his lust filled ones, and I turn on my charm. "Martin, I'm so happy you've figured out a way to get me out of this. I can't wait to finally be free. We can be together, my love." *Gag.* Literal vomit just rose into my esophagus. "Now, you must go. Be with your crew so we do not raise suspicions. Set the scene and come back to me, my sweet *Master.*"

Fucking A+, Aria.

A heady groan leaves his lips and I watch his eyes roll into the back of his head. Martin reaches down and palms himself through his pants.

"I will go, my sweet crustacean, but first I need just a little taste."

Crustacean? What the fuck? I'm a siren, not a shellfish.

I shouldn't have let myself get hung up on his idiocy though, because now I'm caught off guard as he sweeps my hair away from my breast and leans forward, pulling my nipple into his mouth. He sucks roughly and clamps down with his pearly whites.

Fuck.

My shriek does little to deter him—in fact, he mistakes it for pleasure and continues swirling his tongue around my areola, while his hand comes up to knead my other breast. Bile rises up my throat. There is nothing I can do but sit here and allow him to assault me.

I can scream, but what's the point?

I realize at this moment that other than using my siren song I have no weapon to fight off these men that hold me captive, and yet, my song will only drive them more wild with lust and the outcome could be worse. There could be more Martins. There could be more Martins with even more repulsive intentions. Stronger Martins. Fucking Martins that are truly men. And once the shift is over, my only weapon will be gone.

Double fuck.

His mouth pops off my nipple, and he rips my hair away from my other breast, his movements harsh.

"You're like a drug, milady. The high you give me is better than Gala Green. What I wouldn't give to—" but he's lost to the lust, cutting off his own sentence to bite down on my flesh like *I'm* a drug.

"Stop!" I heave out. "Let's talk!"

But he moans in response, muttering something about having me before anyone else.

Irritation flares through me. "It's the lust, you piece of shit. My song—"

"THIS IS TRUE LOVE!" he bellows, making me jump at his unexpected ferocity.

I roll my eyes and look away from him, tears lining my eyes as I focus my gaze on the ocean beyond the porthole. "Whatever you say."

"Tell me I'm yours—"

"I'd rather die."

A dark look passes over the man-child. He suddenly looks demonic. Raising his arm, he flattens his palm and wields it back. "You will treat me with respect, or as your master, I will beat it out of you!"

I'm too distracted by my repugnance, readying myself for the blow, to notice the dark shadow that appears in the doorway, or the heavy stomps that shake the floor. Before I can fully register what is happening, a sickening *CRACK* permeates the air and Martin's head rolls to the side, hanging in an unnatural way. The two enormous hands that hold it pull it to the side before releasing, and Martin's body falls to the floor in a heap.

Captain Erickson's jaw is clenched and his chest heaves with unsteady breaths as he searches my face. His eyes are as dark as the ocean floor, and I can't help but notice the sheen of sweat that threatens to drip from his hairline. "Did he hurt you?" he grits out, voice thick and gravelly.

My eyes follow his movements as he lowers himself to crouch in front of me. Even in my shifted form, I suddenly feel so small. I'm temporarily disarmed by the emotion that dances behind his eyes, almost as if he is... *fearful* for me?

I'm definitely feeling that fear right now. Unfortunately, it's difficult to hide.

"Did he hurt you?" he repeats.

My head shakes on its own accord. My response is flat. Dead. An attempt to bury what I just experienced. "No, he just engaged in a little nipple play." I try to shrug, but it's a challenge when my arms are still hanging above my head.

His hands ball into fists, and he stands quickly, giving me his back. Anger shudders through him. I watch with fascination, and I wonder if I pegged this man incorrectly. Maybe he has a shred of humanity after all. Or maybe it's just the effects of my song.

The bracelet...

And yet lust rolls off him in waves...

Then again, it rolls off me, too. An inexplicable force lies between us, like...perhaps he's enchanted me, too.

The thought is startling.

Several minutes pass before he turns around to face me again. His hands cradle the back of his head, fanning his bent arms out on either side. His eyes close and his nostrils flare before he says, "He put his mouth on you."

His words are not a question, but I answer him anyway. "Yes."

He stands unnaturally still, but there's a look of torment in his gaze as it pierces me. The rage—I can feel it so strongly. It's like a bitter taste on my tongue as it rolls off him; whatever is happening, I know we're linked somehow, like there is a tether between us now, solidifying. Yet despite the wrath, he appears so calm, the storm raging within him tightly buried deep, until he whispers, "He fucking touched what's *mine*."

It takes a moment for me to comprehend his words.

"Excuse me? *Yours?*" My stomach twists with an unwarranted feeling, almost like a tornado of small flutters, which I quickly squash. I let out a sardonic laugh, hoping it disguises how brittle I feel. "That's funny. The man's got jokes now, ladies and gentlemen."

This man is the *enemy*. I remind myself. *I don't just hate him—I loathe him.*

He stops and turns, his eyes locking with mine. With a sinister smile, he prowls toward me in four long strides and couches down once more. "Yes, Siren. *Mine*. Mine to *torture*, mine to *touch*. Mine to *fuck*, if I so choose. The screams that come from this pretty little mouth are either going to be screams of pain, or of pleasure, or of *both,* but they belong to me. That tongue is mine, Little Fish."

Something about his possessiveness spurs me on. Makes me bolder. Hotter. Desperate to push at his buttons.

"I bet you wish you could fuck something other than my mouth, don't you, *Captain?*" I spit mockingly, baiting him. A rush of excitement zips through my body, and I bite my lower lip to keep from smiling.

He opens his mouth to retort, but his eyes catch on my breasts, still fully exposed from when Martin moved my hair, and he squints. Tilting my head downward, I follow his line of sight and find my skin raised and red with a ring of teeth marks imprinted onto the swell.

My vision raises just in time to see every torture device laid out fly through the air as he swings his arms across the table in anger, sending them scattering across the floor. A strangled growl erupts from his mouth as he bends to pick up the meat mallet that landed near his feet. His behavior is unexpected. This is not my aura that drives him into such a rage.

This is something else entirely.

"He fucking *marked* you." Stalking over to Martin's lifeless body, he raises the meat mallet above his head before slamming it down brutally against Martin's skull, bashing it over and over until there is nothing left but a pile of brain matter.

I'm no stranger to blood and violence, but the sight has me scooting back as far as I can, trying to become one with the wall. Blood spatter sprinkles across my tail, which is beginning to dehydrate and crack once more. I say nothing while I watch him stand and move toward me, covered in bright red blood.

Breath doesn't leave my lungs as my eyes run over him.

His white shirt, rolled to his elbows, looks like an abstract painting, the blood traveling up his neck and face, and covering his arms. As he approaches, his shadow looms over me and I'm almost fearful to look up at him from below my lashes.

Crazy.

He's crazy.

"I'm going to ask you once more, Siren. Did he hurt you?"

I know the answer he wants.

He wants me to say *yes* so he can feel validated about murdering his crewmate in cold blood.

A slight look of remorse shadows his eyes momentarily, but just as quickly as it appears, it's gone.

I should tell him no. If I tell him yes, I'm giving into his demands, letting him think he has a hold on me. He's not my knight in shining armor and I'm not his damsel in distress. Him killing *for* me changes nothing. I should tell him no.

Say it, Aria. Say *it.*

"Yes," I hear myself whisper instead.

No sooner does the word leave my lips does he grab me by the base of the jaw, his fingers curling around my throat as his thumb directs my face upward. We hold each other's gazes, a burning hatred reflecting from both, and I tilt my head further upward in a challenge. My heart thunders in my chest, threatening to burst from my rib cage and explode. My skin burns everywhere, yet goosebumps pebble beneath his touch, my nipples hardening into painfully tight peaks.

Slowly, he crouches to my level, and our stare intensifies. His hold is still tight, his eyes hard, but as he tilts his head slightly, I'm met with a loathing that intertwines with a possessiveness I'm not familiar with.

My breaths pick up.

My cheeks burn as I see this bloodied man for what he truly is: monstrous, violent... *mesmerizing.*

Just when I think he's about to release his grasp, his lips slam against mine. He catches me in a punishing kiss, which quickly morphs into a frenzy.

My eyes shut as his tongue prods the seam of my mouth, begging for entrance, which I unwillingly surrender. Melting slightly under his hold, I let him gain access.

The kiss is all teeth crashing, labored breathing, and tongues exploring. There is nothing warm or romantic about it. Instead, it's the complete opposite.

A threat.

A promise.

A power struggle.

A traitorous moan glides up from my chest, and he groans as he catches it.

I gasp as he sucks my tongue into his mouth, swirling his own around it before he bites down hard. Hissing, I jolt my head back and break our kiss, the taste of blood on my lips.

If our gaze was full of loathing before, now it's full of venom.

"Fuck," he snarls, his body faltering like it wants to fall back into me. Instead, he comes to a stand, his chest heaving up and down. He runs a hand through that sinful black hair, his eyes distant now with thought.

No more words are spoken.

Not from me.

Nor from him.

Casting another quick glance my way, he turns on his heel and throws open the door of my prison, stomping over the threshold and slamming the door behind him. Footsteps quickly fade away, and I look down at the corpse of my fleeting rescuer next to me. Vision spotting, I expel a deep breath out.

What the hell just happened?

CHAPTER 12

James

I'm fucking shaking.

The taste of that fiery siren is still hot on my tongue. The feeling doesn't fade the further I am from her. If anything, the distance feels like a burning itch in my chest. It *hurts* to be away from her.

This isn't the power of a siren coursing through me, weakening my equilibrium. This is something else entirely.

"There's a curse afoot," murmurs Grimy as he stands before the shelves. We're on the starboard side of the ship, in my captain's quarters. I peer out the skylight, at the fog still encompassing the boat as it continues to bob lifelessly in the ocean. The ship isn't moving. The water is getting higher in the bilges, and while Luca and Briggs have been spending every minute patching the damage and bailing out the water, I can feel the tension on the Tempest. Can feel its bones grimacing and weakening around me, like it's groaning in agony.

It's breaking me apart.

This ship is all that tethers me to my bloodline. It is the only evidence they existed once upon a time. That we thrived on a beautiful piece of land, on a part of the map that is now marred with superstition.

It was once called Goldspince for all the riches we mined from the earth.

The maps now call it Calamity Isle.

We deserved it.

"If what you've told me is correct, she is no ordinary siren," Grimy continues, running his fingers down the spines of countless old books. They were once my father's books. And before that, my grandfather's. Even longer so, my great-grandfather's, and so on. Sometimes I feel like I'm in a time prison, that they got to escape in death, yet I'm shackled to this fucking ship, my fate undetermined.

Rex whimpers from my berth, his tired body digging under the covers. He's affected, too. We're all weary to the soul. Especially Grimy, who pauses for a moment to run a handkerchief over his sweaty forehead.

"Is she the one who's plagued your dreams, boy?"

"Respect, old man. I'm still your captain."

Grimy throws me a look that very much says, *respect your elders*, but I let it go, relenting and answering his question. "It's hard to say."

"She fits the description—"

"I'm saying it's plausible, but I can't know for certain."

Finally, he pulls out a large black journal from the shelf. His movements are slow as he settles it down on my map desk. The irony is not lost on me that the book covers the entirety of the Calamity Isle, as if destined to be forgotten, even now. Flipping through the pages, I watch Grimy run his weathered fingers down the lines of old ink. The penmanship gradually changes, the strokes different as the fountain pen passed on from one generation to the next.

"What are you looking for?" I ask. I've read this notebook hundreds of times, searching for clues to set us free.

"There was a story passed along, mentioned only briefly at the beginning," Grimy explains. "Of the sorceress who imprisoned humans to be hunted for eternity. She roams the seas, elusive and hidden."

I shake my head, having mastered the journal from beginning to end. "You're talking about Mathis Erickson —known to be mentally unhinged. He spoke nonsense."

Grimy pauses to look over his shoulder at me. His mouth curls into a dark smile. "You would say that, wouldn't you? An Erickson. How evil to have the truth hidden in plain sight. Lines that may be our undoing, their meaning invisible to you."

I take a moment to understand his words, and then I'm stomping to his side, peering over his shoulder at the page he's stopped at. I lean in. "This entry has no coherent thought," I say, looking over the thoughts of the poor Erickson cunt that inherited the pen. "Mathis was a woeful fuck, never stopped talking about getting off the Tempest, kept dreaming about—"

"An enchantress who whispered promises in his ear."

I shoot Grimy a dry look. "Said he had a pet serpent,

Grimy, that nobody else could see. These entries are madness."

But Grimy picks the book up and slams it into my chest, forcing me to grab it. "What if they're true? After all, the sorceress in his dreams predicted this would happen."

Another groan rips through the Tempest, this one long and grieved. Grimy's eyes lose focus, and his throat bobs as he looks at me. "She's hurting," he whispers, speaking of my ship. "She was hardly hanging on as it was—"

"We'll fix her," I say resolutely, but even I can't deny the struggle it is to draw a breath in. To think for a moment she might break apart around us, sinking to the bottom of the ocean. She doesn't belong here. She should not be laid to rest at the bottomless, rotten depths of the Black Sea. Where sirens and other vile monsters roam.

It's not the first time the ship has endured destruction at the hands of a siren, I remind myself as memories pummel through me.

No, it's certainly not the first time.

The Tempest screams as the waves pummel the ship, bursting through the open portholes. I'm ankle deep in water, and never in my life have I felt a fear like this come over me.

My father screams orders, and I watch him, awed by his strength, as we try to ride through the storm nobody predicted. The skies were so clear. We had spent the afternoon anchored down just off a beautiful little island. The men had been rowdy, there had been beautiful girls from the island, and a few of them had boarded the ship. Music had played, couples had danced, and drink had floated around the deck.

For once, my father had not sent me down to my cabin.

For once, I wasn't shut away.

"You're thirteen now," he had said in his drunken moment of glee. "Almost a man."

"But not quite," murmured a flat looking Grimy, sober as a nun.

I never liked Grimy.

He was always trying to isolate me from the fun.

And this fun made my skin hot, and my pulse quicken.

I was watching a crewmate stick his tongue into a woman's mouth, his hand gripping her nearly exposed breast when a palm suddenly slammed against the back of my head. "It's rude to stare," Grimy growled, forcing me to look away.

To spite him, I continued to stare. "If I want to look, I will."

"You are too young."

"I'm nearly a man," I retorted. "Just like father said."

"Your father says a lot of things."

I watched as the man continued to fondle the woman; I studied her sounds and her reaction as he took her into his grip and pushed her against the handrail.

"Go down to your cabin," Grimy ordered.

Anger pounded into my head as I glared up at the ancient, skeletal man. "Father said I'm allowed up here—"

"Your father is currently preoccupied with a whore, and now I'm in charge," he seethed, peering into my eyes with his cold gaze. "Unless you want to interrupt him, you'll do as I bloody say."

I scowled, unafraid of the old man. "You're miserable,

Grimy, and one day I'll be bigger than you, and you'll be following my orders."

He slapped the back of my head once more, uncaring. "Until then, Prince James, you'll be in your cabin, safe and sound."

Safe and sound from what?

Why did he always act like the sky was falling?

Huffing, I stomped to my quarters, slamming the door of the cabin so hard it rattled the walls. Frustrated, I kicked at my dresser before dropping onto the bed, right next to the large lump buried beneath my covers. The lump squirmed, and a moment later, a matted head popped out. Rex looked up at me, his tired eyes roaming along my face before he stuck his tongue out and licked along my hand. I stroked him, still angry, still frustrated by Grimy.

"I'm alright, old boy," I told him as he nuzzled into my side. "It's alright."

Rex was on his last stretch. The old dog nearing his end, and suddenly everything felt all the worse now. My father was rutting a woman, Grimy was still in charge of me, and I was tossed in here like discarded trash, forced to watch the animal I grew up with struggle to keep his eyes open around me. I dug under the covers with him, cuddling him to me as I shut my eyes to sleep the fun away.

The next time I'd wake up, the ship would be swept into the sea, its bow raised to the sky, and most of the crew dead.

And that song—

That song would be playing the melody of death as Grimy burst through my cabin before my father even thought to.

"My prince," he said, shakily. "I will protect you."

"What if Mathis is right?" Grimy asks, pulling me from my memory. He sounds desperate—anxious. "What if we're being hunted, and the siren's attack on the Tempest was deliberate?"

"Then we end her," I say pointedly. "Before she ends us."

"But if this strange bond you've developed with her grows, then what?"

I stare at him, evenly. "Then we pay Vanya a visit."

I HELP Luca and Briggs in the bilges, thinking of Grimy's words. The burning in my chest hasn't eased. If anything, it rages on like an inferno. To be free. To have this fucking bracelet off my wrist. There is nothing I want more. I clench my hand for a moment, peering down at the bracelet's inscription.

We're down there for a solid while, and both men don't speak. Briggs is still gaining focus after coming to, though the Gala Green he'd gulped down was only a small amount. His movements are still a little sloppy.

Luca, on the other hand, is disturbed. He ignores his hard-on, even as a distant echo of a song wafts over us. Ankle deep in water, I watch Luca carefully as he adjusts himself, his cheeks reddening. Briggs notices and scoots away.

"She's using her voice," I say.

Luca pauses from the patch work to look at me. His eyes are glazed, the pained look of arousal taking everything out of him to resist. "Aye, Cap, there's a song. Distant, but I can feel it just the same."

My voice is tight. "I'll bind her lips shut—"

"Distant," Luca cuts in now, staring at me like I'm not understanding. "It's not coming from *our* siren."

My body stiffens, the haunting realization hitting me in full force. *Another one.*

We make quick work of the holes. It's not a permanent fix, but we're buying time. As squeamish and dramatic as Briggs is, he is damn good at ship maintenance. I give him a solid pat on the back, acknowledging his work.

If we can get the Tempest to crawl toward land, it means we still have a chance at saving her.

By the time we're done, the song of the distant siren fades away, and I don't know if that's more troubling. Part of me wonders if they're searching for her. For our siren.

"Anyone know where the fuck Martin's scurried off to?" Luca asks now.

"I'd like to give him a piece of my mind," snarls Briggs.

Wincing, I decide not to tell them his mutilated body is lying next to our prisoner.

For reasons and such.

We climb out of the bilges. Grabbing the spyglass from the pilothouse, I storm above deck, ears straining for the soft echo of a song. Luca follows, his gaze trapped to the waters. Still obscured in fog, I'm not looking into the horizon. I tread my sights along the perimeters of the waters that are visible to us. Sometimes I see the head of a creature surface, its large curious eyes gleaming at us.

They can feel her. They come to her like she beckons for them. Aside from the Tempest being hit earlier, none of the ocean dwellers have attacked.

"That one has one large eye," Briggs points out, sounding offended. "Glaring at me, Cap."

"Tell him to stop," I blandly reply, focusing my attention on what actually matters.

"Stop," whispers Briggs, bending down to point at the large eye of the purple looking sea blob that blinks slowly back at him.

I turn away. I fucking can't with him sometimes.

My skin heats suddenly as that waft of another song washes over us.

Luca runs a ragged hand down his face. "There is only so much I can fucking take, Cap, before I plummet off this ship and swim to that sea whore."

The last thing I fucking need is another set of hands gone. "Then drink, Luca. If it saved you once, it'll save you again."

"Not if that Little Fish below deck starts." He storms off, cursing as he stomps away.

I stand still for a moment, my body tight. The burning itch in my chest is growing worse. I'm exhausted.

Like Grimy.

Like poor fucking Rex who is hiding in my berth because he's ready to die but this fucking curse won't let him rest.

There's a roar in my ears. Of blood rushing. Of chaos zipping along my veins. My mind battles with my body, with that burn. It tells me to take care of her. To remove the fucking blade from my pocket and plunge it into her chest. But that new and foreign feeling deeply rooted within my chest holds me back. It could be why I'm breaking apart, desperate to be close to her. Why my chest feels like molten lava and the only reprieve is to be around her glow.

One thing is certain: If she continues to breathe, she will be our destruction.

But if she's dead...

If she's dead, she might just be our salvation.

CHAPTER 13

James

The debilitating burn recedes the moment I open the door and enter the room. It's like my blood has cooled, the fire in my center burnt out. The smell of copper and death lingers in the air. Martin's body is where I left it. His blood has soaked into the wood, staining the Tempest. As if she hasn't seen enough death.

"Enjoy your company while I was gone?" I ask vacantly, putting down the supplies I've brought down.

My siren is quiet as I come near. She hardly moves to look at me. We're treading familiar waters already. In such a short amount of time, my visitations have become routine.

"All that blood and gore—you truly know how to spoil a woman," she says, her voice bone dry.

"Kinda figured you weren't the chocolate and roses kind of gal."

Despite her dead eyes, she blows me a kiss. "You figured right. Anymore brain matter to spare? Perhaps Luca. I sense he's having a...*hard* time."

She heard the song.

My stare is long, cool. "Will we be expecting another visitor?"

Her lips twist up. "Are you feeling hospitable, Captain? Because she's quite the handful, this other siren of mine."

"So you know the fish beast who's haunting us then?"

"Perhaps," she states coolly. A hint of sparkle shimmers in her eyes, deviousness shining through. "Why? Scared?"

She's lying. I can feel the insincerity wisp through my chest with the falsity of her words.

I decide to not call her bluff, curious to see the extent of the web of lies she will spin to try to make me think she's in control. "I'm not concerned about her."

"Not afraid of dying?"

"If you couldn't finish me off, what chance does she have?"

"You speak as though you don't have an advantage." Her eyes drop to my bracelet. "You're protected against our ways." But then her gaze dances along my trousers, and triumph overshadows her expression as she whispers, "At least... almost." I carefully watch her every move as she tilts her head to the side, giving me that lustful look again. "You're more composed, Captain. Have you fucked your hand yet? How many times? Did you come with my face in mind? Was my tongue that you're *so* possessive about running along your cock in your fantasy?"

Still—*still*—she thinks she can manipulate my

emotions. Like I'm Martin. Like I'm the men she's ripped the hearts out of.

If she's expecting me to spar with words, she's wrong. I have other things in mind.

Crouching down before her, I bring a bucket of water between us. In a separate bucket, I pull out a bathing sponge. She watches me warily as I drop the sponge into the water, wring it out and then bring it to her face.

Her head twists away in rejection.

My hand with the sponge pauses, and I quirk a brow. "What's wrong, Little Fish? You were blowing kisses at me a moment ago—now you're afraid of a little water?"

She's not afraid of water, though. She's growing afraid of *me*. I can see it in the way her chest rises and falls. The moment I splattered Martin's brains all over her, she lost that goading edge to her.

"What are you doing?" she asks, distrustful.

Mirroring her former charm, I smirk. "You asked me if I felt hospitable. I believe I am, Siren. Now hold still."

She goes rigid—she thinks it's a trick.

But as I run the wet sponge over her face, wiping away the blood spatter on her cheeks, her body immediately softens beneath my touch.

I glide the wet sponge slowly down her throat, watching as the water immediately absorbs into her skin. The dullness fades, replaced by a warm glow. She bites her lip, holding in her relieved moan, not wanting to give me her pleasure. She wants to pretend I'm doing nothing for her, but her body betrays her intentions. It quakes—the chains I've bound her in clinking together audibly above our heads.

I drop the sponge into the bucket, wring it, and bring it back to her bare body. Gently, I run it between the curves of her tits. Her body shudders, twisting beneath the sponge and I watch the water disappear beneath her skin before doing the motion all over again, wiping away the blood spatter. The scales of her tail glow with what little water I've given it.

Within minutes, her body is jelly, her eyes half-open from respite. Even under the circumstances, as fucked-up as it sounds, I can't ignore her otherworldly beauty. The glow of her skin. The shimmer of her tail. She is a stunning creature. There is nothing subtle about her.

Looking at her, I keep my voice casual. "What's your name, Siren?"

She lets out this heavy breath, her voice shaky. "Siren."

My lips bunch up, amused. "That's not very original."

She barely responds, her sole focus on the sponge I'm gliding up her smooth skin. I look down at my movements, noticing the vague little scars that decorate her stomach. Interesting that as she's healing, these scars are growing more raised. I pause for a moment to run a finger along a few. "Battle scars?" I murmur now. I sound amused, but I'm paying close attention to her reaction.

Her blinks are slow. "We all have a story, Captain."

"What is yours?" My voice is quiet, thoughtful. I look right into her eyes as my fingers continue to run along the scars. I'm looking for a crack. A moment of vulnerability. Something that tells me she is more than just an unfeeling sea beast.

"You wouldn't understand," she replies now, and

while her words are meant to be scathing, her tone doesn't fit it.

"No?" I question.

She doesn't look me in the eye. "No."

"Because of how you acquired them?"

"No."

"So, it's because I'm human," I state. She doesn't immediately respond, but her eyes betray her—I've hit the nail on the head. I give her a long, cool stare. "Are we truly worlds apart, Siren? Already we've established we're more alike than we care to admit—"

"You're a lowly mortal with a witch's bracelet fused to your wrist," she cuts in coldly. "Just because you aren't dropping to your knees for me doesn't make us equal, Captain. It just means you'll die some other way."

"What do you know about the bracelet?"

Her smile is sour. "More than you do."

I nod once, repeating what she said to me before. "If I knew what the inscription read, I'd be on land. Isn't that what you said?"

"Protection comes at a cost, Captain," she retorts. "You should have stayed on land where you and your humans belong. Here, in this sea, in *our* world, you belong to us, and you will face our wrath. Bracelet or no bracelet. You'll never truly be a part of our world. And I'll never be a part of yours."

I ignore her words for a moment, allowing a chilly silence to fill the void. She looks at me, waiting for my rebuttal. I give her nothing. Looking down, I resume cleaning her, my thoughts buried in her words. In her utter fucking disgust of me. That disgust bothers me more than it should.

Standing up, I slowly pour the bucket of water over her body. I do it in long rivulets, along her tail, over her head, soaking her colorful hair. She looks up at me, the streaks of water running down her face, and once again, as the water settles, more marks along her body are raised, like I've drawn them out. All of her hurt reflects back at me. Telling me a story of a tortured past. Just how old is she beneath that glow and beauty?

I put the empty bucket down at my feet, but I don't move to leave. "Do you think because I'm human that my scars are no match to yours?" I ask in a low voice as I peer down at her, mining what I can from the fleeting cracks of emotion that escape her.

Wise girl says nothing. She knows when to stay quiet. Senses when a bad man begins to change form.

I was right. There's *something* different about this siren.

And in her eyes, I'm just an unmarred man without so much as a scratch on him.

"Do you think I choose to be a pirate?" I ask next, studying her intently. "That I want to be in the Black Sea with sea whores like you?"

I pull the strings of my dirty, white tunic, loosening the knots along my neck and breastbone. She watches me carefully as I slide the tunic over my head and drop it to the floor. Her eyes run over my chest and abdomen. They linger heavily along my broad shoulders and corded arms. Surely, this is pleasing to her eye. The form of a perfect man. She still says nothing, working hard to remain indifferent. Pretending the tether between us isn't tightening from her own desire.

I move to her now, feeling her gaze along my smooth, unmarred skin as I pull out the key from my back pocket and remove the chain to one hand. She doesn't expect it. Her body beneath me tenses, her breath pulling in sharply as one arm drops to her side. Closer to freedom. At least, that's what she thinks as I crouch back down to her level. I look at her earnestly, my desire exposed, transparent.

Her lips part as I edge closer, my large being crowding her. She's so small before me, I overwhelm her with my size. I want the siren to feel tiny, vulnerable, at my mercy.

With the silence interrupted only by our breaths, I drop my head between her shoulder and throat. My lips skirt along her skin. Her skin is cold and smooth. After a flick of my tongue, I taste her. Sweetness and sex and the salt of the ocean. A maddening concoction that makes my cock that much harder. Oh, to take her fucking mouth. I'd bury my cock so deep I'd make her gag. It would fill me with sick satisfaction to warm her belly with my seed.

This little siren would sing—but it would be *my* song she'd be singing.

Her breaths come out shakily as I run featherlight kisses down her throat while my hand is running up her abdomen, settling beneath the curve of her tits. I only lightly cup a breast, feeling its weight. I run my nose along her hair, breathing her in. I'm slow, methodical.

I want her to feel like I'm assessing her taste, touch, and smell.

Like I'm inventorying what's mine.

My body burns with hatred and lust. At the same time, I'm not doing something she doesn't want. I listen to the cues of her body, taking note of the way she shuffles closer.

Her head turns to the side, exposing her throat to me at the same time she pushes her tits out, embracing my touch. I flick a thumb along her nipple and watch her eyes become heavy lidded and her lips part as she looks back at me.

My smile is slow, seductive. "You like that, Little Mermaid?"

"Fuck you," she breathes, but there's no vitriol in her tone.

"Just how does one fuck a little siren like you?"

She swallows, the glow in her skin intensifying as I gently palm her breast. "You don't," she says, looking down, watching what I'm doing with fascination. "Not until..."

"Until what?"

She doesn't answer, and I don't give her a chance to. I squeeze at her breast, harder than she expects. She sucks in a breath, about ready to yelp when I smash my mouth against hers, but I'm not kissing her.

I'm tasting.

Taking.

Fucking.

I bite at her bottom lip when she doesn't open her mouth to me. The second she gasps, spreading her lips apart, I run my tongue along the seam. I feel the sparks in her being, and I press my lips harder, pulling at her lust the way she uses ours like a weapon. She squirms now, gasping again, this time in pain. The sparks intensify, the yearning growing, and a moan escapes her, and then terror.

Stark, cold terror.

The rot is present. The black goo seeping from the floor around us like tar, surrounding us as it wisps into the air like a dark, dank fog.

Death, death, death.

I pull back suddenly to look at her. Tears stream down her face, her lips puffy and raw, her eyes wide and fearful. The glow in her body is gone. The scars are hiding once more beneath the surface of her now dry skin. She's stunned, horrified. The question bleeding from her gaze as she trembles now: *What the fuck have you done to me?*

My smile is cruel this time as I growl, "Icht Nara A'benIff."

She freezes at once as the bracelet around my wrist begins to glow, the inscription bright as the rays of a sun. My wrist burns something fierce as the pain morphs into a black glow that spreads up my arm slowly. Her eyes widen as my skin transforms before her eyes, banishing my handsome, *princely* exterior and uncloaking what lies beneath. Revealing the scars. The bullet holes and the burns. The deep stab wounds and abrasions. My face splits from the scar that runs jaggedly through it. Tattoos cover every inch of my skin from my neck down, blending my tanned flesh with black ink. The very hair on my head grows longer, wilder, untamed. I smile, feeling my severed lip pull as she looks into the demonic eyes of the brutal man I truly am.

"My body speaks a story, too, Little Fish," I say, my voice darkening as she looks back at me. "You asked me if I was afraid of dying. No, siren, I'm not. Because I fucking can't."

CHAPTER 14

Aria

Around the age of thirteen, I began sneaking out of my shared bedroom window once a month and tiptoeing my way across our front yard. I'd sprint down the dark gravel road to the main boulevard that my home sat adjacent to, before sinking into the shadows and dipping behind bushes whenever a passerby got too close. I'd hide until they were far enough where I could move freely without fear of being seen or heard. It took me nearly forty-five minutes on foot to make it down to the docks, but it was worth it every time.

The docks were where my body would ignite simultaneously with fear and excitement.

For a solid year, I stood in the background, watching, learning, and locking every movement to memory. At fourteen, I began inching closer to the crowd, blending in with the people who were too drunk, high, or focused on the show to pay me any attention. The scent of sweat, blood, and alcohol permeated the air, and at first, I found it repulsive, but it was a smell I quickly craved.

By fifteen years old, I had gathered enough courage to get in on the action. With a bag filled to the brim with essentials, I signed myself up before slinking back into the shadows to ready myself, both mind and body.

I remember my hands shaking when a boy who looked no older than seventeen shouted my name through the crowd. You could have heard a pin drop from the silence that quickly spread as I made my way through the throng of people who blocked me. I was nearly a head shorter than everyone as I pushed past the sticky bodies and made my way to the center. The sounds of their whispers made the pit grow in my stomach, and when I finally made it to the ring, the boy who had called my name cocked a brow, not bothering to hide his surprise as he looked me up and down. Out of my modest dress and into trousers and a loose tunic, I was ready. After assessing me with scrutiny, he read the rules to both my opponent and me..

There were only two rules: No guns. No death.

That was it. He read both rules from a tattered paper in his hand, though with rules so simple he should have been able to recite them from memory. *So dramatic.*

Then, he blew his air horn, and the show started.

The first time someone ever stabbed me in a street fight was that night. And, unfortunately, it wasn't the last.

After I had successfully lost my first fight ever, I bandaged my abdomen up and made a mental list of what I had done wrong, what I could improve on, and how to never lose a fucking fight again.

The wound was mostly superficial but gaped slightly, so I knew I'd have to watch it overnight and give myself stitches in the morning if I needed it. With any luck, I wouldn't bleed through my bedgown, and my sisters wouldn't notice and tell our father. Norborne is way too conservative; a girl had to be discreet.

Fighting wasn't something that I wanted to do. I actually really hate it, but a voice inside of me urged me to bend my moral compass. It told me I needed to learn, train, and harness a skill set that none of my other sisters would ever dream of. The voice inside encouraged me to keep my fighting a secret and to hold the power that I had when I wielded a knife close to my heart.

So I did just that. I sought the gritty streets and learned to fight, stalk, pick locks, and thieve. Anything you could imagine. Not that I used everything I learned, but...the more you know, and all that. It's probably what made me such a ruthless siren.

Growing up in a house full of sisters, it was difficult to navigate not only being the awkward middle child but also trying to keep your true personality at bay. Father had expectations; we were all to be proper, polite, and obedient. To fit into Norborne, where witch-hunt is still a major thing, we had to enmesh ourselves in their rigid customs.

And on the surface I was, but the Aria I kept locked inside had a different story to tell.

EXHAUSTION AND WEAKNESS knocked me out again.

The shock of his admission and seeing his skin change in front of me was too much for my body to handle, and my vision swam, the dangerous effects of the moisture he removed from me had swiftly pulled me under.

I think so, anyway. Or maybe he injected me with another hit of Gala Green.

How long have I been out for this time?

His perfect, god-like body transformed in front of my eyes.

Questions rapid-fire through my brain as the vision of the captain's marred skin flashes behind my eyes.

Does he possess magic? Is he not human?

Scars upon scars trailed across his body intertwined with ink, like a map, sprawled out and marked over the surface, leaving an illustration of the pain he's endured. The hellish way he smiled as he told me he couldn't die.

Impossible, the history books... Ericksons are mortal—

Maybe they were wrong?

Protect. Resist. Revenge.

Nothing about the inscription translated to immortal, so how is it he's alive after all the trauma his body has endured?

Clearly the bracelet harbors some sort of enchantment spell, hiding the ghastly sight of his mangled skin...yet, despite the horrors of his past being revealed through brutal scars, I'm not any less attracted to him. If anything, I want to run my fingers against every raised piece of skin, trace the lines that decorated his flesh, and kiss each scar as it tells me its story.

Stop it.

Jiggling my wrists against the shackles once more to reaffirm their strength, my breath catches in my throat as I remember and *feel* one of my arms loose. I circle my wrist and shake it out, trying to regain some of the feeling that I lost over however many hours had passed. Quickly, I move the hair away from my face and tuck it behind my ears, overjoyed to finally have that bothersome feeling gone.

My fingers trail along the scales of my tail, assessing the dehydration. I wince with pain and quickly pull my hand back as though I had burned myself. The momentary reprieve I had when *he* sponge bathed me is nothing but a distant memory, clouded by irritation from my worsening condition. He must have done it on purpose—washed me, only to drain me again.

This is my chance.

With one arm free, I can somehow get my other out of the cuff and make an escape. It'll be hard as hell with this tail and fin, but I know I can do it. I'll figure it out. I *have* to.

Looking out the porthole, the sky is dark save for the little moonlight that reflects off the water. I have no idea what time it is, or how the time passed so quickly, but if my exhaustion has anything to say about it, I can safely assume that we are rapidly approaching midnight. Maybe around ten? Who fucking knows? I've been locked up for hours, in and out of consciousness. Delirium is starting to set in.

I scan my surroundings, looking for anything close by that can help me free my other arm, but the only thing within reach is Martin's lifeless body, still laying in a heap on the floor next to me. Rigor mortis is setting in, and the man-child's once rosy skin is paling further. *Ew.*

I don't need to touch him to know his body is stone cold by now.

He deserved it, I tell myself. I can still remember the slimy feel of his mouth on my skin—

I can feel the captain's mouth, too.

That's beside the point.

The least the bastard *Captain* could have done was clean Martin up before he stormed out earlier, but no. Of course not. He pulled a *"look what I can do"* and left... *again.*

Such chivalry.

How can I release my other arm?

Looking around the room, I take a quick inventory of everything that is within a short distance of my fin. A dozen or more instruments for various forms of torture have crashed to the floor when Erickson had his outburst, and two were close by, though neither appear to be a viable option to get me out of this.

Still, I scoot down on my tail as far as I can. My teeth grit and tears form behind my eyes—the wood sliding against my tail feels like fileting knives skinning my flesh. The overwhelming desire to scream courses through me. I do my best to ignore the pain and slowly flip my fin in an upward motion, encouraging the screwdriver to roll centimeter by torturous centimeter closer to me.

Using my loose hand, I hoist myself back to a seated position and spin my lower body as I reach out in an attempt to grab it. My fingertips barely graze the metal. My shackled arm is pulled so tightly I swear my shoulder is about to dislocate, and my wrist is raw and burns, but I bite down on my lower lip and heave my upper body toward the screwdriver again. When my fingers close around the cool steel, I let my eyes flutter closed as I exhale a shaky breath and momentarily celebrate my small success.

Congratulations, Aria, here's a fucking medal.

Screwdriver in hand, I make quick work to pry any part of the shackles apart with the tool. The chain, the cuff that grips my wrist. *Anything.*

Nothing budges.

I take that congratulations back.

Tears sting my eyes as more panic sets in. I hurl the screwdriver across the room, knowing it's not the answer.

I don't move for a long while, wallowing in my despair. For once, I let myself succumb to it.

I suck at being a human, and I suck at being a siren, too.

Just how fucked am I? I search around the room again, quickly analyzing my surroundings in the dim moonlight.

I don't know how long I have left until I shift back to human form. If I don't get out before then, I won't have the power to get away from him. I don't even want to consider the ramifications if he saw my other form.

That would be disastrous for our kind.

Father would have a field day with that.

An unfamiliar trickle of emotion I recognize to be fear filters into my being and I worry I may not escape this fucking prison without the key that the Erickson keeps in his pocket.

His pocket.

I glance down at the dead body beside me and think back to how Martin got inside my prison.

Steel scraping on steel.

He picked the lock.

He picked the fucking lock!

But as a cloud shifts in front of the moon, it pitches the room in darkness, and I stare helplessly at the body, knowing I'll have to figure this out in pitch black.

Shit.

CHAPTER 15

James

S he's stalking me.

Everywhere I go, I see the silhouette of her in the dark water. I can feel her eyes as they tread along my form.

She will fucking eat me.

Consume me like she does everything that tries to live in these waters.

No wonder the sea is dead.

I try to change direction, to move through the seas under the moonlight. It's about the worst thing you can do, navigating blind in unfamiliar territory.

My skin feels cold.

Her eyes—I can feel her fucking eyes as a clock ticks in my ear, reminding me it's only a matter of time.

Tick-tock.

Tick-tock.

My breaths cloud around me as I breathe in the cold air, approaching the deck rail in search of her.

She's there. Her head is above water, blue eyes glowing; I feel enraptured for a moment. At her sheer beauty. At the *pulse of life I feel stirring in my chest. We used to swim together. She never used to hunt me.*

I try to block her out. She's death and she's darkness—

But she's a colorful current, and my blood is roaring in my ears, and yet that clock is ticking even louder, growing faster.

Tick-tock.

Tick-tock.

I know what this means—I've seen it before.

Sometimes I run.

Other times, I plan my attack.

This time, though, I don't turn my back on her as I step back. My movement instantly triggers her. The blue eyes flicker off like a light. Her silhouette shifts, skin gleaming in green and black scales as she takes on a monstrous form in the waters. She rises from the ocean, touching the sky, the beast with the blood-black eyes, jaw wide, mouth gaping; serrated, conical teeth the size of man. On either side of its mouth, razor-sharp teeth elongate until there are so many crammed in together.

My being freezes as I accept my fate.

I know what happens—

It's happened many times before.

Ticktockticktockticktock—

I shut my eyes as she swoops down and consumes me whole.

I jerk awake, inhaling sharply as I glance around me.

Everything is dark in the pilothouse.

I've managed to nod off sitting down, arms crossed. Yawning, I run a hand over my face as a tug pulls at my chest, reminding me of my captive. Warmth and longing stir within me. That fucking dream and then her—my world feels uneven beneath my feet. Like I'm trudging into unfamiliar waters, and it awakens parts of me I haven't felt stir in eons.

I get up and grab a bite to eat below deck, finding Briggs in the kitchen already, sorting through canned food with nostrils flared.

"Anything make it?" I ask.

"I'm not sure what'll kill us first, Captain, this ship never moving or scurvy."

"You're being dramatic."

I grab a random can.

Canned pork brains in milk gravy.

Never fucking mind.

"It's fucked up, ain't it?" says Luca as he descends the steps behind me. "It's like the Goddess is having a right fucking laugh at us. Give 'em food, but make sure it's fucking rancid as all fuck." He lets out a half-shriek. "Oh, ay, Cap. Your tattoos are back!"

Briggs' gasps. "His hair's long again!"

"His Royal Darkness has returned," chuckles Luca.

"I'll lend you my spare comb, Cap, just say the word."

I don't say the fucking word.

They cough and avert their eyes.

"So, who even packed this?" Briggs demands now, spinning his can for us to see. "Creamed opossums in sweet potato juice?"

"Get fucked," Luca replies, doubtfully. "What the fuck is potato juice, you liar?"

Now Briggs picks up the can and thrusts it in Luca's face. "Right there in front of you. There's no biotin in this! My hair is going to fall out—I need better suste-nance, Captain."

I crack my can open and shove it into his chest. He squeals like a fucking opossum himself, disgusted by the repugnant smell as I stare at him evenly. "So go find better food then, Briggs."

He whimpers and Luca cackles. I turn around and leave and within moments they're arguing, but that doesn't stop Luca once again from calling out, "Where is Martin? Whatever happened to him?"

For the second time, I don't let him know.

For reasons and such.

To have the men behave this normally, it must mean our siren is asleep and not channeling out that fucking horny spell of hers. A notion further confirmed when I'm above deck and catch sight of Grimy. He's on the ground, his back pressed against the rails. Rex is on his lap, and he's cutting an apple with a pocket knife, feeding slices to Rex.

My lips flinch as I come to a stop in front of him. "We have apples?"

Grimy gestures to the basket next to him. "This is what I could find. They'll go off soon, so best have at it."

"Don't tell the others that."

"Why do you think I'm up here?"

Chuckling, I bend down and swipe a couple apples, pocketing one as I sit down on an empty water barrel. Staring out into the fog and then the obscured sky, I spin the apple around in my hands.

I long for the stars already.

For dreamless nights as I take over nightwatch.

For the same stagnant descent into madness.

Yet, at the same time, I don't long for it at all.

For once, time's held still since the siren came aboard. My journey derailed, my supposed purpose all gone, all shifted, and now I know it had no meaning to begin with.

It was just a way to keep the cogs turning. To keep me moving. Otherwise, I'd have ended up like Grimy: fucking empty.

It's my fault he is the way he is. If I hadn't been so selfish...

I take a bite of my apple. "Imagine if I'd married that Barrhaven girl, Grimes. She'd have had a fucking field day with this."

Grimy lets out an empty laugh. "For once, you've spared another soul from suffering."

"Think the Goddess will let me through her pearly gates?"

"You have to be able to die first."

I pause. "Oh, yeah."

Grimy studies me now. "Why weren't you even interested in that girl? She was of quality, wasn't she?"

I squint, trying to remember what she even looked like. It was hardly a year ago we were in Barrhaven, and he won't let the matter of leaving to rest. It was the longest I'd been on land in so long—I wonder if he thought I was looking to stop moving.

Well, he was wrong about that.

"You know why," I simply answer.

He grunts his understanding.

I demolish the apple, tossing its core as far out into

the ocean as I can throw it before turning and patting Rex as I come to a stand. "I'll take over the nightwatch in an hour."

"What'll you be doing before then?"

I don't answer.

He already knows.

I STAND in front of the door, spinning the key around, unmoving.

The last time I saw her, I'd shown her my true self.

All the ugly.

Inky black oozed from my body, spreading along the floor around me like black lava.

I had frightened her and sucked her dry.

Idly, I rub at my chest, teeth clenched. The fire from within always grows when I draw near. Whatever has happened—whether she's responsible for it or not—it's getting worse. This whatever-the-fuck-tether, if you want to call it that, isn't visible, but I swear to fucking Goddess, I feel like I can almost reach out to touch it.

You frightened her, I repeat, shutting my eyes. *You fucking monster.*

I don't feel remorse for it, per se. It doesn't work like that with me—to regret an action is moot. If something happened, there's no point dwelling. And yet...I think of it in another way. I wonder how else it could have gone if I had behaved in a different manner. It would have placed our interaction on another trajectory; I might have kissed her, but not to prove to her I was powerful, too.

I might have kissed her because I wanted to do it.

And how absurd is that? How fucking abhorrent to consider kissing a monstrous creature as she—the very thing that was made to tear hearts from chests and proclaim it's just part of her nature.

Like the nature of man, I tell myself, *to pillage land and take women and proclaim victory through death and destruction.*

I open my eyes as my chest burns brighter.

Perhaps then, we aren't so different, her and I.

I stick the key in the lock and turn it.

CHAPTER 16

Aria

I'm blacking in and out, exhaustion plaguing me like never before.

I feel outside of my body, hovering over myself.

In and out, in and out—until I jolt awake to find a large silhouette standing in the room. My heart pauses for a beat, and then it speeds in my chest. I don't have to see him to know he's there. There is no mistaking the large, muscled shape of this man for someone else.

A surge of adrenaline rushes through me as I take him in. I wonder what he wants. Whether I'll be played with yet again. My brain is so mushy I'm not sure I can bother with any more mind games.

I might not see his eyes, but I can feel his gaze on me, heavy and lingering. I try to stay still, but it's hard to miss the rattle of the chains above my head.

He takes a step forward, his head dropping down to Martin's body. I'm suddenly worried he might remove him, but then he looks away. He rummages around now, and I hear something skid along the floor—the chair.

The chains continue to rattle, unease running through me as he draws near.

I keep waiting for him to speak, but he doesn't. The silence is loud as he situates the chair he's dragged in front of me and sits down on it. I watch as he ignites the lantern and sets it down by his foot. The light is dim, the colors in the room lukewarm and vague. Facing me now, he shoves a hand into his pocket and removes something. I spot the knife in his hand straightaway. I'd be spooked if he wasn't so laid-back in his movements. There's nothing menacing about him right now—well, as non-menacing as you can get with a massive captain watching you in the dim glow of night.

The next look he gives me is lazy, bored. I can hardly look him in the eye long enough because he's back to removing other treasures from his pocket.

An apple.

I blink hard, brows coming together as he runs the knife along the green fruit.

He cuts a long ribbon of skin off, and my stomach growls. He pauses at the sound, staring at me. An expectant look. Like he's waiting for me to start another round of verbal sparring. There's no point being snarky or cocky—I don't have it in me. Too weak, I run my tongue along my dry lip and wait for whatever he's doing to be over.

He must be playing with my head because he goes back to cutting the apple, saying nothing.

My gaze lingers along his perfect profile, and that grizzled torn lip.

His stare crawls along my face, stopping at my mouth where I run my tongue along it once more.

We're battling each other in a way, aren't we? Refusing to speak. Not addressing the vile fucked-up things that have happened in this room, like Martin's body by his foot, or the jagged scars running along this Captain's body as he revealed himself to me, or the fact he keeps coming around to throw water on me—and I have a feeling it's not a torture method like he's been insinuating.

Curious, I look at him now, feeling that flutter in my chest again. The one that tells me he's trouble, and I shouldn't want his company.

Why the fuck is he here?

And why did I *want* him to visit me?

Why do I feel forgotten when he leaves?

This is not good, Aria.

I finally break the silence.

"How long has it been since you captured me?" I ask, my scratchy voice barely above a whisper. My mouth salivates at the sight of the apple he continues to cut apart.

The blade cuts through the crisp fruit, its juices running down the Captain's thumb. He slips the thinly cut apple slice to his lips, his tongue running along the underside of the fruit as he takes it into his mouth.

I can't take my eyes off the movement.

My belly warms, a different type of hunger growing like a storm within me.

But I can't let him distract me.

The clock is ticking, and I need to make sure he isn't here to *finally* dispose of Martin's body.

"About three days." He slices another thin piece of apple, but this time he brings it to my lips in offering. Narrowing my eyes, I drop my gaze to the slice, conflicted on whether to take it. He catches my hesitation. "It's not poisoned, Little Fish."

There is something in his tone that makes me feel uneasy, but he's eaten from the same fruit, and I'm past the point of hunger.

So, what's his motive?

Our eyes connect, and my lips part just enough for him to glide the apple slice between them.

Cool, tangy flavor explodes on my taste buds, and though I'm not naïve enough to think this one bite of apple will curb the hunger that hollows my stomach, I allow myself to enjoy it. I chew slowly, taking my time before swallowing it down.

With another swipe of his blade, he frees another slice and brings it to my lips again. This time, I don't hesitate before opening my mouth fully and allowing him to place it on my tongue.

A strange current flickers through my chest, an unexplainable pull from the tether that somehow links us. I have so many questions about the dark creature in front of me. He hasn't bothered to mask himself again behind whatever magic his bracelet possesses, and instead shows me every inch of his true self.

His grisly appearance should be off-putting, but instead, it fills me with curiosity and an urge to know more.

I'm staring. My gaze is soft—interested. Who is Captain Erickson, really? Something tells me there's more than meets the eye with this human, and though every inch of me burns with learned hatred for my captor, the organ that beats behind my rib cage thaws in his presence.

He peers up from slicing the apple and catches me staring at him. A ghost of a smile breaks through that lazy stare, but even then, I can't read this man.

"So," he drawls. "Are you ready to tell me about yourself, Siren?"

"What exactly are you wanting to know, Captain?"

"How many others of you are there?"

For a moment my heart seizes, thinking he knows about my sisters, before I realize he's speaking of the sirens as a species, not my direct family.

I'm not sure how to answer his question.

Over the decades, sirens have spread out. We blend with the humans. When side by side, it's nearly impossible to tell the difference between the two, until you look closer and see subtle differences. The faint glow we exude—even in our human state—for example. Unnoticeable at first, but once you recognize it, it's impossible to ignore. Our kind has done an impeccable job at camouflaging.

Even if I had a solid answer, I'd never tell him.

So I shrug my unchained arm instead.

"Where do you sirens go?" he continues, undeterred by my silence. "After you attack a ship, you guys throw a party under the sea?"

"Yeah, we throw a party under the sea," I say, straight-faced.

Now his lips flicker up and he lets out a deep chuckle. "Take glory in all your kills?"

I do my best to smile devilishly. "Wouldn't you, Captain?"

His body certainly highlights the glory of his kills, if his scars are any indication. Stab wounds, bullet holes, lacerations—every single wound has a story to tell, I'm sure of it.

"We're not so different, you and I," I muse, watching him cut another piece off the apple.

He pops it into his mouth, thoughtfully chewing. "Pray tell, Little Fish." His voice sounds flat and unamused, so I put some extra enthusiasm into mine.

Laughing weakly, I say, "Now, why would I point out our similarities? You already have more than enough ammunition to use against me, both in the literal and metaphorical sense, I'm sure. If you can't recognize how much alike we truly are, I prefer to leave you blind."

His eyes darken as he lets my words sink in, and for several minutes, the room is quiet, yet again.

I allow the time that passes to ground me, pulling me away from the curiosity growing within.

He *must* leave. And without Martin.

Playing on his arrogance, I decide to try a little reverse psychology, hoping he'll fall into my trap and leave the body here longer. I can't let him take it—I *need* that lockpick.

My gaze lands on the carcass next to me, my chin tipping toward the body. As I hoped, his eyes follow mine to Martin's lifeless heap. "It's starting to smell," I state blankly, void of all emotions. "You need to get it out of here."

The inexplicable wonder from a moment ago has disappeared from both of us, and when he answers, his voice is back to being venom-filled. "Can't stomach a little rotting flesh? How sad for you. I thought I'd leave him just a while longer—serve as a reminder of what happens to those who cross me."

"You can't—"

"I can."

"But the tox—"

"The toxins, what? Will make you sick? Weak? Do you think that's a negative for me, Little Mermaid? You're my *prisoner*. You think I give a fuck about whether you inhale some fumes from a decomposing pirate?"

I let my head fall as though his words defeat me and try to emulate the emotions, afraid that the tether between us will reveal my truth if not.

Neither of us speaks after that.

Neither of us backs down, either.

We continue to glare at one another as the captain finishes the apple, sinking his teeth into every bite and drawing out the time it takes to chew. Finally, the apple is down to its core.

He stands, and I know he's about to leave yet again. If I escape, this will be the last time I see him.

I stare at him deeply now, committing every inch of him to memory as I whisper, "What's happening in my chest, Captain?"

He goes still, staring down at me. I can't see his eyes

from here, but I sense him looking me over, too, the same question running through his mind. "I don't know," he answers, and for once there's nothing cold or snarky about that response.

"Is it your doing?"

"No."

"I want it to stop."

"Can't handle my feelings, Siren?"

"What feelings?" I retort. "You're cold, Captain."

"Yes, I am."

"And lonely."

He doesn't respond for a heavy moment before uttering, "As are you, Siren."

And just like that, a feeling runs through my chest. An emotion I'm all too familiar with. The captain's melancholy. An ache that runs deeper than flesh and sinew. He reveals it to me fleetingly before the feeling is replaced by another sweep of coldness.

His sadness brings a tear to my eye as he stomps to the door and leaves.

THE MOMENT HE'S GONE, I attempt to recover from the weight of that sadness he let me in on. Then, I take deep, calming breaths and spring into action. Time is of the essence and I'm screwed if I don't do *something* fast.

Without hesitation, I throw my body toward Martin's lifeless one, wincing again when my wrist tears into the cuff. A trickle of blood drips from beneath it and rolls down my arm.

I turn back to the heap of blood and brain matter in front of me and chant, *"Please, please, please,"* in my head while I maneuver my hand into Martin's front pocket. He got into this room—now he was going to get me out of it.

"Fuck," I curse, my fingers touching nothing but the fabric of his pocket. I yank my hand out and fumble for his belt loop, using it to tug him closer toward me. Completely stiff, he barely budges.

Why the hell did this man-child have to put whatever he broke into the room with into the pocket furthest from me?

How can I roll his entire body, one handed?

It seems like an impossible feat.

But I have to try.

Encircling two fingers around the belt loop of Martin's pants, I use all the strength I can muster and pull him toward me. He moves a few inches, and it's just enough for me to slide most of my hand into the waist of his pants and close it in my grasp, leveraging a better hold to propel him even closer. By the time he's directly at my side, a sheen of sweat covers my body and I feel nauseous.

Nauseous from exertion.

Nauseous from the deterioration of my body from the lack of water.

Nauseous over the thought that maybe whatever he used to open the door wasn't even in his pocket and all this is for nothing.

There's never been a time in my life that I can remember *wanting* the shift to end so I could return to my human form until now. I would give anything to rewind my shift and start anew. To stay away from this part of the ocean and never be captured by an Erickson.

Using my free arm, I wipe my brow with my forearm and take a large breath to steady the thumping of my heart, then I roll the stone-cold body toward me.

As my hand reaches into his pocket, I am immediately greeted by a smooth metal surface. I dig deeper and pull out three different picks that slightly vary at the head. One of these should surely unlatch the lock on the cuff.

A newfound confidence blooms inside my chest, knowing that I have practiced picking locks for years and this will be child's play. I'll be unlocked in just a few short moments, and then I can figure out how the hell to get out of this room... without legs.

One obstacle at a time.

The first lockpick is too large to fit into the keyhole. I toss it across the room with a groan of frustration and watch it bounce off the wall, coming to a stop next to a butcher's knife on the floor.

This better not be a fucking Goldilocks situation or I swear to Goddess, I will get out of this room and rip the hearts out of every single one of the worthless piece of shit humans on this ship.

Deep breaths, Aria. You've got this.

A shaky breath escapes past my lips as I grab the second lockpick from beside me and bring it to the keyhole. It slides in easily and I send out a silent prayer to the Goddess looking down upon me.

Seconds tick by as I work silently, listening to the soft ramblings of the men on the deck above me. They complain about the darkness that surrounds the ship, about the fog obscuring their vision, while some idiot named Briggs is searching for a comb—

In the distance, I catch an eerie melody as the ocean breeze carries it toward us. The hairs on the back of my neck stand on edge and my spine straightens at the familiarity of the song that sweeps through my core.

Another siren.

The lockpick falls from my hand, landing on the floor with a small *clang.*

My body involuntarily freezes. An enchanting harmony lulls me into a sense of calm and I close my eyes, letting the sound wash over me. It's beautiful, this song. I had hoped that one of my sisters was in close proximity to the ship, but this song...

This isn't the song of one of my sisters, but it's one often sung when the shift is beginning to wind down.

A subconscious sway rocks my body as the song washes over me, the echo of the melody burying itself deep into my core.

Remembering the task at hand, I force myself to refocus.

Scooping up the lockpick, I jam it into the keyhole and hastily jimmy it again, biting my lip painfully as I try to concentrate on getting the pick in just right so it will unlock.

Please, unlock.

A shrill scream catches in my chest, heavy with the impending feeling of defeat. Tears prickle the back of my eyes, and I know time isn't on my side at all. The longer this takes me, the less chance I have of breaking free before *he* comes back. And if he comes back, I know he'll lock my other arm up again. There's no way he'll make the same mistake twice. Hell, I can't believe he made this mistake once.

When I hear the soft *click* of the lock disengaging, relief overwhelms me and my entire body slumps against the wall as my arm falls heavily to my side. I massage it and roll it around, stimulating the blood flow. With both arms free, this is my chance. My *only* chance.

And there's zero chance I'll waste it.

I look around the room, shrouded in darkness, and recognize the severity of my situation. There is one point of entry and exit, which I know is locked, and one porthole, which from where I'm sitting, may be too small for me to squeeze through. I weigh my options, realizing that even if I picked the lock to the door and escaped, I'd be dragging myself through the ship like a floppy fish— the image in mind so fucking ridiculous, I'd rather die first. My end goal is the ocean, and the quickest way to do that would be to squeeze through that damn pothole.

Unfortunately, it's my *only* option.

Using my hands as my means of movement, I ignore the lacerations that throb against every fluctuation of my joint and drag my tail across the planked floor. The surface peels some scales, revealing the raw flesh beneath. My jaw clenches from the searing pain, but I push forward, desperate to make it to the wall with the porthole.

When I reach the base of the wall, my chest rises and falls. My head spins so fast the room blurs. I can physically feel my eyes roll back into my head as I attempt to remain alert.

I lean to the left and retch beside myself, emptying my stomach of the only thing that it has: bile and a few bits of apple.

A succession of dry heaving plagues me and I feel so weak, but I know I'm almost there. I just need to make it through the porthole and I'll plummet into the deep blue beneath me. Once in the water, it will immediately seep into my skin and I'll regain my strength, and from there, I'll make a swim for it.

Get far, far away from this motherfucking ship.

And even further away from *him*.

A dull ache radiates through my chest at the thought —whatever connection it seems to think I have with the *captain* burns. I ignore it.

Reaching up, I grab the porthole with both hands and send another prayer to the Gods and Goddesses that I have enough upper body strength to hoist myself through.

CHAPTER 17

James

"This is all your fault, you know!" I snap at Grimy as he sits in the galley of the Tempest, opening the top of the last can of beans from the shelf.

"Pray-tell, James, how is it my fault that the Tempest hit a storm—"

"You knew that wasn't an ordinary storm. If you had just told father to change paths, we could have avoided it."

The old man purses his lips, steepling his fingers together and tapping them against his mouth. I hate when he does that. It means he's thinking, and I don't like it when Grimy thinks. When he thinks, he fathers, and he is not my—

"You can look at me like that all you want, James, but the fact of the matter is, you're my responsibility now. I vowed to keep you safe, and I plan to."

How could he possibly care for me when he couldn't care for himself? When he couldn't care for the dog?

Not to mention, we're starving to death and he's feeding me the bigger portions.

The thought sends a blast of icy-terror down my veins.

I can't lose Grimy and Rex. They're all I have left.

I watch as he counts out fifteen beans for him and Rex, places twenty in front of me.

My selfish, teenage heart twinges in my chest, and I don't like the way it makes me feel.

Still, as much as I resist him, I know Grimy cares for me. And I know I'd be wise to prove I am growing into a man, and stop acting like a boy.

I've watched him grow gaunt, watched the ribs on Rex protrude, and I want to cry but the tears have been spent. I fear every breath Grimy pulls in may be his last, and I can't be without this man.

"I'm sorry," I say, though the words feel foreign on my tongue.

Grimy stops, fork mid-air, and looks at me with one gray eyebrow raised.

"I don't want to watch you starve to death. To...to watch you and Rex die would be the end of me. I can't survive the seas alone, and yet, because of this bracelet my father forced onto me, I'll have no choice but to endure death time and time again. Alone. I'm going to starve after you're gone for who knows how long—"

"You'll never be alone, my boy. Not truly."

"Yes, you'll be gone, and I'll be here in this waterlogged prison."

From my feet, Rex whimpers sadly. I glance at him, then back at Grimy. He sets down the fork in his hand and reaches for mine. "That's the natural way of things—"

"It doesn't have to be!"

"Remember your lessons, remember that you're capable—"

"I'm going to be this age forever, aren't I?" And the thought terrifies me.

"No," he assures me. "You'll develop into a man and then you'll stop. Your father made sure of it. You're the last of the Ericksons, he wanted to be certain you'd be alright."

But I'm not alright.

I'm watching the only two people I ever truly cared about slowly perish before my eyes.

I run a hand through Rex's matted fur, feeling my chest split apart from desperation. "I need you, Grimy. Don't leave me! I don't want to be alone. I can't do this alone."

He swallows, voice hoarse as he whispers, "You'd want me and Rex by your side for eternity, my boy?"

Without hesitation, my head bobs. "Yes."

And I mean it. Grimy and Rex are all I have left.

"Don't leave me, Grimy. Please stay."

He looks at me thoughtfully, as though making a decision, but then he reaches down and places his other shaky hand on top of Rex's head, and with a firm voice, he says, "Lives tied, immortality bestowed, eternal life unbound."

A sudden feeling—like a bubble popping within my body —pulses through me as wisps of darkness release from my chest and plunge into both Grimy and Rex. The old dog whimpers at my feet again, this time lifting his head as though wondering what just happened.

I too, am wondering what the hell just happened.

Asking is at the tip of my tongue, when Grimy cuts through my confusion. "Tomorrow, we will set sail to the closest island and do our best to stock the ship with supplies and such. It is going to take a long time to get there. We will suffer before then, but we must never leave each other's *side. It's going to be okay, my boy. You'll never be alone now."*

"THE FOG IS CLEARING," Grimy tells me when I'm back on deck and away from that temptress. "And the other siren's song has faded—" His words die when he turns to look at me. His frown lines return in full force, his eyes tracing along the jagged scar cutting down my face. "Your mask is still down, James."

"Too much beauty for you, Grimy?" I ask flatly.

"We went over this," he says, sternly. "Appearance is everything to the family name—"

"Who am I impressing out here?" I cut in, jaw locked, as I turn my frosty gaze to meet his. "Fucking tired of that spell anyway. Makes my skin itchy."

"You think if someone saw the amount of bullet holes, burn marks, and stab wounds, it wouldn't arouse suspicion?" he counters, not letting up. "It's my duty to be your eyes and ears, and not even the ocean is an escape from your family name. I would have thought our prisoner was proof of that."

I'm not in the fucking mood, but I can't tell him off because—*sans two*—my crew is dead, and he no longer has to keep up with the façade without an audience. I ignore him as I peer into the waters. He's right. The fog is clearing, but visibility is still nonexistent in the dark.

"It should be clear by morning," Luca says nearby, his footsteps stomping around the bow of the ship. "The anchor was dropped when the ship went topsy-turvy. I need to secure it so we can drop it the moment we find safe harbor."

My head pounds suddenly as I demand, "How far did it fall?"

Luca avoids my eye, and I have a feeling it's to do with my face. "It's been skimming the waters—"

"So, it swung against the front of the ship."

He lets out a hesitant breath. "Aye, Cap, it has."

My stomach dips. "How bad is the damage?"

"Hasn't broken through from what I've seen, but it may have hit the foundation, and with the seawater battering it, let's just say there will be a bit of rot if we don't ready it for repairs within the next six months. We don't want the Tempest to go through a winter in this condition."

He states the obvious. I simply grunt in response.

"Cap? Have you seen Martin recently?"

His question freezes me in my tracks. I can't lie to him again, but I also feel unprepared to defend myself against my actions. I feel Grimy's judgmental stare burn through my back.

"Around," I stiffen out.

Luca is no fool as he narrows his eyes thoughtfully before nodding. He walks off, leaving me once more alone with Grimy. I cast a few glances his way, catching the frail way he moves about, purposely looking over the handrail and into the sea, avoiding my gaze. There are abrasions along his bare arm, and his brow is bleeding. They're minor wounds in light of what we've gone through, but seeing him hurt never gets easier.

Here is a man that continues to stand alongside me, even at my cruelest.

It sinks in, in that moment, that the Tempest could have very well gone down. That another Siren may still come to finish Grimy and Rex off and I won't be able to find them, that they may be outside the reach of my bracelet's magic, and I won't be able to save them, or continue to prolong their lives. If she were to tear them apart, how would I be able to hunt their pieces in the ocean? It's why I had to lock them in the cell when this shitfuck went down.

There is only so much this bracelet can do. Its magic is old—strong, yes, but fucking old, too. It'll keep me going, sure, but that siren has put its powers to the test, and I don't know whether it's because the strength of my bracelet is waning, or because there's something else happening beneath the surface.

Something I need answers to.

Vanya will know.

I feel suddenly vulnerable. That siren has done something. Mined emotion buried deep inside the void at my center. Because I can't help but feel a sense of profound loss. If I lose Grimy, or Rex, I will be utterly alone.

I may know time, but I don't know loneliness.

"Just like last time, you knew it was a siren," I say quietly. "How?"

"The water went dead," he answers somberly. "Not a sign of life, no breeze, either. And the saltwater scent in the air? Gone. All gone."

"I should have listened."

He knows I'm referring to the last time, too. There's a weight of regret in my words.

Now, Grimy looks at me knowingly. "Everything I had done before, I did it to protect you. Not your father. You."

"Why?"

"Your father was no saint."

My voice is filled with derision. "Neither am I."

Not one bit.

For what I have done—continue to do—for the things I *will* do. There is no repairing a man like me, never mind redeeming. And the title to my name? It's useless. My kingdom is gone. Because of *her*. Because of her kind. *Because of what my family did, too.*

Abruptly, my chest burns hotter.

I massage it, frowning, because it only ever gets this way when I'm close to that fish.

Rattled by these strange emotions, I begin to turn away from the quiet waters when I hear a sudden cry, followed by the sound of a loud splash. It takes a moment to understand the sound, but I catch the stillness in Grimy.

Luca erupts into shouts. "Captain! Captain! She crawled out of the porthole! She's out! She's out!"

"Oh, Goddess," Grimy utters breathlessly, giving me a horrified look. "She's escaped."

CHAPTER 18

James

She's been in the water only a few seconds, but in that time my heartbeat is pulsing through my veins as I stomp up and down the deck, trying to find her in the darkness. I hear another splash and turn back, racing to the other side of the deck. Grimy is by my side and his hands are shaking. He shoots me that look of terror again, and then another softer look follows, one that tells me she will use her song and that this is it, he will be plucked apart in the sea, and there will be no possible way I'd be able to find all the pieces of him.

"No," I growl with urgency, and then I'm shouting orders. I tell Luca to grab his speargun from the armory. Mine is behind the ship's wheel.

"Why not the gun?" Luca shouts back as he races below deck, hot on my heels. "Put a bullet in her heart, Captain."

"Because the speargun reel ensures we bring her back," I say, grabbing at my speargun. "And I'm not fucking finished with her."

When I'm back above deck, Briggs is on his hands and knees vomiting and Grimy is walking along the arm rail, shining his torch along the waters. "She could be gone, James."

"She's injured," I say. "She'll be water loading."

Grimy tosses a questioning look. "What did you do to her?"

My eyes narrow. "Let's just say she won't be fucking off for a while yet."

No, in the water, free to use her song, she will be invincible in a matter of time. I should have just killed her when I had the chance, and yet my heart strains at the fucking thought of it. My body hums as we quietly move about, Grimy aiming the light along the waters, searching for her. The heat inside me burns stronger, and that tether—that strange pull at the center of my chest—intensifies.

I follow the feeling, stopping at a spot. I peer into the black water below, knowing with certainty she's there. I don't let Grimy know, not yet, but I can feel her gaze on me, and for a moment, I sense we're staring at each other in the quiet.

"It doesn't have to be this way," I say calmly, just loud enough for my voice to carry through the still night air. "You run, Little Fish, and I will hunt you down. I don't care how far I have to sail, or how long it will take—I'll find you and take you back."

Because you're fucking mine.

Because I've seen that hair before.

Seen those blue eyes in the darkness, stalking me in my dreams.

The light shines in the exact spot I'm staring as Grimy comes to a stop beside me. I hear the faint dip in the water, and right there, right where I was fucking looking, there's a disturbance in the water. She's hiding. Not singing, either. *Hiding.*

Why is she hiding?

"The sea creatures have gone," Grimy whispers to me. "Maybe she's called them to her."

I continue staring into the water just as a light breeze picks up.

Then...rain.

Soft drops of it fall around us, and I look up, mesmerized for a moment at the clouds dispersing from the night sky. The moon is visible now, and so are the stars. The boat suddenly bobs as the soft waves of the ocean ripple all around us. I look at Grimy, and he looks back, sensing the change.

What the fuck are we in for now?

Before either of us speak, his pocket watch glows from the breast pocket of his vest, and a soft chime sounds. The midnight alarm, one he uses on his overnight shift. He absentmindedly shuts it off, but I stare at the blue glow a few seconds longer—my brows pulled together in thought.

Something feels off.

A panicked scream erupts—*it's her*—and that pull in my chest worsens as Grimy aims the light toward the direction of the scream. We still, our bodies tight with confusion as we watch our siren surface and flail in the water, her arms splashing around her like she's struggling.

Her screams are that of terror, the cries so pained and broken.

My skin blazes, her sounds of distress cutting into me in a visceral, unnatural way.

The tether, it burns.

I'm suddenly hit in waves of sadness and fear—so much fucking pain in my chest. Her terror sits in my gut, twisting, leaving me breathless.

My Little Mermaid needs help.

"I got her locked in," Luca calls out. "About to shoot, Cap—"

"Stop!" I hiss, already grabbing at the pile of rope by the water barrels. "I'm going in after her. Tie the rope end around the Capstan and pull us up when I have her."

Grimy watches me, confused. "It's a trick, James! She's luring you in—"

"If it was a trick, she'd be using her song to pull you and Luca in," I retort as I wrap the end of my rope around my waist, once, twice, three times. "Something is wrong."

And if I don't pull her out of the water, I'm going to lose her.

The thought is so troubling to me. I begin to shake with adrenaline.

Her sounds go quiet as she flails underwater, her head barely visible now.

It's wretched to watch and worse to feel as her fear of dying sits like a brick in my chest.

She's not ready, the tether screams. She's not ready to die.

The wind picks up, and the boat is no longer frozen still. It's moving along with the light waves, and she's growing more distant from us every second.

I have no time to spare.

I cast one final look at Grimy before I jump off the ship. I fall for seconds before the cold water entombs me, leaving me breathless as it rushes through me, immobilizing me for a split second.

It's quiet in the sea.

The silence is welcoming for those few moments. The cold is almost a relief to my heated skin. That is, until a knife-like pain twists in my center, reminding me of her anguish.

And then I'm kicking to the surface. The waves are picking up the second I surface. I spin around in search of her. I barely have to search as I move; the tether tells me exactly where she is. I follow the tugging, swimming toward that cooling feeling right to her. I hear Grimy's shouts, along with Luca. They're trying to tell me where she is, but I can hardly hear them. My pulse thumps in my ears as her cries spur me on. I move faster, closing in on her as she gasps and flails. But she continues to float further from me. Every time I'm about to close in, the waves take her further away.

Then she sinks into the water and does not surface. My heart is in my throat as I dive under, chasing after my turbulent Little Fish, searching for her in the dark sea.

I'm not through with her.

If she thinks for one fucking second, she'll be rid of me through death—she has another thing coming.

I can't see anything, and I'm so jolted by dread. I lose

focus and break through the surface, gasping for more air before I dive back under, following the tether.

There's a different sort of stillness beneath the Black Sea. A world right under our nose. In the blackness, I don't see the creatures, but I can feel their sentient bodies brush along my form, as though figuring me out. It should occur to me I might have followed the tether to my death. That my siren may have tricked me from the start.

That, here, in this flowy ether, she might swim right up to me and claim my Erickson heart.

But the tether twists with her anguish again.

No, this is not a trick.

My chest tightens as I push through the urge to grab another gulp of air. I swim faster, arms outstretched, searching for her as the cool tether intensifies—

I feel her body, and my skin hums.

Her anguish is suddenly absent, and I realize right then my siren is no longer moving.

She's unconscious.

I hold her tightly to me as the men reel us in. I can hear the Capstan whirring, the rope pulling us closer to the ship and then up into the air. All the while, I'm grabbing at her face, slapping at her cheek, trying to jolt her awake. Her head bobs lifelessly, and then I'm pressing my hand against her bare chest, searching for her heartbeat. Do sirens even have a fucking heart? My body grows anxious as arms come around. Grimy and Luca pull us over the taffrail, and we collapse on the hard deck. My hand is under her head to soften the blow, my body covering every inch of her as I lay overtop of her.

"Cap?" Briggs whispers, sounding off.

I ignore him as I brush the hair away from her face and press an ear to her parted lips.

"Cap?" Luca repeats.

The light puffs of air instantly calm me. "She's alive," I say, gruffly.

"James," Grimy hisses now.

"That's not all she fucking is," Luca squeaks.

I pull back further to look up at the men standing over us. "What?"

But they're not looking back at me. Their eyes are pinned to my legs, looking utterly horrified. Have one of the sea creatures latched onto me? I immediately push off the siren and look back at them. "What?" I demand.

"The siren," Luca whispers shakily.

I look her over, and it takes a moment to compute because of how disoriented I am.

But the second I see what they see, I feel my lungs deflate and my chest sink. Bewilderment fills the void as I slowly come to a stand and look down at her in awe. My head shifts sideways as I study what lays before us.

Our siren's shimmering fin is gone...

Our siren has *legs*.

CHAPTER 19

Aria

Whispers uttered by men sound very different from the whispers of a woman. I've been around whispering women my entire life, from my sisters keeping secrets, to the women who whisper judgements as we pass through town. Fucking Norborne. Always gotta worry you'll be accused of witchcraft. Nearly soundless, the whispers of a woman are often passed through a quiet murmur from behind a hand, or a single look shared with another.

Men, on the other hand, are less conspicuous. Their whispers are louder and sharper in tone than a woman's. Less hidden. They offer no semblance of concealment with their secrets. If they think you're a fucking witch, they'll shout it from a rooftop and proclaim they whispered.

The whispers that surround me now as I drift in and out of consciousness are that of men. They border on whisper-shouting. There's a frantic undertone mixed with a hint of aggression, yet I can't quite make out their words.

Where am I?

The scent of salt water floods my senses while pops of light shimmer behind my still-closed lids. My body aches. With a throbbing head, I groan, but the sound stays internal.

The porthole.

I escaped out of the porthole and dropped into the Black Sea.

The squeeze was tight—it took several minutes to maneuver my hips and tail through the round opening, but I made it.

And for a few blissful moments, the comfort of the water that I so desperately needed to relieve the pain enveloped me.

Then the alleviation drained from my body, sucked completely from my soul as the shift happened.

There was no warning—no feeling from within or sign from the heavens that the shift was about to begin. One moment I was revived to my most powerful being, and the next I was drowning.

Debilitated with fear, my lungs filled with water as my legs kicked wildly. I flailed my tired arms like that would somehow magically teach me how to swim.

Then, I passed out beneath the surface of the water, and now I am...*where?*

The sound of a familiar voice—a voice that plagues me with mixed emotions—cuts through my brain fog. My heart sinks, recognizing that I am back aboard the

Tempest, and I strain to hear the conversation being muttered around me.

"How the fuck is this possible? How could we have missed this?"

"I'm not sure, Captain. I don't understand any of this," says Luca.

"Can she still use her song?" questions Briggs. "I don't think I can take being around anymore boners!"

"Shut up, Briggs," Grimy retorts. "Just shut up."

"How does my siren have legs?" demands the captain.

"Your siren, James?"

"Yes, *my* fucking siren, Grimy. She is my prisoner, is she not?"

My head grows fuzzy, and I feel myself losing control of my consciousness again.

The shift has drained me dry.

When I come to, a violent tremor racks my body.

My eyes snap open and I stare up into the midnight sky. The stars are unmasked from behind the dark gray clouds of earlier and the air is still. The evidence of a storm completely gone, along with my powers. My memory floods back once more and I can feel that the shift is over, without even needing to wiggle my toes.

I nearly drowned.

This was my fifth shift and I nearly fucking drowned. I fight against the shame that threatens to overpower me.

This screws everything up. It's not common knowledge that sirens can't swim while in human form. Purposely, that detrimental fact is kept hidden—a curse that our kind keeps buried so it can't be used against us. The sirens have always known the humans will use it against us if they find out.

And now I'm so, so screwed because the one man I can wholly count on to use it against me knows my secret.

I don't move from my spot on the damp wood planks of the deck despite the shivers that plague my body, or the awareness that I'm completely naked...and not alone.

My senses are sharp as his shadow looms closer. It falls over me completely, and his devastatingly handsome face inundates my line of vision.

"You're blocking my view," I emptily tell him, refusing to look him in the eyes as I continue to stare up at the star-filled sky.

"And you're all I see, Siren."

His tone throws me off; it's soft and quiet, and full of...*wonder*. My gaze connects with his and I silently assess him.

My guard stays up.

Surveying my surroundings, I can see the remaining three men watching a few feet away. When Erickson does nothing, I sit upright with the intent of standing. Schooling my features, I reach a hand into the air. "Well, are you going to just stand there, or are you going to help me up and get me some clothes?"

He hesitates, his eyes grazing down the length of my body. A thought runs through his head, one that makes his gaze harden on mine. A strange look of determination is there, and just as I'm about to question that look, he reaches down and scoops me into his arms effortlessly. The air leaves my lungs in a *whoosh*, the surprise of his touch catching me off guard. He's holding me bridal style as we wade further into the ship.

Is he going to take me back to that room?

Lock me up next to Martin's decomposing body?

I can't be chained up again.

Panicked, I thrash wildly in his grasp, but his arms only secure me closer to his chest. "Let me go," I hiss. "I am of no use to you, *Erickson*. Let me fucking go!"

His head bows as his mouth hovers next to my ear, his warm breath sending unwanted goosebumps skating across my skin. "So, you figured out I'm an Erickson, did you, Little Fish?"

I look back at him, hating how gorgeous he looks so close to my face. *And that scent.* His delicious scent is everywhere. The fight in me gives out. I realize I stand no chance of overpowering him. His grip is so strong, he's likely going to leave bruises along my waist and thigh. I have to play this differently.

Feigning arrogance and boredom, I say with derision, "It doesn't take a genius. I've known who you are since you captured me. Your bracelet is a dead giveaway."

"And yet you said nothing," he states blandly, disguising his own emotions.

He stops in front of a closed door and drops me to my feet. My knees buckle beneath my weight, my head swimming from the sudden movement—still not fully coherent after nearly drowning and passing out twice. I reach out and grab the doorframe to steady myself while he watches me closely. He says nothing as he reaches to turn the knob and throws open the door, pushing me inside. He follows me in, slamming the door harshly behind him, and I can *feel* his movement cease, purposely blocking it.

I scan the room for another exit point, but I know better than to hold hope of there being an alternate way out. I keep my back to him and continue to take in my surroundings, looking for something I can use for a shred of clothing. The linens from the bed lay haphazardly, unmade and ready for the taking. A brown belt is draped over the back of the chair in front of a small desk. That'll have to do. Knowing he's watching, I saunter over to the bed and reach forward slowly, pulling the sheet from beneath the throw.

"So, what's your given name, Captain?" I ask, daring to face him as I fold the sheet in half before I wrap it around my body. I knot the top around my breasts before grabbing the belt off the chair.

His eyes watch my movements as I secure the belt mid-waist, and I don't miss the look of desire that dances across them. He surprises me when he clears his throat and answers me. "James."

"Ah, so *you're* James?"

His brow shoots up. "When did you hear my given name?" he questions, taking a step toward me. I lean back against the desk, crossing my ankles.

He's baiting me. Holding my gaze and challenging me to back down first. I won't. "Does it matter?"

"Yes, Little Fish, it very much does."

For whatever reason, I don't feel like lying. "I started to regain consciousness briefly before I lost it again. I heard you speaking with your men, and one of them said your name. You answered, and, well, your voice is very distinguishable, Captain." He moves toward me with precise movements, coming to a stop only when we're toe to toe. "So, I'm *your* siren, huh?" I bite down on my lower lip to keep myself from laughing at his audacity.

"We've been over this." He pushes his hands down on the desk, caging me in. "You're mine. Mine to torture, mine to touch. Mine to fuck too, remember?" His words echo what he told me before.

"How convenient that I no longer have a tail and fin then," I counter.

James' smile grows sinister as he takes the edge of the sheet I've made into a dress and rubs it between his two fingers. "Tell me how you lost them. Your tail and fin."

"Fuck. You," I spit, the knowledge that he now holds my biggest secret in the palm of his hand, a bitter reminder that I'm fucked. Glaring at him, I push his right arm out of my way and walk over to the porthole. The water has calmed and the ship bobs rhythmically across the sea. James doesn't move and instead takes my position of leaning against the desk.

"Why couldn't you swim? Why did I have to save you from drowning?"

Refusing to look at him, I continue watching out of the porthole and train my breathing to match the flow of the waves.

"Answer me," he growls, his voice nearing, though his steps are silent.

I roll my neck, releasing the tension that has built. It pops under the stretch. For a few moments, the only sounds that fill the room are our breaths.

My body stiffens when I feel James' body brush against mine, the heat from him rolling off like the desert sun. He uses his calloused hand to pull my hair to one side, exposing my neck.

"You can't ignore me forever, Siren. You forget that you're my captive, and I'm not letting you go. You'll wear eventually, and I'll learn all your secrets," he breathes against my jaw, his nose nuzzling me in a way in which I would think is affectionate if it had come from anyone other than Captain James Erickson.

His words fuel me. "You won't break me, *Captain*. I will die before I give up more secrets of the sirens. You'll have to kill me."

With a fluid motion, his hand grips around my neck as he spins me toward him, slamming me against the wall. Nose to nose, he chokes me with just enough strength to remind me I'm at his mercy. "You will fucking tell me *everything*. I don't care how long it takes—I will know everything about you. Every detail. Every secret. Every strength. Every imperfection. Because no one, Little Mermaid, is as perfect as you allude to be."

His words confuse me, but before I can think too much into it, his lips edge closer, brushing against mine. He wouldn't dare kiss me. I try to turn my head, cutting off any possibility of his lips colliding with mine. His hand tightens around my throat, the rejection possibly triggering him—and it's that squeeze that compels me to look back at him, to catch his expression.

I'm wrong.

He's not angry.

Not at all.

His lips form that ghost of a smile that makes my lower belly warm. Flutters form, soft tingles spreading across my chest. I swallow, narrowing my eyes at him in warning as he hovers there, his mouth close to mine.

"Not so close, Captain," I warn in a whisper, and even then, it's hard to force the words out when my heart is thumping so loud.

I wonder if he can feel my pulse.

The way his eyes burn brighter, I think he does.

"Or what, Siren?" he whispers back, thickly.

Now my breaths heave out of me quicker. I look into his eyes and see thunder, but...desire, too. So much of it. The want so thick, I'm sure it'd come out of him like the black ooze of his magic if he let it.

"Or I'll bite your fucking face off," I manage out, clenching my teeth as I raise my brows.

"Maybe," he murmurs, his nose bumping along mine. I go completely still, my hands balling, nails digging into skin as those flutters intensify. He stares into my eyes, into *me,* and I feel suddenly transparent. Like maybe my own desire is bleeding out of me, and if it were magic, it'd be colors. A rainbow against his black tar.

Now I'm angry. Angry at him for these feelings, at myself for wanting him to fuck my mouth the way I know he'd fuck my body.

I snarl, "Not maybe—"

His mouth crashes into mine, silencing me.

Immediately, my body hums, and a fire licks my veins. The warmth of his lips makes my knees weak, and I don't hesitate in giving him access to my mouth, parting my lips and allowing his tongue to dance with mine. A deep groan vibrates through him, his hips rolling into mine. And I'm weak—so fucking weak—because I moan into his mouth, unable to stop myself from falling into his taste.

Arousal overcomes me as his hands reach down to grab my thighs, encouraging my legs to wrap around his waist. The sheet I'm wearing makes it difficult to secure my positioning, and James quickly rips it away from my lower half, exposing my naked skin once more.

With the barrier of my sheet gone, he tilts his waist and grinds his cock against my center. The friction from his hardness and the fabric of his pants draws another moan from my throat.

I reach my hand up to the base of his neck and grip his hair that he's tied back, pulling the secured strands roughly. "I hate you," I breathe into his mouth. Our teeth clang and tongues meld together as we continue to explore.

"I hate you, too, Siren."

His hands grip my ass as he moves away from the wall and carries me over to the unmade bed. He drops me on it and kneels one leg between mine, dominating over me with a satisfied smirk.

"So easily I can turn you into putty in my hand, can't

I?" he goads, taunting me with a look that says much more than the words he speaks.

"I can say the same of you. My siren song, like my tail, is absent, James, yet your cock is as hard as quartz. Your body betrays you."

His eyes follow mine down the bulge in his pants, stopping at the wet spot I clearly left behind.

"As does yours," he quips. "No victors in this battle, are there?"

My nostrils flare. "I suppose not."

His eyes burn deeper as he urges, almost needily, "Tell me your name, Siren."

I shake my head and come to rest on my forearms, propping my upper body so I'm not flat on the bed. "No."

He peers down at me, running his gaze along my body. "You know mine—it's only fair that I know yours. Unless you prefer to be referred to as Fish. I'm sure that'll start to feel real old real quick when my crew takes the piss out of it."

My eyes roll. "You know, for a captain, you're quite a twat."

James' arms cross in front of him. He continues to kneel with one knee between my legs, staring down at me curiously. His eyes rake down my body once more, slowly this time, lingering on my core. I watch as his fingers dig into his biceps as he holds his stance. His voice is calm but lethal as he demands once more, "Tell me your name."

Dramatically, I sigh and roll my eyes again. "My name is Aria. Now, are you going to hate-fuck me or am I just laying bare before you for your amusement?"

"You want to be fucked by your captor, Little Fish?" James asks in a condescending tone.

"Ugh. Siren, mermaid, fish. Pick a nickname, James, I can't keep up." I swish my hand absentmindedly for dramatic effect. "And you're hardly a captor since I escaped successfully once already, would you agree? What makes you think I won't escape again?"

"Will you?"

"Obviously." I grin at him with confidence.

"You sound like your escape was a success."

"A minor hiccup."

His tone is dry. "Yes, drowning was very minor."

I fight the blush of embarrassment in my cheeks. That escape was such an epic failure, I can't even think about it without wanting to shrivel up and die.

Very unbecoming of me.

He studies me now as the silence swallows up the room. Then he says, "What if I told you that I won't hold you prisoner again, if you agree to stay on the Tempest?"

Bewilderment coats my face before I can stop it. I stare at him with what I can only assume is a look that mimics if I had just watched a dog lick its own asshole, trying to figure out what he's playing at. I fix my face before answering him. "Why would you want me to stay on this ship, *Captain*?"

The corner of his mouth twitches—he doesn't miss the way I spit sarcasm into his title.

James takes a moment to ponder my question before he removes his bent knee from the duvet and kneels on the floor in front of me instead. "Because as I much as I fucking hate you—and make no mistake, I absolutely fucking *detest* the mere thought of you for what you've done to my ship and men—I'm also mesmerized. It's a problem for me, Aria, to wonder what you taste like."

Grasping my hips, he slides me down the bed until my ass is at the very end. My heart thunders in my chest and I pray to the Gods and Goddesses he can't hear it. The way he affects my body is clear, but my heart...that's another secret I must keep to myself.

My enemy may also be my undoing, in an entirely different way than what's expected.

"Tell me what you're thinking," he breathes, that voice low. His sex voice.

I'm shaking. I have to clench my teeth to stop them from chattering. I feel heat in my core just staring at him inches away from tasting me.

I puff out a shaky breath. "I'm thinking..."

I'm thinking you terrify me.

You make me want to scream, both from rage and from want.

You make my heart throb in a way I've never felt before.

And I hate you for that, too, Captain.

Instead, I tremble out, "I'm thinking you should ease your curiosity, Captain."

He lets out a deep breath, like he'd been holding it for some time, waiting for my response.

James guides my left leg to drape over his right shoulder and repeats the process with the other leg, draping it over his left. Once situated, he brings his fingertips to trail up the inside of my thigh, caressing it slowly. My body trembles beneath his touch, anticipation thick in the air.

This is so fucking wrong.

"Does the captain have permission to taste, Aria?"

More heat settles low in my belly. I am so deliriously fucking lost right now. Staring into his eyes as he peers deeply at me is no easy task. I hold his gaze regardless of how much I want to give in. I can't let him defeat me—not in this.

In this, we're equals.

"Since when does an abductor ask his captive for permission?" I counter quietly, allowing my body to drop back on the bed, no longer interested in propping myself up. I stare up at the ceiling of his room, in mere disbelief that I've committed myself to whatever he wants to do to me.

Does the captain have permission to taste, Aria?

Goddess, I'm in trouble.

A new wave of desire floats through me and I know I'm drenched for him. I know *he* knows I'm drenched for *him*. I don't bother hiding or denying it.

A dark chuckle floats past his lips, but even then, I can hear the tightness in his voice. I almost want to look at him, to see his desperation mirrored in mine.

Until I feel the warmth of his breath on my pussy.

Oh, fuck. Now I'm lost.

I curl my fingers around the throw blanket beneath me and my back involuntarily arches in a silent plea for what's coming, giving him not only permission, but an open invitation.

Roughly, his mouth closes around my clit and he sucks it into his mouth, teasing it with varying pressure as he scrapes against it with his teeth. I cry out in pleasure, and he instantly removes his mouth, moving it to bite the inside of my thigh as he laughs again.

"You're right, Aria. You're my prisoner, and I'm not so sure I'll ever set you free," he tells me before he laps my pussy with the entire length of his tongue.

James

She makes this noise when I taste her. A deep moan that she tries to swallow down. Her body quakes as I run my tongue along the seam of her pussy. She's painfully sensitive, like pleasure is unfamiliar to her. I wonder about that. How a beautiful creature as her could suddenly look so innocent.

I eye her as she writhes, my fingers digging deep in her thighs as she tries to buck and squirm. Her tits bounce from the movements, but she's going nowhere. Not with my punishing hold, and it's a beautiful thing to wield the power now. To not have to worry about her fucking song.

Yet even in her human form—or whatever the fuck she is now—I'm still pulsing for her taste. I'm licking at her tender flesh, not to rile her up, but to feed *my* hunger.

The bracelet.

Its power must still be tainting me.

Because I suck at her like a starved man, and when I hear her moans, I feel like a fucking god.

My wrist burns where the bracelet is. I've never felt power like this before. The pulsing strength surges through my veins, and I can feel my form changing again, returning to the untarnished prince of my past.

And it's that feeling—that horrid fucking feeling of perfection—that hits a nerve inside me. That overwhelms the needy, hungry man that wants to fuck her with my tongue. It gives me the focus to pull away just before she's reached the apex of pleasure. My skin itches, the rage I feel masking into a look of disgust as I let her go and come to a stand. Without her fin, she's fucking tiny. Her legs are long, smooth, and womanly, and they're spread open for the taking. Her cunt is swollen and wet from my tongue and her desire. One more lap of it with my tongue and she'd have exploded.

But why give this little mermaid pleasure?

I don't owe her it.

Certainly not after she's massacred my crew and left the Tempest in disrepair.

Not after she disrespects me, continues on with her verbal sparring even straight after I foolishly offered her freedom if she was willing to stay aboard.

What the fuck was I thinking?

The bracelet begins to cool as I step back from her, the burn of its power waning. I glance down at my arms and see that even my unmarred skin has retreated, my ruthless exterior still present.

Regaining my equilibrium is hard, but I'm resolute. I'm not a man that bends to the whim of a beautiful woman, even as she writhes for pleasure. I'm stronger than that—better than that. Like Grimy says, I need to honor my family name, and that doesn't start by fucking the very species that aided in the destruction of my lineage *and* my kingdom.

I don't trust her.

Her clouded eyes flicker open. She stares at me as her chest continues to rise and fall rapidly. Her cheeks are flushed, her bottom lip puffy from biting down on it. For a brief moment, I see her yearning. Her body is still trembling for release, but I just stare numbly at her.

"Not going to finish what you started?" she asks, and it's meant to come off as dry, but there's an ache in her voice, one even her own malice can't hide.

"Finish yourself," I growl.

At the tone of my voice, she snaps her legs shut and quickly pulls the covers back over her. Her teeth are chattering as she fights the whiplash I've given her. I don't expect the silence to last too long. As her bewilderment fades, her hands begin to clench. "You can't do that, you know," she seethes. "Fuck with someone's body like that."

"I just did."

"You're a prick."

"Doesn't feel so nice, does it?" My smile is all bite. "Imagine walking around with that feeling—"

"Fuck you," she says, harshly. "I can't help what I am."

"You made us suffer—"

"You're alive, aren't you—"

"My men are DEAD!" I suddenly shout as my body

looms over her tiny frame. She doesn't fucking get it. What she's done. Not just to my dead crew, but to my ship, and to the men still alive on it, that pent-up lust and hunger for a woman's heat—she doesn't comprehend the agony she's responsible for.

A hungry man can only take so much.

And within that wanting man, desiring a woman and not being able to have her is an ache that runs through our bloodstream in a cruel, visceral way.

She's making herself even smaller. Bringing her knees to her chest as her face grows pale. She looks up at me with her large blue eyes, and fuck me, she looks so damn innocent, so damn young. "Imagine chasing that feeling—that raw, aching lust—to your death. Fuck, I'd do it to you just to watch you suffer, Siren."

A flash of emotion passes over her, but I can't tell what she's feeling, and it doesn't make a difference. I'm fuming. My mind's not so clouded anymore by her presence. The tether is there, the pull that sits in my chest, but I can hear my fucking thoughts, and they're damning me for touching her.

The taste of her lingers on my tongue.

I grab my black rain jacket off a nearby hook. "Regain your strength. We'll need you out there come morning."

"Need me for what?" she asks, confused.

I slide the jacket on and eye her dryly. "I need a crew."

Now it dawns on her. Her face falls with alarm. "I don't know anything about being a crewmate on your nasty fucking ship."

My sour smile grows. "We all start from somewhere, Aria, and if you want to eat, shit, and sleep on my ship, you'll be pulling your fucking weight around here."

"You don't get it," she hisses. "I'm not..." She takes a moment, fuming now as her chest rises and falls faster. "I'm human, like you, James. While I easily had the same strength as you in my other form, once I'm shifted back...it takes time, okay?"

So, she *is* human then. It feels better to hear that than to wonder if she's a monstrous creature that can shift form as she pleases.

I look threateningly at her. "There are other ways to earn your keep."

Without waiting for her response, I leave her in my bed, still wrapped in my sheet, looking like the sky is falling.

Yeah, it feels fucking good to wield the power now.

LUCA AND I TAKE SHIFTS. We spend the night alternating between sleep and navigation. The rain isn't coming down hard, but it's steady. The night is long and cold and spent bailing out the water in the bilges and organizing the deck space. I've lost a lot of inventory, including most of the water barrels. The food from the cold boxes flipped over when Aria struck, so most of the meat and perishables are off or saturated by salt water. Grimy's going to be fuming when he finds out his entire stock of cigars are soaked. There are puddles of blood and shards of broken glass from shattered windows. The interior of the ship is filled with mountains of crap strewn off shelves and tables.

Tempest is a fucking mess.

I refuse to clean anything, and suddenly, I know exactly what Aria will be doing tomorrow.

As Luca lays in the hammock above deck, I know he's not sleeping like he's meant to. He watches me pace for some time before grunting out, "I can't get any rest. You want to trade places?"

I shake my head. "Won't get any sleep, either."

"Because everything's a fucking mess, aye?"

"Yeah," I grit out. "A giant fucking mess."

He's quiet for several minutes, then he asks in a hushed voice, "What is she, Cap?"

I stop to stare at the black waters, always sensing that we're being watched, being followed. The feeling is unnerving. With a tired sigh, I answer, "A pain in my fucking ass."

CHAPTER 21

James

We've been moving slowly at a pathetic two knots an hour. Right before Aria struck, we would have taken a few days to close in on the Isle of Morda. And while our intention was never to dock on that cunt of an island, we have no choice now. It's the nearest land —if "near" is the right fucking word.

I instruct Luca and Grimy to secure the cargo room. Locks won't cut it. When you have a room full of black market goods and your next destination is an island notorious for outlaws and crime, you want to make sure your shit is hidden away. At the same time, I can't have Aria snoop through my shit.

Before long, we'll be a broken-down ship, crawling to a dock with no crew, no weapons, and a sexy as sin hostage who—I'm damn certain—will spare no time trying to escape my clutches.

It's fucking fantastic, isn't it?

We spend the next day salvaging what we can of the sails. Even after a quick patch up, parts of it are torn to shreds, and as we raise it up, it flaps lamely against the wind. As I sip on my bitter coffee—most of it spoiled from that Siren's shitstorm—I send hand signals to Grimy as he stands behind the steering wheel.

Briggs is naked and hanging up a laundry line of our clothes. He's huffing and puffing that he's had to wash our clothes in arctic waters, and how his are all soiled from the storm.

"No appreciation," he whines. "It stunk of fucking armpits and dick hair! I won't do it again, Captain. I won't."

As he sobs and dry heaves, I smirk and peer out into the horizon, seeing only the ocean. At the pace we're sailing, we're around fourteen days—possibly longer—from reaching Morda. It's fucking painful because on a good day, when the Tempest was sitting pretty in the ocean, we'd have gotten there in less than three.

Luca's knocked out in the hammock nearby, snoring into the air. I glance fleetingly at him, about ready to kick him awake, when I hear the soft patter of footsteps. The tether grows heavy in my chest, and I instantly know she's drawing near. I've been sensing her all morning, pacing around in circles, restless. She's been antsy, taking steps in and out of my cabin. I know she's behind me, pretending to be insolent and broody, but I feel her uncertainty. She's lost, out of her depth, and it's taken her a tremendous effort to get out here. I don't turn around to face her. I keep my eyes pinned on the ocean, but my focus is now lost.

I bring the mug back to my lips, and before I take a sip, I rumble out, "To what do I owe the pleasure?"

"I'm hungry," she announces plainly.

"All those hearts didn't satiate you?" I ask.

"I don't *eat* them, James."

I take another bitter sip. "Watch it, Siren. When we're away from my quarters, you will call me Captain."

"Captain," she icily corrects herself.

"So, how's your hunger my problem?"

She huffs, irritated. "I need to eat."

"So, eat."

I finally twist around to look at her. My heart stills for a fraction of a beat as I glimpse her over, making sure my emotions are hidden away. She's wearing a gray knit sweater of mine from my closet, and it's so big, it ends just above her knee. She's taken one of my worn-out leather belts and fastened it around her waist, accentuating her hourglass figure, and her colorful hair is tied up in a messy bun using the leather shoestring of one of my boots.

So she's resourceful, then—gets quick at work to make herself appear put together. These are the actions of someone who's used to being a human. I lock that thought away. I keep my expression neutral as I watch hers deteriorate. She's giving gross side-eyes at Briggs, though she does appreciate his ripped figure. It makes my blood spike with irritation.

"Where's the food?" she demands, crossing her arms while tapping her bare foot like she's fucking *waiting* on me.

Oh, she's fucking pushing me.

"Do I look like I'm your fucking servant?" I bark out roughly. "Need I remind you that you destroyed my ship, and while you did that, you destroyed what food we had. The flour's drenched in sea water and the meat's been picked off by the Black Sea Ravens. You can forage through the mountain of debris below deck for some canned meat or jump into the ocean and catch us some fucking fish."

She narrows her eyes at me. "Captives don't walk around and feed themselves."

"Consider yourself lucky."

"To be on this shithole with you?" She rolls her eyes dramatically. "So fortunate."

I curl my lips up into a mocking smile. "Would you rather another captain, Aria? You think his crew would be more hospitable?"

Her chest stills with sudden clarity. My words have struck a chord. Good—she's aware of how bad it could be. She knows very well she'd be on her back getting fucked by a train of men if it were up to another captain.

Straightening her body, she keeps her voice level, bored. "Fine, I'll forage then."

Just as she's about to turn, I tsk. "Not so fast, Siren. You gotta earn that food, you know."

Her teeth gnash together as she tries to rein in her emotions.

I walk to her slowly, closing the small gap between us. Tilting my head, I look over her body inch by inch. I take my time, wanting to watch her squirm. But Aria holds herself well. She looks up at me, meeting my gaze with a fiery one of her own. In a low voice, she states, "I'm not your whore, Captain Erickson."

I smirk, bending down to whisper, "You're not a

fucking guest either, Little Fish. You're on my ship, and like I told you last night, I'm in need of a crew."

She swallows as I pull back slightly to stare at her. I can feel the heat of her body from here, can hear the thump of her heart because of that fucking tether between us. It speeds in her chest when I blink down at her mouth, and I try my hardest to keep my pulse from roaring. Because if I can hear hers, surely she can hear mine, right?

It's hard to know with Aria.

But like with this curse, I've got a lot of time.

Time to dig deep into her being and dredge up everything she might know about my curse and how to break it.

And time to fuck with her head, too, because that body? That body might beckon me to touch her, but I've got the power now, and I want to fucking play with it slowly.

"What do you want me to do?" she whispers now, lips parted as I pull away and turn back to stare at the never-ending ocean at our feet.

Now that she can't see me, I smile broadly and reply, "Get dirty."

LUCA'S SINGING a chirpy tune as he climbs the mast, a half-soggy piece of bread sticking out of his mouth. We couldn't find a halyard, so he's been acting like a monkey, his arms and legs wrapped tightly around the mast as he climbs it without a single trace of fear in his eyes. It's dangerous work, one that could break his neck in two seconds flat if his grip loosens and he falls, but Luca's always been an adrenaline junkie. As he looks over the rigging, Grimy is still standing behind the steering wheel, his attention solely on the seas, but I can see him bob his head to the beat of Luca's song.

Rex is running around the deck, his tired bones surprising me as he leaps into the air, trying to catch my attention. Instead of giving it, I toss a dried piece of jerky at him.

Briggs is done with laundry, and he's been patching up the holes on the deck with wood he's pulled out of an unused cabin, still in his birthday suit. At least when he works, he's fucking good at it.

While the men are busy, I've been in the anchor locker, spreading out the chains, looking for damage. I give what I can a quick coat of grease, stopping every few moments to look at the huffing figure as she gathers the broken glass into a pile with a soaked broom. There's been intermittent rain, so she's wet, the sweater clinging to her like a second skin. Her bun has loosened, and tendrils of purple and pink hair fall around her face, framing it. Her heart-shaped face is set in a permanent scowl as she brushes the glass into the dustpan and chucks it into the sea. She's been at it for several hours now, and I gotta hand it to the siren—she's not immune to getting filthy. The deck space is clearing at a rapid pace, and to boot, she hasn't uttered a single complaint.

I climb out of the anchor locker and stride past her. "Take a break. You've earned it." To make my point, I kick at a nearby barrel with a bowl of unscathed jerky resting atop it, inviting her to eat. I can feel her stare as she twists her head to watch me for a moment. My skin prickles with awareness, my chest stirring as her pulse quickens. Ignoring the feeling, I enter the pilothouse where Grimy is and begin leafing through the latched drawers and cupboards.

"What are you looking for?" he asks.

"From memory, Morda takes silver coins."

He grunts, irritably. "The silver's below deck, in one of the safes I hid away years ago. I'll fetch it as we approach. We've got a long while yet."

"We'll need to make a list of what to grab."

Now he's wary. "Expect to be taken to the cleaners on that dump of an island?"

"We have no choice."

"Their chandlery will be primitive."

"Again, Grimy, we're out of fucking options here."

He nods stiffly. "We need food, water, and we have to patch up that giant hole Briggs can't fix on deck somehow, and the bilges. Even if it's quick work. You'd better hope this island has a poor memory, otherwise you'll be driven out the second we step down."

I shoot him a smirk. "They won't recognize me in my true form. They only remember the prince—"

"They'll remember the ship."

"Not in this shape."

He levels me with a stern stare, about to speak, when Rex starts barking excitedly. We turn to the sound, catching sight of Rex as he leaps at Aria. His tail is wagging as he stands up, licking at her face as she bends down to pat him. She lets out a surprised laugh, running her fingers through his hair, and then he's down again. She bends over, discarding the broom for a moment as she continues to stroke him. Rex goes full whore on her, dropping down on his back, tongue out as she gives him belly rubs. As she crouches down, chewing away at a piece of jerky, I can't stop my eyes from drinking her in. Her sweater hikes up, her ass practically on display as she bends over him, giving him so much attention, he's going to fucking explode.

I look away, feeling peeved with myself for admiring her and more peeved at Rex for falling for her charms. Little shit should sense her danger, though it's hard to believe this girl slaughtered and ripped out the hearts of my entire crew when my ancient fucking dog probably weighs more than her.

"What are we going to do about her?" Grimy asks gravely.

I'm about to tell him we'll chain her up in my cabin, muzzle her so she doesn't make a sound, but my words catch in my throat. We'll be on the island for at least a few days, and we'll be coming and going. Leaving her locked up in here is too risky, especially now that she's human and I don't know what other tricks she might pull completely unsupervised.

Plus, there's the matter with the tether. Even from here, watching her from afar, I can feel the burn within. A wicked pain that only cools when I'm close enough to touch her.

"We take her with us," I reply after a moment of thought. "Disguise her, make her fit in so she's not sticking out like a sore thumb."

Grimy looks doubtful, and I don't blame him. I have a feeling I could make Aria wear a garbage bag and she'd still have people gnaw their own tongues off just to taste her. Glancing up at the mast, even Luca's stopped what he's doing to peer down at her. Without her song, she's still giving him a stiff one.

Our siren's going to be a problem.

As the hours pass, and the sun falls, I pass the wheel over to Briggs.

Below deck, Aria is still working herself to the bone, sorting through the mess. "I have a feeling this place was a mess before I struck," she mutters under her breath. It's the first thing she's said in many hours.

"You're wrong," I simply say, barely looking at her as I stride into the room with a bagful of silver Grimy's just handed to me from the safe in his room. I throw it down on the dining table she's just cleared, sliding out of my wet jacket. I throw it at her body aimlessly, ordering her to, "Hang it up."

She huffs, biting back a curse, but I don't pay her any mind. Let her think she's invisible to me. She fucking should be. I unwind the string around the bag and dump the silver on the table. Grimy joins me, counting away as I write down what we need. We're planning early. We want to have everything set up so that when we get to Morda, we don't need to do anything last minute.

"It's got to be in and out," he tells me as he goes. "No mingling with the locals."

"Because I'm a social butterfly," I dryly retort.

He sighs, glimpsing at me curtly as he counts. "No whorehouses, Captain."

From my peripheral, Aria's movements pause for a few moments, and then she's back at it again. I look back at Grimy, tapping my fountain pen on the sheet of paper, wondering what's climbed up his asshole to be giving me such a look.

"I can't promise anything," I say in return.

He grinds his teeth, saying nothing. Aria's gaze is now trapped on us, and I can feel that heart of hers pound away. Is that anger I detect? I should smirk at her to rile up her feathers and tell her yes, I am in the mood for a good fuck, but the desire to fuck with her head just isn't there. Not with the mountain of work ahead of us. It's daunting.

Still, I don't correct her assumptions, either. I don't express that I hit these whorehouses to sell a portion of the Gala Green tucked away in the cargo room.

No, fuck that.

Let the little fish think what she wants. I enjoy the prickle her gaze gives me, and the sound of her heart pumping harder in her chest, letting me know exactly what her mouth won't tell me.

"I need sleep," she says wearily a few moments later.

I don't look up from the paper. "You're not done cleaning."

I hear her shift from foot to foot. "I've done everything I physically can—"

"You can wait until you're dismissed."

"I'm still healing," she says a little desperately now.

"The shift... I need rest to recover. Otherwise I'll lag tomorrow."

Grimy stops counting to look at her. "She's not looking her best, James."

I pretend not to hear, keeping my eyes pinned to the paper as I scrawl more supplies down. Then, in a bored voice, I tell her, "You know the way back to the captain's quarters?"

"Yes."

"That's where you're sleeping tonight. Don't crawl into my bed without washing up, and don't think of fucking around on us. I can feel your presence, Aria, so I'll know where you are."

That heart of hers jumps as her breath slows. She doesn't respond, but she doesn't need to.

A second later, she's gone.

I hesitate outside of the captain's quarters, my hand lingering on the knob but not turning to enter. Why has he sent me here, to his room? The man lost the majority of his men—surely that freed up some crew quarters.

"There are other ways to earn your keep."

If he's expecting me to be his own personal whore while he keeps me aboard this ship, he has another thing coming. He can get his dick wet at the whorehouses on wherever the fuck island we're going to dock on because I sure as shit won't be using my body to "earn my keep" on this ship.

He'll be forced to release me or kill me before I comply.

Haven't you already complied? My brain battles against me, reminding me of the softness of his touch against my thighs, and the way his tongue sank through my folds, feasting on me as though he was bringing himself pleasure rather than bestowing it upon me.

Never again.

I've learned my lesson with James Erickson and I know better than to fall victim to my desire around him. He is nothing more than a vicious jerk—*my kidnapper*—and a hard dick I refuse to ride.

If he wants to put me in the captain's quarters, who am I to complain? I'll happily take over the best room on this abhorrent ship after enduring nights in that wretched prisoner's quarters.

Throwing open the door, I step inside and find the room to be exactly how I left it this morning, only now a lantern hangs from a hook on the ceiling, illuminating the space. Two buckets sit on the floor beside the washroom—or head, as I'd heard it referred to by Luca and Briggs.

I'm tired. So tired, my muscles hurt with my movements. As I move closer, I see one bucket is full of water, while the other sits half full and has a dry cloth hanging over its edge. A dip of my finger into the full bucket confirms that the water is warm. Luca is in charge of the water. He must have prepared it. For me, or for James—I don't even care. My excitement rises with the thought of a warm sponge bath and fresh clothing.

I hurry undressing before dipping the washrag into the water, not bothering to wring it before I run its warmth down my arms. A gentle sigh floats past my lips —the warm water heaven-sent. As I rub the cloth within the curve of my underarm, my eyes catch on a deep, royal blue sea-glass bottle sitting in the washroom. A cream label peeks slightly from around the curve of the bottle, and I drop the washcloth into the clean water before walking over to it to see if it is liquid soap.

The label is written in a language I can't read, so I pick up the bottle and smell its contents through the opening. My body instantly perks, and a small moan unwillingly glides past my lips. It smells exactly like James. I hope he doesn't feel this in the tether—that would be so fucking awkward.

Bringing it back to the wash bucket with me, I pour a large amount onto the washcloth and clean myself. The rich lather coats my skin, the scent of sandalwood permeating through the air. I bend to dip the cloth into the half full bucket to rinse the cloth, before moving to the full bucket to gather clean water. I'm soaking the floor below me with my careless movements, but I don't care. I'm sure the *captain* will make me clean it up anyway.

Once finished, I return to the washroom to grab James' towel, leaving a trail of water droplets in my wake. Water drips to my feet while I stand staring at the towel where it hangs, debating on whether I want to use it. The action feels intimate, and the fibers of the towel look worn, as if it hasn't been changed out in numerous years. Still, I reach for it and bury my face into its plush, inhaling the scent of James Erickson.

I have serious problems.

I hope he doesn't feel this in the tether, either.

Just how transparent am I? I try to concentrate on it, attempting to sense what he's feeling. There's a faint bubble of irritation—yeah, this tether shit is for fucking real.

Snapping out of my temporary stupor, I dry myself before wrapping the towel around my body and tucking it above my breasts. As I step back into the room, I loosen my hair from the boot-lace holding it in place, and the tendrils cascade down in a matted heap. I do my best to untangle the strands with my fingers before moving to James' closet for something to wear. His wardrobe is severely lacking, but there's a chill in the air that causes me to reach for another knit sweater—this time a faded black.

Curiosity gets the better of me as I wander his room, my fingers brushing over the minimal belongings he keeps in his space. His space is dull, lackluster in every sense. Nothing within these four walls gives away any hints about the man who retires to his solitude each night.

Two leather-bound journals catch my eye as they sit abandoned on the small table next to his bed, next to a candle whose flame dances from the light breeze carried in from the porthole. My feet guide me to them, and I sink down onto the bed and pull my legs beneath me, making myself comfortable before I grab the top one and crack open its cover.

There are no dates. No titles. Nothing. The pages are so worn, I can't imagine how many fingers it's been touched by. Incoherent words strung together to make sentences, making little sense. Some more so than others. Pages and pages of entries I try to decode, but suspect mean nothing.

I reach for the second journal, predicting the same gibberish as I open it midway—

Another nightmare of her. This time she's stalking me. I can't hear her song anymore. It's just the damn clock ticking in my ears. These dreams are happening more frequently. Either I'm crazy, and she's just my insanity taking form, or she's drawing closer to me.

They're the captain's words.

I run my fingers along the words, admiring his penmanship as I furrow my brows in thought. Curiosity fills the void in my chest. Instantly, I look up, staring at the door like James might sense this.

That would be bad, to be caught eavesdropping.

Quickly, I place the journal back down on the side table and lean forward to blow out the flame of the candle. I wait in the dark for any noises, expecting him to come barreling through, but he doesn't. The same irritability flows from his side of the tether, and I realize he hasn't noticed me at all.

Sinking into the linens, I lay on my back and continue to speculate. I should continue to read, perhaps gather the answers I seek, but the heaviness behind my eyes urges me to let my itching fingers rest.

Sleep overtakes my racing thoughts, and I drift off with questions lingering in my mind.

The slam of a door jolts me awake, but I know better than to open my eyes.

James has returned.

I listen to the gentle clink of metal on wood followed by a heap of fabric being tossed—I assume a candle and a rain slicker—but still, I pretend to sleep as he moves around the room. Shockingly, James' movements are featherlight, like he's trying not to wake me.

I keep my breathing even as I listen to him move about.

"I know you're awake, Little Mermaid." His voice is low, gruff, and incredibly close.

I bite back a smile. "Well, I don't want to be, but you're loud as hell."

He reaches out and brushes the hair away from my face. Flutters swarm my stomach at the light touch. "We both know I wasn't being loud. You sensed I was here."

"I really didn't," I tell him, opening my eyes. As I

suspected, he is crouched down beside where I lay, at eye level. "The sound of the door woke me up."

"I tried to be quiet."

"I know."

"Why are you in my bed?" Now he stands, crossing his arms and looking down at me as though he's expecting me to get up that very second. Instead, I shift against the linens and make myself more comfortable. "And why are you wearing my sweater again?"

"Do you expect me to not sleep and walk around naked?"

"The latter wouldn't be so bad," he mocks with a dead serious look.

I roll my eyes even though the darkness likely covers my irritation. "I don't even have an answer for you, James. It's basic common sense. Is that a skill you lack, along with your inability to bring a woman to orgasm?"

"There's a difference between inability and simply withholding what belongs to me."

"What belongs to you?" I repeat, scoffing.

"Yes, what belongs to me, Little Fish. Your pleasure is mine, and I decide when you will receive it and to what extent. You did not deserve to be brought to orgasm, therefore I did not allow you to."

A frustrated laugh bubbles past my lips as fury digs its roots deep within my chest. "You pompous egomaniac. My pleasure is not yours and it will never be yours. My lapse in judgment will never—listen closely—*ever* fucking happen again."

"We'll see," he mutters, walking toward the head.

Angry, I flip onto my side and face the wall. Why I keep giving this man the benefit of the doubt, I have no idea, considering he's reminded me time and time again he's not a good guy.

You've never been one to go for the good guys, Aria.

What guys? The other part of me questions, reminding me of my miserably low experience.

Great, now I'm insulting my own damn self.

A deep sigh wracks my body, and I snuggle further into the bedding, pulling the thick knit blanket over my shoulder up to my chin. I close my eyes and will sleep to pull me under once more.

A whoosh of air hits my body as my cozy, warm blanket is pulled from me.

"Hey—" I whine, when suddenly the pillow is ripped from beneath my head. Jolting into a seated position, I move just in time to watch James toss my pillow and blanket on the floor next to the bed. He's wearing nothing but a pair of tight, black briefs and the muscles in his shoulders contract with the movement. I remind myself to pick my jaw off the floor, but I seem to have a hard time taking my eyes off him and his enormous biceps. My eyes start to burn from lack of blinking before I realize I'm still staring. James doesn't try to hide that ghost of a smile, knowing that I'm watching him, as he takes his time situating his make-shift bed on the floor. "What the hell do you think you're doing?"

"Setting up my bed," he answers simply.

"On the floor? What's wrong with your actual bed? Give me my pillow and blanket back."

"You mean *my* pillow and blanket? Just because you

made yourself at home, Little Mermaid, doesn't mean you are home. These are my things. And I'm not sharing a bed with you."

"Scared you'll catch feelings, James?"

"As if an Erickson would stoop so low as to develop feelings for a *fish*."

"Ouch, Captain. Your words cut deep," I quip with sarcasm. I would never let him know that they actually did.

"I'm sure you'll bounce back."

I'm about to remark when he kicks off his briefs next. His nudity is so abrupt, I feel momentarily taken off guard. My shock silences any scornful rebuttals as he approaches the water buckets. I wonder if he'll say something catty about me having used it. He brushes his hand in the water, cupping a bit. The soapy suds are still present from when I used his sandalwood wash. He flicks a glance my way, and I immediately look down into my lap, tracing circles along my bare thigh, like this is all so natural, like his nudity is nothing but a giant cock swinging in the wind, and what's not normal about that?

Yes, yes, I tell myself. What is there not to be used to about a big dick?

My throat is dry, my cheeks flushing as I long to bury myself under the covers, but what covers? This jerk took them, and my pillow, and he's washing himself now with soap I used to clean my body—and there's something quite personal about that. Sort of intimate, or maybe I'm creepy, but it's weird, right? That he wouldn't call for a change in water, at least. And what the fuck—but now I'm looking at him again.

Watching as he uses the rag to scrub his body clean. In such a short amount of time, James has soaked his entire body. There is still smeared grease in some places, but he's mostly covered in soapy suds, except not even the wash can hide the speed bumps of his abs. His corded arms flex. This guy has biceps bigger than my thighs...

He gripped those thighs, Aria. Took a long swipe along your pussy and you...you fucking writhed.

Shut up, brain.

And yet I'm still perving this giant man, and I shouldn't, but it's not my fault.

"That tether's running hot, Little Fish," he says edgily.

I drop down into bed, feigning ignorance. "I'm hot without my covers."

"Because that makes sense."

Ugh.

I turn away from the sloshing of the water and rest my face on my arm. Closing my eyes, I do everything in my power to fall back asleep, but it's near impossible when I can hear his every movement behind me. My mouth is parted, too, and my mouth is so dry—I want a drink of water, but I don't dare let him know.

This is torture, isn't it?

Not just the fact that this man is beautifully rough and rugged in ways that make every atom in my body come alive, but the fact he's my fucking enemy.

There's weight in my subconscious, battling my every emotion, telling me it's wrong. This man is bad—the *worst*—and might even be the death of me. And yet our verbal sparring gives me a high. I feel like I'm being fed Gala Green all over again just by being near to him.

Finally, this sick punishment is over. The water stops sloshing, and he's back to fixing up his bedding. I hear him slump down to the floor, burying himself in a nest of blankets. I turn back around to glance quickly down at him on the floor. He's lying on his side, pushed up on his forearm to blow out the candle he placed on the chair to his right. As he lays back down in the darkness, he gives me his back.

With an annoyed huff, I flip back onto my side and give him my back, too.

He makes me feel petty and childish.

Since he stole my blanket and pillow, I'm left with only a thin cotton sheet which I bundle around myself, tucking it between my body in an attempt to shield myself from the cold ocean air that comes in through the open porthole. My body trembles with repetitive shivers as I struggle to regain warmth.

"Could you at least close the porthole since you stole *my* blanket?"

"Thought you were hot."

"Well, it's getting colder."

"You should probably think back on what made you hot to begin with," he growls back. "That should take care of the problem."

This bastard.

"UGH! Why, James? You're insufferable. Why must we feud? We're obviously stuck in this fucked-up situation together and since you won't release me, the least you can do is treat me with some kindness."

"You think you deserve kindness after you murdered my entire crew?"

Oh, fuck, not this again. "It was only a few guys—"

"Thirty men, Siren."

"Okay, a few dozen. It happened. Quit living in the past, James. You still have Luca, and that older gentleman. And that guy with the long hair that's disgusted by everything and is still searching for his comb."

"Yes, great, a drunk that drank himself out of following a siren's song, an elder who's had one foot in the grave for the better part of four decades, and a man obsessed with his appearance. What a wonderful line-up to get the Tempest nursed back to health."

"And me!"

"Conscripted work."

"Well, it's better than no—"

"No, it's not," he snaps. "If you had any idea how long it took me to acquire that crew, you'd be apologizing instead of arguing."

"Doubtful."

"And you call me insufferable. Go to sleep, Siren. Daybreak comes fast while out at sea." Blankets shift against the floor's wood planks as James situates himself where he lays, likely trying to get comfortable on the hard floor.

At least he left me the comfort of a mattress, albeit having seen better days. Still, it smells like him, and that soothes me for some strange fucking reason. *I'm crazy.* I close my eyes, my inner monologue trying to talk me off the ledge of going full on bitch-mode, and I bite my tongue, knowing that if I throw more fuel to the fire, I'll end up saying something that will dig me into a deeper hole.

But I also decide not to allow him the final word and ask the question that has been burning in my mind. "Whose journals are on the small table?"

I want to know about his dreams. About the siren he sees, and why that unsettles me.

"Found them, did you?" he retorts. "Didn't your mother ever tell you it's rude to go through people's shit?"

My heart sinks slightly, but my voice is all bite. "My mother died when I was a child after she delivered my baby sister."

For once, James has nothing witty to throw back at me. For several seconds, the room is silent.

"I'm sorry," James finally says.

"You're not, but it's fine. And for the record, my *father* taught me that, but I've never been one to give a flying fuck about what people think about me, and I happen to love snooping my captor's shit."

Again, he stays silent, but I refuse to not get an answer out of him. I need to know who wrote the journal and what connection to my kind they had. "Sooooo...?"

A deep growl reverberates through his chest and up his throat, warning me he doesn't care for this topic. Not my problem.

After a few long, silent moments, he demands, "What journal did you look into?"

By his tone, I realize he's worried I might have ventured into his.

"Uh, some crazy man went on about talking serpents or something."

He's quiet a moment. Then, "Mathis Erickson."

"Mathis," I whisper, trying the name on my tongue. I've never heard that name before and it feels old-timey. "When was Mathis alive?"

"He lived until the early-eighteen hundreds before he was lost at sea. The Tempest made its way to shore off the island of Suna, where a couple of stevedores were able to get aboard and guide it to the docks. The Tempest was abandoned, and what happened to Mathis still remains a big fucking question mark in the Erickson family lineage."

"Your family never sought answers?" I ask.

"Before my time, Siren. What they did or didn't do after Mathis disappeared has no relevance to me. My family recovered the ship."

"So, it was ready when your father fled with you?"

"Don't," he says sternly.

"I'm just trying to build a timeline in my head. Trying to figure out how old you are."

"Older than you, and that's all you need to know. Now sleep."

As much as I want to push back, I don't.

Instead, I pull the sheet tighter around my body and close my eyes.

"WHAT DO YOU WANT?" James' groans fill the room, and I

hear his body thrashing on the floor below me. "Why are you following me?"

I rub my eyes, regaining my bearings as I try to figure out what's happening. A heavy breath leaves his throat and I recognize the sound of his fear as night terrors. My sister Celeste has been plagued with them since before I can remember, and it's always been my job to help ease her out of the darkness while she sleeps. I know the drill, having been through this countless times.

Like clockwork, my body takes over. Half asleep, I sink to the floor and peel off the blanket that's wrapped around James' torso and arm. He's trembling, a clammy sheen of sweat layers his body. Once freed from the blanket, I slide in close, pressing the front of my body against his back. My mind begins to stir, registering how different this body is to my sister's. She was so puny, I'd wrap my entire arm around her to bring her close. But with James, it's different. Once I position myself against him and snuggle in, I wrap my arm around his middle, barely making it all the way around. He's huge, his abs flexing as he bucks. A giant mountain of a man—I feel almost helpless trying to calm him down.

"Stop... Don't... Don't..."

"Shhhh," I console. "Shhh, it's okay, James. I'm here. Listen to my voice. Everything is okay. You're here on the Tempest, having a nightmare."

"Please don't..."

I circle my hand along the planes of his abdomen, pulling him tighter against me as I continue talking him through the hold his deepest fears and traumas have on him. At one point, he goes impossibly still, and his breath is so ragged, it's like he's fighting to draw a breath in. "James, it's okay. It's okay, James, I'm here. Shhhhh, you're just having a bad dream."

His body lets go suddenly and then quakes. I nuzzle my face between his shoulder blades, repeating that he's okay, that everything will be alright. Then I feel the change in his demeanor. He settles, and I feel the exact moment the nightmare has retreated. The tension in his body fades and he relaxes against me. Although asleep, the vulnerability humanizes him, and I find the anger I carried from our conversation earlier dissipating as I hold him in my arms.

I think about the journal, about his fears.

He's just a man, I remind myself.

It shouldn't feel this good to hold the enemy so close, but the feel of his skin against mine is doing something to my insides that I'd much rather deny than accept.

Every fiber of my being is telling me to get up and go back to bed, but as his body heat melds with mine, the chill that settled in my bones starts to evaporate.

I MUST HAVE FALLEN BACK to sleep because, for a third time, I am jolted awake. James startles in his sleep, the violent movement ricocheting into me. A breath catches in my chest as James pushes my arm off his waist. He sits up quickly when he discovers someone is touching him. When he realizes it's me, the anger in his eyes only intensifies.

"What the hell do you think you're doing, Siren?" he spits out, scooting his body away from mine.

My brows furrow with confusion. I don't expect him to remember his night terror—my sister never remembers hers—but I don't expect this reaction from him, either.

"I—you had a night terror, James. I helped you calm down, and I must have fallen asleep again," I stutter as I explain myself. My brows furrow again as I wonder to myself why I'm suddenly acting so timid. Watching him with wide eyes, I wonder if he's in some sort of dream state, sleep-wake situation.

"Get up," he growls suddenly, causing me to jump. James stands quickly and yanks my arm, forcing me to stand, too.

"What the hell?" I rasp. "A simple 'thank you, Aria' would be great, thanks."

Not even my sarcasm can ease my nerves. I shrink into myself, wrapping my arms around my chest as I move back. With every step back, James steps forward, removing any distance I'm trying to gain from him. I only stop when my back hits the wall, and now I'm cornered, feeling small and vulnerable. He stops before me, his rage emanating from him. I've pushed this man's buttons countless times before, but this time, it's like I've hit a nerve I didn't know he had.

I have to crane my head up, staring up at him with wide eyes. My heart pounds behind my ribs and there's a lump in my throat so big, I struggle to swallow. I can honestly say that, until this very moment, I have never felt truly afraid of Captain James Erickson. But now, there's so much malice in his eyes; the way he's looking at me, it's like he would truly, honest to Goddess, chain me again.

My eyes dart around the room, looking for a quick escape.

When my eyes connect back with his, he grits his teeth. Any warmth left in my body dissipates as he voices his wrath in a terrifying tone. "You're lucky I'm not gutting you like the filthy fish you are. Don't fucking touch me again, Siren."

The door to my room rattles on its hinges as I slam it shut, stalking out of the cabin with my hands balled into fists and my teeth clenched.

A nightmare.

I'd had a nightmare and my enemy—the one person on the ship who shouldn't have a full look into my weaknesses—saw me at my lowest.

Or at least that's what she claims.

I woke disoriented, my neck kinked and throbbing from the discomfort of sleeping on the floor. A soft warmth radiated against my back and for a few fleeting seconds, a wave of bliss washed over me...then I realized I was in the arms of Aria. Instantly, all the heat rushed to my chest, along with my rationality.

I allowed myself to lie in her arms and feel the soft air expel from her mouth as she slept soundly behind me. Curled into me like I was her personal teddy bear.

Want to know what I did with the one and only teddy bear I ever owned? I sliced it open with the first switchblade my father had just gifted me and tossed the stuffing, along with the plush bear's carcass, into the ocean. I still remember that vacant feeling in my chest as we watched Goldspince fade into the horizon, along with every happy memory I'd ever had of a home.

"Good," my father had said. "You're not a child anymore."

No. I would not succumb to letting her think I was her teddy bear—she'd never have the satisfaction of slicing me open. After all, the first rule of the ocean is to never give your enemy your back. Regardless of how fucking good that enemy felt cradled against it.

I make it to a spare cabin and slam that door behind me. The room is tiny, dark, with just a thin cot and nothing else. My eyes take a moment to adjust. I should have made the fucking siren retreat to this room, or better yet, one of the coffin rooms, but instead I drop down onto the thin foam and cradle my head in my hands.

When did this get so fucked-up?

When did I start enjoying the touch of this woman I hated so passionately?

Aria may have cut open the chests of my men and ripped their hearts out, but I can feel the tight grasp she's holding around mine.

And that's even worse.

Thrashing around in my nightmare was unbecoming of me.

Waking up to find my enemy curled around me like a lover? Intolerable.

The heels of my hands dig into my eye sockets—the pressure pushing against my eyes is enough to cause bright lights of spotting to appear. I let the sound of my breathing echo in my ears and exhale through my nose.

Anger still flows through my veins and I let it, knowing the strong emotion is likely pushing through the tether and allowing Aria to feel my aggressions. She needs to remain fearful. I'm wary of the day she no longer fears me and realizes how quickly the power can shift to her.

I'm not arrogant enough to think she isn't strong. The mental sparring and the physical torment I've put her through since her capture has proven that. My Little Mermaid is tough, and I'd be foolish to underestimate her *again*. I never did investigate how she was able to break free of her chains and escape, but I wouldn't make the same mistake twice in thinking I had any true hold over her.

My mind spirals, snapshots of Aria flickering through my brain like a movie, dancing behind my eyelids along with the bright bursts. They move together —the light shimmering around her and making her even more ethereal than she already is—when out of nowhere my body freezes, and the nightmare from earlier slams into me.

Tick-tock.

Tick-tock.

Blackness, coldness, the never-ending clock winding down my life. And running. I'm running on a ship that screams of the Tempest, while a giant beast in the water stalks me. Finds me. Darts out of the ocean to ensnare me. Curls its thick, slimy serpent-like body around me, and I'm pleading.

Please.

Please.

Please.

Water crashes over the side of the ship, knocking several men over the side.

"Run away!" a man shouts as he races for cover.

Just then, a bolt of lightning strikes, shooting through a pair of massive sails. A spark ignites and the entire mast goes up in flames.

Shouting.

Chaos.

Still ensnared by the dark creature, its grip around my middle tight, I look over my shoulder at the men who flee. But more bolts of lightning cut through the sky, connecting with every man, causing them to fall lifelessly to the ground.

"Stop," I plead, twisting helplessly. "Stop!"

I turn to look at the creature.

A pair of dark, inky eyes stare back at me.

"Don't do this! Stop!"

Then suddenly, all is silent.

The storm passes, the crew is gone—vanishing into nothing—and I fall from the arms of the serpent, colliding with the wet boards of the deck. On my hands and knees, I begin to weep as the large creature shifts before my eyes.

"Please..." I plead. "Don't..."

Blackness devours the form, and I scoot back, terrified.

Suddenly, the blackness fades, and the creature before me lays limp on its side. The sight is jarring: bare flesh, colorful hair, a tiny feminine form of ethereal beauty positioned on her side, her back to me. I slowly crawl to her and shakily touch her shoulder, pushing her on her back. Tears fall down my face as I stare into the lifeless blue eyes of the siren who watched me, who stalked me.

Tick-tock.

I look her over, horror devouring me now as I see blood pouring from her stomach.

Blood everywhere.

Her skin cold as ice.

Cold like death.

MY NIGHTMARES ARE GROWING MORE vivid.

Happening more frequently. Every time I awake it's the same: I'm drenched in sweat, my heart through my chest. Straight away, I know what sort of day I'm going to have.

Grimy, Briggs, and Luca know, too.

They keep their distance, and even Aria catches on. There's quiet in the tether. She's cautious, her emotions turning to dread when I lurk nearby. This is good—she needs to keep her distance from me.

I assign her the shitty jobs. Mop the deck, wipe down the portholes, do the dishes; it's the work I used to assign my lowest ranking crew. The ones still finding their sea legs before climbing the ranks.

It's the work that keeps her away from me, and after what happened with my nightmare in the captain's quarters, distance is exactly what we both fucking need.

CHAPTER 25

Aria

The captain is cruel.

He assigns me my tasks and acts like I don't exist. I feel like a servant, and I get it. I do. The damage I did to their ship...it looks so fucking wrecked by my siren powers. I actually am beginning to pity James for the havoc I caused.

I can tell this ship means a lot to him.

And to Grimy.

They've both been walking around the last couple of days with somber expressions. Grimy, while reserved and unpleasant, at least looks at me and will acknowledge my presence. I get nothing from James.

The guy gets to taste my pussy and leave me hanging on the precipice of a giant orgasm, but one mercy cuddle during a bad dream in the night and *I'm* the asshole.

I shake my head, feeling a surge of frustration yet again.

What's wrong with me? I'm surrounded by human men—my enemies. I shouldn't care if my storm broke their ship. Caused damaging holes and tattered the sails. Spoiled their food and diminished most of their clean water supply. They deserved it.

At least, I try to tell myself that.

As I toss a barrel of rancid meat out, I glance out into the ocean. My sanctuary. If I had my tail, I'd be on the other side of the world, getting sun-kissed by the tropical heat of Avangail. I hear it's the most beautiful land, and I long to visit. Rumors speak of giant, burly miners that built a treehouse utopia deep in the forest. Of apples so juicy, they're the base of every sweet. And the men. Oh, I hear the men in Avangail are breathtaking. My sisters get giggly just speaking of the land. Why couldn't I have been kidnapped by them instead?

Sudden movement derails my thoughts. I blink out of my daydream and feel the tether burn hotter. A flicker of longing pours into me, mixed with a tinge of lust. It's not coming from me. I turn and catch the captain's gaze on me and quickly the tether fills with repugnance. The captain barrels past me like I don't exist. The guys follow behind him, and within minutes they're getting the only intact fishing boat ready for launch. Or so they say.

I pause to stare, my hair whipping over me, carrying the scent of the rancid food I've been handling for the last hour. Briggs has made it a mission to keep away from me. Just like now when he takes gigantic steps around me to get to a pile of rope.

"I'm not infected," I snap at him.

"Not infected," he agrees, taking another large step around me, "but you smell like my grandpa's ass in the summertime heat."

My mouth drops open in shock as he hurries past me. My cheeks heat, embarrassment thick as I drop my chin to my chest and try to casually smell myself. The horrid stench brings tears to my eyes, and now I feel pissed. Angry that I'm doing this. I'd throw the whole barrel into the sea if I was strong enough, but in this form, I can barely lift it two inches off the ground. And never mind asking the men for help. They've been given explicit orders to leave me be.

Thanks, Captain Asshole.

I turn my back to the men now as I grab handfuls of the spoiled food and toss it into the sea. My movements are brisk as my frustration takes over. My shoulders feel weak. I'd been roused from bed since four in the morning to do these dumbass tasks. I haven't even had breakfast yet, not that I can stomach anything with this gross smell in my lungs.

I'm muttering curses under my breath as the slime gets under my nails.

A shadow falls over me, and I pause to glance at Luca. He's been slowly approaching me for the last couple minutes, looking almost nervous.

"What?" I hiss at him, unable to hold back my irritation. "I'm not diseased, Luca."

He's rubbing his hands with a rag, nodding. "No, I know, I know."

"If it's breakfast you want, you'll have to wait until I'm finished, unless you want me to serve you with *these*." I raise my filthy hands at him.

He keeps nodding. "Of course not! No! I can make

breakfast, no worries. In fact, I don't even think we have breakfast to make. All the food's in that barrel."

I stare blankly at him, waiting for him to get to the point. He clicks his teeth together. "On that note, Cap requests your company aboard the fishing vessel."

It takes a moment for me to compute. I glance over my shoulder at the guys propping the boat along the side of the ship. Captain Jerk-But-Fuck-He's-Beautiful-When-He's-In-That-Dark-Sweater doesn't hold back, grunting up a storm as he helps haul the boat across the deck. Those grunts send flutters in places that have started growing cobwebs.

I look back at Luca. "He requests my company?"

"Yes."

"Requests?" I repeat dryly.

"Uh-huh."

"So I can refuse this request."

He pauses, coughs, pauses again. "Well... more like demands—"

"Of course he fucking demands—"

"Oh, well, you know, Siren, it's my duty to form his demands into proper etiquette—"

"Why does he want me to accompany him?"

Now he blows out a breath. "You know, that wasn't disclosed, and if you want, you can ask him that yourself."

"Won't ask him for me?"

"I'd like to keep my fucking head today."

"So only I should withstand his wrath."

He sighs, looking tired now. "Don't shoot the messenger, fishy. You've got a quarter of an hour to get ready."

He stomps off, leaving me no time to respond.

*Q*UARTER OF AN HOUR TO *get ready.*

He could have just said fifteen minutes. But Luca gets all weird when James is in a mood, I've noticed. He's extra cautious, trying his damned hardest not to fuck-up. I should ask him for pointers. Like, *hey Luca, any tips on how to behave after a person destroyed a dude's fucking ship and all? Asking for a friend.*

Fifteen minutes isn't long enough to get myself cleaned up. I still smell like rotten meat when I make it back. At least my hair is out of my face, and I might have squeezed my cheeks a few times for a natural glow. Not that I'm trying to look decent to the man that almost ate me out to orgasm or anything. No, no, not at all. Did I rub his soap all over my skin? Yes, but so what? His room is my room now, at least temporarily, and as his ~~captive~~ guest, I can use what's available to me, right?

I am not rocking my hips back and forth as I walk toward him on purpose, either. That's just my normal strut. I run a hand over my ponytail only to keep the flyaways out of my face. And is he looking at me? I sneak a peek—

No.

He's not looking at me at all.

And the tether is cold as fuck from his end, so you know what? Fuck this.

I cross my arms and stop beside him. Without

looking at me, he gestures to the tiny boat dangling on the side of his ship and says, "Climb in."

IT'S A BEAUTIFUL SCENE, I won't lie.

The sea is quiet as James rows for some time, approaching a tiny spitball of an island. I can't even call it that. It's rocky looking, and there are only sad looking plants that rise up from whatever bits of grass there is. You could probably take thirty steps and get from one end to the other. But it's land, sort of.

He stops rowing and begins to gather the supplies he took with us. Apparently, Briggs had been working on this makeshift fishing rod all morning. I stifle back a grimacing expression because it's the saddest looking fishing rod to ever exist. The line is strong though, and to demonstrate that—more to himself perhaps—James tugs on it, this dead look on his face telling me nothing of what he's thinking.

He's grabbed bits of that rancid meat and is using it for bait. *Poor fishies.* He slips it through a tiny hook, checks on the sinker and then flicks it into the water.

For some time, we sit there, me on the bench seat opposite him, hands clasped together. We bob there for who knows how long in the silence. The sun isn't strong, so it's not overbearing. I'm not hot, either. The cool wind is pleasant, almost chilly.

I look at him intermittently. Running my eyes over the jagged scar down his face and through his lip. I stare at those lips, brush a strand of loose hair behind my ear, stare back at his lips and then sigh, wondering what the hell I'm here for.

"Did you take me out here to finish me off?" I ask, half-joking, half-serious. *Fuck me, but what if he did?* "Didn't want to do it around the others? You can call it a boating accident, and they wouldn't for one second doubt it. Since I almost drowned already and all."

James' obsidian eyes dart to mine. It's the most he's looked at me in *days,* and for a while we're trapped in each other's gaze. My heart beats faster, and I swear I can feel his mirror mine. Then he looks away and starts to run that tattooed thumb across his bottom lip, heavy in thought.

"I don't need to secretly murder you, Siren," he finally says. "My men wouldn't blink twice if I told them I'd done it."

This is strange. Because on one hand, I feel jittery that he's acknowledging me. On the other, I feel this vacant despair at the notion that my death wouldn't even be a blip on anyone's radar. Especially his.

I swallow the ache that surfaces, smiling joylessly at him. "How sweet of them. Bros before hos, I get it, Captain. Sweet squad you got."

"Thank you, Siren."

Siren.

That's all he's calling me.

Not Little Fish, or Aria, or Little Mermaid.

I'm just Siren, like he is Captain.

Well, two can play that game.

My fake smile grows as I sweetly ask, "I won't lie—

I'm flattered you invited me, but I'm curious why you chose me over your buddies."

"They're too busy to keep an eye on you."

"I don't pose a threat."

"You're not to be trusted unsupervised."

"Scared I'll cause damage in my human form? All five foot five of me." Now I tilt my head to the side and give him an award-winning smile, my tone turning seductive. "Or is it my mouth, Captain? Are you worried I'll use it on your men behind your back?"

If I thought the tether was cold before, I'm in for a rude awakening. An arctic blast runs through it as those eyes narrow on mine. I'm distinctly aware of the double meaning I've just implied, and I'm also acutely aware that I'm seeking his attention, even if it's negative. A reaction, anything, I just want to know what he's feeling. Even if it's rage, it'd be better than this emotionless wall he's been giving me.

"Careful, Siren," he warns, gravely.

"Or what?" I press.

But he doesn't answer for a while. His stare is intense, dangerous. The warning is very clear. That I'm not to say that again, and Goddess help me if I did anything to his men at all.

He'd kill me.

But I don't believe that.

He'd kill them.

Ah, yes, now that...

That is more believable.

The realization is troubling. I glance away first. Yes, let him know he's won this round. I don't even care. I stare down at the water, feeling all kinds of fucked-up. Defeated, even.

More quietly, I say, "Why am I here, James?"

He sighs. "I said it was to supervise you, but really I don't want them to see there's nothing out there."

I look at him, frowning. "What?"

He throws the fishing rod down. "The Black Sea is dead, Siren. Why do you think we stockpile food onboard? There is nothing out here."

"How do you know that—"

"Because I know." His teeth clench as he stares solemnly at me. "I've starved out here. Starved and starved for weeks and weeks and because I can't fucking die, I know it's the most awful fucking way to go. I think I died a dozen times during that time."

My voice has dropped to a cautious whisper. "What time was this?"

He runs a hand over his face, bunching his brows like just the thought of it hurts. "When I escaped...when we escaped the siren that killed my father..." He stops there, and his jaw tightens as he shakes his head. "I can't go through that again."

My heart picks up at the wretched look on his face. A siren killed his father? The realization is a dreadful one. I almost want to reach a hand out and run my fingers across his cheek, assure him that everything will be alright, like when he had that nightmare—

"Don't," he growls sharply, glaring at me now. "I don't want your fucking pity."

"It's not pity—"

"*Enough.*"

Feeling frustrated, I cross my arms and spin around, giving him my back. "It was sympathy," I hiss. "Not pity, Captain. Sympathy for your pain. I'll be mindful to keep it at bay next time."

"Good."

I roll my eyes. "Yeah, good. You know, I'm such an annoyance. I'm surprised you don't just drop me off right here. It's a pretty island—"

"It's not an island—"

"I'll starve to death right here and you won't have to see it—"

"Not happening."

"You can let me go and never have to worry about a soul giving a shit about your feelings—"

"I'm not letting you go."

A strange knot forms in my chest, and it has nothing to do with our tether. "For how long?"

"That's undecided."

"One more month? A year?"

"It'll take ten lifetimes to pay off what you destroyed."

"I can't give you ten lifetimes, Captain. I live and die like everyone else."

The silence that returns feels loud somehow.

As if ruffled, he lets out this deep grunt. Suddenly, he comes to a stand and throws his clothes off, one layer at a time. I know this because I'm peeking shamelessly over my shoulder, unable to look away from those muscled legs and tatted torso.

Captain James Erickson is the most gorgeous creature I've ever seen, and I'm in serious trouble.

His movements are rough, like he's angry. I wonder if it's something I've done, or if it's the food situation. Maybe both.

In just his briefs, he grabs the speargun by his foot and, without a word uttered to me, he dives into the ocean. I lean over, watching him disappear under the water.

Anxiety engulfs me when he doesn't surface for a while. How long can this man hold his breath? Before I can properly worry, his head pops up from the other side, and he takes in a lungful of air.

"Anything?" I ask.

He shakes his head stiffly and then dives back under. I see his form under the water glide over the reefs of the sad island-but-not-an-island. He swims even deeper, and I can feel the desperation now. He needs food. Needs to feed his crew.

They're all he has left, I realize.

A sad weight sinks to the bottom of my stomach as I continue to watch him surface, only to dive back under.

For the rest of the morning, we don't speak. The sun moves across the sky. I grow hungry, tired, my lips dry. All the while, James takes breaks between bouts of spearfishing. The man doesn't stop. He's desperate to feed them—feed *us*. I sense trauma in him and reflect on the fact this man starved for weeks and died of starvation.

He's caught a couple fish, and they flop there at my feet for a while. Being a siren, I feel my heart wrench at the sight of any sea life perishing. But at the same time, my stomach twists, and Goddess help me, but I'll take any stew—even if it's fish.

"These'll hardly feed a single man," I mutter as James climbs back into the boat, wet chest heaving for breath. I glance up at him as the sun kisses his dark skin. His briefs leave little to the imagination, and as I drink him in—he's soaking wet, his hair loosening around the bun—I relive the memory of him undressing and bathing in front of me in the bedroom. He's been neglecting his beard the past few days, so it's been growing in thicker, and it's not fair—for the rest of us to look so gaunt and at the mercy of nature, while James looks like a god of the ocean.

"A bite is better than nothing," he replies, sitting down. Elbows propped on his knees, he sinks his face into the palm of his hands and runs his fingers through his hair. He's exhausted. The man's stamina is fierce.

Imagine how hard he'd go in bed. Man would probably last all night long, Aria, just in and out and in and out—

I suck in a breath and look away from him, peering into the clear blue waters. My heart is thumping violently, worried he'll feel my lust. Quickly, I bury the anguish that is horniness and bring my hand into the water.

The sea is refreshing. Taking a cupful in my hands, I run it down my arms, and then my face. I do it over and over again, trying to dull the ache at the pit of my stomach brought on by this man. I refuse to look at him, refuse to feel that heat reignite. Goddess help me if he stared me in the eyes—

What is happening to me?

Am I crushing on my abusive captor?

When I get back to Norborne, I'm going to do exactly as father says. I'll be the best shut-in Norborne has ever seen. I'll never fight again—never sneak out to the docks and try to prove myself. I'll even call Sadie, our judgmental neighbor, a witch. That bitch has been itching to call me one, so I'll beat her to the punch. And when I shift, I'm going to just play tag with the fishies and leave the bloodlust behind.

Speaking of fish, one tiny blue one darts into the palm of my hand, rubbing its head against my skin. I smile softly, allowing it to swim around my hand like it's doing a dance. I run my hand back and forth, playing with the little guy, when another one joins.

Then another.

And then another.

Before I know it, the boat is swarming with these little guys. My hand tingles, the faintest reminder of my powers as a siren.

"How are you doing that?" James asks suddenly. I've been so distracted, I didn't notice him peering over the edge to look at what I'm doing.

"I may not be in my human form, but I'm still a siren, Captain," I say quietly.

His awe—an emotion I haven't felt from him before —pulses through the tether as he watches the fish come to me, each wanting their turn to say hello. I'd be pretty awed, too, I guess, if I were a human. Still, I can't help the smile it brings to my lips. The positive emotion he's silently offering almost feels like the smallest of olive branches. Perhaps more like an olive twig, or maybe just a piece of stripped bark from the olive branch…it's miniscule, but the teensy white flag it waves is present.

A larger fish bumps the swarm of little guys away to have a play with my hand, and just like that, I don't feel quite so alone. I open my mouth, a song about unity with the sea at the tip of my tongue—

The water in front of my hand suddenly explodes before my eyes as a spear is driven through the fish. I let out a horrified scream, whipping my hand out of the water as fish blood coats the surface. Spinning around, I look up at James, heart battering in my chest with shock and horror. He stares back at me, a determined, cruel glint in his eye when he orders, "Put your hand back in."

I gasp. "No."

"No?"

"No!"

"Either you put your hand back in willingly, or I'll do it for you."

I glance back down at the water, the swarm of fish scattered in all directions. "They trusted me!"

"That's good."

"And you killed one!"

"And we're going to kill more."

I cross my arms, enraged. "I won't have you use me."

"We need food, Siren," he says gravely. "Would you rather kill a bunch of brainless fish, or are you that determined to kill the last of my crew?"

"They're not brainless."

"*Aria.*"

I don't speak, but I can't help the way my heart jumps

at the use of my name. He waits for me to decide, and I know I have no choice, but still. I take my time stewing.

Finally, I stand up and crane my head to look up at him. My eyes narrow, and I try my hardest to look strong, unyielding—even though this man is terrifying.

"I'll do it," I speak slowly, firmly. "But only a few fish, and we'll be giving thanks to the sea for every kill. If you want more, you'll have to dive back under and catch them yourself."

"Only a few fish," he promises resolutely, black eyes holding my gaze. "Now stick your hand back in."

Aria

The crew cheers as James unleashes net after net of fish. The deck looks like an unrolled carpet of dead fish.

I glare at the bastard as he grins at his men, a satisfied look in his eye.

"Don't thank me," he says, that voice laced with arrogance. "Thank our siren. She lured them to us."

I shake off Luca's pats and push away Briggs as they swarm me. I begin to walk away, heading toward my room when James says, "We're not done giving thanks, Siren."

Ha fucking ha.

If I'd known he'd be using that damned net, I wouldn't have agreed to stick my fucking hand in the water again.

WITH SO MUCH FISH, we get to work over the coming days. We gut them and hang them up to dry. The sun is fierce at noon, so within a few days they're dried out and ready to be taken down. We gather the fish jerky and load them into a clean, dry wooden container. I gather the meatier fish and prepare them for a large stew.

It's been full-on.

By the time the sun goes down, I can't wait to crawl into bed. I sleep so deeply; I don't even dream.

I can't say the same for James. I don't know what's become of him in the night. Sometimes I hear his footsteps above deck, stopping above my room. Other times, he's just outside my door, standing there. The only reason I know this is because of the tether. Cold as it may be, there's a faint heat still radiating from him. I can sense him, like the way a person can sense when they're being stared at.

Sometimes, when I concentrate hard enough, I can feel the echoes of his curiosity. He wonders what I'm doing. He wonders where I am. It's the strangest thing to know this. To be so acutely aware of the manner in which he's thinking about me. I have no explanation for it. Just a feeling at the pit of my stomach that tugs me down a train of thoughts on their own.

But he keeps his distance.

He hates me.

I'm his enemy.

A siren killed his father, after all. I understand the depths of his loathing, and I can't fault him for it. And so I have to be extremely careful. I can't let my guard down, no matter how much the men have warmed up to me.

Any minute, they can decide they've had enough.

Any minute with my unpredictable captor can be my last.

IT'S AN OVERCAST DAY.

I'm collecting the last of the jerky from the lines. Stopping at the mast, I line the jerky in a cool wooden container. I'll have to ask Briggs to help me carry it below deck when I'm done counting every piece we've made, a stupid task Grimy gave me just to keep me busy. I'm onto my fortieth fish when I idly glance around. Briggs is moving up and down the ship, retying some of the lines that have gone loose. "Not hard to tie a knot, Luca," he whispers under his breath.

"I heard that," responds Luca from above my head. He's climbed the mast again, doing a paint job with a black brush.

"Well, it's true," snaps Briggs, stopping to point at him. "You're supposed to be a seaman!"

"I am a fucking seaman!"

"Your bowline knots suck!"

"Oh, fuck me, we ain't fucking at port, are we?"

"I don't care! I almost tripped over the pile of rope you left on the starboard side—"

"So watch where you're going!"

Briggs gasps. "Motherfucker, I could have fallen overboard and *died*."

Luca scoffs. "Oh, you're being dramatic."

Briggs huffs loudly, and his hair blows off his face. "Dramatic, my ass! You wouldn't have heard me."

"Quit being a baby. You're here, ain't you?"

Briggs snarls, "That's not my point!"

"Wah, wah."

"I hate you!"

I have to swallow down a laugh. And here I thought the captain and I had bad fights.

As they squabble, I see movement from my peripheral. My face falls when I glance at Grimy as he runs a palm along the handrail, lost in thought as he strolls along the ship deck. There's a buried ache behind his eyes.

It's the look of a man that wants to let go but can't.

As if the old man can sense me, his eyes flicker to mine, and I feel my heart skip. I wait for him to scold me, tell me to get back to work, but he simply nods once in greeting at me and walks on by.

Now Luca's voice is softer as he calls, "Hey, Siren."

I look up, momentarily shuddering at the view. I'm right under him, and he's only in his underwear.

Underwear with giant, fist sized holes in all the tasty places.

"If you got a voice people would die for—" Luca pauses to chuckle at himself at that. "—does that mean you got a nice voice outside of being a crazy fucking siren?"

I wish I could sing like my sisters. Like I can open my mouth and let out a fairytale chorus that brought in the birds and the fishies. *Yeah, let's not forget what happened the second I* wanted *to sing to the fishies*. But, sadly, I respond, "Nothing like yours, Luca."

"But she can dance," Briggs cuts in, smirking at me. "I've seen her move when you sing, Luca."

"Is that right?"

Now they're being cheeky, teasing me as Luca breaks out into another song. I shake my head, suppressing my smile despite the strange giddiness I feel at their light-heartedness. I'm responsible for all this carnage, and they're going about their day cleaning it up and cracking jokes, treating me as though I'm not an outsider to them. They go from calling me Siren to Aria and I can't really decide how to feel about that development, or the ease in which it happened. Like it was so natural. Like I'm just another deckhand, part of their crew.

Even Grimy chuckles as he walks back, doing his second lap of the ship. "Put another underwear on, Luca!" he calls up at him. "No one deserves such punishment."

"Don't cramp my style, old man," Luca cackles down at him. "I'm trying to flirt with our sea guest, after all."

"Yeah, that ballsack will win hearts," Briggs mocks.

"Not tryin' to win hearts. There are other places in a woman's body I long to win."

Now a laugh escapes my throat.

"See, I made her laugh!" Luca carries on. "That's how you win 'em, boy. Crack a few dirty jokes, and next thing you know, there ain't nothing wrong with being in a half-torn underwear."

"Disgusting," Briggs retorts.

"Did you know when you're turned on, you can tolerate all sorts of disgust?"

"Fuck off, Luca."

"It's true. Just make 'em beg for it long enough and suddenly they'll do anything for your tipper."

"Your tipper?"

"Cock, Briggs!"

Now the laughter grows louder. My chest vibrates and I can't fight the sudden glee that races through my being. It's been too morbid until this point, so I relax my shoulders and give in to the jokes.

My face is flushed as I shake my head up at Luca just as Briggs' laughter dies short. Grimy stills from beside me, his gaze trapped behind me. I've been so busy and entertained, I didn't really pay attention to the tether until now. It tugs sharply as I slowly spin around, staring directly into the eyes of our captain.

There's emptiness on his side of the tether. More so than normal. It's cold and distant, like a black hole you're dangling your legs over. You can't know how deep it goes, and you're too scared to goad yourself into going over.

No wonder I felt like the tether had gone quiet.

Captain Erickson is mastering the way of silencing it.

My laughter fades straight away. He peers at me shortly, the stare so dismissive and unfeeling. I'm suddenly nervous, extremely aware now of how dangerous this man is, and how silly I've been in pushing his buttons. If he wanted to sever our connection entirely, he could so easily throw me off the ship and I'd sink to the bottom of the sea, and I'd be gone.

Just a bump in his past, a fleeting problem he solved and forgot about.

And that thought stuns me for a moment.

Would he so easily forget me?

Luca is mindlessly cracking jokes about all kinds of vulgar things, unaware of how fucked up it is down here. With his hands behind his back, James continues to stand there, unimpressed and threatening. Briggs is back to his job, and Grimy is slowly walking away, like he doesn't want to be here for the outcome.

I haven't gotten back to work. I'm still standing straight as an arrow, heart thumping steadily faster as I glance up at Luca and then down at James. Finally, Luca realizes he doesn't have an audience. "Why are you guys so quiet? Did I offend your sensibilities—"

And then he goes dead quiet. He stares down at his captain, the brush limp in his hand, the black paint dripping down, hitting my bare feet. He looks absolutely ridiculous, his privates swaying in the wind that's just picked up. A spattering of rain hits the deck, and Luca begins to pack away his supplies, putting them in a pail he's dangled up there.

His climb down is uncomfortably long, but when he gets to the bottom, he acts nonchalant. "Hey, Cap," he says sweetly. "Didn't see you there."

James flicks his dead eyes at him. "Are we finished, Luca? I didn't want to interrupt you. Don't stop on account of me."

But Luca shakes his head. "Just takin' the piss, Cap."

"So I hear."

He clears his throat. "Gonna work on another job 'cause can't do much with the rain coming, can I?"

Now James' voice turns icy as he retorts, "Rain? You've been up there fuck-assing around, and all you saw from that high vantage point was *rain* coming, Luca?"

Luca looks up, and I follow his gaze and realize very quickly what James is getting at.

"There's a storm coming," James growls out. "Clear the fucking deck—we're battening down the hatches and riding through it."

Storm is an understatement.

Within minutes, the wind has picked up so much, whatever we haven't been able to tie down or store below deck flies away into the sea. The rain has turned to a full-blown downpour, and thunder continues to crackle overhead.

I'm still on the deck, pretending to be a try-hard. I'm putting away the paint supplies into the deck box. I try to slam it shut when I'm done, but it's overfull. Opening it back up, I remove some things, spinning shit around to get it all to fit.

"Time to come in!" Luca shouts from behind me. "Aria!"

"In a second!" I shout back.

I'm doing this purposely, taking my time so the men can disappear back inside. I toss a glance over my shoulder, watching Luca's back as he turns it to me, waiting for me to finish. Quickly, I dig into the tools, searching for a weapon small enough to conceal. My heart kicks up, anxiety gripping me, but I need something, anything, that could protect me.

I may have exchanged a few laughs with the crew, I'm still their prisoner.

His prisoner.

And he's been so cold—so damn cold.

If he's silencing his side of the tether, it could mean he intends to do something, and I'm not going to take that risk.

I find a pointy screwdriver and slip it up one of my sleeves. My fingers are numb by the time I close it back. Coming to a stand, I turn around, take a quick step and nearly scream at the broad chest I slam into.

Nausea travels up my throat as I fearfully look up at my giant captor. He stares down at me, the feeling of rage vibrating down the tether. *Cold. Cold. Cold.* He's scaring the shit out of me as his gaze flicks up and down my drenched body. I'm frozen, trembling, teeth chattering as the wind and rain continue to batter us. His white tunic is like a second skin. I can see every muscle, every dip of his chest when he breathes. His raven black hair has loosened around the bun, long strands frame his wet face, some sticking to a high cheekbone.

"What are you doing?" he demands in that quiet, deadly calm tone I'm beginning to think is scarier than if he were screaming.

"Packing," I answer, but I can hear the tremble in my voice. "Like you ordered us to do."

He's suspicious of me. He scans my face, those empty eyes looking almost black. Without the sun, the captain looks like he belongs in the foggy gloom, with the rain cascading over his skin, the puffs of cold air coming out of his parted lips with every calm exhale. He's your worst fear come to life, and yet he has this allure about him, the sort of aura that is tangible and magnetic. I feel drawn in, mesmerized by the blackness he exudes.

Yes, your worst fear, but an enchanting enigma, too.

I wonder how long he's been standing over me. Did he see me conceal the tool?

"If you took something," he says now, studying me intently, "put it back, Siren. I'll give you just one chance to do the right thing."

The right thing, I repeat internally. I nearly want to scoff. The right thing would be to plunge the tool into his heart and end his life. I can feel that itch there, however vague it feels. I may be tethered to this man, but it still hasn't dulled the voice inside my head, reasoning that he is an enemy and he might just kill me. His kind —*his family*—wiped enough of us out as it is.

You have to kill him first, that voice inside says. And for an instant, I almost don't feel like the voice belongs to me. It's like the bloodlust of being a siren still stirs inside me.

My brows come together with indecision.

The man proclaimed he was immortal. He showed me his magic. His true skin. He's proven he can evade my song—but I haven't seen proof of him being more than mortal.

I consider that as I stare up at him, wondering how long I'll be held here on his ship. Wondering even more what his intentions for me are.

Keeping myself calm, I reply, "Put what back, Captain?"

He doesn't respond for several moments. The wheels are turning in his head. I know he knows I took something. It's obvious. I won't blame him if he searches me—I would search me, too.

But the captain just gives me that lingering, lazy stare, before saying, "You're wanted below deck. We're hungry."

I don't even breathe. I just stiffen a nod. Any other time I might say something catty, but not this time, not when I can barely breathe, much less think.

I hurry past him, heart in my throat. The second I'm below deck, I don't stop moving. I make it to his quarters and lock myself inside, trying not to vomit because I'm certain he knows I've got this stupid tool. Lamely, I bury it under a pillow and remove my clothes, finding another sweater of his to pull over my head. I don't even bother to fasten it around my waist. I let it sit baggy, like a tent over my body as I fix up my hair.

Then I take my shaking ass out of that room to make food for these shitbags.

CHAPTER 28

James

She's got something.

Probably a screwdriver. What else could she have found in that toolbox?

The little fish is irritating, but her arming herself is amusing to me.

She's wearing another sweater of mine—I don't find it in me to give a fuck about it anymore. I'd rather she wear my clothes and be covered in my scent over Luca and Briggs.

I watch her as she sorts through the kitchen, cracking open cans, being a good little fucking slave tonight. Probably because she's spooked. I felt her fear— could almost taste it—and I'm glad for it. I'll take her fear over her arousal, because the latter puts distracting thoughts in my head. Thoughts I don't want to have.

I'm quiet, broody. I know it's unbecoming of me. The men have gravitated away, and I'm alone at the table while they're drinking the rationed ale we managed to recover. I haven't touched mine. I idly tap the table, watching the girl make a mess of things. She's been at it for a while now, the smell of fish stew heavy in the air. We're so hungry, I know it won't last long. Maybe a couple days worth. Certainly not enough stew to make it to land, possibly not enough to make it through this damned storm. But we've got the jerky tucked away, and that'll have to do.

"You responsible for this storm, Little Siren?" Luca chuckles as the ship groans with the force of the wind battering us.

He better not call her Little Siren again.

I crack my neck, tapping my steel cup faster as she turns away from one of the rancid fucking cans and blows out an exhausted breath. "I'm just making dinner, Luca."

Briggs laughs. One of those sweetheart kind of laughs. I've heard it before on land, trying to woo his next fuck.

He better not laugh at her like that again.

"Aria, is your hair naturally that color?" he asks. "It's exquisite."

"You should see my sisters." Her body freezes the second that line leaves her mouth. She looks away quickly, asking, "How do you get your hair so nice, Briggs?"

They're idiots for not paying attention to her admission. That she has sisters. That they have hair like hers. Possibly in their human forms as we speak, because if she's shifted back, they might have gone through the same transformation.

Briggs dives into a discussion about his hair, and next

thing I know, Luca is pulling out a chessboard and clearing off another table. Briggs sits down across from him to play, talking about a tail comb and a detangler comb and honestly, I couldn't fucking care less. Aria serves them their food bowls just as Rex scurries in, smelling the fish stew in the air.

She doesn't serve me.

Not yet.

I see my bowl on the counter, growing cold.

She's patting Rex's head, prolonging the inevitable.

She feeds him first. Forgets about me.

I'm patient. Let her take however long it takes.

I just want to look into her eyes when she does it. Coming so close, the tether will burn in a delicious sort of way.

The ship rocks from the waves, and I know Grimy will be growing hungry behind the wheel.

I check the time. One more hour and then it's my shift.

One more hour of watching her. Wondering what to do with her. Wondering how long I can keep her for. Whether I want to even keep her at all. Whether I ever want to let her go.

And could I?

Keep a siren—*my enemy*—aboard my ship, forever.

An interesting thought.

With very grave consequences.

It troubles me that it doesn't trouble me. That I could very well do it. Have her aboard my ship forever. Desire her at the same time. Taste her occasionally. Perhaps even fuck her—

I grind my jaw, regaining my equilibrium quickly before she senses my wayward battle. She turns to look at me. I stare straight back, not bothering to disguise it. She picks up my bowl and walks slowly to me, every small step measured. Those blue eyes flicker up once—just once—to look into my eyes.

As I look into them, I smile cruelly.

Yes, I tell myself. Yes, I think I do want to keep her. Forever. To ruin her. Put her back together.

The bowl rattles from her trembling hands as she sets it down, and I wonder if she senses it.

If she's caught on to my wicked thoughts.

Aria

The storm rages on and doesn't relent.

For days, we're trapped below deck, riding through it. The ship groans and rocks around. On an empty stomach, it makes me want to vomit. On a full stomach, it, too, makes me want to vomit.

I've never had to seek sanctuary from the ocean. I've always been part of the storm, not in the eye of it. It's a horrible feeling to be so vulnerable to the elements. I can't help but extend respect to any human brave enough to cross the ocean.

"Sit down, girl," Luca tells me when I've begun to clear the table off after breakfast.

It was, you guessed it, more fish.

Fish jerky, fish stew—if I live through this storm, I'll never touch a fish again, I'm certain of it.

"I'm just doing my job," I remind him, bringing the cutlery and dishes out of the room and to the large sink in the kitchen, or galley as the boys call it. I dump them in, slightly feeling overwhelmed at the mountain of work I have ahead of me.

The ship shudders as it braces against the fierce wind. I stop and rest my hand on the counter, shutting my eyes as a bout of dizziness hits me.

"You get used to it."

I open my eyes to James' voice and turn my head to look at him.

His hair is wet and let loose around his shoulders. He's in clean trousers and a white tunic, both freshly washed by Briggs before the storm had hit us. The smell of sandalwood wafts to me, and I can't help but blurt out, "You showered."

His arms are crossed, one hand holding a steel mug, steaming with the coffee I just made for the boys. "Do you often point out when one cleans themselves?"

"Only to let them know the difference is quite potent," I return swiftly, even though I'm thinking this man was just in my room—*his* room, whatever you want to call it.

I expect yet another retort, something to challenge my response, but he just stands there, staring at me, *into me*, and I've never felt so transparent.

"Having fun with my men, Siren?" His voice is deep, low, almost a whisper. The question is loaded and unexpected. There's double meaning in them, I can sense it. The lethal calm in which he asks it is raising all sorts of red flags.

I turn around fully and press my back against the counter. Leaning back, I casually relax my elbows on them and tilt my head to the side. "They're great,

Captain. Rowdy and fun. A girl can really let go around people like that." Now I twist my features, looking sorrowful as I add, "But you wouldn't know that, would you?"

He doesn't skip a beat. "To be rowdy and fun, or that a girl can really let go around people like that?"

"Both."

"I'm an experienced man, Little Fish."

Yes, the way he's making my knees wobbly, I have no doubt about that.

The way he almost made you come, too, is a clear reminder of how experienced the captain is.

He places the mug on the opposite counter and moves to me. I think he's about to stop in front of me, but then he opens the drawer beside me and rummages through it. He looks at me while he does it, and I look back, trying to remain cool and collected. Like my confidence is soaring even though my life has been falling apart around me since being captured by this man.

Pulling something out, he tells me, "Hold still."

"Why?"

"Because I fucking said so."

I say nothing as I hold still, partly-curious, partly-afraid of triggering his temper. He reaches a hand out and grabs at the torn neckline of my sweater. He closes it for a second, eyeing the split, and then lets go. I've been having to adjust the sweater all morning, and the guys have gotten to take healthy eyefuls of my tits. But I'm running low on clothes, and this thin sweater was all that was left in James' closet.

I look down at the small case he pulled out and is

unzipping, revealing the contents of a sewing kit. Is he seriously going to fix it? *Now?* As I stand in front of him, barely able to keep my knees from shaking? I stare back up at James as he pops a sewing needle in between his plump lips and unwinds a gray colored thread. Within minutes, he's sewing the damn split with his bare hands, his movements quick and experienced. I don't ignore the way my skin tingles as the pads of his fingers graze along my bare chest as he goes. My nipples feel stiff from how hard they are; I'm alive and burning and all he's doing is putting the split together with focused eyes. Like, fucking relax, Aria, you'd think by how tightly wound up I am that this is foreplay.

In places like Norborne, it is.

"Man of many talents," I remark, but the dry tone doesn't quite come across the way I intend it to. I sound breathless instead. I stare at his mouth, running my gaze along that split in his lip, wondering not for the first time what horrors this man has endured.

Also wondering how good they'd feel against my mouth if he'd just stop being such a dark cloud and kiss me. Better yet, he can keep that dark cloud in him. He can kiss me with the force of thunder, and I'd love the jolt of lightning running through me. This man would revive my senses, have me begging for his storm.

I really do need to get away.

But I don't want to at the same time.

When he's finished, he puts the needle and thread back into the sewing kit, but he doesn't move away. He lingers there for longer, turning back to look down at me. His eyes run along the length of me, and they look heavy for a moment, almost satisfied.

"You like how small I am to you, James?" I whisper, bravely.

The tether tightens. I feel a hit of warmth rush through my veins. I hold my breath in surprise, knowing it's him putting it there.

James edges a little closer, and his arms come out on either side of me. He rests his palms face-down on the counter behind me, leaning forward a bit, dropping his head to mine. I'm still looking up at him, and my heart is racing, my skin is coated in that heat he's administered. He hovers there, his mouth barely a breath away from mine. If I moved, our noses would touch, and I want to move—I do—but I'm nervous and scared and I don't know what I'm doing.

With a more searing look, he murmurs, "I'm beginning to think any lack of experience between us is coming from your end."

I narrow my eyes. "I know how to have fun."

I feel his fingers glide down my arm. Even with the sweater on, I'm sensitive to his touch. "No, you don't, Siren. If you did, you wouldn't have gone around, sinking ships to the bottom of the sea."

My resistance is weak. I utter, "That's just my nature—"

"Nature is something you can't control. What you did was targeted," he cuts in, studying me, fingers gliding down the length of me. Down my side, around my hip. "Why else would you have decided to hunt the Black Sea where us marauders are? If you loathed humans so much, you wouldn't have cared. If it was your nature, as you say, then you put yourself as far away from the best of them as you could because you, Siren, didn't trust yourself."

He's more right than he is wrong, but that doesn't mean I'll let him know that. I simply look bored. "Goddess, Captain, if I didn't know better, I'd say you're trying to redeem me."

His fingers pause, as his eyes harden. "Redeem a killer fish? Not a fucking chance. But I'm beginning to think you were right. We're alike, you and I, and that's a dangerous thing."

"What exactly is dangerous about that?"

"You can't tame heat with heat. That's not how it works." He runs his teeth along his bottom lip, eyeing my mouth and then the repaired split along my sweater. "You're a problem for me, Siren."

He suddenly steps back, his warmth replaced by the cold of the ship. Turning his back to me, he grabs his mug off the counter and warns, "You ever show your tits around my men again—there will be hell to fucking pay. Need I remind you that you are the help and not a piece of fucking meat for them to salivate over."

A bolt of anger runs through me as I retort, "Are you jealous, Captain?"

He turns his head, offering me his profile as he growls harshly, "I am *murderous*, Siren. Do not fucking push me."

BRIGGS AND LUCA weren't too enthused that my sweater was repaired. I was in a fog all day, attempting to play chess with them, but James weighed heavily on my mind. He took over the afternoon watch, which left Grimy down here, reading a book with tired eyes. He eventually dozed off on the settee, and I felt bad for the old man because he looked cold. I wound up finding a spare blanket to cover him up in.

"Softie," Briggs said.

And maybe I was.

I didn't know.

I just didn't like the idea of him shivering in his sleep.

By evening, Briggs took over for night watch, and I escaped to my room in an attempt to dodge James. I've been in here ever since, rocking back and forth from the force of the waves, feeling terrified that we'd smash apart and I'd be separated from them. Odd that I'd worry about being separated by them over drowning in the black waters of this relentless sea.

I take my time bathing myself. After I've washed every inch of my body and am satisfied I don't stink of fish, I comb my hair with the brush Briggs lent me. He's promised to braid it tomorrow to keep it out of my face.

As I'm just about done, I hear footsteps outside the door. I pause combing and stare at the door. The heat in the tether tells me James is on the other side. The floorboards groan beneath his feet as he stays there, not coming in, not going away either. I swallow thickly, feeling something heavier than lust through the tether. My heart beats as I continue to hold my breath, waiting, *hoping,* he'll pay me a visit.

But then the footsteps continue, drawing away from the door. My shoulders sag in disappointment.

I crawl into bed and curl under the covers, heart in my throat when a loud groan sounds. Poor Tempest. I run my hand along the wall, whispering, "You're okay."

The ship is tough as nails. I know it'll be fine. Even my siren powers couldn't tear it apart, but still, its groans feel real to me, like it's in actual pain. I rub my eyes to keep the emotion at bay, feeling that horrid guilt in my throat at the devastation I did to it. The pain I see in Grimy's eyes when he runs his hands along the damage fucks with my head. It's like I've ruined his home, and what has he ever done to me? Nothing. The old man would have never caused me harm, and yet my song would have drawn him to me, and I wouldn't have thought twice about ending him.

I close my eyes, needing sleep to come because I don't want to feel this way.

Not at all.

I dream of dark eyes and scarred lips, tattooed skin and needy hands.

I dream of a deep voice growling in my ear as his fingers rub along the folds of my pussy. *"I'm murderous, Aria. I'll kill anyone who looks at you, and I'll fuck you so hard. Punish you for thinking I could let what's mine walk around with her tits out. You're mine, got it? I want to hear you say it, Siren."*

"I'm yours, Captain."

"That's right."

And then I open my eyes just as I'm about to come. I stare into the darkness, panting, the pulse between my legs too difficult to ignore. I run my hand down my body, lightly grazing my fingers along my core. Drenched. Seems I can't even come in my dreams. I run a hand down my face, frustrated beyond belief.

It's only as I'm lying there that I realize I'm not violently rocking around.

The storm has ended, and the silence is deafening.

I almost can't wait for morning just to hear Briggs and Luca have a go at each other. I decide tomorrow I won't try to evade James, either. If he wants to watch me, I'll let him. If he wants to corner me in the kitchen, I won't be a smartass.

I'm tired of fighting him.

I won't lie and say it hasn't been wonderful having the entire quarters to myself, but I also won't lie and say I haven't laid in bed at night, wondering where he is. And now I'm dreaming about him, too, thinking of how violent he looked when he warned me in the kitchen. Murderous, he'd said. He felt *murderous*. And fuck me, but I can't stop myself from liking that.

A few times, the urge to climb out of bed and find him consumed me. I'd made it to the door more than once, holding the cool brass knob in my hand, and even giving it a turn, before realizing my lapse in judgment and crawling back under the covers. With James gone, it means I have full use of his warm blankets and comfortable—albeit flat—pillow.

If I wasn't held captive on this decrepit old boat with a grumpy sea captain and his...*eclectic*...crew, I'd say this situation isn't a total loss. I have a warm bed, after all. A break from my rowdy sisters, who I love and miss, but honestly, the silence is welcome from the constant girlish chatter that could cause a brain aneurysm. But then again, I *am* a prisoner of this ship and even though the grumpy captain is irresistibly handsome, his attractiveness doesn't forgive the fact that I'm not a guest here.

I'm kidnapped, and he refuses to let me go.

Though I'm beginning to suspect his reasoning for not letting me go has changed.

And my reason for not really wanting to go has intensified.

Tonight, I will stop resisting the urge to call for him. I'm so needy, so full of lust and craze, I just want him here. Even if it's to bite my head off.

I focus on the tether. That constant heat in my chest. Then I openly allow myself to yearn for his touch. I know this is dangerous. I'm practically begging him to come to me. To touch me. To *explore* me. To rub me like he did in my dreams and fuck my pussy with his mouth like he masterfully did already.

The images flash in my mind, and I hope they can travel through the tether. I hope he *sees* them. Images of my mouth wrapped around his giant cock. Glimpses of my fingers rubbing along my pussy, aching for him.

I focus mostly on the raw ache and I send it through the tether full-force.

The air feels so unnaturally still. I hear every small creak the ship makes. Footsteps above me make me wonder who's up and moving about.

Is it James, then?

He can feel me, can't he?

Leaning over, I light the lantern and set it on the nightstand as I listen intently to every sound. The footsteps continue, moving down the ship to the door that leads below deck. My heart picks up. I think about him standing outside of my door again, and I need him to be there. To want me the same way I want him.

I focus on the tether, but I can't feel him. He must be muting it again. That's fine, I'll just have to rile him up and break down those barriers.

I climb off my bed just as a sound cuts through the air, coming from the door. I practically feel like I'm floating to it, and my stark desire is the driving force. As I reach for the handle, it turns within my grasp, and my heart stills.

He's come to me.

"Miss me—" I begin as the door opens, but the air catches in my throat as I am met with a large, sickly looking man overtaking the frame. Shadowed, he's as tall as he is wide, and has a face meaner than an ogre. His dark, dingy brown tunic is stained everywhere, and white salt stains line the armpits and collarbone. His face is beet red and covered in a layer of sweat, yet he still looks green with nausea. The man does not look well at all, not while his eyes are bloodshot and misty.

I begin to step backward, my arms braced in front of me as though they'll hold him back. "Stay away!" I shout, hoping my voice is loud enough to garner some backup. Where is James? I keep my barriers down, sending terror down the tether, trying to rouse him wherever he is—

Is he even okay?

"Fancy seein' you down here," says the man, and even his voice is repulsive. "Didna expect a pirate ship whore on here, and in the captain's quarters no less."

He trudges in further, eyeing me in a way I recognize. I back away, sensing the danger. My mind immediately calms, telling me to play this smart. This isn't James.

This man won't stop himself from taking me if I sputtered out a no. The thought has me suddenly appreciating James in that moment—for not hurting me in that way, for never even considering it, despite the empty threats he tried to scare me with in the beginning. I knew they were just that—I could always feel the emptiness behind his words.

"The boys will like you," he continues as he begins to tear off his belt. I glance behind him, at the opened door, and my heart sinks to the bottom of my stomach. If he's not even considering closing it, it means he's confident nobody will stop him.

"I'll not let them know just yet," he continues. "We'll have fun first. On account of my arthritic back, you'll need to get naked for me, sweet thing, possibly need to strip me too. You can take your time with it. I've been told this body is somewhat of a stallion."

Ew, gross.

I feel the bed behind me, and I have to decide how the fuck I should go about this. Screaming for help, or bullshitting my way out of this. I keep my hand out, like that'll somehow stop him and say in a commanding voice, "I'm actually the captain of this ship, and you are not welcome here!"

The intruder goes dead-still, staring at me with confusion. "I'm sorry, what?"

I nod as my hand runs along the bed behind me, searching for the pillow where the screwdriver is. "That's right."

"You're a woman."

I frown. "What century are we living in? You'd think

we're living in mud huts and women are just breeders for you sick lot."

"But we *do* live in mud huts and women *are* breeders—"

"Maybe on land, but right now, right here, we're in the heart of the Black Sea, and you want to board my ship and have your way with me?" I let out a disgusted, disappointed sound. "Excuse me, fellow, but haven't you seen the state of things? We recently endured the worst storm—"

"As did we," the fat man cuts off, eyes bright. "It was fucking treacherous."

"I bet you lost all your food also!"

"Why do you think I'm boarding your ship?"

"Well, for food!"

"That's right."

"Well, look, we have lots of canned food left over. Some pig brains and lamb heart stews—"

"I'm hungry, but that sounds disgusting."

I frown, disappointed. "Now you sound picky for an intruder."

The man's face falls, and he actually looks remorseful. "Fuck me, I'm sorry, sweetie."

"*Captain*," I correct.

"Captain," he amends.

"That's okay."

"We're starving, you know? We ain't thinking straight."

"You know, you could have always just knocked, and I'd have been a good sea neighbor."

"Lots of violence out here, that's all."

"Yeah, well, look, how about I get dressed more adequately? Y'know, in my captain get-up and all, then I can take you down to the storage room and you can pick out some food for you and the other guests."

He nods, considering it. "Aye, that might be the best option."

Oh, my Goddess, I can't believe this moron is falling for my bullshit.

My heart is still thumping when I pretend to search for my "captain" clothes on the bed. I quickly grab the screwdriver under the pillow, making casual conversation as I go. "Did you bump into any of my crew by chance?"

I hold my breath, dreading his response.

"Aye, some blond long-haired man-doll in your wheelhouse."

Briggs. I blink back tears. "Is he...Is he alright?"

"I gave him a good clobber. He went down easy. Shouldn't have such a lighthead in your wheelhouse, Cap."

I stiffen a nod, putting on my best James tone when I retort, "You're right, aye. Best I make him walk the fucking plank come morning!"

"He'd deserve it!"

"Aye, he would! I'll take him down to the starboard side and teach that man-doll a lesson."

He goes quiet.

I cringe, maybe I oversold that. *Less is more, Aria.*

"Port side," he suddenly says, his voice deeper now.

I turn around slowly, confused. "What's that?"

His expression twists, growing suspicious. "Your plank is on the *port* side. I saw it coming in."

I shoot him a casual smile, like it's no big deal. "Oh, starboard, port side, tomato, tomahto. What's the difference?"

He shuffles from foot to foot, sounding bothered. "Well, one is the right side, and the other is the left side."

I give him a thumbs up. "Well done!"

"Thank you."

"You're welcome."

"So, which is it, then?"

I can hardly keep my knees from smacking together as I stutter, "What?"

His eyes narrow. "What's the left side and what's the right side?"

The facade drains from my body as I wield the screwdriver behind my back, holding it tightly. I should know this. I've been working as a crewmate for a while now, but I'm so flustered and frightened, I can barely think straight. "Left is...starboard?"

The red in his face returns in full fury as he darts a sausage finger at me. "You ain't no fuckin' captain! You're just playing me, ain't you? You *are* a ship whore!"

"Believe me, I'm truly not. It's actually a funny story—"

But he doesn't let me finish. The man cuts the distance between us and shoves me down on the bed. My brain jostles from the harsh landing as my legs immediately kick out as his body closes in on me. Terror sweeps through me as I swing the screwdriver at him, and he grunts in pain. I'm not sure where I hurt him because my vision is swimming and I'm screaming bloody murder. He rips the screwdriver from my hand effortlessly and throws it down so hard it slams into my cheek, tearing through the skin. His greasy hands are on my shoulders, forcing me down.

"Wasted my time," he grunts. "Gonna have to just tie you up and take you with us!"

A blast of rage tears through my chest. I gasp, shocked because it's not coming from me—

"You're about to die," I whisper, squeezing my eyes shut as the tether roars.

Not a moment later, he's pulled off me and the room goes pitch black. I blink, stretching my arms out around me, unsure why I can't see anything. Oblivion is all around me, spiking my fear into such a frenzy, I barely breathe. Panic descends and I gasp, trying to breathe.

Where am I?

What is this?

I pass out.

"Wake up, Siren," says a voice. A hand rests against my cheek, delicately stroking the strands of hair from my face.

I blink my eyes open, confused, disoriented. The second the light of the lantern hits me, I jolt, gasping.

"He's gone, he's gone."

But it's not the man I'm afraid of.

It's the blackness.

"What happened?" I tremble out. "Why did every-thing go black?"

I'm sweating everywhere. My hair is still stuck to my face as I pull away from James' touch and look around. I'm in bed. Exactly where I was last when the man was over top of me. But he's gone. He's gone and—

James.

I look at him, bug-eyed. I felt the tether roar with fury, with *his* fury. But he stares at me with a calm look, and the tether sits peacefully between us.

"I'm going to leave," he says. "There are men still aboard the ship, hiding."

"How long have I been out?"

"Seconds."

He climbs off the bed, coming to a stand now, and it's only then do I see that his tunic has been torn down the middle. His knuckles are bright red from blood.

I scoot to look out the bed, and nausea hits me in full-force—

"Don't look at him," James growls.

I twist my face away, but the sight of the man dead on the floor is impossible to scrub out of my mind.

"Stay in bed, and don't move," he tells me.

"You're going to leave me—"

"Lock the door," he cuts in, like I haven't spoken. "Ignore the dead man—"

"Are you fucking kidding me?"

"I'll clean him up when I return."

"IF you return!"

He bends down and grunts, pulling at something from the dead man. Standing back up, I watch as he wipes the blood off his switchblade using his shirt. Oh, my Goddess, he pulled it out of the body. My lips part in disbelief as he pockets it and says, "I *will* return."

Moments later, he's gone, and once again, I'm trapped in a room with a dead man.

CHAPTER 31

Aria

I'm pacing the room, listening through the open porthole for any indication the attack is over—listening for the voices from the captain and crew of the Tempest.

He left me in this room, forcing me to hide until he gave word it was safe.

Safe. Says the man who kidnapped me.

Still, I obey his command and stay put, fighting against my instinct to join them. Fighting against my instinct to look at the dead man lying near the bed. How many dead bodies is this man going to leave me with? First Martin, now this sickly idiot...

I know how to fight—I should be up there. I've trained for it, and if given proper weapons and opportunity, I can hold my own, even against a man three times my size.

Okay, so I guess what just happened with the dead man wasn't the greatest example, but I was taken off guard. One second I'm hot and bothered, thinking I'm about to be face to face with someone who no doubt would give me a mind-blowing hate-orgasm, and the next I'm face to face with a man I'm fairly certain was dying from some disease.

And my weapon was a screwdriver, for Goddess' sake.

It obviously just wasn't my time to show off my skills.

Finally, the tether sparks. The closeness of the connection burns bright, and a rush of relief hits me. I race to the door to unlock it, and pull it open.

James sends me a quick glance as he enters the room, and it's his look alone that has me stepping backward until my back is flush against the wall. His eyes are hard, darkened. His features etched with a firm look that tells me he has a job to do still, and to not break his focus. I watch intently as he moves to the dead man and stands over his body, looking down, assessing, before he bends and reaches for the man's arms.

He repositions the man's arms so they're outstretched above his head, and I think he's going to use them to drag the man out of here, but within seconds James is bent again, swooping his hands beneath the man's disgusting armpits and using them to pick up the lifeless body. James heaves it over his shoulder, swaying slightly from the added weight, and heads toward the door.

A trail of blood drips from the man. As soon as I hear heavy footsteps moving toward the deck, I race to the head to grab a towel and get to work on cleaning the blood spill.

Within minutes, James returns again and he peels the bloodied shirt from his torso as he enters the room.

The door to the captain's quarters rattles on its hinges as he whips it closed, the momentum from the shove of his hand so powerful the door practically bounces back open. Anger radiates off him in waves. The tether between us filled with so much ferocity, I can't help but bring my hand to the middle of my chest as the pain sears through me.

"James," I croak from near the door, hesitant to follow him across the quarters.

He moves like a tornado, ripping his clothes off with savagery, as though he can no longer stand the feel of the fabric against his skin. Removing one by one until he is stark naked.

I can only imagine what demons he's internally battling. I heard the scuffle on deck. Felt the symphony of emotions he'd had throughout. Heard the shouts throughout the hallways of the others. Seeing it must have been so much worse...

And then there was the man who'd made his way into the captain's quarters. The man I stabbed with the screwdriver.

I know in some capacity James is blaming himself for the man making it that far.

"James, talk to me," I plead as I cross the room to him, stopping a few steps behind him. His back is to me as he stares down into the now cold buckets of water I had used to bathe with hours ago. The soap suds have long since dissipated, the hazy water left to be dumped in the morning. "What happened? Is everyone okay?"

He rolls his shoulders, then stretches his neck from side to side, as though the simple gesture might release the tension he carries. "The bastards are dead, and everyone's okay," he snaps. "But we shouldn't have had our guard down. He shouldn't have been able to make it this far."

I'm relieved that everyone's okay. I was so scared...

"You couldn't have known." My voice is small. I reach out to touch his shoulder as I watch his chest rise and fall, but think better of it and let my hand fall back down to my side. The muscles in his back and shoulder blades contract as he breathes through the adrenaline rushing through his body.

"Had I been here, he never would have made it past a step through that door and into your quarters."

It's not lost on me that he says *my* quarters, as though this isn't his space. I try not to let it have an effect on me. A sputtered breath blows through my lips. "You couldn't have known," I repeat, and this time I take a step forward and place my hand on his shoulder blade. His skin is warm, hard.

"You keep saying that, but you know why that's not true."

I shrug. "I don't resent you. That's like saying I expected you to look after me."

"That's my job."

"I'm your captive, James, who fucked with your ship and killed your men," I retort now, irritated. "You don't owe me a damn thing!"

He flinches at my words, turning his head to the right to peer at me without fully turning around. For several tense seconds, he says nothing. Finally, he shrugs his shoulders to remove my hand. "You stole the screwdriver," he states plainly. It's not a question—he knew I had it, yet he allowed me to keep it.

I swallow the lump that's formed in my throat. "I did. But you already knew that."

He nods once, turning his face away from me. "It saved your life."

"I barely hurt him."

"You hurt him," he says unequivocally.

"Probably hurt his ego more—"

"It saved your life," he repeats sternly.

The reality of the situation is that James saved my life. I simply slowed the man down. My knee-jerk reaction is to agree with him—to throw it in his face that I am completely capable. Instead, I hear myself saying, "*You* saved my life."

Again.

He saved my life *again*.

Ignoring me, James reaches into the bucket and grabs the washcloth before wringing it out. I watch as he cleans himself hastily, continuously scrubbing and rinsing. The water turns pink from blood.

Whether it's his or his enemies, I'm not sure.

My eyes scan over his naked body, looking for any signs of injury, searching his already marred skin for any new punctures. A few cuts drag along his side—swipes of a knife—though nothing seems deep or threatening.

"Where were the others?" I wonder.

"They didn't make it far. I heard the tether—heard

your fear. Grimy heard your screams, but one of the men had climbed down a skylight—"

"In his room?" I squeak out, shocked.

"Yeah."

"Oh, Goddess, did he hurt Grimy?"

He looks at me, a soft expression spreading. "Aria, he's okay. He's handled worse, believe me."

My heart is going so fast. "The man said they needed food. Maybe if we'd just given them some—"

"He would have taken you," he cuts in, darkly now. "I don't give a fuck what his intentions were. The second he broke into my ship, his death warrant was signed. I just don't know how you were able to keep him stalled as long as you did. The tether hurt a long while, Siren. How'd you do it?"

I shrug, embarrassed of admitting, "It was nothing."

"Aria."

My heart hiccups and now my face is flushed as I force myself to admit, "I told him I was Captain."

His movements slow and he just stares at me with unreadable eyes. "And he...bought it."

I run a hand through my hair, avoiding his eye. "I was very convincing."

"No siren spell on him?"

"I'm all human, James."

He grunts, and the sound could either be of his wonder at my abilities to feign being Captain, or in absolute fucking dismay that I even bothered to attempt something so ridiculously idiotic.

Saying nothing, he resumes cleaning himself, and I recognize the signs of needing a moment to your thoughts, so I back away from him slowly until my calves hit the bed and I lower myself to it.

For once, the tether is unguarded. His rage still sizzles, along with this grief—grief that it could have gotten worse. As he thinks this, the rage worsens, and I worry he is going to turn on himself.

Every muscle in his back is tight. Thick cords run down his arms in various places, defined under the strength in his grip as one hand chokes the washcloth, while the other's balled into a tight fist at his side. The tether burns with hatred, but this time I'm certain it's not directed at me. It's a welcome reprieve, not to be at the center of his disdain.

At the same time, I'm sad this happened at all. I wonder if the men are dead and in the ocean, but I don't want to ask and have him relive it all over again. I have a feeling they're seafood right now.

After several minutes of watching him scrub himself raw, his tanned skin red and agitated, I sense there's no end in sight. He's in a trance—lost to his own mind.

"James," I call from across the room, but he ignores me and continues to scrub. I raise my voice. "James."

He tenses, but stops. His shoulders heave from the intensity of his breathing. The room is so quiet you could hear a pin drop, yet neither of us break the silence.

Finally, he drops the washcloth, the water splashing up and over the bucket. Turning, he looks at me with so much anguish reflected in his eyes it takes my breath away.

I want to say something, but nothing I think to say seems right, so I continue to keep quiet.

James turns and stalks over to where I sit on the bed, the anguish gone and replaced again with anger. As he approaches, I hold my breath, waiting for whatever cruel words may come. Maybe he does think I'm to blame. Instead, he silently reaches around and yanks the pillow from behind me, tossing it to the floor.

"What are you doing?" I stupidly ask as he grabs the blanket from the bed and tosses it down too.

"What does it look like, Siren?"

Oh, so we're back to Siren now, are we? Which means he's back to shutting me out. I huff out air through my nose in frustration.

I don't bother responding. I lay on the mattress and curl my body into the fetal position, my hands folded beneath my head. Snapping my eyes shut, I silently stew while listening to James turn off the lantern and drop to the floor.

His large body thumps against the wooden floorboards as he tosses back and forth. It can't be comfortable. I almost want to open my mouth to snark at him and tell him I don't bite—

"Fuck this," he growls, and I peek through my lids just enough to see him come to a stand and swipe the pillow and blanket from the floor. He turns and overshadows the bed, peering down at me. "Move over."

My heart rate quickens knowing he's about to crawl into bed beside me. Through the darkness I see him quirk a brow, seeming to feel the acceleration himself. I shuffle over a fraction, hardly more than he needs. The mattress dips below his body weight as he flings the pillow to the head of the bed and comes to lie on top of it.

James rests on his back, one arm curled beneath his head, his elbow bent. He closes his eyes and his breathing finally regulates. Through the dark, I trail my gaze over his features. His face still holds a level of anguish, but he's far more relaxed than before.

Lowering my view, I take in the swirls of ink that stretch across his skin, each individual hill of scar tissue, and the divots from the bullets that had penetrated his skin. As my eyes drift even lower, I become acutely aware that James has crawled into the bed—a bed we're now *sharing*—without a stitch of clothing.

The thin linen blanket covers low on his hips, giving me a view of his toned abs and his delicious Adonis belt. What is it about that part of a man that makes you want to lick it? Desire pools low in my belly at the thought of running my tongue against his skin, tasting him like he's tasted me. I feel my pussy dampen at the mere thought.

"Don't get any ideas, Siren," he grumbles at me without opening his eyes, reading my thoughts—or perhaps feeling them through the tether.

Rolling onto my back, I stare up at the planks of the ceiling, lost in my own conflicting thoughts about this man. When he first brought me aboard—*kidnapped me*— I burned so deeply with hatred for him and the remaining crewmates on this dismal boat. Now... I want to hate them, but it's become so muddied, I struggle to find that line in the sand. Briggs with his ridiculous obsession with hair, Luca with his dirty humor, and the compassion I know is within him. Grimy, though weary and tired, was once a kind soul. I can *feel* it. And then there's James.

My misunderstood captor who is bound to the sea.

My captor who has proven time after time, though he longs to loathe me, that he will protect me at all costs.

It's fascinating, really, how quickly the lines can blur.

I can't be certain how much time has passed since he told me to not get any ideas, but ideas are all that circulate my mind as I share a bed with the one person I shouldn't find myself attracted to. Yet, attraction spurs me, and my body takes over.

Sliding beneath the blankets, my body tents the sheet as I stare down at James' naked lower body. I swallow thickly.

What am I doing?

Staring down at his thick cock, I question whether I should do this. Crossing this line with him. *Again.*

Even flaccid, James is huge. He also hasn't yet objected to me being in this precarious position. That, coupled with his soft expels of air, tells me he's likely fallen asleep. I continue to stare down at his monster cock and debate on what to do. Every fiber of my being wants to take him in my mouth. My pussy clenches in anticipation, practically begging for me to make a move, while the sleeping man I stare at is none the wiser.

Slowly, I reach forward and wrap my hand around his length, feeling the weight of it in my hand. I curl my fingers around it, watching as it instantly begins to harden beneath my touch. Adrenaline races through my veins, causing me to tremble, but before I can change my mind, I lean forward and lower my head, taking him into my mouth.

A sharp intake of breath hisses above me.

Not sleeping then.

Suddenly, a hand curls around my hair, bunching it up tightly. Tears spring to my eyes as James rips the blanket off my body and stares down at me, his eyes alight with desire and...anger, still. For what happened. For what he thinks he's responsible for.

The desire wins over quickly as he takes me in. What a sight I must be, looking up at him with my lips wrapped around his cock. He hardens further and the corner of my lips stretch to take in his size.

Still gripping my head tightly, he allows me just enough movement. Dragging my tongue up his length, I circle his engorged head, allowing my hand to slide up the length of him until it meets my lips. As I slide my hand down to the base, I follow it with my mouth, taking him in as far as I physically am able.

Our eyes stay connected as I repeat the motions, taking him deeper into my throat each time. His grip intensifies, and the sting is painful, but not unpleasant. I take my time, swirling my tongue around, up the vein on the underside of his shaft, and suck at the tip of him.

No longer resisting, James guides my movement, controlling the speed and depth that I take him. The grip is impossibly tight, but he's channeling his strength, trying his best to resist going too hard. I have a feeling when this man lets go, he *really* lets go.

Abruptly, he yanks me off him completely. My mouth releases him with a pop at the sudden movement, and before I have a moment to process, he tosses me to the side and onto my back like a ragdoll, coming to straddle my body as he shifts upward toward my mouth.

His breaths come out hard, strained. "Is this what you want? For me to fuck your greedy mouth?"

I nod once as my fingers skirt down my body and beneath the sweater of his I'm wearing, connecting with my clit.

"Are you wet, Little Mermaid?" There's heat in his eyes as he asks me this.

My voice is hoarse as I answer, "Yes."

My fingers play between my legs, and I'm surprised when he doesn't order me to remove them.

James kneels above my face, his thick thighs on either side of my head. Wrapping his hand around the base of his cock, he strokes it slowly, eyes never leaving mine as he pleasures himself. All I can think is how much I want him inside me. The very last place I should ever want him is currently craving him the most.

"I'm not going to fuck you," he muses darkly as he pumps himself. "At least, not where I know you'd like me to fuck you."

I squirm beneath him. My breath picks up as I lap my eyes over the sight of him above me, all broad shoulders and narrow hips.

"Your cunt will weep for me, Aria. I want it so wet, you puddle the bed. I want it needy and pulsating, leaving you in such agony you beg me to relieve that throbbing between your legs."

The tether between us burns hot, spurring the defiant side of me to take charge. What he doesn't realize is I have no intentions other than his pleasure. After everything he dealt with tonight, something in my being aches to take care of him—to show him gratitude for saving my life—and this is the only way I know with certainty he'll let me.

Nothing says "Thank you" quite like a blow job.

Opening my mouth, I wordlessly invite him in.

And he accepts my invitation without hesitation.

The moment he's back on my tongue, I close my mouth around him and suction, hollowing my cheeks as he glides as far down my throat as he can. He's lucky my gag reflex is nonexistent, or I'd struggle to take him fully, though I suspect he'd do as he pleased, regardless of my abilities.

Pressing his forearms against the wall for better stability, James thrusts into my mouth roughly, fucking my face so thoroughly, tears stream down from the intensity of it. It drives me wild, and as I swirl my fingers around my clit, I feel my own orgasm begin to crest.

"You think you're going to come before me, Siren?" he asks, removing one arm from the wall to whip my arm out from between my legs. "You don't deserve to come."

I want to ask him why, but his cock leaves no room to speak. He's rutting in and out of my mouth with such vigor, I can barely breathe, let alone talk. It's absolute agony not rubbing myself, yet the pain of it riles me up, makes me lose all inhibitions as I moan around his cock, enjoying the bittersweet burn. Saliva drips from my mouth, coating my neck. He looks down at me and smirks wickedly.

"You may have been wise to arm yourself, Little Fish," he continues, slowing his thrusts as he rhythmically pulls out of my mouth to his tip, before rocking his hips back in and meeting the back of my throat. "But you thought you were protecting yourself from *me*, didn't you? So, you stole from me and lied about it. Neither of which I can overlook so easily."

His speed picks up again. My eyes roll back into my skull. Every movement—every deep groan—he makes sends a jolt of electricity directly to my clit, and despite the lack of attention my pussy receives, I can feel my orgasm climb still. Our arousal melds together through the tether, the strength of the emotion so potent, it feels as though my soul may combust.

His grunts spur me on, encouraging me to intensify my suction and take him further down my throat. Overhead, I watch as the veins that run along his forearms bulge, his hands turning into fists against the wall. He's close. I can *feel* it. "You're mine, Aria. So long as you're here, there's no length I won't go, no enemy I won't battle, if it means keeping you with me."

And with his words, he comes with a roar, spilling down my throat as he slams the wall with his fist. I drink him down, taking every last drop of him until he blows out a shaky breath and pulls his cock from my mouth.

I dazedly look up at him, licking my lips to ensure they're clean. As he drops next to me on the bed again, I turn over onto my side, curling my hands beneath my head once more and watch him come down from his orgasm.

I didn't need to come to feel like I'm free falling

through the air beside him. No, he fucked with my head and I feel a buzz beneath my skin. In a way, it's more powerful than an orgasm as it runs through my bloodstream, coating me in warmth. I'm just as content and enjoying his post-orgasm high, and the thought is alarming.

Our eyes connect and a sleepy smirk touches his lips. The first hint of a true smile I think I've ever seen dust his face.

"Sleep, Siren. We'll be busy come daybreak."

"Busy with what?" I ask, tugging the blanket up and over both of our bodies.

"Preparing to dock on Morda."

James

I keep Briggs standing outside her door as she sleeps when I make it out first thing in the morning.

It's still dark as we approach the island, so we decide to anchor for several hours. I don't want to dock in the dark. I need the sun. Morda doesn't operate on electricity; only the rich can afford that luxury, and this place is the end of the line for the desperate. Even at a distance, I can smell the smoke from fires, and catch flickers of candlelight along the shore. Distant music plays even as dawn approaches, and every so often there's a scream or a rowdy bellow of cheers. I don't want to know what's happening.

On Morda, when the sun goes down, anything goes.

We've hung lanterns up the mast and then along the perimeters of the ship. The last thing I need is to blend into the darkness and have a vessel collide with us. The damage would be too astronomical now that the Tempest is fighting for breath. At the same time, we're visible now, which is always a risk. Luca stays above deck with me, keeping an eye out for marauders and passing ships.

None of us speak unless we have to. We're exhausted from the attack. From the mental and physical toll. Mostly, we're rattled that it even happened. Briggs is blaming himself. Wouldn't even talk to me this morning when I told him to guard Aria. An apology was at the tip of his tongue, but I silenced him with a shake of my head. "As Captain, it was my fault."

He didn't seem to think so. "She's okay?"

I hear the wretched tone in his question. "She's okay."

He looks relieved.

Even Luca tells me later that he'll fix Aria breakfast. That she needs to take it easy. The boys have taken a liking to my siren, and on this matter, I appreciate it.

Finally, the sun comes up, and so does the anchor.

We approach Morda at the speed of a snail. The scene is apocalyptic. Plumes of smoke billow from all over the island. There's crying in the distance. Deep in the jungle. Some kind of shit fuckery went down, but it seems to be the status quo. There are residents on the shore going about their lives like fire and wailing is all part of the island's anthem. Some are pushing off on their tiny boats, fishing gear and nets stacked in chaotic order. Others are gathering driftwood or starting little fires. I can smell charred fish and burnt dough.

We've spent the majority of the day hauling everything below deck, stuffing what we can in the safe room and coffin rooms. The rest of the bad food we accumulated over the storm has been thrown overboard, which has attracted the sea creatures. Luca reeled up an octopus and has it on a burner, passing out the tentacles for a taste.

I'm not sure Aria approves.

I've barely looked at her. But I sense her just the same. That fucking tether pulsing despite her quietness. She's thinking about me and doesn't want to, and because of that, she's *angry* at me. Because she huffs every time I draw near, then scoots away like I repulse her. The fucked-up part of me thinks her fear of me has waned. That me returning to the captain's quarters and sharing a bed with her has made me weaker in her eyes.

Or perhaps it's because I fucked her face so roughly it's a shock she's standing upright.

Yeah, but she liked it. Perhaps that's why she's such a dark cloud. I got under her skin like she's gotten under mine.

My movements are brisk. My darkness has Luca pulling away from me. Even Grimy knows to stay away. Briggs is nowhere to be seen. He's tucked himself away in the galley, pretending to clean the pipes. He's refusing to get off the ship while in Morda, claiming he's *"too pretty"* for the island. Is even worried he'll be mistaken for one of the island's whores thanks to his long, luscious locks. His words, not mine. I know it's a facade. He's rattled about the attack, and for once, I won't push him to join us. I need someone to stay behind anyway.

As we get closer, I'm pissed and reactive; this place attracts nothing but trouble. Something is bound to happen, I know it. I can't afford anything to happen to her. I make the mistake of letting that emotion slip through.

Fuck.

I need this tether to break. I want to dig a hole in my fucking chest and tear it out of me, cut it in half and send the fish back into the ocean, and in my rage, I want to hunt her down and tear a hole into her heart like she would have mine had I not been protected by my bracelet.

But you also want to keep her.

And maybe that's what bothers me the most.

That I might want her—*truly fucking want her*—and knowing, if given the chance, she'd likely kill me without blinking twice about it.

I stop to glare at her. In my sweater. Legs wet from the smatter of rain. Long hair pulled back. And she's bending again, her ass teasing, as she picks up more spoiled food. She tosses it into the ocean, her chest heaving from the labor. And she's not afraid of labor.

That bothers me.

Because I suspect she comes from some sort of privileged life. I hear it in the way she talks to me. That condescension. That trained behavior of never letting the enemy sense her fear. I taste it in her tether, and the way she's straightening, her chest stilling, her back taut and facing me—she knows I'm watching her.

She feels my stare.

Feels my rage.

Probably tastes my hunger too.

And what a sick combination.

Rage for what she's done, and hunger for the very

woman I'd like to take down to the captain's quarters and devour.

BY MID-AFTERNOON, we've cleared the deck space and are about an hour from docking. I bark instructions. *Get the ropes ready. Arm yourselves. Test the engine. Bail out the bilges one final time. Empty the waste tanks. Wash up, change, conceal your blades, and be ready.*

Despite the dangers, Luca is high-spirited. "We'll find some good grub, hey, Cap? And then after, I need pussy."

Grimy gives him a long, dry stare. "What sort of pussy do you think you'll find on a place like this, Luca? Don't expect quality."

"Not asking for much," Luca retorts, defensively. "Just a warm one to shoot my load into."

I dip my hands into the wash bucket, rinsing off the dirt. "You got enough coin to spare?"

"Doubt a brothel will be much around here."

"Mark my words, Luca, you get what you pay for."

Grimy laughs while Luca just shrugs his shoulders. He won't follow my advice. Why should he? The only way a man learns is by being burned.

"Disgusting," Aria mutters under her breath just then as she stops in front of another wash bucket and rinses her hands.

Luca hears. "Oh, I'm disgusting?"

"Feral."

"But it's not disgusting or feral to enchant us with your song and then plunge a hole into our chest?"

Aria turns to look at him. "Nature dictates I hunt, Luca."

Luca grabs at his cock through his trousers and sings, "And it's nature that makes me want to fuck, Aria, darling."

Aria gives him a filthy stare, but her lips break into a smile. Luca doesn't stop singing. About fucking. About pussies. About all sorts of explicit shit that sends a rag flying out of Grimy's hand and into Luca's face.

Now they're all fucking laughing, and Rex is jumping up at Aria, tail wagging. She's just washed her hands, but she doesn't care that Rex is filthy. She runs her hands through his old, matted mane, accepting his licks as Luca continues to sing around them and Grimy is shaking his head.

I stand still, enjoying the moment of peace.

It wouldn't be a good time to let them know we've been spotted by the boats. That we've been circled by a fisherman or two. That there is a ring around the Tempest rich with sea life, as though being called upon by Aria, just as it was when she was in the longboat.

But she has no idea at all.

My tether calls out for her just then. It burns more intensely. It prompts her to turn around from her work and finally look at me. I briefly meet her eye and gesture her over with my chin. My face is flat, cool, the indifference more troubling to her than the rage. She walks to me warily, and before she gets too close, I tell her, "Follow me."

I lead her back into the ship and to my quarters. We don't speak as I enter my room and leaf through my clothes. I throw down a sailor's hat, dark trousers, and another black sweater, before pulling out a thick pair of wool socks. Next I find a pair of old leather worn boots on the back of a shelf. I never wore these, nor do I know what Erickson it belonged to, but their feet were smaller, so they're Aria's for now.

She doesn't ask any questions, just watches me silently, and it's unbecoming of her. I expect her sharp tongue. Almost yearn for it at this moment because her quietness unnerves me. She's not sending any decipherable emotion down the tether, but there's a faint sort of defeat. Or maybe I'm confusing it with compliance.

Either way, I don't trust it.

"You're going to change," I tell her just then. "I need you in layers, Siren. The less attention we get, the better."

She's surprised. "You're taking me with you?"

"I am."

"Why?"

"Why not?"

She looks at me for a moment, trying to decipher my intentions. "I just thought..."

I finish her thought. "You thought I'd leave you here, tied up?"

She shoots me a dry look. "Getting tied up seems to be your kink, Captain."

"Only when you're cutting hearts out of chests."

"I've stopped."

"Too late."

She presses a hand to her heart, saying in a heartfelt tone, "Can't a woman start over without being condemned for her past mistakes?"

I quirk a brow. "You're getting ahead of yourself."

"I'm a new person. You've woken me up and shown me the way."

"I'm relieved to hear that."

"My enlightenment is all thanks to you."

"Don't be too much of a sweetheart."

Her face falls, tone hardening. "I don't want to go, James. Tie me up, I don't care. I'd rather you men do what you came here for and leave me out of it."

"So you can escape?"

She tosses her hands into the air. "Because I have so many places to escape to."

"The ocean."

"You forget I'm missing a tail and a fin." Her gaze dips to the floor as though she's sad about the loss of her siren form.

I narrow my eyes, not sure how I feel about her sudden emotion. "Gonna tell me about that?"

She snaps, "No."

"Then stop wasting my time and get dressed," I bark, crossing my arms over my chest. I watch her closely, not trusting she'll actually do as asked. And as suspected, now that I've told her what to do, she purposely takes her time, testing my patience.

She grabs at the clothes I set aside, inspecting every one of them. She picks up the hat, spins it around, and I swear she's about to gag, but she stiffens a smile. "You spoil me, Captain."

"Would you rather go naked, fish?"

Faking a gasp, she tilts her head to the side, her eyes practically sparkling with mischief. "What on earth for? Didn't you know, James, that I've aspired for some time to look like a wretched vagrant?"

"I didn't know, but I'm glad to hear it."

She picks up the trousers next. "Charming."

"Aren't they?"

"Been washed recently?"

"It's been a decade or two."

"Lot more recent than I would have guessed from the likes of you."

I run a hand over my jaw. "You're wasting time, woman."

Now she grabs the hat again and waves it in the air, staring at me with challenging eyes. "You really think this is going to disguise me? I have colorful hair that reaches my ass. I'm far more slender than a man, and my tits can hardly be hidden under this sweater as it is—"

"You don't want to wear it, then don't," I sharply cut in, tired of our back-and-forth nonsense, and frankly, tired of her shit. "But I'm not saving your ass when we're stalked by a rapist or two. Either try to blend in or accept what happens when you're a piece of meat in a lion's den."

Her expression twists with anger, but her words are deathly calm. "You're disgusting, Captain."

I smile coldly. "I am."

"A complete scoundrel."

"Quit flirting, fish."

She scoffs and begins to undress, her movements

sharp and irritated. "Oh, I'm such a flirt! Can you blame me? I'm trapped on a ship with a scarred mongrel whose only shield against me is an ancient bracelet with a curse that's waning. Do you know what that means, *Captain*?" She throws her sweater down, completely topless as she spins around to face me. Her tits look heavy, full, her nipples pebbled—*perfect*. I don't directly stare at them, keeping my gaze locked with hers as she smiles cockily. "It means one of these days you won't be so impenetrable. You've already shown me what a simple swipe of my tongue can do to you, and if that's not defense crumbling, I'm not sure what is."

I move slowly toward her, my frame towering over her tiny body. I love that she doesn't step back. That she stands fixedly in place, challenging me. She has to crane her head up to look at me once I reach her, and I don't speak for a moment, allowing the silence to fill the room. I give her a moment to understand just how vulnerable she really is. And then I say quietly, with a tone reserved for a lover, "You'd better hope that doesn't happen, Little Mermaid, because if it does, I'll have no reason to hold back. You think my lapse in judgment was unrestrained? With that conceited little mouth of yours, it would be fair to assume you've never truly seen a hungry man let loose. Have you?"

No response.

She doesn't need to.

The tether burns.

Her desire combined with her fear and—

Challenge.

She is resisting me, like I am her.

And for a moment, I feel a little sad for the two of us.

Because if we gave in fully, I have a feeling we'd set each other on fire.

"Quit stalling," I icily say now. "Tired of your shit, woman. If you're not dressed in five minutes, you're going as you are."

I briskly leave, not bothering to look at her over my shoulder.

I let her think her bare skin has no sway over me, and I thank my cock for not bursting through my pants to prove otherwise.

"Forward!" I shout as Luca and I race to throw the lines overboard.

Grimy is steering the ship, keeping us level as we approach the shoddy docks. The sun is out in full force, casting an orange glow along the waters. I don't know whether to be relieved or wary of how empty the marina looks as we pull in. Large sections are unfilled, allowing us complete passage through. One spot has a mast sticking out of the water, the sunken ship impossible to see through the murky waters.

Fuck that.

I shout at Grimy to steer left, as far away from the mast as possible. I worry about collisions beneath the waterline. The Tempest will not endure more damage kindly.

Already I can see a small crowd of liveaboard form on the dock, watching us and whispering. Not a single offer of a helping hand. I expect nothing less from these bastards.

I shove the starboard ropes to Aria who's been following me like a lost doe, unsure of what to do. She makes an *oomph* sound, stumbling back. I grit out, "You need to throw the lines to me when I'm on the dock."

She does as she's told, and then I brace myself, preparing us for arrival.

WE DOCK WITHOUT A HITCH, tying off along the sad slip we've pulled into. We make one final check, ensuring every deck box is locked and the deck is as clear as possible. Don't want these ancient liveaboard fucks sniffing around, hungry for the slightest crumb to thieve. Once done, we lower the ramp and step off. Briggs remains aboard the ship, staring down at us. He's got a speargun in his hand, like he's prepared to use it, and that seems to keep the liveaboards away.

Aria stands behind me, blending in among Luca and Grimy. She keeps her head down as we cautiously step over gaps in the boardwalk.

I gotta hand it to the fish: I didn't give her much to work with, and she's done well with her getup. The clothes hang off her, but she just looks like a well-starved crewmate—nothing unusual there. She's balled her hair up in a tight bun, and it's completely concealed under the tricorn hat. She scrubbed her face with dirt, so even her cheekbones are impossible to spot. The only thing she can't fucking hide are her plump, feminine lips.

Aria has the most sensual mouth I've ever seen.

And sometimes, when she stands there all fucking doe-eyed and clueless, those plump lips part... Fuck me sideways, no amount of dirt or a hat can hide how utterly sinful that mouth looks.

Imagine it wrapped around your thick cock.

Again.

Her mouth hardly fit.

I grit my teeth, sensing her stare as she feels that warmth through the tether. Here I am, on one of the most notoriously violent islands, and I'm thinking about Aria's mouth around my cock.

The bracelet's powers must be waning.

But I can't even be sure it's that.

My heart gallops behind my rib cage as we prepare to disembark the Tempest, a range of emotions weighing heavy on my chest. Mostly nerves. The last time my feet touched land was in Norborne, the night before I was captured.

I feel homesick at the thought of my homeland. Norborne may be a Goddess belt of crazy worshippers, but it's beautiful—full of sunshine, flowers blooming, and the most crystal waters surrounding the land. I miss its familiarity. I miss my sisters. I even miss working at their school, helping those Goddess worshippers remind those cute little angels of brimstone and hellfire. To think, one day I was going to sleep in a room full of my sisters—hearing their chatter and feeling their warmth as I planned my shift—and the next, I'm captured by a ruthless sea captain with a craving for vengeance and a heart of stone and a cock as thick as my forearm.

Deep breaths.

James casts a glance my way as I follow him down

the ramp leading off the ship. He can feel my apprehension as we move lower down the incline. I'm a fool to hope he'd offer some sort of reassurance, but he turns his eyes forward, scanning our surroundings as our feet touch the aged wooden dock. Crossing my hands over my chest, I rub my arm that's now bulky from the layers I wear to disguise myself. I blow out a shaky breath.

From behind, Luca speaks low, just loud enough for me to hear. "It'll be just fine, fishy."

"Let's hope so," I mutter in return, but I'm not sure he hears me.

My knees buckle slightly from a sudden onset of sea legs, but my body barely sways when a strong hand juts out and fingers encircle my bicep, steadying me. James and I share a look. His eyes look heavy, a hint of reassurance lurking in their depths. Just as quickly as he comes to my aide, he removes his hand, turning away from me and striding down the dock.

Still stopped, I take in my surroundings. To my left and right, I'm encased by the ocean, but the water looks different around the docks than it does out at sea. Darker. Dirtier. There's a hazy film that sits on top of the water, mixed between the floating trash, spurts of rotting plant stems, and dead fish carcasses, and shit. Literal shit. *Human* shit. It's not unlikely to assume the marina harbors infection and anything it touches is plagued by death. In front of me, the dock stretches until it reaches land and meets a dilapidated shack. The windows are boarded up and the door sways in the wind. I begin to think it's an abandoned shithole, but there's a fairly new slab of wood with the word *stop* with an arrow pointing to the door, so I suspect there's some sort of grisly dock-hand inside collecting fees.

James keeps walking toward the "building," not bothering to confirm we're following him, and I can't help but wish I had stayed on the ship with Briggs and Rex.

"Aye, it'll be fine. Keep a move on." Luca pokes me in the lower back, urging me to follow. As I put one foot in front of the other, he blasts around me, jogging to catch up with James.

Grimy walks alongside me, fidgeting with his fingernail. I bet he'd give anything for a cigar. I stare down at my feet in the too-large boots that clip-clop against the dock as we approach the shack. I'm not paying enough attention to see that James and Luca have stopped, and I walk face-first into the brick wall that is James' body. My head whips up as our bodies collide, and I'm unsurprised to find him looking down at me with his eyes alight.

"Sorry," I mutter, not because I am, but because it seems like the appropriate response for when you run into mean giant men. He grunts before taking a quick look around where we all now congregate, before turning back to me and his men.

"Luca, you wait right outside the office with Aria. Attempt to conceal her if she comes into view of the stevedores. Grimy and I will go in and pay the fee to dock the Tempest," James barks orders, speaking under his breath so our names aren't heard by the men lingering around.

Luca gives a nod and turns to me. He reaches up and

pushes the tricorn hat down on my head, even though it's already as far down as it can be. "This will never work. Even grubbed down, you're still enchanting. You're going to start riots if we're not being careful." His hands shoot to his waist where he rests them as he assesses me skeptically. It makes me uncomfortable, and I shift from foot to foot, re-angling my body to peer over his shoulder.

Inside the small building, a man sits on an overturned bucket behind a lopsided metal table. His skin is sun-rotted and dirty beneath his tunic and vest. He looks like he's been waterside for the better part of his life, his skin overly tanned, wrinkled, and leathery. His grayed hair sticks out haphazardly from his flat cap, and as I watch James and Grimy interact with the man, a wave of nausea rocks through me. *Yuck.* I suddenly have a bad feeling about this man, and as a slimy, missing-toothed smile crawls across his face while he watches Grimy pretend to count coins to pay the toll, I have a feeling as to why.

I'd been warned that in Morda everything goes. And my instincts tell me the dock keeper is one of the island's most prominent sets of eyes and ears.

My eyes track the movements of Grimy's hands, watching as he carefully slides a single coin out of the small bag he holds, one at a time, setting them down individually on the steel table in front of him. I have to hand it to him, for as aged as Grimy is, his mind is fully functioning: the man is smart as hell. From an outsider—from the dock keeper's point of view—he moves with the quickness of an old man. To someone who has spent time with him, Grimy is putting on a show, purposely moving slowly to appear as though he has to count each coin carefully to be certain he has enough.

Genius, really. Then again, marauders living in the Black Sea with a ship full of Gala Green and Goddess knows what else, you had to be smarter than your enemy.

Those truly should be words I think carefully about. Be *smarter* than the enemy. Not fall in love with the enemy.

Goddess, I couldn't be falling in love with James, could I?

The line between love and hate is so fine...

I stop watching Grimy and move my gaze to James, but before it reaches him, they catch on a set of muddy brown, bloodshot eyes staring straight at me. *Appraising me.* Looking at me like he knows exactly what I am.

Terror shoots through me and I turn away, positioning my body so I face outward toward the ocean. I watch the Tempest bob with the light movement of the waves, feeling Luca step closer to my back. He says nothing, but for some reason his presence calms me, if only a little. I cross my arms across my chest and bring a hand to my mouth, chewing on the corner of my thumb, fighting against a crushing feeling of overwhelming anxiety.

After what feels like an eternity, I feel James' body brush up against the back of mine and his hand meets my lower back. Grimy stands beside James, blocking the visual of how close James is to me.

Bowing his head, his lips brush against my ear. "What are you afraid of?"

"Many things," I say quietly. "But right now, the dock keeper. He stared at me for longer than what's appropriate. I think... I think he could see right through this ridiculous costume."

His fingertips graze the back of my neck sending a current of electricity through my body. I shiver and force myself not to lean back into him. "He knows nothing. And even if he did, I'd never let him lay a finger on you. You have my complete protection."

My body hums from his words, my lips parting in awe from the surge of possessiveness that crashes through the tether—coming from him. Entirely from him. A great wave of it that is comforting just as it is terrifying. Before I can respond, he pushes me forward, and the four of us walk toward the horror scene that is the Isle of Morda.

CHAPTER 34

James

It's evening when we make it to what I can only assume is Morda's village square. I say this only because there is a grouping of structures that aren't burnt to a crisp and seem to be relatively intact. These buildings are actually standing, albeit not all of them whole. Morda is a gutter of antipathy and perversion. The cobblestone path is almost entirely swallowed up by weeds, and piss, and shit.

We walk past decrepit stone structures. I see shadowy figures smoking. Little fires burning for light. That burnt smell of fish over small fire pits. A moan sounds from one of the "homes" and our interest is inevitably drawn to it. Against the white washed stone wall, a man is fucking a woman that must be part chicken; she squawks and he grunts and then another man is demanding his turn. An exchange of coin follows, and the squawker begins to squawk seconds later as another man fucks her, the slap of his balls against her used pussy impossible to ignore. She's being filled to the brim with cum, and she sings her chicken song like it's just any other day.

I'm a marauder, I've seen some fucking shit during my doomed eternal life, but goddessdamn, this is so beneath me right now.

I side-eye Luca, noticing his face has grown paler, the reality of Morda's grotesque sex life hitting him. Disgust radiates down the tether...and curiosity. Fuck me, Aria is such a contradiction of feelings; that she can see something as feral as that and not be entirely turned off by it. Dare I say I'm impressed, and so I try to heighten her curiosity by sending a pulse of lust down the line, just to fuck with her head and make her question whether that lust could be coming from her own being.

I'm paying too much attention to the tether because I don't take notice of the shadowy figure that follows. Not until he's suddenly coming out of the shadows to Grimy's right. I catch his jerky movement from the corner of my eye and turn my head just in time to see the figure prod a gun at Grimy's head. "Empty your pockets, old man."

He's fucking filthy.

Missing teeth, spotted, red face, the stench of alcohol a sudden cloud around him—fucking ugly as fuck. His own mama must hate him.

We come to a stop, and I feel amused as Grimy sighs deeply and replies, "We've not been on land for more than two minutes, and we're getting robbed—"

"I told you Morda is no joke," I cut in, smirking. "I warned you, old man."

"It's not like we had options," Grimy retorts. "You

sound like we could have kept plodding along and not been underwater by now. Unless you wanted to manually pump out the bilges twenty-four hours of the day, we had no choice—"

"Oi!" the robber shouts, pissed. "I'm fucking robbing you, old man. Empty your fucking pockets or I'll blow your brains out."

Grimy turns his seething glare to the robber. "Do you know how many times I've been robbed, you stupid little shit? How many times I've been *fired* at and *stabbed* and *hanged—I've been hanged three fucking times!* Now I've had a shit fucking week, I'm tired to my fucking bones, I haven't slept, smoked, or ate, or had a proper shit, and you know fucking what? For once, I'm not even going to object to my captain blowing your pigheaded skull away!"

"Really?" I ask, surprised.

"Fucking really," Grimy retorts.

It's never a good sign when Grimy is swearing. He's truly at the end of his fucking rope. Which means one of two things: he's hungover, or he's hungry as fuck.

And I know which he is.

Without looking at the robber, I remove my gun in less than a second and let out a shot. A thud of a body lands by Grimy's feet, and with my eyes still on him, I say, "You choose dinner, old man."

ON THE SHORT walk to the pub, we see a person get robbed, another get shot, and two more people fucking a one-eyed whore with swinging tits who coos at a bug-eyed Luca. "Hello, blue eyes."

Luca visibly shudders.

Aria lets out a cough mixed with a laugh.

And Grimy just wants to fucking eat.

The pub is the only structurally sound building that I've seen so far, at least three stories high, advertised as an inn as well as a bar. It's backed against the jungle that overtakes a large majority of this island, and the surrounding area is spotless and crime-free. You'd think the fucking pub is a temple the way it's being worshipped by gross fucks who—get this—wipe their boots against the doormat just outside the entrance doors. There's even large sconces lit with torches to illuminate the entryway.

We enter the pub, and I take a moment to look around. The interior is all dark wood furnishing with lit lanterns strung from the ceiling. It's packed with patrons —all men since there seems to be a higher ratio of men to women on this shithole island.

They must be able to sniff out new meat because many of the grubby looking men pause to watch us come through, their gazes heavy.

I flick a glance at Aria, and her head is still down, her movements a little stilted. If she doesn't loosen up, she's going to attract attention. My tether calls to her, forcing her to look up briefly at me. I give her a hard look, one that says: do a better fucking job. Her body loosens and she stiffens a nod.

"Table for four? Or you looking to get a room for the night?" asks the man behind the bar, taking notice of us.

He's a middle-aged fellow. Bald. Calloused hands and beer gut. Years of stress lines and exhaustion peppering his face.

As I reply, his eyes scan each of us. "Food and beer."

"You get dinner and breakfast on the house if you take a room for the night."

"Not necessary."

"You'd also get a coupon to shag a good whore, sent from Madam Ruth's Manor itself."

Coupon to fuck a whore?

What is this fuckery?

I keep my gaze steady, considering. "Got a ship at the marina. Don't need a room. But whereabouts is this Manor?"

Anger burns through the tether. I ignore it as the barman answers, "She's further down the road. You can't miss it."

Luca perks up. "I might get a room with that coupon. We talking 10% off or something?"

Grimy grows impatient. "Do we seat ourselves? Where are the menus?"

The barman answers Luca first. "If you're staying longer than a night, you can get one woman at full price and a second half off."

"All in one night? At the same time?"

The barman nods before answering Grimy next with, "Pick a table, menus are just here."

He passes Grimy the menus and we find a free table that's next to a wall covered in posters, photos, and eclectic artwork ranging from ship sketches to pin-up girls with their bare tits hanging out. Luca is all eyes as he sits next to a drawing of a pin-up girl with long flowing dark hair. He runs a finger over her long legs, exclaiming, "This ain't so bad, Cap, is it?"

I merely grunt in response.

This is so much worse.

Nothing like before.

I didn't think Morda could travel anymore down the shitter, but there you fucking have it.

I make sure Aria is across the table from him, also sitting next to the wall. I settle in next to her, aware that my body is so big, she is easily overlooked this way. Grimy sits next to Luca and is already mulling over the papyrus menus. The menu consists of only stews.

Goat stew.

Rabbit stew.

Chicken stew.

Cow stew.

Stews here, there, fucking everywhere.

"I didn't see any livestock on our way here, did you?" I ask Grimy, amused.

"It's probably all one meat," he responds.

"Probably horse," jokes Luca. "I heard a high-pitched neigh, but...you know, it might have been another squawking woman."

"Could be human," mutters Aria.

We stop to stare at her.

She's busy dusting crumbs off the table. "Just saying. We've seen like two deaths in the span of five minutes. It would be one commodity that would remain in high supply."

Silence.

We take it in slowly.

Digesting the thought—even considering it.

Grimy looks to Luca who looks to me, and I stare at Aria, my lips twitching. "Nothing a bit of beer can't wash down, right?"

Aria's lips spread, and she tries to hide her smile, but it's too late. The men laugh and then she's burying her face in her hands, laughing, too. It's a great release after a long, shitty day.

It's not long before we place our orders. Some sort of animal stew is coming our way, along with mugs and mugs of beer. I try to appear laid-back, relaxed, like this is just another night out with the guys, but I don't drink a single sip of beer, and I'm watching. Watching the men that come and go. The men that stop to glance at us. Eyes filled with curiosity. Others suspicion. I keep track of their stares, making sure they don't linger on Aria.

Aria, who laughs at Luca's jokes, whose hat slips with the motion of her shoulders.

My hand darts out to keep the hat from falling off. Her body seizes in horror, and then relief. She gives me a warm look, her own hand flying out to touch the same spot, and her skin connects with mine. Warm. Smooth. Feminine. My body hums from the touch, but I fight to contain it, and with the sensory overload, it doesn't appear like she's noticed.

I drop my hand and fist it under the table, trying to clear my mind.

I watch people, spinning the mug round and round. Even when the food is placed in front of me, I barely eat. I catch the gaze of a man or two. They watch me, watch the others, their gaze lingering a little closer on Aria than I'd like.

She's *my* fucking siren, I want to say.

I caught her fair and square.

Mine.

And I'll shed more blood to keep it that way if need be.

The possessive feeling is so thick in my body, it heats my skin and boils my blood. The skin around my scars tighten as I attempt to rein back the sudden emotion. It's unnatural and unexpected. Nothing I've ever felt before. It must be the fucking curse. My bracelet begins to glow, but it's hidden under my sleeve, and only Aria—

Only Aria can sense what I'm feeling.

I turn to her, and she's staring right at me, eyes wide.

And for a moment, it's like the room has fallen away, the noise muted.

Her gaze on mine.

The tether tells me she's resistant to my possessiveness. That she doesn't agree with it. That she will *fight* it —fight me.

She's the first to look away, focusing her sights now on the wall of pictures. Abandoning her food, she disengages as the tether fills with hate. Hate for me. Hate and—

Horror.

I still, blood pumping harder in my veins as I follow her line of sight.

She's staring at a black framed photo. I look at it closely. It's a black and white sketch. I see the ocean, waves rippling under a storm. Clouds and lightning. The seas depict madness, and the ship is suspended at the very edge of the highest wave, its nose facing downwards, like it's about to crash into the murky black sea. It's a death sentence; it won't survive the cataclysmic crash. There are pieces of the ship missing, like parts have been blown to smithereens, its mast broken in half. There are vague outlines of sailors, and they're not bracing themselves against the impact.

No, they're not even staring down at what lays at the bottom.

They circle a grisly kill with their arms up in the air. Blood flows along the deck, and that's the only part of the picture that has color. Bright red. Puddles of it everywhere; it's so vibrant, it looks like paint on their hands.

When I focus on the kill, I feel the air in my lungs whoosh out.

Strung up on a piece of mast line is a dangling, dead body of a woman.

Not just a woman.

A siren.

Her tail has been cut deeply, and it's bleeding out, like she's being drained.

Her face is vague, but there are shadows of her opened eyes as she lifelessly stares at the whooping men. Aria's eyes trail over to the framed image next to it, depicting a similar scene, and again to the two that hang even further above those. All with sirens strung up and being drained. All with triumphant men celebrating their victories. I don't tell her I recognize one of the ships depicted with its black and gold sails. That the name of it jogs a memory of a ship departing from Goldspince under my father's direct order to find him more treasure.

More sirens, he meant.

I didn't know.

Aria's response is immediate. The horror is a vortex within her. An all-encompassing weight filled with fear and despair, my heart speeds in my chest as it reaches the tether. She bolts up on her feet, hand covering her mouth, and she makes a break for it. I grab her arm on reflex, gripping it tight. "Aria," I warn.

She tries to shake my hand away. "Let me go, James!"

Her voice is louder than it should be. A feminine lilt escapes, and I'm gritting my jaw, wanting to force her back down again. But then she's rubbing at her stomach, and I think she might be feeling ill. I let go but immediately follow her as she hurries across the bar and to the entrance. I brush hard against shoulders, feeling pissed that her tiny form manages to slip through the bodies while I'm pummeling these fuckers down.

At one point, someone growls at me, swinging a fist at the back of me. He tried to aim high but missed, his punch landing on my upper back. I spin around in one instant and slam my fist into his face, knocking him cold to the ground. Now I've caused a fucking scene, and the men are sizing me up, but all I can think of is that Aria has just slipped out of the pub, that bun of hers coming loose, sending colorful tendrils down her neck.

Fuck.

I chase after her, and this time, the men part.

I'm two seconds out the door when I hear him come barreling through it. The already cool night air is frigid against my sweat-damp skin. I wrap my shaky arms around myself and rub my hands against my skin, trying to erase the goosebumps as I take in my surroundings.

The Isle of Morda truly is a wasteland.

Realizing I have little options on where to go, I slow my movements to a stop, listening as James' heavy boots slap against the uneven street.

He's right behind me—stopped so close he's practically touching me.

Blowing out a shaky breath, I spin to face him, and he looks down at me with mixed emotions carved against his striking features. A wave of anger rushes through the tether as I glare up at him with wet eyes that sting with tears.

Crashing my fist into the middle of his chest, I lose control of my emotions all together and scream, "Is that what you were going to do, James? String me up and bleed me out—"

"Calm the fuck down, *sailor*," he cuts in sharply, silencing my sentence.

He's still putting on the ruse that he's worried about my safety amongst the vile humans that inhabit this island.

I smile cruelly at him and narrow my eyes into a glare. Despite my best efforts to conceal them, a single tear squeezes from the corner of my left eye, and I wipe it from my cheek quickly. "What does it fucking matter if anyone sees me? They won't know what I am in this form—"

"If you don't lower your voice, I will fucking muzzle you."

My head shakes slowly in disbelief, and I give James my back, tilting my head to the night sky. The stars twinkle as though trying to taunt me with their simplistic beauty. "I hate your kind for what you've done to us," I admit. My voice is barely above a whisper, but I know he hears me. "I hate the fear you've put in us. We barely have any of our kind left. We've spent our existence being hunted down—"

"Can you blame us?" he growls. "You come after *us*, Siren. You use your song on *us*. Ensnare us only to kill us—"

"Back when you had your kingdom, you had a lot of land, did you not?" I cut him off, tired of hearing his version of the story. He thinks he knows, but the stories he's been told are far from the truths we have lived.

He blows out an exasperated breath. "I did."

Turning back toward him, my chest is heavy with a feeling I haven't felt in a long time. *Grief.* Sirens deserve better. "When a predator encroached on your land, did you let it take what it wanted, Captain? Did you let it fuck your women? Did you let it suckle away at your power, using you for its own gain? Or did you kill it?"

James glares at me, and I catch the way his hands ball into fists. "This isn't like that."

Frustration slaps me hard across the face, anger rattling me to my core. "Don't tell me what it's like," I hiss. "You don't fucking know—you didn't live it."

"Did *you*?" he bites back, searching my eyes. "Or are you on a warpath just because you were told it's what you're meant to do?"

I scoff, completely taken aback by James' words. "I've seen what men like you do—"

"And I've seen what sirens do. They hunt humans, *my* lineage. They live to see the day my head is on a fucking pike. You were wrong, Little Mermaid, about my bracelet's power waning. It's *you* that distorts it. Something about *you* drew us together. It's how you found me. You sensed when an Erickson was near, and for so long, my bracelet had stopped your kind from finding me. But now here you are, and here I am, and now we're stuck, tethered to each other, and I don't understand why—"

"Just let me go, James. Tether be damned," I retort, but it comes out more like a plea. "So it'll hurt, maybe that's what we need it to do before it breaks comple—"

"No—"

"Let's try it—"

"I fucking won't—"

"It might set us free—I might be able to leave you—"

"But you're *mine!*" James growls, his voice taking on a rough tone.

The possession that courses through the tether startles me; it's rooted so deeply, its intensity takes my breath away.

Staring at James, neither of us back down, and I lift my chin to further solidify my defiance. I will not submit to him. Not now, not ever.

He is my enemy.

His family killed so many of us.

And now he means to *keep* me?

"What does it mean to be yours?" I question him. "You keep me locked up on that ship to serve you until I'm old and wrinkly? I get to fuck your cock with my mouth whenever you kill a man that tries to rape me? How about when I shift, James? Are you just going to chain me up in that hellish room and pour buckets of water on me?" My voice is growing now. "What the fuck does it mean to be yours?"

"That's not fair," he says, sharply. "I never attacked you first."

"You could have let me go at one point, and I would have never returned."

He just stares coldly at me. "You know that's not true. You wanted the last Erickson dead—"

"I didn't even know who you were!"

"If I'd have let you go, you'd have brought the Tempest to the bottom of the ocean—"

"What does it even matter anymore? I want to be

gone," I argue, my voice contorting with conflicting, overwhelming emotions.

Do I want to be gone? The greater part of me screams *yes*, while the smaller part—the part that holds compassion for this man that has brought life to a hidden part of me—whispers *no*.

"I can't do that," he states, his gruff voice firm and unwavering.

"Because you're selfish!"

"Yes."

"Because you don't care about my misery!"

"The tether speaks otherwise."

"Fuck the tether!" I shout now.

He doesn't back down. "You want me to come to you at night. You *ache* for me. I've felt it for a long time now. You don't want to admit it, but you don't need to. I feel everything, even what you think you're hiding from me. We've both been hiding, Aria." He takes a deep breath, his hands balling once more. "I want you."

He wants me?

I'm rattled.

He wants me.

But I shake my head. "It could never work."

"Give me a chance."

"No."

The rejection is swift... and painful. I feel my heart ache, the connection growing painful under the weight of his anguish. He's angry, I can see that in the way he trembles, fighting hard to restrain himself, but there's acute sadness funneling through that outweighs the anger.

His loneliness is a storm: dark and gloomy, and it's been hurtling through his being, ripping his soul apart until it's nothing but flying debris that swirls within him, wreaking havoc.

And I just made it worse.

"We're going back," he demands now.

"I'm not going to that pub."

"Back to the ship."

I step away, shaking my head again, knowing these feelings will only grow worse. *"No."*

After a moment, James' eyes begin to darken, even more so than their regular deep shade. They're so dark, they almost take on a glowing hue. I'm not sure what's happening, but that sadness feels like knives piercing my chest. I rub at my chest as his emotions grow out of control. Everything fades away. The colors. The sky. The pub and the trees surrounding us. Darkness swallows us whole, obscuring the world, like it's just the two of us.

"James," I whisper, taking another step back on instinct. The darkness he's concealing us in has put me on edge. "You're scaring me."

"Aria," he begins.

"Make it stop."

"I don't know how–"

"Make it stop!"

Just like that, the darkness evaporates, and we're back on the cobblestone path, back outside of the pub. My heart is battering so hard, I'm disturbed and shaky.

James' expression calms. He watches my reaction to him and takes a tentative step forward. "That's never happened before, Aria—"

But I take another step back, shaking my head.

"Aria, *please*."

He's never pleaded before.

It's so foreign to hear that word fall from his lips, but it changes nothing.

I continue to inch back on the uneven cobblestones, trembling. My legs feel tingly. My flight response is like a ticking time bomb.

He senses it, and a look of panic runs through him. "I'll chase you down, Siren. Don't you even think of running—"

"I'm not yours, Captain," I counter quietly. I have precisely one second to make my decision before he reaches out and grabs a hold of me. Every atom in my body tells me to *go*. Tells me that this darkness he's shrouded us in will follow him wherever he goes, that he might trap me in it so I never escape.

"Siren," he growls. "You can't escape from me. I won't let you—"

I don't let him finish.

I run.

And not back down the path we came from.

Straight into the jungle instead.

I would be a fool chasing after her into the jungle in the dark of night.

What the fuck had come over me?

How did I lose control of my emotions and allow my darkness to shroud her?

For several moments, I'm rooted to the ground, horrified by my possessiveness. Frightened how deeply she has dug under my layers and slid into my being.

Aria.

The dreams of the colorful haired siren—

It was Aria following me.

Aria that sought to ensnare me.

Aria that lay in a puddle of her own blood, dead before me.

Jolted by that visceral realization, I run after her, but I barely get far when I come to my senses. I'm not thinking straight. If I want to track her, I need the right supplies. At least a torch. And my men by my side.

The tether is still hot when I turn back and return to

the pub. My breaths are fast and hard, my being screaming to chase after her. It takes everything in my nature to stride in the opposite direction.

I'm loaded with adrenaline, my head still pounding from lack of food and drink when I come upon the crowd of men outside of the pub. Luca's in a headlock, the large fat man's arm only tightening as he growls, "You think you can cut the fucking line and get away with it, you little rat fuck?"

I search the crowd for Grimy and catch him in the doorway of the pub, having a spat with the barkeep. It's a heated argument, with fingers pointing in each other's faces. The barkeep doesn't look phased as he stands over Grimy, but little does the fuck know that Grimy—if push came to shove—can incapacitate him in two moves. It would cause Grimy a lot of harm—he might be out of it for days just trying to recover from the energy he'd need to expel, but I can tell from his vehemence that he's prepared to do just that.

How the fuck did everything deteriorate in such a short amount of time?

The tether jerks. I can sense my siren's distance growing.

I don't have time for this.

Teeth clenched, I jump straight into Luca's brawl, swinging a fist into the grizzly man's face. It's a king's punch—I'm not proud of it. I feel like a fucking dirtbag as he falls to the ground a moment later, knocked the fuck out, taking Luca down with him. He's landed on Luca, and I can hear him screaming curses as he tries to push the giant man off him. Sighing, I roll the giant fuck over and when Luca stretches his arm out for me to take, I ignore him and turn my gaze on everyone else.

"Where's your colorful haired bitch?" one suddenly hisses.

"What are you talking about?" another asks.

The man smiles a one toothed smile at me. "I sawed it. He came with a woman—not just a fucking woman, neither, fellas. She had pink and purple colored hair—"

"Fuck off," someone else shouts, doubtfully.

"And all her teeth," One-Tooth continues. "And smooth, clean skin."

The crowd hushes down for a moment. A series of men look at one another, their eyes growing larger than their heads as One-Tooth adds, "Them top couldn't hide them tits, neither. Nothing like them whores at Ruth's— she was young. Fucking tasty sorta young, no white- haired, scraggly looking whore."

"You're wrong," I say flatly. "You're talking about my crewman—"

"No, I sawed it me-self. She done ran into the jungle, some sort of lover's spat with 'er Cap'n."

One-Tooth's conviction seems to draw the men in. I guess they take this fuck's word as gospel. *Fucking great.* Their hunger can be felt across the crowd.

"Does that mean she's free for all?" one asks.

"Ay." One-Tooth grins. "Gotta catch her first."

"You won't want to do that," I growl calmly. "It won't go well for you."

One-Tooth barks out a laugh. "You and what fuckin' army? The old man by the door?" His laugh grows stronger. "Or the idiot that's already hugged the ground after Freddy put 'im in a headlock?"

The men are excited, laughing along with him. Others are already spreading the word. Of a pink-and-purple-haired girl in the jungle. Some have already disappeared from the crowd, and I suspect they're looking for her already.

Well, fuck me sideways in the asshole with a razor blade, we are fucked.

Grimy's no longer arguing, staring solemnly at me now as the situation begins to worsen.

I can deny it all I want, but what's the point? They've already made up their minds, and it doesn't help that Aria did slip up on her way out the bar. I didn't think we had an audience listening. I'm waiting for the hammer to fall. For One-Tooth to say she's a siren, but he doesn't.

Fear shoots down the tether, but it's losing its intensity. She's got a head start. No one will have found her so soon, but she doesn't have much time.

My head feels like it's splitting open. I don't know if it's the tether, or if I'm at the end of my rope.

I keep my gaze glued to the crowd while I whisper to Luca, "You need to run. Now."

Instead of questioning me, Luca takes one look at the menacing crowd. He wipes the blood across his mouth with the back of his hand and then he begins to step back. Further and further from my peripheral he gets. Soon, he disappears from my view entirely. I glance back at Grimy who's standing deathly still now as the crowd's chatter intensifies, the circle growing tighter around me as they carry on about the colorful haired girl, firing demands at me. Demanding to know who she is, how old, if she's been fucked, and is she my whore. A lanky, unkempt man brags that he'll fuck her so hard, she'll see stars—

A bullet rings out, searing through his forehead. He drops to the ground, and the silence is deafening as eyes turn to gawk at me and my raised gun. I raise it to another head, gritting out, "No one's going after the fucking girl, is that understood?"

But now One-Tooth smiles a large gummy smile at me. "Looks like we got a fuckin' hero on our hands."

"I am no hero."

"We'll see 'bout that, hey, fellas?"

Within seconds, pandemonium descends as they come at me.

I'm bigger than most. I pistol-whip heads and kick down men. I shoot another head or two.

But they just keep coming.

And soon one is jumping on my back, while another is kicking into my gut. Fingers claw down my face. Someone chews at my shoulder. I throw the man off my back, and kick back the man who's kicking at my stomach. A thick arm wraps around my throat while another comes at me so fast, I don't see the blade in his hands until it's too late.

He plunges it into my chest, sinking the knife deep into my heart while the arm continues to grip me, blocking off my airway. I see flickers of Grimy fighting and losing. I see him fall to the ground, and then my vision blacks out as the blood flows from my body and I'm lying in a puddle of it.

Flashes of purple and pink hair float in the darkness.

I wheeze, tasting blood, feeling pain, as flashes of a distant future barrel through me.

Blue eyes and shimmering skin in the water.

Stargazing on sandy beaches.

A kiss under a waterfall.

She stands on the Tempest, watching the sun rise.

I brush my nose along her hair, whisper, "Where to, Little Fish?"

"Home," she says.

I stop breathing.

PART

II

My feet carry me instinctively, the large boots clomping hard against the ground as I weave into the unfamiliar jungle. I travel in jagged lines, turning and continuing my path at random so I can try and lose James. Darkness surrounds me as I traipse further into the shadows, using the large bushes and tree trunks to hide.

I know he's chasing me, but as I push myself to move as quickly as I can, the tether dulls. It's the first time since he's captured me and we discovered the strange connection that I've felt it's waned, and I know this discovery should be my salvation.

I can break free from him if I get far enough away.

Only when I can no longer feel the tether at all do I stop, doubling over to catch my breath. My lungs burn like I've breathed in broken glass, and sweat layers my skin from the weight of the clothes. I wipe at my hair-line, wiping away a bead of sweat that threatens to fall.

Moving to sit beneath a tall tree, I find solace in its

wide trunk as I lean against it, satisfied that I'm safe for the time being. My heart still races though.

Images of the gruesome scenes that hung proudly in the pub race back into my mind, and I shudder at the possibility of that happening to me. At the *probability* of it happening to me. If not for the tether, would James have done that? Slaughtered me while he gathered his men around to cheer him on?

He kept me alive after he took me prisoner because of his curiosities. But I can't say for sure that if I hadn't changed back to my human form when the shift ended that I wouldn't have ended up exactly like that siren in the sketch.

The sketch that hung like a trophy in a pub.

On an island I'm now stuck on.

It's a vicious reality—if I'd been in the hands of another captain, that could have happened.

Still, I blow out a shaky breath as I sit and think about the consequences of my actions—*of me running.* It's like ice flows through my veins, my entire body instantly freezing, and I swallow thickly, looking around at the jungle that surrounds me.

It's only now in my solitude that I realize how dark the night has become and how still the forest is.

Nearby, something rustles between leaves while the wind whistles through the branches overhead.

I've traded one evil for another.

I'm alone in the jungle being hunted by at least one demon that I know of. I have no idea how large this vile island is, how far this jungle runs, nor do I have any solid plan on how to make it out of here alive.

Well done, Aria. You really fucked up this time.

But he terrified me. The darkness he swallowed me in...

How did he do that?

There's so much blackness in that man—

He was scared of what he felt for you.

Was he though?

Pulling my legs to my chest, I cling to myself and look around in the dark. I'm terrified of seeing glowing eyes watching me from the bushes. To meet a predator I have no way of defending myself against.

A man I can take on, but a beast of the wilderness? With sharp teeth that literally would rip me to shreds and enjoy me as a meal? At the very least I needed a knife to have a fighting chance, but that's a luxury I wasn't given before stepping off the ship.

The possessiveness James harbored radiated through the tether—the silent promise of protection—was the only glimmer of safety I had clung to since stepping off the ship and onto the island of Morda.

But possessiveness doesn't mean shit when the man himself might want to skin me alive.

Fleeing had been the right option. The *only* option.

And seriously, why are we tethered? What exactly is this magical bond between us that allows us to feel what the other feels? Of all the men on the planet to be tethered to, why him? *My enemy.* Someone I was born and bred to hate. Someone who hates me with equal fervor.

And where did it go?

Is this tether situation temporarily disabled because

of the distance, or is distance the key to breaking it entirely?

My mind spirals with all of the questions that have no business infiltrating my thoughts at the moment, but a single notion keeps pushing itself to the forefront of my mind: whatever this tether is, if it's not truly broken yet, I need to break it before it breaks me.

And I'm sorry, but why the fuck did this happen to me? Shouldn't this be the oldest sister's responsibility? The firstborn? Isn't that how curses and stories and bullshit typically worked?

'The firstborn child, blah blah blah.' How the hell did it skip over a couple sisters and land on my shoulders?

A frustrated growl rumbles low in my chest and I shudder out a breath, shivering as the cold breeze settles onto the sheen of sweat still dampening the back of my neck. My eyes scan my surroundings again, but I'm only met with darkness. Still, my gut tells me that I need to keep moving, so I stand, choose a random direction and begin to walk. This is a recipe for disaster, but I pretend to know what I'm doing, and this is all part of the plan. If I dig a little deeper in myself, I'd hear nothing but profanities of my idiocy, so I don't do that. Not yet. Not until I'm desperate and dying, which won't be too long from now.

My movements are slow and deliberate, my focus solely reserved on my senses. I'm not foolish enough to think I'm alone in this jungle despite the stillness that surrounds me. It's too good to be true and I know better than to let my guard down or find a place to wait out the morning.

With any luck I can move through the forest and make it to the other side of the island by daybreak. Though, I'm not sure what I expect to find on the other side. Based on the look of where we came from, I'm in the middle of literal hell. I just hope Hades doesn't find me before I find safety.

I envision him scratching his head. Imagine him asking me, *"What...what exactly were your intentions?"*

The jungle begins to groan as I move further into the tangle of trees, the sounds intensifying as if to warn me away. Screeches sound from animals—birds, maybe—are high up in the canopies above, and raspy creaks and squeaks from the creatures that hide within the shadows, are on the ground. Branches rustle, twigs break in the distance, and I swear I can hear the sound of footsteps from behind me, but I refuse to turn around and look. Not yet.

My stomach flips from the unease I'm feeling, and I force myself to swallow down the bitter taste of bile as it rises into my throat. I'm hyper aware of every noise, the loudest being the hollow echo of my thundering heartbeat ringing in my ears.

I'm confident enough to admit when I'm scared and right now, I'm utterly fucking terrified.

This is worse than when I used to sneak out to the docks as a teenager—at least I knew my way to and from the docks, and there was moonlight. I'm grateful my eyes adjusted quickly earlier, because the moon is now completely eclipsed by the canopy coverage overhead. There's no light to guide me as I move through the jungle, and I have no choice but to travel carefully, watching my every step so I don't trip or slip. Or worse: step on something.

Oh Goddess, what if there's a snake?

Give me all the sea creatures, but the scaly reptiles that inhibit the land? Hard pass.

The terrain starts to change the further I progress and the soft mud is met with large river-type rocks, causing me to watch my footing as I still wear the boots that are far too large. But my choice is to keep them on or brave the jungle floor barefoot, which seems like a recipe for disaster.

To my left, the trees unveil a small valley, thick with tall green grass that looks like it'll reach beyond my knees. As I move toward it, my fingers run across the weeds. Large beads of dew transfer to my trousers as I pass through, and its moisture seeps through the fabric in some places on my legs. The cold prickles of water against my skin send a ripple of chill through me and I shiver involuntarily.

Fuck, Morda is a cold place.

By now I have the feeling I've been walking for a couple hours, and I'm officially reaching the end of my metaphorical rope. I need to sit, rest, and try to devise a game plan.

Because why would someone wander around a jungle housed on the most depraved island without a game plan?

Seriously, this was one of the dumbest impulsive moves I've done to date.

Some of these ingenious plans include finding a boat and getting the fuck off this island. Maybe even stealing one. I saw a bunch of fishing boats—no, no, they wouldn't weather the ocean.

Then maybe I can wait around for a ship and smuggle myself on.

An ear-piercing scream stops me in my tracks and instinctively I drop to a crouch. My mouth goes dry as fear settles in, clutching deep into my soul. What the hell was that?

Again, this was the worst idea I've ever had. Not even being on that damn sinking ship with a bunch of men who kidnapped me had instilled this raw, bone-chilling fear. But throw me into a jungle for a couple hours, alone, and I'm a scared little girl who wants to return back to her captors.

Geez, Aria. Stockholm syndrome, much?

The scream that fills the air goes silent, but immediately an equally horrifying sound takes its place. A demented cross between laughing and barking echoes into the air, as if possessed monkeys are swinging in the trees directly behind me. The sound is far too close for comfort and despite the terror I feel, I quickly talk myself into getting the hell out of there.

Standing, I take off running in the opposite direction of the sound and further into the valley. As I move along the edge, my eyes stay peeled for any sort of shelter I can find, but it's mostly just open grass, which offers zero protection.

Veering to my left, I find another grove of trees along the valley's edge and head into it, stepping over tree roots and mud puddles. I walk until yet another break reveals what appears to be a mountainside, though I'm not so sure that's what it is. I'm hesitating, but I push forward, knowing my options are pretty fucking limited at this point.

My fingertips trail against the rocky hillside as I continue to move, using my sense of touch to guide me further. A symphony of sounds float through the air from beneath my feet: mud sloshes, leaves crunching, and the occasional twig snaps.

My feet start to ache within my boots from both the walk and the ill-fitting footwear. *Stupid fucking old boots from a stupid old Erickson.* Why couldn't there have been a woman on board at some point who had left behind something better fitted for me?

And with that thought, the toe of my boot catches on a thin root and I stumble again, thankful for my hand on the mountain to brace me from falling. I take two more steps, then suddenly, my hand is met with nothingness.

Way to jinx yourself, Aria.

Cut into the mountain—*hill,* whatever it is—is an open alcove. My hand grips its edge as I peer into it, not that I can see much since it's pitch black, but it looks just big enough for my body to fit into.

I think.

Worth a shot.

With a fleeting look over my shoulder, I make the snap decision to squeeze in. Though the frame is small, I pass through without needing to turn my body—my shoulders have just enough room on each side to get by. Inside, I am able to stand fully and stretch my arms out, though I don't dare step too deep into the cave, unsure of how far it goes or if it drops off. It's too dark to see, and

I'm not willing to take the chance just to get further from the alcove. From here I have a vantage point anyway. I'll be able to see if there is movement outside to know if I'm being followed or found.

Other than the creatures who lurk in the jungle, it's been quiet.

Too quiet.

And that's what scares me the most.

The air feels damp around me and the smell of pungent, wet soil burns my nose. I scrunch it, not loving the aroma of my shelter, but this is literally as good as it gets for now.

Lowering myself to the ground to get comfortable, my palms meet wet dirt, and as I lean my back against the side of the cave, I feel how soft the structure is. The amount of mud that makes up this cave has me feeling claustrophobic, and I send up a quick, silent prayer to the Goddess above to keep me safe until I'm able to leave.

Please don't let me get buried alive.

Leaning my head back, I feel heavy with exhaustion. I finally allow my eyes to close, but as I sit and try to relax, the pressure builds behind my lids and my heart rate accelerates.

Tears start to form.

From exhaustion, from despair.

Tonight has been so fucked.

My father's voice rings through my mind as I sit in the cold, damp space, lost in the middle of the fucking jungle on an island that is depraved and ungodly.

Aria, I told you. Humans are vulgar, vile, unkempt crea-

tures who will stop at nothing to hunt their prey. You are their prey, Aria, and I fear that if you keep acting out, you'll fall victim to their savagery.

I wish I could say I should have listened to my father, but I know there's nothing I could've done differently to have changed this fate. I followed my natural instincts the night of the shift, acting on par with every protocol—what I'd been taught. Getting captured by James had been a fluke; there was nothing I could've done to avoid it.

It was the unfortunate path I'd been led down by some outside force.

I *know* that.

We're a part of a bigger plan.

His curse. It has to be.

I felt the tether just as he had. The tether I wish I could still feel so it could lead me home.

Home.

At what point had James begun to feel like home?

Literally just hours ago I'd been desperate to get away from him, and now I was, what? Desperate to get back to him? To the ship, and the crew who barely tolerate me?

Confusion sits heavy in my chest as I exhale a shaky breath, and something happens that I haven't experienced in a long, long time.

I cry.

CHAPTER 38

James

I know what dying feels like.

I've been there so many times. The searing pain. The loss of blood. The way the world spins like it's off its axis.

I know what it's like to feel my breaths thin out, to feel my heart slow down as it struggles to beat.

Yes, I know the fucking feeling, but there's one thing I don't know.

Actual death.

The first thing I feel is the searing burn of my bracelet as its magic reignites, flowing through my veins. My whole body aches. Fire courses through me, zipping through my bloodstream. The healing hurts more than dying.

I groan, cracking my eyelids open as my heart tries to mend over the splitting ache. It takes effort to raise my head and look down at my chest. There's a handle sticking out of me, its blade still settled in deep. With a shaky hand, I wrap my fingers around it, teeth clenching as I try to remove it.

I feel weak, and it takes effort, but within seconds, I slowly pull it out and let it drop beside me. Then, I'm raising my sweater to see the hole in my torso, over-flowing with blood. Dropping my head back down to the earth, I stare up at the night stars as the hole begins to heal faster. Now that the blade is gone, I feel my heart begin to beat, and I groan again as the muscle rebuilds itself.

Close by, I hear similar groans. Grimy lets out a curse. "Just...wanted...to...fucking...eat..."

I crack a smile. "Yeah..."

"That...siren...is...a pain...in my...fucking...ass."

I just grunt in response as our bodies continue to mend.

Footsteps sound out, racing from me and then to Grimy. Before I dread that we're going to get stabbed again by another illiterate yokel, I recognize Luca's terri-fied voice. "What do you want me to do to make it better? Captain? What do I do?"

"Quiet," I breathe out weakly.

"But they've gone. Everyone's gone."

My breaths are ragged. "How...long?"

"Been five minutes, by my guess." He sounds panicked now. "What if they find her, Cap?"

He's genuinely terrified for Aria.

This fucking mermaid is winning hearts instead of destroying them.

When I get my fucking hands on that fish, I'm going to teach her a lesson about running.

I go still, feeling suddenly haunted at the absence of the tether.

Fuck this.

I groan loudly as I roll over to my side and slowly—fucking painfully—attempt to climb up on my feet. I'm still saturated in blood. It rolls down my arms and hands, leaving a trail on the ground. I grip the hole in my chest that's now closed over, grunting painfully as my heart begins to regulate to its normal thump again. Sucking in a large, full breath, I turn my sights to Luca. He stands before me, always awed by the transformation, and I don't blame him.

"I'm sorry for leaving," his voice breaks. "I'm sorry, Cap."

"I told you... to," I manage, still healing. "Because I knew...you'd be dead."

But he shakes his head. "I should have stayed—should have fought—"

"Stop with the dramatics," Grimy snaps as he, too, comes to a stand. It's the first time I get to look at him to see what happened. His head has been twisted so that his face is looking down at his back. He grips his head, growling out another curse as he twists it in one sharp movement, locking it back in place.

Luca dry heaves at the sight while I let out a low whistle. "Fucking shit way to go, Grimy."

Grimy just flares his nostrils at me, looking unsteady for a moment like he's off-balance. His mangled looking neck begins to smooth out, and when he's finally in one piece, he looks murderous and declares, "I'm going to kill every last fucking one of them."

WITHIN MINUTES, I've regained my equilibrium. My blood has multiplied, pumping through my veins. There's a dull ache in my heart, but it's nothing compared to the agony of not feeling that fucking tether.

Luca explains that the men have fled into the jungle in search of Aria, but Grimy's more interested in burning down the pub because of the tiff he had with the barkeep. "Wanted to charge us more," he gripes. "Orchestrated a fucking fight with Luca to justify charging us—"

"That's not our priority," I quip back. "We can come back and burn that place to the ground later—we need to find Aria first."

But Grimy is shaking his head. "Your tether can find her straightaway—"

"I can't feel her."

Grimy and Luca pause to stare at me with surprise. I fume, "Just before they stabbed me, she'd grown fainter."

"Is she dead?" Luca asks in horror.

My heart sinks to the bottom of my chest at the thought. "No."

But I don't know.

I can't be sure.

Except my head is still splitting wide open with a migraine, and I have a feeling it's to do with our separation.

"We need to find her. I need to get closer to her and the tether will come back."

Grimy doesn't look too certain, but Luca is nodding his head. "Tell me what to do, Cap. Anything, I'll do whatever you ask."

"Quit being such a kiss ass first," Grimy retorts. "Best plan would be to split up."

I nod as we come to a stop out front of the jungle. We're at the exact spot she disappeared in. "It would be best for Luca to go with you, Grimy. He needs protection."

Luca huffs. "I can take care of myself—"

"We'll meet back at the marina by sunrise?" Grimy asks, ignoring Luca.

I let out a sigh, thinking. "You both will be back at the ship by sunrise, but I might take longer."

"We need to know you're alright—"

"I'm fucking immortal," I remind Grimy. "I'll be fine. What won't be fine is Tempest sitting in the waters, protected only by Briggs, especially after what's already happened. They might pillage my ship."

Grimy frowns, stiffening a nod. "Then Luca and I will be back by sunrise."

Good.

I toss Luca my gun and he catches it. "Use it if you have to. Kill any one of those cunts that you find."

Gripping the knife that was plunged into my chest, I take a look into the jungle and take my first step forward. Grimy and Luca follow, and within moments, we're shrouded in wet greenery. Immediately, the environment is bursting with animal life. It's so dense with shrubs and trees, my boots drag through thick foliage along the uneven ground.

Just as much as we need to be mindful of the fucks chasing after Aria, we also have to watch out for the jungle dwellers.

On cue, a shrilling scream sounds out, ending in a bark-like sound.

"What the fuck was that?" Luca squeaks.

Grimy tosses a wary look my way. "There are creatures that live deep in the jungle of Morda. Creatures watching out for trespassers—protecting their land. We aren't welcome here. They're already hunting us."

I wonder if they've found Aria.

I wonder if that's why the tether is mute.

Panic floods my being.

"If you find her," Grimy says. "What will you do?"

"Discipline her," I fume. "Then take her to Vanya."

"That is a dangerous path, James. There is too much scorn for you to show your face—"

"What other choice do I have?"

He doesn't respond.

Without looking back at them, I press on, praying to the Goddesses that I feel my siren.

I wake with a startle, a strange sound jolting and disorienting me out of a sleep I hadn't knowingly fallen into. Reaching up, I rub my eyes, remembering where I am and wishing it had all been a bad dream. But it hadn't been, and I'm very much sitting in a dank, dark cave.

How long have I been out for? It couldn't have been too long.

The strange jostling movement sounds again, but this time it multiplies. My heart sinks and I wonder what the hell it is. The cave's so shrouded in darkness that even though my eyes have adjusted, I still see nothing.

As time passes, the noise continues, and my mind begins to play tricks on me. I see shadows dance along the walls across from me, hear phantom footsteps further into the cavern. *It's not real,* I tell myself...but what if it is? The logical part of my brain tells me I'm making it all up, but the side that's terrified to the fucking bone shuts my eyes tight.

It's too dark for there to be shadows.

I can't even see my own shadow.

The rationality does nothing to ease my terror.

When James prepared me for this visit to Morda, he warned me of the repulsive humans who lived here. I saw it firsthand as we passed through the town—if you could even call it that. The poverty and sad little flames, the desperate fishermen on broken down boats, trying to catch food. The visual of the appalling, offensive men who openly fucked the town whores, the unsavory looks the four of us received as we passed…I'll never forget it.

And let's not forget the lovely gentleman who tried to rob Grimy. He was a peach.

Morda is no joke and now more than ever I wish I'd heeded James' warning to follow his lead. If I'd taken a moment to *feel* the sincerity in his promise to never do what those sketches flaunted…

Suddenly, the swift movement of something flies by my face, the air shifting in front of me as it does. I continue to sit still, racking my brain for any clues of what the fuck that was and where the noise I keep hearing is coming from, but nothing comes to mind. For a few fleeting moments, all is silent and I doubt what's fiction and what's reality.

My doubt dissolves the second the jostling increases and another *whatever* flies by. Then another…and another.

And then I realize what the fuck is in this cave with me.

Shit.

A shrill squeal leaves my lungs as my legs ricochet

me upward, and I'm rushing toward the alcove of the cave, racing through it, just as no less than seventy-five bats follow me out. I take off in a sprint, frantically trying to get out of their way, but before I make it less than thirty feet, I trip over my own boots—*these goddamn too big boots*—and plummet into the loose mud beneath my feet.

A bloodcurdling scream leaves my body, releasing the fear and frustration that has plagued me for hours, as my body connects with the jungle floor. My wrists break my fall, but it's no use against the muck that splatters over my clothing, face, and hair. I give myself no time to dwell and jump back up, spinning in place as I try to figure out which direction to go.

Picking one, I move in the direction that I *think* I came from, following the edge of the cave back to where the trees gather and back into the jungle. When I spot the tall grass from the valley, a thick lump clogs my throat and I swallow it down. This has to be right. It looks familiar, but at the same time, it doesn't at all.

I'm moving slowly, listening to the jungle around me, when suddenly I feel the flicker of something deep in my chest. My hand flies to my chest, fingertips connecting with the exact spot I feel it.

James.

The rush of relief that I feel in that moment is so intense, it practically brings me to my knees. My breathing accelerates, chest heavy, like I'm on the verge of a panic attack. The connection is faint, but I can feel him again as it reignites.

Instinct tells me to start moving again, to follow the

connection until it burns hotter, but before I can consider it, voices cut into the air from a distance. I sink behind a bush, ducking down as low as possible to conceal myself. I hold my breath to stay silent.

The voices grow louder, more hurried, as they close in on the valley.

"I 'eard a scream!" a man says. "It's that girl, Jon. We're getting closer, ain't we?"

"Not if you don't move fast enough!" another retorts, grumpily. "There are over a dozen men scourin' this fucking brush for her, and I'm the only one stuck with a legless man."

"Oi, I got a fuckin' leg—"

"Yeah, you got one of them, not two!"

"My wooden leg's faster than yours, you arsehole."

My face falls, confusion filling me as they turn on each other. With just the smallest of movements, I peek around from where I hide to watch them. Next thing I know, they're beating each other up. They're far too close for comfort, and I jump, spooked, as the slams of their fists connect and their pained groans tear through the air. "You...bastard..."

"I told you me leg's fine!" the one-legged man growls.

"Aye, you're right, Spike, you're right..."

After a tense silence, they begin to apologize to each other. "You think we stand a chance finding this girl? I hear she's got all these colors in her hair, Spike."

"Bottle colored, surely."

"Did you know sirens have colorful hair?"

Now Spike laughs. "She ain't no fuckin' siren. They's dead, they is."

"Deader than that Cap'n, eh?"

Now Spike roars. "Oh, he ate it good, apparently! Took a knife straight to the chest. Bled out when we left. Total goner. So that girl's ours."

My heart sinks to the bottom of my chest as my hand squeezes tighter around my mouth. Tears fall from my eyes, running down my face endlessly. I'm not even sure when they started.

They stabbed him? But...I can feel him...feel the flicker in my chest... A horrifying thought passes that I'm feeling him dying instead. *No.* I immediately push the thought away.

The men come closer, done with their fighting and back to the hunt. It takes everything inside me to remain still as they pass by. They come so close, their footsteps feet from me.

"Think she'll massage me foot?" Spike wonders aloud.

"Aye."

"Even me wooden one?"

The jungle is so dense, it'd be impossible for them to see me obscured in the bush, but I still feel dread. Their filthy faces are in full view as they focus more on their discussion than on their surroundings. There are over a dozen of these men searching for me, I realize, each of them determined to be the first to get their hands on me.

What have I done?

When they're long gone, I stand up and hurry in the opposite direction. The boots slosh beneath me as I take off running, letting the intensity of the tether guide me while I run through the valley. Screams ring out; they're not of men, but of the creatures high up in the trees. My confidence grows, recognizing the sound from earlier. I must be on the right track, and with every step I can feel the tether burn deeper.

He's alive, I tell myself. *He's alive because he can't die.*

Calling his name seems like a foolish thing to do, but it is so tempting that I open my mouth to yell out anyway, only to be met with the sound of the fear-inducing laugh-bark. Something about it sounds pure evil and another wave of nausea rolls through me, chilling my blood, making me want to drop into a ball and hide within the blades of grass.

Forcing myself to keep moving, I creep through the valley, breaking into a jog until I make it back to the tree line and into the jungle. A shaky breath passes through my lips, the tether radiating so intensely in my chest, I no longer resist.

"James?" I call out, looking all around as I continue walking in a random direction. My eyes connect with every tree, every shrub—I'm even looking on the floor for footprints left in the dirt—but there's no sign of James.

A thunderous roar sounds, answering my call from moments ago, and I scream again, tearing off into the fastest sprint I have ever managed. I race through a grove of trees, unaware of how I am staying upright as I navigate myself around trunks and barrel past the branches that lean into my path. They catch my hair and whip at my face, leaving small cuts and likely bruises. Adrenaline is so potent in my veins, I am unfazed by any pain that they may have caused.

I keep running, pushing myself even though my lungs burn, and my legs wobble and threaten to give out.

The tether drives me, the adrenaline fuels me, and the terror clutches deeper. Gasping, I try to take in small inhalations of air. It's hard to breathe. My body quakes. The roar sounds again, but this time it's far behind me, almost as though it is an echo in the wind.

"Aria!" James' faint voice beckons to me, and I swallow a sob, relief overhauling my senses.

I spin in a circle as I attempt to figure out which direction he is. "James!" I yell back, but I'm afraid to move, afraid that if I do, I'll never find him. My muddy hair whips around me as my eyes search.

The jungle stays silent.

There's no sound of his voice. No footsteps. Not even the snap of a twig.

Too scared to call out to him again, I scan the tree line for any immediate threat and start to jog, hoping that I'm going in the right direction.

Something rolls down my cheek and I swipe at it, frustrated that after all these years, *now* is when the floodgate of tears reopens. Only, it isn't a tear that has slid down my face this time. I stare down at my hand, surprised to see blood staining my fingers. I lift them to touch the cut on my cheek, sucking in a sharp breath at the pain that sears through it with the graze of my fingertips.

Fuck.

Blood trickles down my cheek again and I wipe it with the back of my hand, instantly moving my hand down to my oversized trousers to wipe the blood there instead.

And with my concentration broken, I stumble over a loose rock.

These fucking boots.

My hands fly out and the balance it spurs is enough to narrowly catch myself, only just. My feet still have a mind of their own as they take me a few more steps forward, and I slam full force into a huge tree trunk. The wind knocks out of me in a *whoosh*.

There's no time for me to regain the air in my lungs before I'm faced with the startling realization that the tree trunk isn't a tree at all. I've slammed straight into the smelly chest of a man. Immediately, arms wrap around me and I'm lifted into the air by him. I scream, a loud, bloodcurdling scream, as I pound at his back.

He lands a smack on my ass and proclaims to absolutely fucking nobody, "Caught her! Fair and square, fellas!"

"No!" I scream into the quiet jungle, continuing my assault and landing punch after punch against his back.

But the bastard doesn't even flinch.

"Don't worry, darlin'," he assures me. "We'll take good care of you at Madam Ruth's. You'll be the most sought after whore this island's ever seen."

CHAPTER 40

Aria

No. *This can't be happening.*

The weight of the man's arms around my middle, caging me in a tight hold against his body, sends my heart into the pit of my stomach. I'm still punching his back, adrenaline pumping through me with such intensity, my vision spots. I'm exhausted, but I continue to fight, because if I let the fight in me go, I have nothing left.

Sending hit after hit against his meaty back, his neck, and even his head, I'm hoping that I land one good enough to disorient him enough to loosen his grip. Then I'd be able to slide out of his hold and run. It's a long-shot, but I have to try.

My fist connects with the nape of his neck and the large man grunts. "Caught meself a fiery one, haven't I? Ah, you'll be a fun one to bed, darlin'. I'll break you in real good."

A small whimper escapes through my lips at the vile

image this man just placed in my mind. I should have never fled. I should have stayed with James...

As though summoned by the very thought of his name, the tether roars, rage burning so intensely I feel like my chest has been lit on fire.

Instantly, I know he's here, and this man is about to die.

I stop pounding his back and close my eyes, wrapping my arms around my head as a large force slams into the front of the man holding me. The world tilts as he falls to the side, with me in his grasp. Again, wind is knocked out of me, and for a brief moment, I'm dizzy and trying to catch my breath. Disoriented, I manage to crawl away, scurrying a few feet away. Pulling my legs to my chest, I look around, disoriented, as the commotion grows louder. There are two bodies on the jungle floor next to me, but only one of them is moving with the speed of a wild animal.

James.

He's here.

His hands are locked together, raining down on the man's body ceaselessly. He's in a trance, his hands rapidly coat in blood from the knife wound he's slit across the man's neck. It's so deep, he bleeds out quickly into the muck beneath him.

The sight is so jarring, my brain can't keep up. "James," I whisper, wanting to get his attention. It's over. He's won the battle against the man who had me in his clutches.

But he's lost to the motions, this possessed rage

rolling off him so thick and untapered, the darkness eclipses us once more. The same terror washes over me.

I rise to my feet, and this time, I don't run away from him, but *toward* him. Dropping to my knees in front of him, the man is now between us, unmoving. I lean over the body and place both hands on his face, frantic of what may happen if he loses control of his darkness even more. "James, stop, stop! It's okay, I'm okay!"

My voice breaks through his haze and he stops suddenly. His chest heaves, mouth parted. James' unfocused eyes look at me, but I know he's not seeing me, so I keep repeating myself, telling him I'm here, that he needs to stop, that everything is okay. Slowly, the focus returns to him and the blackness recedes until we're back under the trees, under the spitting rain that hits his face. It merges with the spatter of blood along his cheekbones and mouth, and I wipe the blood away from his lips. His eyes shutter momentarily at my touch.

"We have to go," I tell him, panicked. "We have to leave, James. There are more!"

Eyes still closed, he shakes his head. "They're dead, Aria."

"No—"

"I killed them."

I pause in disbelief. "What?"

He opens his eyes, staring at me solemnly, his exhaustion heavy. "I killed every man along this path. There's no one left. No one's hunting you."

I look him over, catching the blood on his clothes and the bruises along his arms and bloodied knuckles.

"James..." I breathe out, brokenly. "What have I done?"

"Shh," he whispers.

Suddenly, he's up, his arms wrapping around my tired body. He lifts me to my feet and cradles me to his chest. I shut my eyes, breathing him in.

"Shhh. I've got you, Siren."

I look up as he spins us around in a circle, his eyes scanning the entire jungle around us—every tree, bush, and the canopy overhead. Several minutes pass in complete silence, the only sound coming from the wind as it hisses through the trees and the light rain that lands on the leaves.

"You're shaking," James whispers, wrapping his strong arm around my shoulders. "Are you cold?"

I shake my head no as he pulls me further into his chest.

"Stay quiet," he presses, his eyes never leaving the jungle.

My chest rises and falls in rapid succession as I catch my breath, finding solace in the arms of my enemy.

Is he even truly my enemy at this point?

Either way, I'm so fucking happy he's here.

I tilt my head back, watching James as he looks purposefully into the jungle around us. My fingers cling to his shirt, the fabric bunching in my hands as I hold onto him. Still, I'm half convinced he isn't real, and this is all some sort of sick nightmare I'm having.

Any minute, I'll wake up alone in that cave.

But the way his abs flex beneath the garment between us reminds me that he is really, truly with me.

Possessiveness burns through the tether again, but this time it's mixed with fear.

If James Erickson is fearful of what dangers hide in this jungle, then I know I should be too. I make a mental promise to myself that later, when I'm beating myself up over the fact that I should have somehow been stronger, or that I should have fought harder to find a way to escape this island instead of running back to James, I'd remember *he* was afraid too.

When James is satisfied we aren't being hunted, or whatever he's keeping an eye out for is absent, he looks down at me, meeting my eyes. His large hands come up and envelop my shoulders as he takes a step backward, looking over my full body.

"Are you hurt?" he asks, cupping my face and rubbing his thumb over the gash on my cheek. "Why are you covered in mud?"

"I fell," I state, trying to keep the sarcasm out of my voice but failing. "Obviously."

His hands continue to touch every part of my body as he ignores my attitude, scouting for any injuries. Once he's taken a thorough look over, James' gaze and hand travel back to my face—the only part of me with actual physical injuries, which I could have easily told him, but why complain about some scratches when he's covered in blood?

"The gash on your cheek is deep, but it's clotted now, which is a good sign. It probably doesn't need stitches to heal, but if you don't want it to scar as badly, we'll need to tend to it once we're back on the Tempest."

I nod wordlessly, my mouth dry as I lick my lips and

acknowledge his statement. James' gaze follows the movement of my tongue before trailing back up.

He's taking me back to the Tempest.

I wait for the fight in me to return—to refuse his claim—but it's desolate.

He senses it, too, but where there should be relief, I see hardness. "You ran."

I look down at my feet. "You scared me."

He sighs. "I lost control."

"You covered us in darkness—"

"That's never happened unintentionally before."

"Why did it happen at all?"

"It's complicated." His face doesn't soften. "Don't run from me, Aria. Not again."

I feel the hurt and anger in him. He doesn't want to let it go. He wants to roar in my ear that I ran, and he wants me to assure him I won't ever do it again.

Instead, I swallow and stiffen a nod.

A ghost of a smile plays on his lips, likely from feeling the lack of defiance through the tether. "Does anything else hurt, Aria?" he asks, his voice low.

I can hardly breathe around the look he's giving me. I read it clearly. Silently, I press a finger against my muddy cheek. "Just here."

His eyes follow the movement before his head drops. His breath comes out light as he brushes his lips against my cheek. I shut my eyes at the feeling. "Right here?" he asks.

I nod.

"Anywhere else, Aria?"

The tether pulses within me when he speaks my name.

My hand grows shaky as I point to my mouth. "Here."

His lips brush along my lips, and I can't help the light moan as he runs his tongue along the seam of my mouth. My blood turns to lava. Around us the air's charged with electricity as we stand hypnotized in the trance of one another. I feel the layers of my resistance come down. Just as quickly, I feel the wall he's built around our connection drop.

Relief and lust mirror as we hold each other's stare.

"Do you want me?" he asks, his lips brushing along mine as they move.

I barely blink. "Yes."

"My darkness, too?"

"Yes."

"Even if it terrifies you?"

I shake, unable to resist this man a second longer. "Especially because it terrifies me."

He lets out a shuddering breath, then whispers my name like a prayer, "Aria..."

And just like that, the world tilts on its axis.

Our bodies act in unison, our mouths slam together and we connect through a punishing, passionate kiss. He spins us, slamming my back against the trunk of a tree, and I gasp on impact. He steals the air from me, literally sucking it out of my mouth, as his fingers work to unbuckle the belt that cinches the oversized trousers around my waist. As the belt gives away, the pants fall from my body and pool at my feet. His hand glides down one leg, and I raise it to allow him to remove the boot and pants from around my foot. He does the same to the other leg.

"Stupid fucking things," he says bitterly. "I'm a fool to think they could have disguised you."

His movements slow as he works my sweater off, delicately sliding it over my head and discarding it on the ground with my pants and boots.

I'm completely naked and feeling extremely vulnerable.

Even pressed against me, James looks me over—a look of reverence coating his features. I cling to that look as his hands roam my flesh.

I can't see anything but this man, enveloped completely by him as my back presses against the tree. There's no escape. No way out. But I'm not looking for one. Not right now, at least.

I suck in a breath when his fingers run along my inner thigh. I'm weak for his touch—my body begging for the faintest brush of his fingers against my core.

"James…" I breathe out, running my gaze along his torso. I'm so needy, I think I'd come from just the feeling of his body against mine.

As if reading my thoughts, he takes my hand and presses it against his shirt. "Take it off. Do what you want to me, Siren."

I reach for the hem of his shirt, untucking it and working to pull it up and over his torso. He's just so damn big, it's not an easy task, but he works with me, bending down enough for me to push it up higher. He's patient, watching me with that look that sets my skin ablaze. There's no smirk, no cocky glint in his eye.

Just pure desire.

When his tunic reaches his neck, he takes charge, pulling it over his head. He tosses it on the ground and now he's bare to me. It's not something I'm unused to—but there's a huge difference right now. I can touch him. I can taste him. And fuck me, but I want to do it all to him. I want to know every inch of this man's body—I want to commit it to memory.

His muscles contract with every movement, and I watch with heavy eyes. Even in the darkness, I appreciate how irresistible this man is, scars and bruises, blood and all. I think all that wildness about him drives my lust into overdrive.

I'm ravenous for him.

Raising up to my tiptoes, I kiss along his shoulder, flicking my tongue out to taste his skin. He goes impossibly still as my hands run up and down his torso, nails scratching along the muscles in his biceps and forearms. He doesn't move as I kiss his collarbone, run my lips along his chest, brushing them against his nipple and loving the air he sucks in at the contact.

He's sensitive.

Extremely so.

It reminds me how unwound he was when I took his cock into my mouth.

My captain may be experienced, but he's easily triggered, his desire raw and transparent.

His lips find mine and our tongues dance wildly as he fists my hair, weaving his fingers through the vibrant strands that tumble around my bare shoulders. A moan catches in my throat and I completely stop thinking. In this moment, he's not my captor, nor my enemy, nor the prince I've been taught to hate.

He's just a man.

And right now, I'm not a siren his family would have urged him to kill.

I'm just a woman.

My fingers reach for his belt, shaking as I work to unlatch the buckle, fumbling against the leather with unsteady hands.

Without breaking our kiss, James reaches down, taking over as he unbuttons and unzips his pants. His fingers dip below the waistband and he pushes them down his hips, freeing his thick cock.

"This is what you do to me," he strains out. I catch the wonder in his eyes, the look of a man drunk off desire and want. "I almost forgot what this felt like, Aria..."

Fisting his cock in his hand, I watch through hooded eyes as he pumps it from base to tip. It's so engorged, its veins protrude angrily and an abundance of pre-cum leaks from the tip.

The urge to take him in my mouth until I'm choking and unable to breathe has my knees buckling. My voice is cracked, desperate. "James..."

But before I can think of dropping to my knees, it's James that does. I don't have time to think before he nudges my legs apart. I look down exactly as he buries his face in my core, lapping his tongue along my folds like a starved wild animal.

Oh, my God.

My body shudders and my knees buckle, unable to stand upright. His hand grabs my thigh to steady me, making sure I won't fall, before he guides my leg over his shoulder. He brings his other hand to grasp my hip, keeping me firmly in place as his tongue tastes me. He's ravaging me, making my breath come out quick and disoriented.

I feel like I'm on cloud nine. Everything about this is so dirty and wrong, but it couldn't possibly feel more *right*. James fucking me with his tongue in this dangerous jungle where I could still easily be hunted, with a dead man feet from us. Yet I throw my head back as he swirls his tongue up and down. He skates his tongue across my clit before suctioning his lips around it and sucking it into his mouth. The intensity makes me cry out, and my knees buckle again.

His fingertips bite against my bare skin as he tightens his grasp, pulling his face away from my pussy slightly to say, "Press your body into my face, Aria. Use my mouth to stabilize if you need to."

His words confuse me, the lust induced haze fogging my brain so intensely, it takes a moment to process what he means. But as I stare down at this ruthless man on his knees, he grabs my hips and guides me back to him, attacking my pussy as though it's his last meal. And as he buries his tongue within my folds so tightly that I'm sure he can't breathe, I understand.

My body relaxes more against his hold, letting more of my weight press against his mouth, and I tangle my fingers in his hair, gripping him harshly as I ride his face.

He eats me out like a man possessed, and with every roll of my hips, I moan his name. "James… James…"

Raking his fingernails down my skin, he brings his fingers between us and prods at the wetness between my legs. Feeling how soaked I am for him, he leaves no room for mercy as he plunges three of his fingers inside me. I suck in a breath, shaking from how tight I feel. Immediately, his movements curl upward to reach the most sensitive spot.

His fingers thrust inside me as he sucks roughly against my clit, pushing me toward the edge. Eyes half-closed, I barely take in the swirling green of leaves overhead, or the dark cloudy sky jutting between the small breaks of the branches.

He growls his satisfaction, the sound vibrating through me, and I'm coming—

Hard and long, crying out as my fingers dig deeply into his thick hair, and he doesn't let me go anywhere. Not when I buck, not when I thrash through the intensity of the orgasm.

I'm free falling.

There's buzzing in my ear—the blood whooshing around my body, my heart thumping like never before. I've disconnected from the external world and am floating there through the high, subtlety aware that he's pulled back and is standing. That his arms are around me now, and he's lifting me up, hands tucked under my ass as he presses my back against the tree bark and runs his tongue along my lips.

Weakly, I part them, allowing him in, and the taste of him—the taste of me—brings me back down to earth.

I blink at him, refocusing on the glazed look in his eyes. I understand him well, and I can feel what he wants through the tether.

He wants me.

He wants me now.

And he won't be gentle.

My knees bend and tighten against his waist as I nod once. An acknowledgement of his desires.

James' chest moves rapidly, the realization that this is truly going to happen hitting him. He presses his cock between my legs, rubbing it against my wetness. My clit throbs as he slides the head between my folds and up to my clit, giving it a slap with his cock. I moan shamelessly, desire pulsing through me yet again as my body rocks against his, chasing the next explosion of pleasure.

My pussy tingles and I feel my inner walls clench with anticipation. I wrap my arms around his neck and let my fingers bury into the hair at his nape.

"This is your chance, Siren," he strains out, the ache in his voice present. The tip of his cock pushes against the soft flesh of my pussy, but not entering. "This is your one and only chance to stop this from happening. I won't be gentle. Fuck, Aria, I'll split your pussy in two and won't relent until I've filled you so thoroughly with my cum that you'll drip for days. This pussy is *mine*, Little Mermaid. *You* are mine."

The conviction in his words practically incinerates the tether, burning it so brightly that I physically hiss from the stab it ejects in my heart. The look on his face tells me he feels the same pain, and it's a pain he welcomes.

This is dangerous, I want to tell him, but I can see the same thought reflected in his gaze.

What are we fucking doing?

We're too alike.

We're two burning fires, and we'll consume each other.

I send these images down the tether, catching his understanding.

"We'll burn out," I whisper in my despair, eyes welling with emotion.

"Best thing about a fire, Aria, is we can spark another one," he replies softly. "And another one... And another one."

Relief runs through me in that moment. I smile slowly, my heart expanding with the defeat. With the utter surrender of giving my being to him—and not just my body, but all the layers beneath it.

I drink him in, knowing that there is no turning back from this once the words leave my mouth, yet I have no interest in stopping them—no matter how catastrophic they may be later on.

"I'm yours, James," I whisper.

And without a single hesitation on his part, he slams into me, connecting our bodies and uniting the tether between us.

I want to be gentle with the siren. The instinctual part of me longs to be tender, and for a few moments, that's exactly what I am.

The walls of her pussy are tight. Her warmth and her slickness—I don't want to just fuck this pussy, I want to devour it whole. She makes me so fucking wild, and then there's her scent. That sweet ocean scent. The one that reminds me that the sea is my home, and it beckons me—beckons *us*.

After I've slid into her completely, there's stillness.

She hasn't even let out a moan, much less a breath.

Neither have I.

My cock throbs, but my heart throbs faster. As I hold her up, her back braced against the trunk of the tree, I feel my fingers tremor under her ass. My entire body breaks into a sweat, urging me to move.

I pull back my head to look at her. Eye-to-eye. The variations of blue in her eyes are so intense, they keep me rooted there, unable to look away.

If she's still got magic, I'd wager she's using it on me now, much like she did as a siren. Pulling me in, she could so easily rip my heart out of my chest, and I'd let her—anything she wanted—I'd let her fucking do it to me in this moment.

But she ran.

My head throbs from the reminder. The anguish of it.

She took off from me, and she didn't even look back.

"You ran," I accuse, just then in a whisper.

The tether throbs with lust and...something more.

Something sweet, something deep.

It is not the weight of magic, either.

There is no magic in my little siren.

It is just us.

Her magic is gone—depleted—and she's giving me the same awed look as I know I'm giving her.

Like she's under *my* spell now.

She doesn't respond.

She's too far gone, chained to the moment.

Her plump lips are parted, and she lets out this shaky breath, letting me know she can feel every inch of me inside her, and she wants more.

I pull out just barely before pushing back in. The spark of pleasure is immediate and I feel myself grow impossibly hard from within her. The feeling of our bodies connected is too much, but at the same time, not enough.

Her hands slide down my body, digging into my chest as though she's trying to claw her way in.

"You ran," I repeat, and this time there's a bite in my

voice as I withdraw from her tightness and slam back into her with more vigor than before. She lets out a light moan, saying nothing to my accusation.

I'm filling her whole, pushing as deep as our bodies will allow, and I know she'd be squirming if she were any less wet. Instead, her legs want to spread wider, silently begging for me to use her—

And I do.

I withdraw almost completely, and this time, I plunge into her in one rough stroke, gritting out in a harsher tone, "You fucking ran, Siren."

But she's not listening to me, not when I'm fucking her like this: in harsh strokes, hissing my distaste along the way, telling her as I fuck her wholly, "You didn't even look back. Where the fuck did you think you were going to go?"

She tenses at my anger, but her eyes are still glazed. She takes my punishing rhythm, wincing slightly from the pain I'm causing—and oh, how I love to cause this siren pain.

And pleasure.

I love to give her both.

We're nose to nose. I'm pissed at her, and she's looking back at me with a little more focus. Her gaze turns to anger like she's pissed at me, too. But what the fuck for? I didn't throw her in the jungle—she chose to flee.

She was scared, I tell myself.

I frightened her.

But I would never have hurt her.

My cock swells as I move, pumping into her, driving her wild. Panting, Aria swipes her tongue along the seam of my mouth, asking for entry. I pull my head back before she can kiss me, and she doesn't like that one bit. With a challenge in her gaze, she brings her hand up to wrap around the back of my head and uses her strength to pull me back to her. My teeth are clenched, but she doesn't care. She runs her tongue along my lips, over my teeth, before sucking at my bottom lip, groaning as she does. I relent, kissing her back with ferocity.

Oh, we're fucking beastly, aren't we?

Two wild creatures playing a dangerous game.

There's so much of my pre-cum shooting inside her, and I groan at the thought of drowning Aria with my cum. "I'm going to fill you with my cum, Siren. I'll fill you over and over, so much so, you'll have me leaking from you for days. Maybe I'll make you eat it, too," I growl through my rage. "Make you slide your fingers inside your pussy to draw out my cum, and you'd fucking lick it clean for me, wouldn't you?"

Aria is thrashing against me, lost in her pleasure, moaning, "Yes, yes, yes..."

My balls feel heavy as I fuck her against the tree trunk. Our bodies are slick. This feverish fucking is dangerous—so fucking dangerous—to be doing out in the open. I step even closer to her, shielding her with my body should anyone attack her. They'd have to go through me first—

And that startles me.

Draws my pleasure back enough for me to blink in

my astonishment that, yes, I would take a fucking bullet for this mermaid. A thousand more. They could set me on fire, cut my throat clean—I'd do it for her.

This sexy as sin, vibrant-haired beauty with the sharp tongue, who has withstood weeks of hard labor and cold nights on my ship. And she took it, didn't she? Never uttering a single word of protest, she accepted the hurdles we threw at her—

How could you flee from me? After everything? Because it wasn't so bad, was it? We were good to you, too. You know it —you fucking know it!

I'd hold back on my pleasure if I could—I'd fucking stop this very instant because the choking feeling in my throat is tight, telling me I'm fucked.

She's gotten into my head, and into my heart. *And she fucking fled.*

But I'm too far gone—the feel of her pussy, her tongue sucking along my lips, her loud moans and bucking hips, the feel of her meaty ass in my hands—

She tremors, coming hard, body shaking, but I don't stop to let her ride through it. I pump into her, hard and fast, and I follow straight after. Fucking her in a few harsh strokes before stilling as the long orgasm rocks me to the core. I feel it rush through my veins, that delicious euphoria drawing out, and I try to savour every fucking second of it, because I know what will happen when it's over.

I'm going to be plunged into darkness.

Bereft without her tight walls.

Maybe I don't want to sever this tether after all.

THERE'S an ache that won't die inside me.

It pulses and pulses as I stare at her. She looks back. The lust isn't over, but our bodies are spent. Her teeth are chattering as I carry her away from the tree and drop us down onto the cold earth. I shield her for a while, my body over hers, my dick still hard because of her. She wraps her arms around me, running her hand up and down my spine. She traces the long jagged scar that runs down it as I kiss her jaw and throat.

The jungle is silent.

It's just the rain pattering around us, picking up speed.

Aria is still in her lust fueled haze. Her tongue darts out, running along my shoulder and neck. Her legs are stretched wide, and she bucks her hips, moaning for me, whispering words I don't quite capture.

I shake uncontrollably from her touch, my lust merging with unrestrained urges to mark her. That's what I should have done instead—I should have fucked her before we stepped off the Tempest, and I should have marked her in teeth marks for all to see. To let every fool know she's been used, marked, and taken.

"My mistake," I utter. "To leave you like that. Never again."

My instincts kick in. The savageness in me is unrestricted. She's lost in us, too busy licking my throat when I pull away. I shake my head down at her. *No,* I want to say. *Not like this. Not while you look at me.* I can't let her see the darkness threatening to burst from me. Like the black ooze when my mask came off—this one will frighten her.

I roll her abruptly to her stomach. "Close your eyes, Siren," I demand heatedly. "Whatever you do, don't open them."

I leave her no chance to respond when I slide into her in one vicious stroke. Oh, the fucking pleasure. I shudder over her, groaning deep in my throat.

And there it goes.

All the color is ripped out from my periphery. The jungle disappears and it's just her in the all-encompassing blackness. She gasps in shock, sensing the shift, the blackness inescapable, even with her eyes closed. I pull out, and then drive back into her harshly. Her hands ball together by her face as she squeezes her eyes shut tighter. She brings one fist to her mouth and bites hard as I repeat my actions, fucking her in long, fast strokes. I'm volatile and shaken. My cock so hard, I want to go in as far as humanly fucking possible. This fucking siren has awoken the serpent within, and he's demonic and cruel, and all he wants is to claim her.

My siren.

All fucking mine.

I fuck her until her groans fall away, and it's just the animalistic strokes. Fucking her until she's out of breath. Fucking her until my legs quake and my heart might burst. And I tell her this. Somewhere along the way. I let her know she's my undoing. That she's woken me up from a long nightmare. That I've seen her in my dreams—

And it's all too much at once. The flood of emotion—

the rage of her running—the crest of pleasure as it approaches—the tightness in which she grips me. And it's not just my cock she's squeezing tight; it's that fucking rock in my chest I didn't know could still beat with purpose.

I come hard, my release pummels through me in one violent swoop as I erupt deep inside her. Coating her walls. Filling her up. Oh, how she'll drip of me, how I'll run down her legs...

The darkness dissipates with every calming breath, and as if to compensate for my recklessness, I cover her body whole with mine and hold her to me until we've come down from our high.

WE'RE UTTERLY silent as I pick her up off the ground. She's covered in mud and leaves. A gush of our fluid slides down her thighs, and I have the fucking audacity to glide it back up to her pussy and rub it around her folds. She trembles at that as I set her down on the ground slowly, delicately. She sways, nearly falling over, but I catch her, and her hand shoots to my hip, using it like an anchor to stay upright. Her head is down, that hair a curtain over her features now as she peers at the ground, saying nothing.

I don't expect her to talk, but I do want answers.

Eventually, I step away from her, and she is quick at work, collecting her clothes. Now that her breaths and moans have ceased, I can hear clearly. The jungle sounds of birds and insects buzzing, the sway of leaves and distant howl-like calls.

Nothing is out of the ordinary.

No ominous shouts.

No footsteps crunching along the foliage to signal an enemy is nearby.

Oh, the blood I've had to shed to find her...

I look back at Aria and clench my jaw shut. I tell myself to hold back, to wait until we're back on the Tempest, but I've just been inside her pussy, and I feel like I'm going fucking mad because—

"You ran from me," I grit out, darkly. "Why?"

Aria doesn't meet my eye. Instead, she focuses on the clothes littering the ground, collecting them one after the next. If she thinks she can get out of answering me, she hasn't learned a fucking thing about me.

"Why did you run from me?" I repeat, my voice growing harder.

"Let's not talk about this now," she retorts, sliding her shirt back on, covering those round tits. But you can still fucking see them. Of course those men knew she was a woman. Her tits are impossible to hide.

How could I have been so fucking stupid?

"I'm not taking you back until you answer."

Her eyes narrow on mine as she pauses to look back at me. "Keep threatening me and I'll do it again—"

"What, run?" This time I smile cruelly. "And put yourself in danger all over again? Don't be a fool, Aria—"

"I didn't say I'd run *now*," she cuts in, holding still now to hold my gaze. "It won't happen on this island, and maybe not on another shithole island, either, but when the time is right, I *will* run, James, if you keep pushing me."

"How did I fucking push you? I don't even know why you fucking ran!"

"I couldn't be in that pub, around your kind—"

"Those men are not my kind!"

But she's shaking her head. "They are, James. They're all as wicked-hearted as you! You've told me countless times you should have killed me, ripped my heart out instead, and these men? They would do the same if they knew what I am! And I knew that, okay? I understood. But to see it in the pub like that...us sirens bleeding to death like art porn on those fucking walls... I don't fucking belong here in your world, and certainly not with you."

"A lot of the stories told are just tales, Aria," I say. "Those pictures weren't all of real sirens—"

"That's not true, and I don't care, James," she cuts in vehemently. "I made a choice in that pub. I decided I wasn't going to be some painting on the walls of the fucking Tempest."

"You won't be. Ever." I clench my fists, adding, "Why do you think I chased after you? If I wanted you dead, I wouldn't have bothered."

"Because you're stubborn," she guesses. "Because you want to be the one to kill me—"

"*Never*," I say.

"Then you want me as your personal slave again." But she knows that's absurd.

"You're really bad at being a slave," I say.

But she's carrying on with that theory, reminding me

harshly, "I am not one to be controlled, and I am not the type of female to submit."

I want to tell her she submitted just fine around my cock, but I can tell she knows this fact. Her cheeks redden, and she looks annoyed. "Don't read too much into it," she mutters, putting one foot into her pants. "I was horny—so were you. We fucked each other, and it was grand and all, and your dick's pretty big—"

"Pretty big?" I question. There's the most subtle tinge of playfulness to my tone, and it's something I hardly recognize from myself. I can't recall the last time I was playful about anything. *What is she doing to me?*

She shrugs her shoulder nonchalantly. "Yeah, it's pretty big. You want a fucking medal, James?"

"I want you to slide your fingers in your pussy and eat my cum like you said you would."

She's so shocked by that response, she stumbles as she puts her next foot in and falls to the ground with an *oomph*. Trudging to her slowly, I watch as she flails pathetically, attempting to put the pants on while lying on her back. My face is stoic, but internally I'm pushing down a laugh. Maybe she's trying to save face, to say she wasn't being clumsy—that she wanted to fall and slide them on—but her efforts are in vain. She lets out a frustrated grunt and goes limp. Her chest is moving rapidly as she stares up at the tree overhead, her face flat. I stand right over her, smirking as she doesn't meet my eye. "What's wrong, Aria?" I ask. "You only talk dirty when you're horny?"

She doesn't answer.

"I won't make you do it," I say, coming to kneel beside

her. I study her face, catching every twitch and gulp of her throat. "In light of being hunted down by half the island's horny men, I'll save that cum-eating for another day. But I want you to do it—"

"Not fucking happening," she hisses, stubbornly. "This was a one-time affair—"

"Silence," I growl, and just to spook my siren, I force the tether to burn hotter with my rage, just to teach her that I'm not to be fucked with.

She surprisingly goes still.

"You put us through hell. If Luca is still alive and Grimy hasn't been killed again, I'll be fucking impressed—"

"Again?" she asks in a whisper, her shock inescapable.

I glower. "Yeah, Aria, *again*. We got killed when you left—"

"I didn't know. Not about Grimy." There's pain in her voice, but I don't let it get to me. "He can't die either?"

"No. And neither can Rex. My bracelet's power protects them too, because I..." I let out a shaky breath. "If you put them in danger again, I'll leave you to fucking die, tether be fucking damned," I threaten, and despite my instincts roaring that I can't do that, I know in my soul that I must. I can't endanger Grimy, not when I owe him my life. "You want to pretend this was a one-time thing? Fucking be my guest, but what I said when I fucked you still stands. You'll come around once you realize the only thing standing in your way of what we are becoming is yourself. In the meantime, you have a lot to make up for. You're going to get up, get dressed, and you're going back to the Tempest with me, and Goddess fucking help you if you utter a fucking word of protest about it."

With trembling lips, she doesn't protest at all.

WE HAVE to be stealthy on our way back. I take the same route to make sure no one has trailed the bodies I've left behind. Aria is in fucking shock at the grisly scenes.

"What happened?" she whispers in shock at the first body we come across.

"It got complicated." There's no point telling her how close she was to falling into the arms of man after fucking man. Frankly, it'd surprise me if there were any men left on the island after the shitshow we left behind.

It's another stark reminder to Aria that nothing will stop me from getting to her. And I'm fucking capable of it—of getting what I fucking want. Her silence tells me she's understanding.

There's a stillness beyond the tree line as we step out of the jungle and down the familiar path to the dock. We pass a few elderly locals, but they don't make eye contact with me. Heads down, they carry their buckets of water and fish back to their make-shift homes.

Some of the whores are more brazen, one of them whining, "You killed Fred, y'know. He was a fucking regular. Never slapped me around, neither."

I toss a healthy handful of silver coins their way to silence them, and they grin their toothless smiles at me as they fetch for it like rabid dogs.

I'm tense, looking in every direction, feeling slightly fearful. What if Grimy and Luca weren't at the dock waiting? What if they didn't make it out? The thought is heavy on my mind as I trudge along, the walk feeling like a never-ending marathon. I'd have to hunt for Grimy. Not the first time I've done so. But Luca... Luca would be a loss I'm not prepared to face.

Halfway down the path, Aria's legs buckle. With all her adrenaline sapped from her limbs, she flags behind, unable to keep up. I stop to collect her in my arms, picking her up and over my shoulder like a sack of potatoes. My hold is awkward, but I can't hold her in both arms in case we get attacked.

I expect a witty curse to fall from her lips, but she hasn't said a single word since our talk. With her over my shoulder, I move faster in the direction of the docks. Anxiety grips me, the thought of Grimy gone or dead again—

"About time!" shouts a familiar voice.

My heart beats harder as relief crashes into me. In my hold, I feel Aria sigh a breath of relief too, though whether it's my relief or hers she's feeling, I'm unsure.

Has my mermaid taken a liking to my crew?

Grimy is on the dock, next to a neatly stacked mountain of crates, while Luca is hard at work, loading the crates into the ship with startling speed.

I approach him, glancing between the crates and him. "I got sidetracked."

Grimy wrinkles his nose like he can smell the sex on us and frowns. "You weren't meant to reward the siren for running off—"

"Quite the opposite," I assure him with a dark smile.

Grimy still doesn't look happy. "I don't want to look at her face, not for a fucking while yet, James—"

"She'll be in my chambers."

"Being punished?" he pushes, and I can hear the cheeky doubt in his voice.

"Being punished," I repeat on a nod.

Luca bristles as he stops to nod once at me, his glare razor-sharp as he takes Aria in. "Was hoping you wouldn't find her," he grumbles under his breath. "She's nothing but trouble!"

He grabs a heavy crate and continues on his way.

"What are in the boxes?" I question.

"We ransacked the chandlery," Grimy answers.

"We had the currency, Grimy—"

"They weren't complying," is all Grimy says, shooting me a foul expression. "And I'm not about to tell you the other bullets I had to heal from—"

"Where?"

"Doesn't matter."

I look him over just as Luca calls out from the deck, "Had to push out a few bullets from his ass cheeks, Cap! Was a gnarly sight!"

"Shut up," Grimy growls as Luca erupts in laughter. The familiar sound of Briggs' dry heaving fills the air, relieving me once more. My men are okay.

I hold back a grin. "Better than having your neck broken, right, Grimes?"

He just shakes his head and walks up the ramp, muttering, "It was a literal pain in the fucking ass, James."

"We got everything!" Luca continues to shout down at me. "We're ready to get the fuck off Morda, Cap! And then where'll we go?"

As the tug of the tether tightens in my chest, I decide right then I know exactly where we're going.

Within the hour, we leave this cunt of an island behind us.

Boarding the Tempest again should have felt like a death sentence, but the moment James sets me down onto the waterlogged boards of the dock, a sense of peace washes over me. I shouldn't feel safe with the men who have held me captive, but I know James will never hurt me, despite his constant threats. I can feel it. Something between us has shifted, and he can continue to spew whatever hate he wants, but his words no longer align with the truth behind his eyes. He's given me a glimpse of the man hidden beneath. He *cares* even though it's the last thing he wants.

Following Grimy up the ramp that leads to the ship, I step aboard the Tempest and breathe a sigh of relief. Around me, I take in the sight of the crates Luca had brought up and dropped wherever space had allowed. There had to be twenty of them, and I wondered what was inside. Food? Supplies to fix the ship? Even though I know the Tempest is in rough shape and needs repair,

I'm grateful the men have no intention of sticking around this creepy-ass island to work on it.

I allow my eyes to flicker closed as the ocean breeze brushes against my skin. I'm surprised that the feeling that rushes through my system isn't animosity toward being back on this ship, but dare I say gratitude? Though my time in that goddess forsaken jungle was relatively short, it's more than I ever hope to experience ever again. The Tempest feels like a safe haven in comparison, though I know better than to let my guard down more than it already is.

I hardly take two more steps before James catches my wrist and pulls me toward him like I'm a human yo-yo.

"Hey–" I protest, but before I finish my thought, his fingers circle my hips, nails biting against my skin as he tosses me over his shoulder. My stomach slams into his shoulder bone, expelling the air from my lungs.

Like a caveman, he stomps down the corridor of the ship toward the captain's quarters. My head bobs with every step he takes, pushing us further down into the belly of the ship as he makes his way to his bedroom, only stopping long enough to kick the door in. It's cold in his quarters, the porthole left open for the sea breeze and mist from the fog to slink into the space.

My body slides down his front as he lowers me to my feet, and my breathing hitches as he dips his head closer to mine—our lips just a hair's breadth apart. Our chests touch, the gentle rise and fall mirror each other before he pulls the rug from beneath me, flattening his palm against my sternum, pushing against it with a small shove so I stumble back into his living space.

"James, what are you—" I start, but before the sentence can fully form, the door slams in my face.

Without hesitation, I reach for the knob, grasping it firmly and turning it so I can push the door back open, but he must be holding it, because there is no give. The metallic sound of a lock clicking tells me all I need to know as I slam my palms against the solid wood that stands between me and James.

Once again, I'm a prisoner.

"You can't do this again, James!" I scream through the door, still pounding against it. "I shouldn't have run, okay? But I won't try to escape this fucking ship again." *At least not right now.* "Let me out."

I'm met with silence, but I don't hear his footsteps retreat either. He's still on the other side of the door.

"Please."

A fierce burning radiates beneath my breastbone, and I know he's igniting the tether between us. It burns intensely, rippling with frustration and desire, and even a flicker of remorse.

"You have to earn our trust, Siren," James' deep voice floats through the door. I drop my head to the wood, annoyance pulsing through me.

I have no idea how the tether works or how we're able to push emotions through it, but I hope he can feel my irritation now.

"I never had it to begin with," I spit, my hand floating down to the knob again. I twist it hopefully, but it doesn't budge.

"You had more of it than you do now. Grimy and Luca would rather leave you here than have you fuck them over again. Even Briggs is hurting. As it stands, the only creature on this ship that doesn't want to throw you overboard is Rex."

"How long are you keeping me locked in here for?"

"Until I decide I'm not going to kill you for running." The weight of his boots reverberates against the floorboards as he retreats, and I can't help but to slam a fist against the door.

"Fuck!" I scream, letting my hands fall to my sides. Turning from the door, I step further into the room and scan my surroundings.

The lock wasn't necessary. I realize the damage I've done with Grimy and Luca. The skepticism they all felt about me was slowly drifting away with each passing day of me on the ship. I played the part—put in the work, earned my keep—did everything asked of me, and I knew they were cracking, but then I went and ran and blew their trust right out of the water.

It was because of my actions that Grimy got killed, though being that he's immortal, that's neither here nor there, except I clearly burned my bridge with the old man.

The only creature on this ship who doesn't hate my guts is Rex.

So now I'm starting over again from the ground up. But I'll earn their trust again—get back in their good graces. Someone is bound to open up to me sooner than later, and then what? If I earn their trust again, what becomes of me in the long run?

I move to the two buckets of water on the floor by the washroom and dip my hand into the water, finding it cold. Still, I pull the day-old towel from the bottom and wring it out before bringing it to my face to scrub the dirt and grime off. There isn't anything I can do about the dried mud that's caked in my hair, but I do the best I can to wash the rest of me.

Stripping from the oversized clothing, I run the cloth along my body and remove as much of the jungle as I can from my skin. The water swirls murky and brown from the dirt, and as I dip the washcloth back into the clean water bucket, I realize my upper legs are sticky and pull the waterlogged cloth to the apex of my thighs. The fabric is frigid against my skin, a sharp hiss whistles through my lips from both temperature and sensitivity as I run the cloth between my legs, removing all evidence of James.

I want nothing to do with him.

Us fucking in the jungle was nothing more than a moment of weakness. A silly momentary loss of sanity.

Then why does the memory of him pounding into you keep racing through your mind?

My clit throbs involuntarily as another pass of the cloth rubs against the sensitive bud, and I briefly think about fucking myself, simply so James isn't the last one who had.

What would Captain James Erickson do if he found out the siren he captured had sprawled out on his bed and finger fucking herself? Would he stand in the doorway and watch as I brought myself to orgasm? Would I toy with him and let his name fall from my lips as I came?

My fingers brush my center and dance along the

seam. I'm already so wet, my pussy contracting from the memory of James buried deep inside me and the thought of pleasuring myself on his bed.

A loud thump jolts me from my daydream, my fingers ripping away from the wetness they trailed against.

"I can feel your fucking desire all the way from the bow of the ship, Siren. Unless you're asking for me to come in there and fuck you until you can't breathe, I suggest you stop replaying the way you came all over my cock and find another way to make yourself useful."

Fucking asshole.

Shaking my head with disbelief, I hold up my hand and flip him off, even though he can't see it. How easy for him to discard me in here and forget all about me, knowing I'm going nowhere. Feeling closed in and defiant, I back up until my calves hit my bed, and a thought enters my mind: *I won't make this easy on him, either.* Smiling disdainfully, I climb onto the bed and kneel on his rumpled linens. I bring my right hand to my mouth, licking my middle finger before I bring it down to my clit and begin to rub slow, soft circles.

Nerve endings magnetize and my body awakens as I continue to play with my clit. Moans fall from my lips and already I find it difficult to stay seated on my knees, my body begging me to lie down and spread my legs wide.

Tossing my head back, the loose tendrils of my hair tickle against my spine, and I reach up and cup my breast. It feels heavy against my gentle touch, and as I skate my thumb against my nipple, it peaks. A low moan escapes my throat as I drift my fingers from my clit into the wetness that's pooling from my pussy.

A deep growl, followed by a loud smack, emanates from the other side of the wooden door separating me from James. "Aria, I swear to the gods, if you don't stop this goddamn game you're playing, I'm going to come in there and fuck you so hard, *again*, you won't be able to walk straight come morning."

Possessiveness cracks through the tether, and like a jolt of electricity, it surges down to my core. My fingers dip further into my pussy, and I begin finger fucking myself to a rhythm that alternates between riding my own hand and maneuvering my fingers to pinch my needy clit.

"Aria," James growls again. His voice is low and predatory, despite the door that blocks us. I imagine his dark eyes—likely nearly black from the mix of anger and arousal he's feeling. *I* can feel it through the tether.

I want him so badly.

As I continue to fuck my hand, my orgasm builds, sparks igniting like tiny fireworks through my body as I move my fingers to work my clit.

Fists pound against the door again, but all it does is urge me to rub myself faster, to get to the edge faster. Instead of his shouts, his eerily calm voice breaks through the silence. "Just remember I warned you, Aria."

His boot slams against the door and it flies open, revealing a very pissed off, very turned on James Erickson.

Even from across the room, his cock threatens to burst from his pants, the outline straining against the material—engorged and heavy. I let my eyes linger on it before I trail them up his body, and a surprised gasp escapes me. Gone are his tattoos and scarred skin. His split lip has healed, the jagged scar hidden beneath the princely mask, yet again. I take in every cord in his arms, every ripple of his muscles, accentuated by his smooth skin. His hair is trim—cut short on the sides, and a little longer on top, neatly combed—his beard short and groomed. My eyes meet his, and I see the surge of desire that pulsates through my body from the tether mirrored through his eyes. I never waver from the hold he has me in, still pleasuring myself as he watches me like he wants to kiss me.

Or possibly kill me.

It sends ripples of pleasure straight to my core.

James takes huge strides, covering the distance between us within a second. He reaches out and grabs my breast, roughly massaging it before moving his fingers up to my throat. His legs press against the side of his bed as he stands in front of me. I'm still kneeling, my hand buried between my legs as he presses his palm against my esophagus.

"I should fuck that pretty little mouth of yours and stifle those moans."

His suggestion draws out another throaty moan, and the sound spurs him on, his hold tightening around my throat.

"Fuck, Siren. What are you doing to me?" he murmurs, leaning forward to capture my lips. But before he can, I wrench my head to the side, arching my back slightly to put distance between us.

"No," I state firmly.

"No?"

"No," I repeat. "You don't get the privilege of fucking me again, James. Not my mouth, nor anywhere else."

"I'm not a good man, Siren. We've been over this. If I want something, I take it. We both know that includes you."

"You won't though," I argue, lifting my chin. "You'd have done it already. You may be a selfish prick, but you like your woman willing."

"Which you are."

"Not anymore. You lost my willingness by turning that key." I lift my head to gesture to the door, as if he doesn't know what fucking key I'm talking about.

"You think that matters to me? I'm a marauder, Aria. A fucking pirate. We take what we want—do what we want. And I told you, Siren. Your pleasure belongs to me. *You* belong to me." James puffs his chest out more, his firm muscles bumping into my bare breasts—the fabric rubbing against my sensitive nipples. I have to stifle a groan from the pleasure it delivers. "If you think for a second that I won't fuck this pussy—" He reaches down and cups my core, settling his middle finger just slightly inside me. "Or this mouth—" He growls and leans forward to trace the seam of my lips with his tongue. My lips part, willingly giving him access for more. "Then you *haven't* learned a fucking thing about me, have you?"

James doesn't give me the opportunity to answer before he withdraws, stepping away. He brings his middle finger to his mouth, licking away the taste of me, then he turns and walks back to the door.

"Where are you going?" My voice is shaky. I hate myself for letting him affect me this much. Why couldn't he have a small dick that he *didn't* know how to use properly? Why couldn't he have just simply fucked me in that jungle and not claimed me for himself? The intensity in which he did it sits heavy in my chest, making my heart squeeze.

James grips the doorknob, turning his face so his profile is on full display. "I told you, you're mine. You think I'd risk the crew seeing you like this, Siren? Dripping for your captain? As dear as they are to me, I'd still fucking kill them if they got in my way." He pushes the door closed, slamming it roughly. "Lay down on the bed, Aria. Spread your legs and let me see my pussy."

His pussy.

Fuck, his possessiveness makes me yearn.

I do as he demands and immediately drop to the bed, laying on my back. My feet press into the soft linens and I drop my knees and spread my legs wide. My fingertips flutter back to my clit on their own, and I draw lazy circles against the sensitive bud as I watch James undress.

He moves toward the buckets and skims his body with the washcloth, removing the layer of dirt still on his skin from the jungle. I almost want to tell him not to worry about it. That I like him dirty. Once finished, he stalks toward me, a dark hunger in his eyes that tells me I'm in for a long night with this man. My body clenches in anticipation. Stopping at the edge of the bed, he watches as I touch myself.

My orgasm crests under the weight of his gaze, and I

touch my clit harder, tracing circles around the sensitive spot between my legs, working it harder, then softer, than harder again. A rhythm builds and warmth blooms within my body. Tossing my head back, I bring my legs up so my feet sit flat on James' bed, feeling that I'm right on the edge of teetering into bliss. Soft moans tumble past my lips, and I picture him replacing my fingers, his tongue flicking against me. It's here, I'm so close, I'm—

I cry out from a mix of pleasure and pain. In one swift movement, James digs his fingers into my hips and drags me toward him, thrusting into me in one, punishing movement. *Fuck yes.* He fills me to the hilt before he pulls out almost completely.

"Harder," I gasp, pulling my legs around his waist. My hands move to his shoulders and I dig my nails into his skin. "Fuck me harder."

A gush of desire pools in my core, making it easier for James to slam into me again. He feels so fucking good, and it's still not enough—I have a feeling it might never be enough.

He catches my bottom lip between his teeth, clamping down hard before flicking his tongue against where he's just broken skin. "'*You don't get the privilege of fucking me again, James,*'" he mocks. "Such big words for a woman whose body blooms for me like a flower. Can you hear how wet you are for me, Siren? *Feel* how easily my cock slides through this perfect pussy?"

All I can do is moan at his words. He's right. My being fucking blossoms for him. He owns my body, and with all the time I've spent fighting against this, I want nothing more than to just finally give in.

I meant what I said in the jungle. *I'm his.*

It was inevitable—written in the stars. My fate was sealed long before the night of the shift.

I was destined to be his.

His lips hover above mine, brushing inadvertently with every movement. Our skin slaps together, the harsh sound filling the room. My skin feels like it's on fire, hypersensitive to every place he's touching. He hovers over me, using his forearms to hold himself up, but the space between us is minimal, and my body begs to close even that small distance.

The moon shimmers through the porthole, casting a slight glow throughout the space—enough that allows me to see his unmarred, tattooed skin. I know what lies beneath the smooth exterior when the magic falls, and I brush my fingers over the places where the scars lay hidden. Every nerve ending in my body craves to be close to him, more than just proximity.

"We shouldn't do this, should we?" I groan as he circles his hips, pushing impossibly deep within me. Stars explode everywhere, the pleasure so fucking intense, I'm almost lost to the feeling.

"We shouldn't," he grits out as he pushes up onto his palms and angles his head down. Torturously slow, he pulls out of me, leaving only his engorged tip inside before pressing halfway in, then withdrawing again.

"It's going to end so badly."

"Probably."

"James."

He stares at the space where our bodies connect,

watching himself as he fills me. "Do you want me to stop?"

"No."

He looks at me now, eyes heavy as his body shudders with the urge to move. "Then what do you want, Aria?"

I watch him for a moment, realizing quickly that he's been taking it easy on me. "Are you being gentle with me, Captain?"

There's no humor in him. "Stop talking in circles, Aria, just tell me what you want."

"How about letting go?"

"Which means what?"

I bring my head up and run my tongue along his lips. "Fuck me *harder*, James."

His eyes blaze as his gaze connects with mine. He slams into me with the full weight of his body, picking up his pace now. The pressure threatens to rip me in half before pleasure radiates through me, eliciting a moan from my lips. "Fuck yeah, Siren, take every inch of me. Let me take what's mine."

James brings his hand between us and pinches my clit, rolling it between two fingers. My eyes flutter back into my head as he rubs it in time with his thrusts. Incoherent slurs and curses pour from my lips and I thrust my hips forward to encourage his movements.

"You're mine, Aria. You'll never run again."

There's a guttural edge in his tone, a pain he mistakenly lets slip. My heart clenches in response, the guilt mixing brutally with the pleasure. He alternates his touch between soft and rough, his fingers never continuing the same pattern and driving me absolutely wild.

"Say it, Siren."

His fingers pinch my clit again roughly, but his thrusts slow as he begins his deliberately slow movements, now showing extra attention to the spot that pushes me toward my climax the fastest.

"Say what?"

"That—" James slams back into me, rocking his hips when he's deep inside. "You'll never leave me."

His words cause me to freeze, and I open my heavy eyelids to find him staring down at me.

James stays inside me unmoving, waiting for my response. My mind and my heart are at war with one another, logic fighting tooth and nail to stay relevant, as my heart trumps through all the doubt.

Before I realize what's happening—without James ever pulling out of me—he shifts me so I am above him, straddling him as he sits on the bed. From this position, we're eye to eye and, if it's even possible, more connected physically than before. I moan again, the new angle feeling tantalizingly erotic as our bodies press against each other. His hands grip my hips tightly, holding me firm, but I don't miss the way his thumb brushes lazily against my skin.

"Aria, when you ran, it gutted me. I'm not a man who shares, or gets attached, or *cares* about anyone beyond the very few members of my crew, but you running... don't fucking run from me again, Siren. I won't survive it."

My hips rock against him, seeking the friction his body offers. "You're immortal," I respond lamely, my mind still reeling. This is a whole new side to James—a side that I can't help but swoon over. But there's still that part of me that's hesitant. It's diminishing, but still there. So many 'what-if's' and red flags.

But one of my favorite colors is pink, and that's just a lightened shade of red, right?

This time it's him who seeks pleasure and his hips pulsate upward. I bare down, my pussy clenching around his cock that's seated to the hilt, and I move my hands to cup his face, bringing my lips against his.

He catches them, kissing me with fiery passion, so different from all the kisses we've shared before. "Losing you forever would be the death of me, immortal or not."

"Prove it," I whisper, my own words jarring as I hear them aloud. What is it exactly what I want from him? A truce? Admission of lust? A declaration of love?

Love?

No.

Hate.

Right?

The line between hate and love has blurred to the point of being gone completely.

Sucking in a sharp breath, I flinch from my own thoughts and pull my head backward, drawing space between our faces. James' eyes soften and search mine. Unspoken questions race between us. The air feels thick and I struggle to swallow down the lump that's formed in my throat.

I wait for the pushback—the snide comment that surely sits on the tip of James' tongue—but it doesn't come. Instead, his eyes narrow slightly as if he's also at war with himself, struggling to piece together what exactly is happening between us at this moment.

Because it feels like *something*.

It feels raw and real, and utterly terrifying. It feels like I just put a piece of my heart on a shiny little platter and offered it to him, simply by uttering the words *'prove it'*.

Tears prick the backs of my eyes and I'm still frozen in place, speared on James' lap with his cock still inside me. My brain screams for me to scramble off him—to flee from this situation—and that seems to be my knee-jerk reaction to everything, isn't it? To run? But I don't think I want to run again.

James has me pinned in his gaze and what I don't expect is the tenderness behind his eyes, or the way his head slowly moves toward mine and bridges the gap between us.

He presses his lips against mine, his tongue tracing against the seam for access. Once I grant it, our tongues connect and dance, exploring with a gentleness I wasn't aware he possessed. Leaving one hand on my hip, he brings the other to cup the base of my head, his fingers weaving through the brightly colored strands of my hair as he kisses me with abandon, breaking only when we're both breathless and practically gasping for air.

"Let me try," he whispers, and before I can say anything in response, his hips thrust upward and cause me to cry out.

Flipping me onto my back again, James' fingers find my clit, rubbing it with just the right amount of pressure that makes my hands grip the bed linens. I cry out again, not caring who hears—not like there's many of us on this ship anyway. He fucks me so hard and fast, I see those stars explode before my eyes. Bearing down, my walls clench around him as he expertly massages my clit, pushing me higher and higher. I know I'm moments away from soaring, and there's nothing more I want than to come with his cock inside me.

"You're the fucking North Star, Aria. The only light in the night sky guiding me through my darkness."

Me.

Not my body.

Not my pussy.

Me.

My vision blurs as I squeeze my eyes tight, my entire body on overdrive, including my mind. I am so close. Warm tingles radiate throughout my body. I lift my hips, matching him thrust for thrust. "*Please*, James. I'm so... *so* close."

As my walls clench around him again, James growls low. "Come, my siren. Drench my cock and prove to *me* you're mine."

It's as if his words possess magic because I come on his command, screaming his name as my hands fly to the back of his head, pulling him down into a sloppy kiss that's all teeth and tongue. James matches my energy and roars through his own release, slamming into me relentlessly as we both chase our highs.

I lose all control of my body, and just like in my dream, the feeling of free falling overtakes me, but this time, instead of falling through the darkness, I can feel myself falling in love.

CHAPTER 43

"How long have you been immortal?"

Her question comes at me a few hours later, after she finished riding my face. *Again*. When I turn my head to look at her, a smile touches my lips. Aria's hair is a mess, all just-fucked and flowing around her shoulders. I love the creamy tone of her skin. Love the stark difference against my bronzed skin when I run my hands down her body. Like I have so many times tonight, and like I plan to do for the rest of eternity.

How quickly the tables can turn. Mere hours ago I burned hot with anger at the siren who was crawling under my skin, and now... Now I find her touch soothing, like it's a cooling balm to a burning wound.

This is a problem.

Because I didn't even know I was hurting in this way until now. And now it feels like I've found everything I didn't realize I was missing.

On her elbow, her hand is pressed against her face as she looks at me, waiting for an answer.

I look away from her, staring at the ceiling as I answer in a guarded tone, "A while."

She waits for more. I feel her staring at me intently now, but I don't meet her gaze. I *want* to tell her more; but I've never spoken about it to anyone beyond Grimy.

Telling her more might mean revealing the bitter scorn I left behind.

A scorn I must revisit.

"Do you not trust me?" she prods. "Even after we've exchanged bodily fluids *multiple* times—"

"It's not that," I return swiftly, frowning as my movements slow. "Grimy and I...and Rex...it's been the three of us, you understand? The three of us...for so long. They've been my only form of everlasting, Aria... Beyond that, everything else is temporary."

I expect her to take that the wrong way. To seethe and question whether she's temporary, but Aria doesn't do that. She just watches me closely, her eyes still warm and filled with curiosity.

"Tell me about Rex then," she states, a teasing smile forming on her lips. "Please don't say he's only ever been on the high seas with you, never having even rutted—"

"You are a dirty girl."

"I just want to know my boy lived a life of adventure."

A smirk pulls at my lips as I look down at her now. "Your boy?"

She chews her bottom lip, cheeks growing red. "Rex is my buddy now, James. We're pretty tight."

"He doesn't know you ran, that's why."

"Probably does, actually, probably commends me for it—"

I push her back, forcing her off her elbow and flat against the mattress. I wrap my hand around her throat, my smile growing as she runs her tongue along her bottom lip, making this soft moaning sound at my dominant touch. "Rex would have wondered where you went," I say lightly, though my words are serious. "He has a master...but he sought for a mistress of the ship, too."

"Got a damsel in distress instead," she replies, also lightly, but her words are a reflection of how she feels; when she ran, she was vulnerable, at the mercy of whomever would have caught her. Not the all-powerful siren she was in her other form. This form frightens her, and that makes me wonder...

"When I caught you, I assumed you lived a privileged life, but I'm wrong. The tough act is all a ruse. You were sheltered before the transformation, weren't you?"

Her amusement slowly fades, and the silence stretches as she attempts to form an answer. "Because of what I am, he always needed to know where I was."

"Who?"

Her lips turn down. "My father."

"With that dirty mouth, he was failing, wasn't he?"

She looks at me dryly. "I may have been sheltered, but I'm a woman, and I know what I want and what I like."

"So you managed to sneak away from your old man and get fucked?"

"Have fun," she corrects, rolling her eyes.

I try not to feel disdain over the fact that others have

touched her, but my jaw clenches just the same. I feel my grip along her throat tighten as I strain out, "How much fun are we talking, Aria?"

She likes to press my buttons, so I'm not sure why I'm prodding. Sick fascination. The dreaded part of me feels like just another fucking number to her. But Aria's not wrathful in her response. Her tone is gentle. "Not much, James, and even then...well, no one compares to you, do they?"

Good answer—*wise* answer.

I let go of her throat and run my thumb down the side of her face, brushing away the strands of hair. Why does she have to be so fucking beautiful?

I know I've been looking for her.

For my One.

But the Goddess has a sick sense of humor delivering everything I've ever wanted...in a *siren*. And now I don't know what to believe anymore. The slaughter of my kind at the hands of hers—and yet I can't loathe her, not a single inch, nor even a strand of hair.

Yes, the Goddess has a sick humor.

She's mortal, my mind whispers. *She will come and go, James. This is not everlasting.*

The thought makes me breathless.

Aria's eyes drift closed as I touch her, and it's a break from her gaze, aiding me with enough courage to admit, "I've been alone, Aria...much too long. I almost forgot what pleasure felt like. You ask me how long I've been this way...I don't even know. My aging progressed slower once I grew from a boy to a man, ceasing completely around my thirty-fifth year. Somewhere along the way, time slipped. Decades, maybe?"

It's a black and white admission.

I can't remember a face before hers. Not in my arms. Just decades of the sea and the cold and the numbing despair that comes with the lack of decay gained from aging. It pulls the life out of you, much like death does. I see it in Grimy, too. The will is gone. The search for meaning depleted. He longs for death while I wonder if I've ever felt alive at all.

It's cruel to feel this alive knowing it's through the hands of a mortal creature. Our intimate moments are healing me, though I know in the long run, when she's dust in the wind, they'll aid only in my destruction.

I need to break this curse.

At least Rex is trudging along amiably. Aria sparked a chord in him, brought him back to life, like he's a puppy again in an aged body, but he doesn't seem to mind.

I can hear him now, at the door, scratching at it. A whimper sounds, and I shake my head, tossing my legs over the bed and standing up straight. "Your biggest fan seems to have heard you."

I begin to pull on clothing, dressing in my usual trousers and tunic, strapping my belt through the loops of my pants to secure the holster for my pistol. It's early morning now—the sun is ready to rise, and there's much to do.

Aria's smile is small as she watches me, but the smug look is impossible to ignore. "What'll you be doing?"

"We'll be closing in on the Straits of Calla in a week's time, depending on the weather."

She gives me a blank stare.

"It's a harbor city."

Now she's uneasy. "Not this again."

"Calla is tame, Aria. There's governance there. We need to abide by the rules, and I need to find a crew... and sails... and supplies——"

"Goddess, I fucked-up your ship..." she groans before refocusing on me. "Is Calla the reason you've hidden your true self?"

I smirk as she drags her gaze down the portions of my visible, smooth, unmarred skin. "Can't be a dignified captain sporting a split lip, can I?"

She shoots me a perplexing look, like she can't believe my words. "Dignified?" she deadpans.

I slide into my boots. "I was a prince once upon a time, Aria," I quip now. That foreign, playful feeling is back. Leaning down, I rest my fists on the mattress, caging her body as I catch her lips in a heated kiss. Her lips instantly part, and I meet her tongue with mine. She hums against my mouth, deepening the kiss as she reaches up to slide her fingers through my hair, tugging on it sharply as I slide my tongue along hers.

The temptation to strip from my clothes and take her on all fours hits me fiercely, and I quickly realize that's her desire pushing through the tether, planting that tantalizing image into my mind.

It takes great strength to break the kiss, and when I do, I stride from the room without looking back, knowing if I do, I'll never leave.

Aria lets out a squeal as Rex barrels through the door and leaps onto the bed, attacking her face in wet, sandpaper kisses. I smile, overwhelmed by the sense of contentment that settles deep in my chest.

I could get used to this.

CHAPTER 44

Aria

It takes a lot of bravery to leave the room.

For most of the morning, I've hidden out in James' room, planting more images of him fucking me in his head, hoping he might just come and take me on all fours.

I was successful.

Just once.

He practically kicked the door down, and I didn't even get a chance to sputter a single word to him when he simply threw me on my hands and knees and took me on the edge of the bed. It was a fast and hard fuck. There was nothing gentle in the way he gripped my hips and drove himself into me.

"There'll be nothing gentle about this, Aria," he strained out, landing a smack on my ass that nearly sent me over the edge. He didn't pleasure me for most of it, either, which just left my pussy feeling swollen as my orgasm built. He used me like I was a fucking sex doll to empty his load into—and fuck me, it was everything I didn't know I needed and more.

When he came, that deep growl spilling from his lips, I felt his cock jerk within me, and then I felt his fingers brush along my folds, rubbing at my clit once, twice—

I came so hard, moaning loudly into his pillow, feeling like I might finally catch a break and not need him anymore. He slapped my ass again, sharper this time, as he pulled out of me, growling, "Careful what you wish for, Little Mermaid."

But when he left, the desire simply returned, the want to fuck and be used growing once more from a spark to a flame to a roaring fucking inferno.

This is a problem.

And I think it's the tether's fault. I'm not feeling the desire of one person, but two. I'm not seeing images of just what I want to do to him, I'm seeing what he wants to do to me, too.

And what a vile, depraved man my captain is.

And what a sick, foolish woman I am for loving it.

HUNGER DRIVES me out of my room. I tiptoe across one quarter to the next, down the long narrow hallways and to the kitchen. Rex follows me, panting up a storm. Every stop I make has him tilting his head up at me, his questioning eyes wondering, "What the hell are you doing?" I'm trying not to bump into anyone, I want to say, but instead, I just give him a half-hearted smile as I risk another step into the kitchen.

It's empty.

Blowing out a relieved breath, I forage for food. There are boxes on the counter, the contents not put away yet. Maybe I could do that myself? Go back to being part of the crew like nothing happened? Like I didn't run with absolutely no plan in mind?

I nibble on some cheese and nuts, and then I begin to sort through everything. I stop to tie my hair back, and then I'm kneeling, opening up drawers and cupboards, emptying everything inside. From flour to sugar to spices and herbs. There's some bread, a lot of cheese, and lots and lots of nuts and almonds. I take another bite out of those. In another box, I'm shocked to find bottles of alcohol. Rum and wine and other bottles with unrecognizable language sprawled on them.

Morda may have been a dump, but fuck, they had a lot of booze.

I not only put everything away, but I develop a system. Every cupboard is sorted with specific essentials, so we're not digging everything up looking for something. Once I'm done, I pull out the flour and sugar. Without eggs or milk, I can't do an awful lot, but I remember growing up how creative my sisters and I would get with our baking skills thanks to an absent father who worked more than he fathered. Luckily for me, we still have butter from before I'd attacked the ship, so I pull that out, too, and get to making powder biscuits.

A way to a man's heart is through his stomach, right?

I'll feed these seamen and have them smiling at me like they used to in no time.

WHEN THEY FIND ME, they don't speak for a while. Trays of powder biscuits line the counter, cooling. The boxes I've emptied are stacked neatly beside the hallway. My bun has come undone, my cheeks are flaming hot from constantly checking on the oven, and I'm sweaty. I spin around at the sound of their footsteps. Stopping outside the kitchen is Luca and Briggs.

I smile brightly, but it's so fake, I must look scary. "Hungry, fellas?"

Luca gives me a filthy look. "It's gonna take more than some fucking biscuits to win us over, Siren."

Briggs scoffs, tagging along with Luca. "Yeah, and I want my fucking comb back, *Siren*."

I watch as they move to the trays of biscuits and take giant handfuls of them. Luca eats loudly, demolishing them two at a time as he walks into the living quarters and collapses down on the settee. I follow after them, wringing my hands with the rag. "Awful fucking biscuits, give me more. And I want rum," Luca declares. "And what the fuck is for dinner?"

Briggs nods and drops down next to him, running a hand through his blond locks. "I want sustenance, also! More of those disgusting biscuits!"

I fight the dry look on my face. They're really playing it up, but I understood it was going to be like this. I keep the pleasant smile plastered on my face. "I'm working on it! Stew and buttered bread sound good?"

"Well, make it first and I'll decide!" Luca does his best to glare at me. "And rum. Lots and lots of rum!"

I do exactly that.

Dinner is stew, cheese, and bread. All the mugs have been washed and the bottles of rum are out. The night is lively on the boat. Everyone's happy to be gaining distance from Morda. I'm mostly ignored, except for when they want a refill. Luca or Briggs will extend their arm out, cups in hand, and I dutifully refill.

"You're not a slave," growls James from behind me. He takes one scan across the room, at the biscuits and the food. His nostrils flare as his eyes coolly regard me. "I don't want you at their beck and call, Aria."

The men don't hear him—they're too busy playing their poker rounds. I squeeze his arm, giving him a soft smile. "I know, but I did everyone dirty. This is the only way I know how to apologize."

"Then just apologize," he simply states. "Don't grovel. My woman does not grovel, do you understand?"

I don't know how to respond to that as he takes a step around me and serves himself dinner. "Is Grimy joining?" I ask.

He grunts. "He's steering the ship. I'll have Briggs up on deck as a second eye."

"He's drunk." I gesture to Briggs as he sloppily takes another gulp. "I can be up there, you know. Just tell me what I need to do."

James turns his head to me, eyeing me for several moments. "You're sure?"

I nod, eagerly. "I am."

He sends me up shortly after. I carry a tray of food for Grimy. There's only one lantern lit in the pilothouse when I enter the room. Grimy stands there, peering out, his hand on the steering wheel as he makes calculated turns. He doesn't speak to me as I set the tray down on a foldout table near to him.

"James sent me to help," I start, clasping my hands nervously. Of all the men, separate from James, I feel most hurt about what I did to him.

Grimy isn't cruel to me, but his lips are turned down into a frown as he says, "I just checked for obstructions along this trail. I might need you back up on deck for another overview."

"I can do that."

He still keeps his eyes out when he remarks in a gruff voice, "Do not run again, Aria. Not from him."

I fidget, the weight of guilt growing worse. "I won't."

"I can withstand dying—I've done it too many times to count—but watching him die...every time it happens, the pain of it is worse." His throat bobs as his face breaks with emotion. "That boy is all I have—not my flesh and blood, but he is my boy." His eyes finally flash to mine, shining with pain. "Every time they hurt him, I die a little more inside."

My lips tremble as my eyes prick with tears. "I am so sorry, Grimy."

"I don't want you to be sorry, Aria. I need you to be certain that he is what you want, because if there is still any flicker of doubt in you, you must let me know at once. If escape is what you seek, I can grant it for you. I can let you go and he would never suspect it, but I'd rather you tell me now than later."

"Why would you want to help me, Grimy?"

A small smile graces his lips before he pushes it back down. "Love is scary. The unreciprocated love can leave a woman feeling scorned and bitter. That's a troubling sort of life. It's one that leads to consequence." He sighs deeply. "I knew love once. Every man deserves to experience the true unconditional love of a woman." His voice wobbles as he adds, "He still has a piece of him held back. A piece he is withholding should you hurt him. If he gives that to you...you don't know the depths of his darkness. He would destroy himself over and over again, hoping each time might be the last."

He says it with such certainty my brows furrow. "He's done it before."

Grimy exhales shakily. "Immortality is reckless."

"*He* was reckless."

He nods once. "How do you think he got all those scars?"

My heart climbs up my throat. "Because he wanted to die?"

"He lost all purpose a long time ago, I don't know when it happened, but it fled from him the moment he realized his kingdom was lost forever, and he would never share a life with a woman, never love, never form everlasting attachments. That does something to a man, Aria. It makes them ruthless, it makes them vacant, it makes them wander these seas with revenge on their mind."

"Revenge at what?"

"At the world. At the monsters in the water, at the depraved villains we cross paths with on the marauder's trail. When you surfaced, he'd just pillaged all that Gala Green from a decrepit shore town. He was going to take over the black market, proclaim himself the dark king of the underpass."

"Underpass?"

"It's the Bridge of Exchange. That's where we sell our product and find buyers."

"In other words, the black market."

"Yes, but they don't like to call it that."

"Is that still his intention?"

Grimy sighs, studying me now. "If I told you it might be, would you still stay?"

I shuffle from foot to foot, feeling almost ashamed when I admit, "Yes."

"Why?"

"There are worse evils than him. Better he be the king of the underpass than a more vile man who enjoys hurting others."

Now he tilts his head to the side, curiously. "James does not enjoy hurting people?"

I raise a brow. He's testing me. "Absolutely not. And there are men that do—that would have caught me and tortured me and done what they wanted to my body. James may be ruthless, he may be scary, and he may kill as a last or even first resort, but he's not evil."

Grimy's face splits with warmth. He stares at me differently now, almost relieved. With a long breath, he nods at me. "Then you see him—truly see him."

"I do."

"Then you must be the one."

"The one?"

His eyes flash to mine. "The one who plagues his nightmares. His other half."

For a couple days, I haven't stopped thinking about what Grimy told me, but I don't let James immediately know. I'm still caught up in our love spell.

The man is insatiable.

I'm dick drunk and lost in a haze.

The hours of my day are a blur. I do my tasks, helping in any way I physically can. I make sure the men are fed and happy. But my core is constantly throbbing, the yearning so great, sometimes I can hardly function.

James hears my pleas. He feels it deeply. And no matter how busy he gets, he doesn't leave me hanging. Like now, with my face pressed against the wall of the supply room and my hands held behind my back in the large grip of his own. I can hardly keep upright as he fucks me ruthlessly, with the vigor I need, with the growls in the air and the dirty words he sputters into them.

He tells me this is how I like it—this is how it'll always be.

And I'm lost to the pleasure, eyes rolling to the back of my head as I gasp for breath, taking his dirty thrusts from behind me. I can't count the amount of orgasms this man has given me. Or how sneaky he's delivered them. Last night, he cornered me in the kitchen in the dead of night and fucked me against the counter, and I had to do everything in my power not to cry out. He swallowed my sounds with his mouth, filling me to the brim with his cum.

Just like now.

His hands squeeze tighter around both of my own as he reaches his climax, but by then I'm already spent, my face sweaty, my breaths hot and heavy. Our connection sizzles, tightening within me, until I can no longer tell where it begins and ends.

James doesn't leave me straightaway. He brings my back into his chest and holds me tightly, kissing up my neck, grazing his teeth along my earlobe. "Aria..." He says my name with so much emotion, I shut my eyes to savor it.

Finally letting me go, he helps me back into my clothes, shaking his head at the latest sweater I've raided. "Next place we go, I'm stocking your closet right up."

I just smile, on a high as he gives me my silly shoe-string so I can tie my hair back up. "I don't want anything too nice."

"Tough. It'll be lingerie and dresses and sexy midriffs and tiny little shorts—"

"Midriffs and tiny shorts? You forget I'm from Norborne, James. We don't dress like Avangail women."

He smiles back, and because of his perfect facade,

even his teeth are ridiculously straight and white. I'm not sure I'm jamming with this version of my man—I'd grown used to the rough exterior, the canvas of the man whose body told a story—and I nearly have a heart attack at that thought. *My man.* Goddess, I'm in deep. The thought sends my heart pounding.

But that's what he is, isn't he? We'd quickly grown to that point—or maybe not quickly at all, depending on how you look at things. Week after week spent at sea has messed with my perception of time, but I can feel in the depths of my soul that with every day that passed and continues to pass, we have grown closer, and slowly, the gap between hate and love bridged.

Though the word has not been spoken by either of us, it's what it feels like.

Undeniable, irresistible, unimaginable love. I can feel it in the way the tether burns, whether together or apart. There's a constant stream of emotions that sparks through it from both James and I.

Lust.

Happiness.

Desperation.

Enchantment.

Longing.

Excitement.

It's endless, really, and my heart soars. It feels like it beats for him, and in a way, it does. I was fated to love him. I can feel that deep down in my bones.

James Erickson, my enemy, has turned out to be my greatest love.

"You're not in Hicksville Norborne, nor in prissy

Avangail, Aria," he breaks my thoughts, still going on about my future wardrobe. "You're on the Black Sea, which means you will dress however the fuck your heart desires."

"And what if my heart desires your sweaters? They seem to suit me, no?"

"Then I will find ten thousand more and bring them to you." He bends down to deliver another chaste kiss. "I've got nightshift later if you want to join me."

I tap my lip, thinking. "I'll check my calendar, Captain."

He makes a deep noise at the back of his throat. "Fucking love when you call me that, Little Mermaid. Better hear you screaming it next time I fuck you."

"So within the hour, then."

He lets out a deep laugh as he buckles his trousers. "Precisely. Let's try to aim for tonight, though. I need to recover, woman. You're driving me wild."

"It's a date, Captain."

Aria

By afternoon, we've anchored next to a sad looking island, as dead as the one we caught all the fish at. The men hung lanterns along the ship to keep us lit in case of passersby, or worse, marauders like the ones that boarded us. It's why whoever is at watch must carry a weapon at all costs.

No one wants a repeat.

The ship is quiet when I step out of my room, freshly washed. I've let my hair down in wet waves. Everyone's crashed by the looks of it—all those long days and late nights, I can see a stark difference in the ship, and I imagine when it's back in good repair, it will look like a ship James will be proud of commandeering.

I find James in the pilothouse, scribbling notes down in that notebook I've seen in his room. He's lost in thought, unaware of my presence. For a moment, I lean against the large window of the pilothouse, admiring him. His hair is wet from the rain, his rain jacket dripping along the floor.

"What do you write in there?" I ask quietly, stirring him from his thoughts.

He turns his head to look at me, a soft smile on his face. He doesn't look surprised by my presence—maybe he knew I was here all along.

"Thoughts," he responds.

"Those pages are worn."

"Yeah."

"You erase what you've written."

"Over and over again."

I think about what I read a time or two. His nightmares. I think about what Grimy said to me the other night.

"What's on your mind?" he wonders, aware of my curiosities. "Voice them, Aria."

I'm a little fearful to ask. Thinking, I run a finger along my lip. "I read some of those passages."

He doesn't look bothered. "I'm aware."

"I also talked to Grimy…"

James continues to stare, waiting.

"He tells me you've dreamed of a siren. In the jungle…you mentioned it, too, but honestly, I was a little distracted." Thank the Goddess for the dim light. My cheeks are burning as I look momentarily down at the floor, asking, "Was it me?"

"Yes," he answers openly.

"I was in your *nightmares*, James?" My voice is growing small as I fight to hide my dread.

"You're bothered."

"It's not the most romantic thing I've ever heard."

He smiles slowly. "It didn't start off that way."

I watch him closely. "Can you tell me about them?"

He rests the pencil down and slowly closes the journal. Looking down at the cover, he traces the dreamy swirls on the front. "They didn't happen very often. Every once in a while I'd find myself in a dream where I'm wandering the ship, and I can feel a woman in the waters, watching me. She has colorful hair, and her eyes are so blue, they glow in the dead of night under a full moon."

"Were you alone?"

"Sometimes. Sometimes I'm so alone, I feel cold and fearful. Other times, I watch everyone I know—everyone I've ever met and cared for—die in front of me." He frowns, and I can feel his pain. "I'd chase after this woman in the water, thinking at first she needed to be saved. I became obsessed with her. I'd wake up from the dreams, and all I wanted to do was go back to sleep and see her again." He shuts his eyes, brows furrowing as he thinks. "Then they started to change. I'd see her, and I'd know she was following me, but then she'd start to sing, and it was the power of the lure that made me realize she was a siren. Still, I didn't consider her wicked. I wanted to go to her. I...felt like she was as lonely as me." He opens his eyes again to look at me. "I thought this woman was real. She *felt* real. When I woke up, Aria, it was like she must have woken up too, in that exact moment, thinking she must have had a dream of me, too.

"As time went on, the dreams changed. I'd get close to her, but I'd never get close enough. Until once I did, and that's when it happened. She shifted in my dream, turned into a giant monstrous looking creature, and in the midst of all that, I'd hear a clock ticking in my ears. Tick-tock. Tick-tock. Over and over again." He shudders, like he can physically feel it. "Grimy believed it was because I was getting closer to her, and in time, I would find her. The woman in my dream. He said it had to be some part of the curse somehow. That it was taunting me—showing me my other half, who I'd never be able to claim as mine in this form. But after so long, when you've lived out here in this vacuum of loneliness, you start to believe in nothing at all... Until you came along. With your colorful hair and glowing blue eyes. A siren, no less."

I've barely moved, enraptured by his words. I don't know what to say. He watches me, eyeing my reaction slowly before he sighs, shaking his head. "I'm no good for you like this, Aria. Not in this way. I need this curse broken, Little Fish. It's the only way for us to work."

"Why?" I ask.

"Because I can't be in a world without you."

I understand what he's saying. "I'll age, you mean. You don't want me getting wrinkly on you—"

"Aria," he says sharply at my attempt at humor.

I smile regardless. "I'm not going anywhere, James, no matter what happens. Even if it means I grow old alongside you—I don't care. So long as I get to spend my days out here in the ocean with you, so long as I can shift and enjoy my true nature those few days a year—that's all that matters to me."

"But my darkness—"

"Stop fighting your darkness," I cut in. "It's why you're scared of yourself. You hold back, James. For too long, you've put on that face, charmed everyone, manipulated and pillaged, and in the midst of it you fought not to embrace your curse."

Now his eyes widen. "*Embrace* my curse?"

"Maybe it's not so bad."

"How so?"

I shrug weakly. "It brought us together, didn't it?"

He just looks at me, dumbfounded. Like I told him a truth he'd never known before. "You might leave," he says in a whisper. "I'm destined to be alone—"

"What does the tether say?"

He goes quiet, and for emphasis, I send a burst of emotion down the line. In doing so, I shut my eyes, allowing my vulnerabilities to be splayed wide open for him to *feel*. It's the only way, I realize, for him to know the truth. To feel that I'm here, that I am falling madly, deeply in love with him.

My cursed Captain.

I open my eyes to look at him. He's gone quiet, feeling everything, and for once his eyes don't look so heavy, nor as dark.

"Tell me about your shift. About how you have legs." I'm surprised it's taken him this long to ask.

I shrug from where I still lean against the window. "We've adapted. You're not the only one whose lineage knows witches, James. The sirens had to make a choice —live a life always being hunted for our fins, or survive. What better way to survive than to hide amongst the very creatures who want you dead?"

"But you still shift."

"Of course we do. Being in the water is our nature."

"But you nearly drowned..." His brows crease together, confused.

"Because my father never taught me to swim," I tell him honestly. "He wanted to keep me and my sisters far away from the water. You saw what happens when we're in it. We attract the sea life."

I watch as the pieces click together in his mind. "And what easier way to reveal your identity than to witness sea creatures flock to you."

"Exactly."

"Come out with me," he says gently, extending his hand out for me to take.

I've been pressed into the corner this entire time, fearful of letting myself fall in. But he's felt every emotion I bared to him through our connection, and in return, I feel the warmth of his radiating back. I bridge the gap between us and take his large hand. He opens the door and leads me to the upper deck.

"Next time we're underway, I can help. Grimy taught me what to watch out for," I say from behind him.

"A fool's errand," he responds, amused. "There are no obstructions in the Black Sea. The sea beasts consume everything in sight."

I frown, reflecting on how Grimy sent me up and down the deck, looking over the handrails to make sure the seas were open. I felt so fucking special when he complimented me, and now I feel stupid.

"Was he laughing at me?" I ask.

James chuckles. "On the contrary, Aria, he has a sweet spot for you. I think he was trying to welcome you in, make you feel like you're part of the crew."

I bloom at the thought. Despite the havoc I've caused, I sense I've developed a relationship with the men around me.

James stops us at the handrail. "I didn't notice until recently that whenever we anchor, you get visitors, Siren."

Confused, I follow his line of sight. Under the starry night, I peer down into the black waters. The thing with the Black Sea is light never reflects off it. It just swallows it whole, and yet...my eyes narrow as I catch the green and blue glow just beneath the surface of the water. The bioluminescent sea life ranges in size. Some are small, others large. Few have tentacle looking structures, like a glowing octopus, but with more arms. As I peer down, the glow becomes more fierce, like they know I'm observing them. My heart jumps at the tangible warmth they radiate toward me.

James eyes me closely. "They never sensed you before, Aria. Why now?"

I'm lost for words, shrugging. "I don't know. Us sirens make sure to stay away from the water when we've shifted back to human form. But I think...being here, in the ocean...I've been more in touch with my nature. It's why it made killing those fish so hard for me."

As if hearing me, half the lights in the water go out, disappearing back into the ocean in the blink of an eye.

James chuckles. "I don't think they liked knowing that."

My cheeks flame as a laugh bubbles up my throat. "I don't regret feeding Grimy and Rex."

"And Briggs?"

"He does my hair, so no."

"How about Luca?"

"So long as he wears pants, I'm happy to go fishing if it means he doesn't go hungry."

"What about me?"

I twist away from the handrail and look up at James, flashing him a flirty smile. "Haven't I fed you enough, Captain?"

He makes a noise in the back of his throat as he takes a step toward me. "Never enough. In fact, I'm hungry now."

I step away from him, blood pumping through my veins harder as I say innocently, "Now, James, don't you know gluttony is a sin?"

He continues to follow me slowly as I move away, approaching the center of the deck. With the holes mostly patched and the space mostly cleared, there's a lot of space I'm able to put between us.

"I'll happily serve whatever punishment is necessary for these sins," he tells me, coming to a stop. His look is absolutely predatory as I, too, come to a stop. "I'm a greedy man, selfish too–"

"You have to be those things if you're the king of the underpass," I cut in.

Now he smiles wickedly. "Grimy's not held back."

"He doesn't need to. Neither do you." But now I tap my chin thoughtfully, wondering, "I'm curious, Captain, if this makes you royalty again."

"Not sure there's an official title in the underworld for such a thing."

"Humor me."

He looks me over quickly, running a tongue along his lower lip. "Sure then, Siren, I'm dark royalty."

"Like I said, a king."

His eyes grow heavy as he plays along. "If that's what you want to call me."

"It doesn't matter what *I* want," I say. "You should be telling me, as your dark king, what *you* want."

"I want you to be mine."

"To serve you tonight?"

"Fuck, Aria, if you want to serve me tonight or tell *me* to drop to my knees to serve you, I'll fucking do it."

I'm sort of breathless at that. Here is a giant wall of a man, a man that can take me however he wants, use me, overpower me—and he's telling me he's at *my* mercy.

How did we come so far, so fast?

I look at him from across the deck, and my heart has never felt fuller. I see him, in his prince-like exterior, and I want the man within. The one that's shrouded himself from the light, thinking his darkness will snuff it out. I want that man to know he can be powerful with me, that I'm not frightened by it. Not after having felt his love through the tether.

Slowly, I loosen my belt and raise my sweater over my head. I discard it on the deck by my feet and stand before him completely naked, with my hair covering my breasts and my cheeks flushed from my desire. James barely breathes, standing impossibly still as his eyes do all the moving for him.

I could go to him right now. Let him wrap his arms around me. Let him drop me to the ground and dote on me. All the passion in him would be spent pleasuring me, and after all those nightmares and revelations, I don't think that's what he needs right now.

I love how awestruck he looks, and I want to push him over the edge. Drive him wild. Make him the one I'm happy to be at the mercy of tonight.

Slowly, I drop down to my knees, and his reaction is impossible to ignore. His eyes flare, and he raises a hand to his mouth, running it along his jaw. "Aria," he strains out.

"Tell me what you want," I demand quietly. I cup a breast, squeeze at it, and slowly trail my hand down my body, over the curves of my belly and to my throbbing core.

I barely cup myself for long when he orders, "Come to me." His voice grows lower. *"Crawl to me."*

I can't help the satisfied smile that stretches across my face. Adrenaline surges through me, and nerves—always nerves that take flight like little butterflies in my stomach. I slowly stretch forward, my eyes focused on his, never looking away as I begin to move to him. They're slow movements, and I should feel like his submissive, but the growing need in his eyes makes *me* feel like the powerful one.

Like the lioness prowling to her prey.

And how desirable must I look to make him so wonderstruck? I can picture myself, naked under the starry sky, crawling to her dark and ruthless Captain like his claimed little whore.

The deck is wet from the rain that's just passed. Its smell lingers with the powerful ocean salt in the air. That would have normally felt like home to me, but now

I need that subtle mixture of sandalwood to round it off. The scent that lingers on James' skin and never seems to wash away. I make it to him, eager for that scent, for the taste of his skin on my tongue—

He's already removing his jacket and tunic, his gaze never leaving mine as he drops it by his feet. I make it to him within seconds, and my hands are already flying to his belt, trying to remove it quickly. He helps me, pulling off the belt, only to wrap it around his hand tightly. I don't wonder about it for long when I free his cock from his pants and bring it to my mouth. His empty hand grips my hair, fisting it as he lets out a shuddering breath.

"Fuck yeah, Aria," he tells me. "Let me in deep. I want to feel you choke, Siren."

And I do.

I take him in as far in as I can go, my mouth already sore from how wide I've had to stretch it. The noises he makes send pulses of heat through my body. I'm already delirious for his touch. I suck him harder, faster, using my hand to run it up and down his cock. He grows impossibly thick, jets of pre-cum shooting into my mouth as he tightens his hand into my hair and uses me roughly.

My knees grow sore, my mouth screaming for reprieve, but the desire to stop does not wane. I want him to come down my throat. I need to hear his gruff release because it does something to me, something that sinks layers deep into my being.

He pulls out suddenly, letting my hand drop. I make a sound of protest when he grabs me by the arm and stands me up. He takes me to a large deck box and pushes me down on it. I settle on my back, raising my head to watch as he spreads my legs apart and jerks over my drenched folds. He stops to glide his length against it, and I quake at the way it rubs against my clit. I bring my hand down to help, swirling my fingers around in circles, moaning through the tiny explosions that rock me.

"No," he demands.

He lets go of his cock and grabs my hands. Within seconds, he's throwing them over my head and to the railing. Using his belt, he loops it into a knot around my hands and the deck. He meets my eye, his lip twitching as he recognizes what he's doing. I grin up at him, feeling like we're back there again, to me being locked up, but it's completely different.

Unlike before, we aren't enemies, destined to hate.

In this very moment, we're lovers, fighting against all odds, curse be damned.

He moves back between my legs and sinks his cock into me. I feel my walls around him, gripping him tightly as he buries himself as far as he can go. The pressure is intense, and I expect him to pull out and then slam back in.

Instead, he doesn't move. Just keeps himself rooted there deep inside me, and it's almost too much. The feeling of fullness is both pleasurable and unbearable. I gasp as I stare at him, eyes misting with tears, and he's just staring down at me, jaw locked as his body quakes, begging him to move.

"This is how deep I'm going to come, Siren," he whispers down at me, still unmoving. "And you want to know the most terrifying part? I want to keep going, fill you even deeper, touch every inch of you, not just this beautiful pussy."

I barely hear him as I throb, my hips jolting, begging him to fuck me.

"How fucked-up is that?" he asks, astonished. "That I'm seated inside you and I still can't get enough of you."

He pulls out suddenly, and I gasp as he plunges into me once more, hitting a spark inside me that floods my being with pleasure. He does it over and over again. Watching his cock disappear inside me, holding it there until I'm begging him to keep going, to never stop. And that feeling of fullness? I'm clawing for it again. Wanting him to do what he's doing because I might come like this with him buried to the hilt, my walls quaking around him, squeezing at his thick length like I'm milking him to orgasm.

He picks up his pace, fucking me in long, smooth thrusts. Always hitting the back of my walls and I lay there after a while, just a vessel of feeling.

Fuck yes, this man knows how to fuck.

My skin is slick with sweat, and I welcome the ocean breeze as it washes over me. My back rubs back and forth along the deck box, that orgasm building to impossible heights. His hands run up bare, slick skin. I feel him everywhere, squeezing my breasts, pinching my nipples, sinking a finger into my mouth for me to bite down on. Then I feel his hand around my throat, keeping me still, squeezing me enough that I can breathe, but it's half a breath. His forearms are corded, veins protruding as he clenches his teeth, squeezing at me tighter—

Without notice, I explode, crying out, my walls gripping him so tightly, he lets out a guttural groan and stills deep inside me. Darkness erupts from him and clouds around us like wisps of black smoke, intermixing with the starry sky. I feel his cock jerk, and I relax now against the deck box, my body limp and exhausted—I'm so disoriented and on a high. I might never recover as all energy drains from my limbs.

Within seconds, the black clouds he brought on by his heightened emotions are gone. James is quick to loosen the belt, picking me up delicately, like I'm this fragile creature he didn't just fuck the brains out of.

As he carries me below deck, he kisses my temple and whispers, "Sleep, Aria. We have a big few days coming up."

He lays me down under our covers, and as I'm about to drift to sleep, content and at peace, I think to myself: *I never want to leave this ship again.*

"James," I whisper, seconds away from passing out.

"Yeah, Siren?"

"I dreamed of you, too."

CHAPTER 47

James

Where Morda was a lush jungle filled with cunts and a plentiful array of sex diseases, Calla's landscape is mostly desert with the occasional drought tolerant plant. Water here is a luxury, so loading up the water tanks will be costly.

Calla's people are the scholarly type; educated and proper, and they're wary of new people. Their sandstone homes are tightly crowded together in miniature communities with a well at the center of every town. Every small community houses a few dozen families, their governance coming from a handful of leaders that speak to King Wilheim on their behalf.

All around, the people of Calla are richly dressed in colorful clothing, their faces usually half covered to protect against the wind and grit, their flowy gowns reaching their ankles. The weather is always dry, the heat oppressive during the middle of the day. From what I've observed in the past, no one usually comes out until the sun begins to set.

They remind me of nocturnal animals, out during the night and shut-in during the day.

As a whole, Calla is a wealthy community; the land is overflowing with natural resources. Under the rule of King Wilheim, they've mastered trade and they educate their young, keeping travelers at a strict distance, sometimes never even letting them dock. The kingdom is secretive and extremely private, valuing their isolation.

But they do fucking *love* Gala Green.

Briggs and Luca have carried up a healthy supply of it, situating it in the pilothouse.

"What if they don't dock us?" Luca asks, sounding vulnerable. We're running scarily low on maintenance supplies despite having been able to get a few necessities on Morda. This constant lack of crew is killing us though, and if we're unsuccessful here, the next safe harbor is weeks away by sail. Physically, that'll hurt us.

"They'll dock us," I tell him confidently. "They'll recognize our ship."

Grimy just looks on at me with this unimpressed stare. I know what he's thinking: the last time we were here and what a shitshow that was, but I don't want to talk about it. He'll just ramble on about the power of scorn, and I'm not in the fucking mood. Luca wasn't part of the crew at the time, so he's oblivious, exactly how I like it to be. It doesn't make me less uneasy, however.

"How about the women?" Luca is really pushing it now. He looks between us, shrugging dramatically. "Come on, Cap, I got balls that need emptying—"

"Calla's very protective of their women, so let's not

break any more hearts than necessary," Grimy snaps. "You got a hand, don't you?"

Just had to land a cheap shot, didn't he?

Luca, confused, grumbles something under his breath as Grimy adds, "Keep Aria inside, will you, James?"

"Not happening," I retort. "After Morda, she's not leaving my sight."

He doesn't tell me why that's a bad idea—

I already fucking know.

"She should stay on board and start preparing our meals, is what she should do," Briggs chimes in.

His words make my blood boil. "She will do no such thing. She's not a fucking slave on this ship, and it'd be wise of you all to recognize that immediately."

"Isn't she though, Cap?" presses Luca, confused. "Thought the siren was supposed to be cleaning 'round here after the mess she made. On that thought, she's always disappearin' these days. Anyone know what that's about?"

"Probably to get away from you," mutters Briggs.

"Fuck off."

"It's the underwear, Luca. Someone has to say something eventually—we can't take it anymore."

"That ain't why she's gone and comin' back all flushed and dreamy-like. I'm frankly curious what's goin' on with our siren 'cause last I heard she's meant to be another deckhand, ya know, on account of Martin disappearin' and all." Luca shoots me a knowing look, not vocalizing I know what he's thinking.

Briggs on the other hand, isn't as intelligent. "Yeah,

where is Martin, anyway? I haven't seen him since... Well, I can't remember when I last saw him, but I know it's been a while."

My hands ball into fists at my side, my jaw clenching to the point of pain. Could this man be so dim that he thought he could exist on a ship for weeks upon weeks without bumping into fucking Martin?

Grimy and I share a look, one where he silently presses me to tell the crew about my newfound relationship with Aria, and to *finally* fess up about Martin's death, the giant fucking elephant in the room.

My nostrils flare as I square my shoulders and force the rage down, but not too down. Like my siren says, my darkness isn't all bad.

"Aria is mine. You will show her the same respect you show me, and you will treat her as though she is superior to you, because she fucking is. Her running off in Morda endangered us all, but she's trying to make amends. And when she finally does utter a word of apology to you dim fucks, you'd be smart to accept it." I stop, sneering at them each individually before I open my mouth about Martin, but Briggs' reaction stops me point blank. I watch him through gritted teeth as he rolls his eyes quickly, looking away as he does, like he's afraid I'll catch him in the act. Too fucking late.

"And if she never does?" he questions, resting his hand on his hip. His stance reminds me how a woman would act, attitude blazing like a child.

How I allowed this man to become my second-in-command is beyond me. If he wasn't so damn good at his job, I'd toss him over the bow of the ship and let him swim with the sharks.

"If she never does, then you will accept that she's now the lady of this ship, regardless."

"The lady of the ship, Cap?" Luca questions, his voice cracking like he's not sure what to do with that information. "What the fuck does that even mean?"

"It means she is the lady of this fucking ship, Luca. And you will treat her as such or you will all walk the fucking plank, just as Martin did." So he didn't *actually* walk the plank, his fate was a much crueler one, but they don't need to know that just yet.

"He means she's his other half, you fucking knob-heads," Grimy adds, irritably. "Now stop talking back."

Both Briggs and Luca stare at me with wide eyes, their mouths slowly agape. Luca audibly gulps, while Briggs immediately turns away and continues to busy himself with the boxes of Gala Green. Nudging into Luca, he whispers, "Martin walked the plank, Luca!"

Annoyance trickles through my body, and I'm done with this conversation.

My Little Fish must feel my anger because a burst of something that feels a lot like love whooshes down the tether and instantly calms my nerves, but I'm still wrestling with myself, combating the conflicting feelings rushing through me. Along with Aria's love, I feel the anger, white hot and raging, toward my idiotic, sorry excuse of a crew. Yet within that anger I feel the flickers of relief for finally verbalizing it to the lot of them that Aria is my woman.

Ultimately, Grimy wins.

I tell Aria to make herself scarce, and she doesn't question me. I sense she doesn't want to be around anyone after Morda. She shelters herself inside my quarters, and it's a load off my mind as we approach Calla.

As predicted, they recognize us.

Men are on the docks when we swing our ropes their way. They gather them, tying them into unmoveable knots along our slip. We're at the very front of the marina, taking over an entire aisle of one dock. It's a smooth transition. This marina is in amazing condition, and it feels like I've journeyed out of a prehistoric era to get here.

Hebnor, the owner of the marina, is already standing along the boardwalk, watching us intently with a wide smile. We drop the ramp with a loud thud. Luca and Grimy stand by the rails as I descend, meeting Hebnor at the bottom.

Like the last time we docked, Briggs makes himself busy below deck.

"It's been some years since I've seen the Tempest on our horizon," Hebnor remarks as I stop to stand in front of him. I tower over him, and it's an unhappy moment for me to see him so withered, his back hunched. We shake hands, and he's friendly, giving me a pat on the back like we're old friends, and we are. "Haven't aged a minute, have you?" he adds, looking me over.

"The ocean's been kind to me," I reply nonchalantly.

He lets out a hearty laugh. "Is that right? Well, can't say the same about me, can you?"

I look him over, at the fine lines and wrinkles along the creases of his tanned skin. "What do you mean, Heb? You don't look a day over thirty."

The old man's eyes grow warm. "I've been waiting for you, you know. I knew you were coming."

"Did you?"

His brows furrow. "Vanya's been having visions. Of a darkness following you. She saw that you'd return here to seek her. Am I right?"

Grimy comes to a stop behind me, listening to Hebnor's words. I keep my face neutral as I stare back at Heb, even though the tether tugs. My siren is curious. She might be inside, but she can hear everything happening through the open portholes. I don't want to bring any attention to her right now, and I don't want to think of Vanya's visions. My horror might flow down the tether. Instead, I say casually, "Among many things. We'll have time to discuss later, Heb. Right now, my boat needs help."

Heb chuckles. "Your boat needs more than just a little help from the looks of it, and it's not superficial damage."

"I need to repair my sails, a patch in the through hull, and a new crew."

"Sail repair won't be cheap," he tells me. "I can have my men look over any work that needs to be done, and as for a crew...well, we have a lot of strays. A couple months ago, a bunch of ships went under. Men washed ashore here—claimed it was the storm of a century that rolled through."

He's talking about the siren storm. I keep my mouth shut as I nod once. "Unfortunate."

"Were you caught up in it?"

"Yeah, hell of a storm." I quickly change the subject. "I don't want trouble. We're seeking safe refuge until my ship's up to scratch—"

"You caused a lot of grief the last time you were here."

"Nothing a bit of Gala Green won't fix."

Hebnor laughs, eyes twinkling with amusement. "You're telling me you have Gala Green safe and sound on that wretched looking ship?"

I keep my smile faint. "I do."

"Wish Vanya would have foreseen that instead."

"What do you think, then? Will I be chased out of here, or will Wilheim welcome me in?"

"I can't say with certainty. You know how he is; grievances can't be soothed with currency, but Gala Green, on the other hand..."

"Tell him I'll take his strays, whatever vagabond he doesn't want."

"The jailhouse is getting full."

My smile is cold and full of bite, "I'll take them, too."

"Wise."

I step back, keeping myself barren of emotions as I say, "We'll stay aboard until you come back with an answer. In the meantime, we need water."

Hebnor nods, glancing back at Grimy with a friendly look before looking up at the ship where Luca stands. Curiosity fills him. "How many heads do you have?"

"Not many," I answer vaguely. "But in the likelihood I get a crew, I need the most you can offer."

"I'll get back to you as soon as I hear an answer."

I'm already up the ramp when I respond, "I'll be waiting."

WE'RE WAITING A LONG FUCKING while.

Luca is standing on guard in the pilothouse, keeping a lookout for Hebnor, or trouble in general. In the salon, I'm looking over the maps, trying to figure out which supplies are low and how many we'll need once we set off. Grimy is standing next to me, staring down at the map, but he's not really looking. His eyes are filled with thought as he rubs at his chin. Nearby, on the settee, Aria is pretending to be occupied by Rex, but she's really just watching Grimy and me with a million questions on the tip of her tongue.

I barely look at her. I can't, or I'll lose focus.

I'm schooling my emotions, but I'm thinking of the meeting with the King, and Vanya. If the witch foresaw me coming, did she see Aria also? And if she did, has she told anyone about the siren I have on my ship?

If she did tell a soul, we'd have been driven out of here by now. Not by pitchforks and lit torches either, but by crossbows and *flying* torches. We'd be in a big rut, too, chugging along the sea with damaged sails and limited fishing gear to catch our food. Not that Aria wouldn't help with that, but I don't want to see the guilt in her eyes when she deceives those fucking fishies.

And don't get me started on water.

I fume, trying to play out how the coming days will be, especially if I take Aria with me ashore. If King Wilheim accepts my offer of Gala Green, he'll invite us over, and it'll be a night of interesting sordid affairs that Calla gets up to when their young are in bed. I'm not fucking eager to put Aria in the center of that.

Calla is dangerous in its own way. Sordid and devious, it's similar to Morda in that we can't trust a single soul.

But I run the risk of not getting to her in time if our visit goes south, and if she's killed—

Intuition demands I keep her here, locked up if need be. Let her stay below deck until we leave.

I can't have her discovered.

At the same time, I know that's not a way to live. I want Aria free and roaming, just not in a place like Calla.

"Cap, Heb is back!" Luca calls from the top of the steps.

I still don't look at Aria as I leave the room and meet with Hebnor at the dock.

WE'VE BEEN GRANTED safe refuge, and the exchange is immediate.

We set up the barrels of Gala Green on the dock for Wilheim's men to take. There are many of them overseeing the transaction. In return, we're introduced to the strays on the island. I meet with countless men: old men with cataract eyes and paralyzed limbs, and young men who still look like sea virgins with barely any ship experience.

It's a shitshow.

Absolutely pitiful.

Out of the thirty men, a mere five are useful, and they're the prisoners of Calla, with hardened gazes and bulging muscles and trouble—fuck me, they scream trouble. But I stiffen a nod of approval, like yes, this is great, this is all part of the fucking plan. One of the men —who calls himself Sparrow, so fucking stupid—tells me he'll be the best fucking deckhand the world has ever seen so long as I drop him off at Avangail.

"What the fuck did they put you away for?" I wonder aloud as I look this pretty boy over.

"I stole from the rich and gave to the poor," he responds simply.

I blink once. "You're hired."

"Half of them won't last a week," Grimy says under his breath as we watch Luca jot down the names of the men. "Half will either walk the plank or defect, and the others will die of some kind of fucking illness. Look at that one with the boils all over his face."

Said man with the boils is sneezing and wheezing, and Luca is stepping back in alarm, a forced smile on his lips as he decides to sign the man's name for him.

"He's wonderful," I return swiftly, sounding upbeat with the King's armed men nearby. "They're all fucking great."

Grimy just blinks in response.

"King Wilheim welcomes you to the castle tonight," Hebnor says next, looking really chuffed with the exchange. "Plenty of ale, plenty of meat—all things you and your own must be in dire need of. They say they look forward to meeting you... and the girl."

I go completely stiff, moving only my eyes to look at Hebnor. I take a few seconds to respond, but a thousand questions are running through my head. What the fuck did he just say? How did they know—

But I can't stall.

I don't want to reveal my alarm, either.

I simply nod once, acting unperturbed. "We'll be there."

My blood is swooshing so fast, my head feels light. I ignore Grimy's heavy stare, his own questions mounting behind that look. I stay calm as Hebnor directs men to assess what can be done on the ship. We fill up on water. Replace our electric coils and begin to stock up on nonperishables. The entire time I'm there, I'm thinking of running.

Nothing good ever comes out of visiting Calla.

When all is said and done, Hebnor leads me to the marina office as Grimy stays behind. He offers me coffee that I pass up before handing me a clipboard to sign in.

I write my name down, feeling my skin prickle at his watchful gaze. The tether pulls just then, the distance between my siren and I unwelcome. I dismiss the feeling.

I pay for the slip and am about to leave when his voice cuts through the air.

"Since when do you travel with your guard up?"

He means the mask I put up to hide my scars and grizzled face.

"Maybe I wanted to look nice for the King, Heb."

"Mmhmm," he hums, not buying my answer, which ironically is the truth. The last time I was in the Kingdom of Calla, I caused havoc. If I want Wilheim to take my request for supplies seriously, I need to act accordingly. Present myself differently. In the back of my mind, though, the end goal is Vanya. Has been for a long time now.

I look up from the sign-in sheet and into his questioning eyes. I decide against bullshitting. "We've barely been docked, and they know of a girl." It's not a question, just a statement I throw at him. "I must act strategically to get what we've come for—which are supplies, and a crew, only—and set sail. This isn't like before, Hebnor. This visit is for no reason other than necessity. I have no desire to form alliances to assist with reclaiming my land. There will be none of that."

"What's changed?"

I sigh. "Time."

"So, the dream of the royal throne is gone."

"I no longer dream of being still."

"And the girl?"

"She's nobody's fucking business."

Hebnor leans over the counter, searching my eyes as he says cautiously, "They have sway over the sea life around Calla. As such, they have eyes and ears everywhere. Those eyes watched you coming. When I told the King you were here, he was unsurprised. He knew already, so if you don't want harm to come to your girl while you're docked here, I would keep her very close to you, and I would coach her very, very sternly not to open her mouth unless it was life or death."

Trepidation coils within me. "She is harmless—"

"Maybe in her human form."

I stare evenly at him, trying my hardest to school my expression.

Hebnor senses my question. "How do I know? Because a siren always senses when another siren is nearby. Be careful, James. If they find out what she is, they'll take her, and they won't kill her, either. They'll want her for themselves, to harness her power and use it on their enemies. Such a weapon would be pivotal for sea wars."

I don't say anything as I slide the sheet his way, and then I'm leaving, the weight of his words heavy on my mind.

His voice rings out one last time as I make my exit. "Make sure you mark her, Erickson."

Make sure you mark her.

Cover her in my scent, he means. Make sure everyone knows she's taken.

Not a problem.

I'm feverish as I approach my ship, desperate to get back to Aria. The need to bury my dick inside her, to *consume* her, drives me.

Hebnor's words have rattled me.

The thought of anyone laying a finger on my siren is enough to make me murderous. Over my dead fucking body will anyone touch her—and I can't fucking die.

I don't consider welcoming the new crew just yet. They're somewhere nearby, being utterly useless as they wait to climb aboard.

I can smell a ruse from a mile away; Jonas Wilheim has dumped his throwaways at my dock, probably because he doesn't want to bury them on the island. Just getting rid of the sick, or infected, or injured.

I don't linger on the dock. Instead, I barrel past everyone and race up the ramp.

Once aboard, I find Grimy in the engine room, taking shit apart. I look down at him as he crouches in the bilge. "How does Wilheim know?" I ask, dumbfounded.

Grimy instinctually knows I'm referring to Aria. "We don't know what he knows yet. He might assume you have a warm body to slip into."

"What if there's been a sighting—"

"We've been careful, James," Grimy cuts in, pausing to look up at me. "She's hardly above deck as it is, and Wilheim's strength is the land, not the sea, so I doubt there've been that many sea life keeping an eye out for him. And anyway, if they even thought for a moment you're harboring a siren, we'd be in a different sort of trouble right now."

I consider that. "Heb knows what she is."

"Because of Vanya."

"Yeah."

"Well, I'm hardly surprised, given what *she* is."

"She's expecting me, so she knows what I seek."

Grimy sighs, turning his attention back to the engine. "Always prepare for the worst, James. Don't get your hopes up. For all we know, this curse may be eternal."

"Or there could be a way to break the curse and be free of this fucking noose around my neck."

"Perhaps," Grimy muses, steepling his fingertips against his mouth.

"You think I'm wrong?"

"Do I think Aria could be the curse-breaker?" He shrugs. "Goddess knows. Your visions have come to fruition. You've developed a tether and she's affected you from the very start, overriding your bracelet's powers. But to be able to break the curse? Sometimes I see it, believe it... Other times I think she could be your ruin."

HE THINKS she can be my ruin.

That she will grow old along my side, or worse, die young.

I'm a fucking mess.

Aria's in my bed, tucked under the covers and napping when I come through the door. My desire to be near her is just as urgent as it was before, though most of the anger has seeped through my pores. No wonder the tether had gone quiet—she's been sleeping. Curled up on her side in our bed, a thin linen blanket is draped across her frame. She looks content—peaceful, even— and so unassuming for what is to come. She's wearing another one of my sweaters, gray this time, and her vibrant hair fans across my pillow.

I stand over her for a few minutes, thinking of what Hebnor said.

"If they find out what she is, they'll take her, and they won't kill her, either."

I would die a million deaths, each more gruesome than the rest, before I let that happen.

Kill as many men as it takes to ensure her safety.

And even if I have her unscathed, even if the curse breaks and I'm mortal, I don't think one life will be enough to cherish her.

Heat rushes through me and my dick hardens, straining to be let out. The carnal need to be inside of my woman overtakes the peace I feel from simply watching her sleep in my bed.

Stripping out of my clothes, I silently crawl onto the bed and gently push her body so she lies on her back. Slowly, I pull the blanket down, smiling as I find the sweater she wears pushed up past her hips, presenting her pussy to me as though her body is begging for me. And I intend to give it exactly what it's asking for.

The warm hues from the setting sun reflect on the water, casting an orange glow in the room. The lighting reflects off her glistening folds—my siren is already wet. Even in slumber, Aria's body calls to me—*craves* me. Is ready for me.

From my knees, I inch my way to her, lightly spreading her legs as I come close enough for our bodies to align. Fisting my cock, I tug it from root to tip as I gaze down at my beautiful siren.

I glide the tip through her wetness, taking it with me and spreading it all around the lips of her pussy and against her clit. This rouses her now, her arms coming up to stretch as she lets out a soft groan.

I take that as my cue.

Bringing my cock to her entrance, I slam into her with one movement, and a guttural sound erupts from me on impact. "*Fuck!*"

Grabbing her hips, I pull her closer, resting her lower half on my thighs as I gain momentum, pumping into her with no restraint. She lets out a breathy moan as I reach down and massage her clit, and her eyes finally pop open and meet mine.

"Sorry to wake you, Siren, but you looked too fucking beautiful for my cock to behave."

Her eyes get hazy and she moans again, bringing her hand to rest over mine as I play with her clit. "Slow down, James. Make love to me."

My heart skips a beat or two.

No woman has ever asked me to make love to her. To fuck, yes, but never make love. The ancient past is full of faceless women who had always used my body as a vessel for pleasure, as I had used theirs.

I'm not even sure if I'm capable of making love, but for her, I'll try.

Slowing my movements, I angle my body so hers slips down my thighs and rests fully on the bed. I lean over, resting my forearms on either side of her head. Her lips find mine as I roll my hips into her—not softly, but not with the intensity of moments ago. I find a rhythm that suits us both and listen to the light lullaby of moans that escape her lips and float between mine. The intimacy squeezes at that muscle in my chest.

Fucking my siren feels incredible, but this...

This is otherworldly.

I feel every muscle within her constrict around my shaft, the walls of her clenching so tightly it feels better than anything I've ever felt. My hands brush against her every curve as I take my time, thrusting in controlled motions. Breaking our kiss, my eyes travel south, the desire to see us too strong to ignore, and I watch with awe the way our bodies unite, the way I glide in and out of her.

This woman was made for me, siren or not. Her species and mine, our burning hatred, curse or no curse—it's all a distant blur. I've accepted my fate, and my fate is *her*. Our bodies, our minds, the way we challenge each other. The Gods and Goddesses created every aspect of Aria solely for me—my perfect fit. The other side of my coin.

With each thought of adoration rushing through my mind, a shockwave of emotion zips through the tether. I'm feeling as though my entire chest will explode from the weight of it.

Looking down at my siren, I know she is feeling the same power in the way that my movements have ceased, but her lips form a perfect O. An overwhelming inclination grips me. It's as though Aria has sliced into my skin and now grasps my heart in her hand, and every fiber of my being screams to tell her so.

My eyes are rimmed red as a declaration pours out of my lungs steadfastly. "Aria, before you I was lost in a sea of darkness. Cursed to a life of misery. You've brightened my days—shown me how mesmerizing life could be if only I'd give it the chance. Because of you, I've reunited with the part of my past I thought I lost—my heart. You are my heart, Aria. The reason it's beating. The entirety of it belongs to you and you alone. With every morsel of my darkness and glimmer of light within, I belong to you. Love is not a strong enough word to grace you with, my siren. Not a single word in any language will suffice."

I don't give her the opportunity to respond as I move

my hand between her legs and use my thumb to rub her clit. Rolling my hips into her, I pick up speed, working her body in the way I know will push her to orgasm.

I need her pleasure more than I need my own.

She tilts her head to reach mine and brushes her lips against me, whispering, "I love you, James."

It's all I need to hear before I pick up my speed and work to make her come. With every thrust, I mutter a different devotion to the woman that writhes beneath me.

"Incredible." *Thrust.*

"Mine." *Thrust.*

"Forever." *Thrust.*

"Fated." *Thrust.*

My words are practically incoherent, my mind and being lost to pleasure. I feel my orgasm building from within, the delicious tingling pulling from my center and overtaking my entire body. My balls tighten as I try to fight off the inevitable. "You feel too good, Aria, I'm going to fucking detonate. Come for me, Aria. Come all over my dick and show me just how much you love me."

And she does.

Her legs constrict around mine, her pussy tightening. Aria screams out, my name falling from her lips in decadent moans. She tilts her head back against the pillow, jutting her chest further into the air. With force, I push the sweater up and expose her perfect, round tits, and lean down to pull her right nipple into my mouth. I suck it roughly, flicking my tongue across the peaked bud.

Her nails bite into the nape of my neck, and the slight sensation of pain sends me over the edge. Two more slams into her and I'm filling her up, my cock ejecting so much cum I can feel a sheen of sweat form across my brow from exertion.

I'm still hard when I finish, and not yet ready to disconnect from her, so I don't.

Sliding my arm beneath her, I cradle her body and hoist it onto mine as I come to a seated position on the bed. Without thinking twice, Aria wraps her legs around my body and kisses me with such burning ferocity, it could scorch the sun.

And once again, we move as one.

I WRAP my arms around her and pick her up from the bed, settling her down on the floor. She's still dazed, cheeks flushed, with her eyes bright and warm.

"What're we doing?" she slurs, half-asleep from our fuck-a–thon.

We went for hours, only stopping when Aria physically could not handle anymore.

"Getting you dressed," I say. "We've been invited for dinner."

"That's a hard pass, James."

I smirk. "Don't be like that."

Her eyes look a little more focused. "I get weird vibes from this place. Plus, it doesn't help that I heard some of your exchange with that man from earlier." Her lips turn down in thought. "Sounds like you burned bridges the last time you were here."

I sigh, tiredly. "Indeed, I did."

Her voice is quieter. "Why?"

"I wanted my throne back. A lot of time has passed since I've been here, and what I wanted before, I don't want anymore."

"You honestly wanted your throne back?"

"I did."

"What happened?"

"The sea happened, Little Fish. It got into my veins."

"But you're a prince. That part of you must still call out to you."

I hesitate, taking my time to form a response. I look into her questioning eyes, then down at her lips, all pursed. My heart rattles a little more in my chest, the tether burning warmly. She senses this, and her eyes grow heavy. It's the most emotion I've sent down the tether yet.

"Former prince," I respond, almost curtly. She watches me, her eyes narrowing in silent question, but she doesn't press further.

I left that life behind long ago.

"It calls out to me," I finally say carefully. "But I'm not that man anymore, Aria."

She tilts her head to the side. "You don't think your people want this man—who you are now?"

My hands slide down her arms, settling at her bare hips, squeezing them as I respond, "With the curse, I thought I was invincible. I thought... I could have every-thing I ever dreamed of, and all I needed was the power. It's what brought me here to Calla in the first place. It's a rich land, an alliance made complete sense. Grimy warned it was a mistake, and I only realized it after I spoke to Vanya."

"Vanya?"

I nod solemnly. "Heb's wife."

Her brows furrow. "What did she say?"

"She said it wasn't part of my trajectory. That if I stayed still, word would travel and the sirens would find me and destroy me once and for all."

Shock flashes in Aria's eyes. The flush in her cheeks is all gone. She looks paler, her lips parted. She's lost for words.

I study her intently now, trying to read into the tether, but she's using considerable effort to disguise her feelings. A split second of doubt rushes through me. That this could still be something she intends to do to me. My instincts tell me to be careful with her, to never let my guard down—

At the same time, I've given her every inch of me.

I'm hers.

She senses my disarray, my surrender, my doubts. She shakes her head. "James... I would never..."

"Don't." I shake my head once and grab for the clothing Luca delivered at my door that Heb sent. "Whatever comes, let it, for it would take equal measure to fight it than to just embrace the inevitable."

Her words sound breathless. "Why would you say that? How can you think that way?"

"Something my old man used to say when the crew would warn him of an inbound storm. They'd try to find ways to go around it, but my father didn't work like that. He believed to brace for it."

"He was right every time?"

I shrug one shoulder, avoiding her eye. "Yeah. Right up until a siren took him from me."

"I'm sorry, James."

"Don't be."

"I didn't know until we went fishing, and even then, given how upset you were, I didn't want to pry."

I turn back to her. "Don't feel bad for me, Aria. My father wasn't a good man. He was an egomaniac and a womanizer, and he didn't value life if it wasn't serving a purpose to him. If he saw your kind, he wouldn't have thought twice about killing you. In the ocean, it's do or die. My father—he lived by that motto wherever he went, ocean or land."

She listens raptly, nodding once when I meet her gaze. Then her eyes are back on my hands, at the white clothing I'm holding. "What's that?"

I spread out the dress she's expected to wear for dinner. It's thin material, the see-through kind. Frilly looking shit that will accentuate her body. Her face falls as her eyes harden on mine. "No. Absolutely not."

"It's nice."

"It looks like it's made of tissue."

My eyes brighten at the thought. "You think I can tear it up like tissue?"

"James—"

"You're coming, Aria. It's not up for debate. I can't leave you here alone, you understand? I need to know you're safe, and I can't do that if you're not under my protection."

She sways easily, taking the dress from my hand

while she makes a big show of looking irritated. "I need to rinse first."

Now I stand taller, shaking my head. "No, just put it on."

"James, I smell like sex—"

"Good."

She's confused by my stern approval, but she doesn't speak a word against me. She slides the dress on, and I nearly groan at the way she slowly pulls it down her body. This woman was made for me—every fucking inch of her was made to torture me, to burn me, to fuck with my head until it's just my cock calling the shots. Her nipples are still hard, pressing against the material, and I want to fuck her in it, want to cover her in my cum all over again. To leave her a sticky, wanton mess. Parade her as mine at the dinner. Look Wilheim directly in the eye and let him know he does not rattle me.

I hand her the slippers that go along with her dress next. They're a little too small, but she doesn't utter a word of protest. I decide right then that I like dressing my woman up, and she can harp on about liking my sweaters all she wants. If I can get her to wear this sort of shit—at least in the bedroom—I'll live on for eternity as a happy man.

Next, I help with her hair, running my fingers through it. She shuts her eyes as I massage her scalp and sort through her tangles. My bracelet burns against my wrist as I take my time running my touch through her hair. It's not long before her brows are coming together in confusion, and then she's whipping her head away from my touch, hissing, "What the hell is that?" She feels the heat of my magic running along her scalp.

"It's temporary," I assure her.

Now her eyes snap open. "What is?"

I step back, motioning my head once to the small shaving mirror on the wall. She turns to it and gasps. "My hair—"

"I had to."

She runs her fingers through the mousy brown strands, nodding silently, understanding. There's no way in hell we could explain away her colorful hair when she's been in the ocean for so long. It would only arouse suspicion. Plus, the aim is to attempt to lessen her beauty, not enhance it. We want Wilheim to believe she is just another whore we picked up along the journey.

It'll be a challenge for me to keep the magic up, if I even can. I've only ever mastered it on myself, but the risk is necessary.

Aria fingers the strands, looking down at them, her face suddenly unreadable. Confusion pours into the tether. "Why didn't you do this in Morda?" Her eyes snap to mine. "If you could have changed the color of my hair..."

Her thoughts trail off, and I see the way sadness flashes behind her crystal blue eyes. She's confused and full of doubts. Doubting *me*. The way she asks raises my hackles—the slight twinge of accusation behind her question instantly sparks frustration in me.

"If you think for one moment that I wanted you to be in any more danger than you already were in, you clearly haven't been paying attention." I take her chin between my finger and thumb, tilting her face up to mine. "I wasn't sure if I could expel the power necessary to change your hair until I just tried it. Truthfully, it hadn't crossed my mind to even try in Morda. But here, on Calla, after I nearly lost you once... The dangers between the heinous fucks who inhabit Morda and a *King* is quite different, Aria. I'll do anything it takes to keep you safe."

I press a kiss to her forehead before I release her from my hold and move across the room. Bending to pick up a spare boot, I unlace it and pull the string through the eyelets. When I finish, I toss the boot aside. Once in front of Aria again, I lower myself to one knee and skim my fingertips up her inner leg, pushing away the fabric from my path until I reach her thigh.

Leaning forward, I kiss her soft skin once before bringing the bootlace up and tie it tight around her. "It must be tight," I tell her as she looks down at me with her big doe eyes.

What is at the tip of her tongue, but she swallows it down as I remove my switchblade from my pocket and tuck it between the bootlace and her inner thigh.

"My father gave this to me as protection, and now I'm giving it to you, Little Mermaid. If you feel as though you're in any danger, use it. Do not hesitate, even if the one you're fearful of is *me*."

She sucks in a sharp breath, but the smart girl doesn't argue—she just nods once and watches as I wrap the lace around her thigh once more, securing the two ends in a clove hitch knot. I touch my work, giving the switchblade a slight shake to test its security. When I'm satisfied it isn't going anywhere, I drop the fabric of the dress and stand back, inspecting the place where the blade hides beneath her dress.

The black bootlace is just barely visible beneath the thin garment, but unless another man's eyes are glued to my siren, they'd be none the wiser.

Stepping away, I start rummaging in my closet and begin to dress. Aria stands beside me for sometime, studying herself in the mirror. Then I feel the weight of her gaze on me. "James?"

"Yeah."

"Why would a single woman's words convince you to leave Calla?"

My movements slow as I run the shirt over my torso. I look back at her, clenching my jaw once, twice. "She's not just a woman, Aria. She's a witch, and she laid the options before me: a short, miserable existence on Calla before the sirens found me, or in the endless sea, searching for the curse-breaker."

She swallows hard. "I see."

I grab for the belt and begin to slide it on, sensing more of her questions.

"Do they know you're cursed?"

I shake my head. "They believe I have powers."

"Of course they would want to form an alliance," she muses now. "To have an immortal king while they took over more kingdoms."

"That was the plan, though they are unaware of my immortality."

She nods. "You must have pissed them off by leaving."

"I did."

"But to form an alliance, to also lead Calla, it would have meant a joining."

Now I pause, looking up from my belt buckle at her glowing eyes. Fuck me, I gotta do something about those eyes, too. "That's right." I simply say.

Aria takes a step closer, eyeing me peculiarly. "Is she still alive then?"

"Who?"

"The girl you were supposed to wed."

CHAPTER 49

Aria

There's still light out when we leave the ship in the evening.

I'm a little disoriented, the revelation that I'll be meeting the woman that was supposed to be united with James fresh on my mind.

It's hard to see James in a different light. To think he might have been so power hungry once upon a time, that he would go to such great lengths to try to claim his kingdom back.

But growing up, I knew the former Kingdom of Goldspince, renamed Calamity Isle for decades, was now a miserable existence for anyone born there. The land has been fought over so many times I don't even think the young inhabitants remember a kingdom ever existed.

The walk from the marina to the city gates isn't long, but I stare enviously at the camel wagons along the path going past us, already feeling hot in this barely there "dress." James is distrusting and uncertain, forgoing any ride in the presence of a stranger. So, I walk strictly between him and Briggs. Behind me is Luca and in front of me is Grimy. I feel boxed in, like a treasure they're trying to protect, when really I'm supposed to play the ship tart.

What does a tart do exactly? I wonder.

Just go with the flow, Aria. Pretend you're having sex with James. Let loose, just not too loose or else he'll break the neck of every man that looks at you too long.

So then, don't act like a ho?

This is confusing.

There are two watchtowers between the giant gates. When we approach, a trumpet sounds and it all feels so dramatic when the guard shouts down at us, "Who goes there?"

James rolls his eyes. "I've been granted safe entry, boy. Open the gates. We're expected at dinner with King Wilheim."

At first, the guard simply points a crossbow at us, and I can't help but wince. We were strictly told not to carry any weapons on us, so the boys had to leave their pistols behind. The only weapon I know we conceal is the one strapped to my thigh. Due to the peace treaty signed in all the developed kingdoms, automatic weapons are strictly forbidden. *Except in Morda. Fuck that place.* Glancing at James, I'm not surprised he has them at all, given his black market hustle. A bad weight forms in my chest, telling me that going into this kingdom this bare might be a mistake.

James sends warmth through the tether, relaxing me instantly.

"Don't worry," he whispers down at me. "Should anything happen, they'll have to go through me first."

"And me," whispers Grimy.

"And me," adds Luca.

"Me, what?" asks Briggs. "I wasn't paying attention."

No one answers as the gates finally groan open, allowing us passage.

PALM TREES SWAY as we walk down a well-maintained cobblestone path. The town seems to have only just stirred with people coming out of their residences instead of retiring in them. The streets are lit up—there's electricity here! It's not frequently common in Norborne, so I'm especially surprised and giddy. Calla is modern, like Avangail. Shops and pop-up food stands come alive, and the smell of food hits the air. My stomach growls, but I know dinner is coming with King Fuckwad.

Just the thought of it makes me nervous all over again.

The guard that let us in guides us through the town. There are plays and music and art displays.

Calla is the shit.

"We can find our way from here," James tells the guard. "I've been here before and dined with the king."

The guard gives him a strange look. "I don't remember you."

"Of course you wouldn't. Likely before your time."

Now the man is confused, and I can see the questions

mounting. The man looks close in age to James. Before he can say another word, James simply dismisses him with a pat on the shoulder and walks off. We follow his lead as the guard stands there in his white robes, looking lost.

Turning back, we take a long path past the markets. James seems to know exactly where he's going. Grimy, too, as he doesn't look over at him for direction. We pass a huge stone building with long columns and black barred windows. There aren't any gardens, but there is a line of palm trees at the entrance. It's heavily fortified by guards in their long robe-garbs. They're not carrying crossbows but swords, and I feel a little queasy thinking of the lame switchblade tied to my inner thigh.

I don't need to ask James to know that's probably where we'll be dining.

But we press on, through quieter alleyways and even quieter streets. Away from the noise and life. By the time he stops us in front of a small looking cottage, it's dark and the crickets are chirping. There is a subtle glow coming from one of the windows of the cottage. It's not electricity running, but candlelight, flickering shadows and a warm, orange shade. We walk down a small trail leading to a curved door. I glance around the place, the tether burning for relief. James offers it swiftly, assuring me yet again that all is okay.

He pounds on the door, and we wait a few moments. Looking around, we seem out of the ordinary. Four large men hovering outside a tiny cottage with a random girl in risque clothing.

The door opens, and a tall, broad-shouldered man appears.

"Hebnor," James says.

The man has a beard and black shaggy hair with white in it. He's hunched from age, his eyes dark and friendly. "James! You're welcome to come in. Vanya is expecting you..." He surveys the men, his gaze landing on me and staying. "And you. Yes, she said to bring your lady friend with you."

"Am I coming in?" Grimy cuts in, raising a brow. "Or has Vanya decided I'm no longer a good friend?"

"Is that Grimy being dramatic?!" comes a woman's voice from the inside. "It's been a few decades, and he still has the jaws of a wee girl, pouting like that. Let him in, Heb, let him in."

Hebnor lets out a deep chuckle as he steps aside. "You three inside."

Grimy goes in first, and then James. He's quick to grab my hand, making sure I'm pressed against his side. Behind me, I hear Luca curse and Briggs pout. "Are we to just wait out here, then?" asks Briggs.

"Shut the door," Vanya commands.

I'm barely through the door when it slams behind me, straight on Luca and Briggs' faces.

I look straight ahead. The room is cozy—there's plush carpet beneath my feet and a chic sofa on one wall painted in creamy pastel colors. The rest of the room is covered in bookshelves and houseplants. Hebnor leads us away from the living room and into a small kitchen with skylight windows. Instantly, I look up to see the star-studded sky. It's a dreamy look with just a few candles lit and the smell of herbs in the air.

The kitchen counters are littered to the brink with

not only kitchen utensils but instruments I don't recognize. *Is this, like, witchy stuff?* I wonder. I don't get far into that thought when I catch the woman sitting at the round table. I hesitate, blinking a few times. She's...not what I expect a witch to look like. Father described them to me once when he was blackout drunk. He'd said the sea witches were like serpents in human form. That you knew not to trust one just by looking into their beady eyes. *"Frightening,"* he said. *"They'll make your skin crawl. Don't go to the docks, and never make deals with witches. Live by those rules and you'll be okay, Aria."*

Well, fuck.

My old man couldn't be more wrong.

Sitting behind the table is a refined woman who sits gracefully, her spine straight like she's being pulled up by a string. She's fair-skinned, her facial structure enviably elegant. With sharp cheekbones, a heart-shaped face, and long flowing black hair, she has gray eyes and plump, red lips. Older, yes, but well-preserved, her beauty still youthful despite the white strands in her hair.

My senses flare, and I tilt my head a moment, staring at her strangely. Why does my being hum familiarly?

She hasn't looked up at us. Her concentration is buried on the wooden mortar and pestle she's holding tightly. She's grinding something down, maybe a herb judging by the plucked stems I see on the table. She's lost in her own world, as though already forgotten of our arrival.

Hebnor rounds the table, standing behind her. He

rests a hand on her shoulder, squeezing it. "Darling, your visitors…"

She pauses, flicking those gray eyes up at us. Her gaze skims me fleetingly and rests solely on James. She looks him over with an indecipherable look in her eye. "I thought you were over theatrics, James, but I see you're still putting great use in your manipulation techniques."

I glance over at James as he crosses his arms. "No manipulation. If you're referring to my mask—"

"That, and *hers*." She flicks a dismissive hand in my direction. "Hiding. You're always hiding."

"I did it to get into this kingdom. To see you."

"You did it to also fix your ship and gain a crew, and no, my dear Heb didn't tell me that. I saw visions of the Tempest limping to shore. It might be time to put her to ground—"

"She can be fixed—"

"So, you've accepted your fate—you and the sea for eternity. Why then bring the siren?"

My heart skips a beat as her eyes look back to mine. There's a subtle glow in her gray eyes, and again, a feeling tugs at my center, warning me of her presence.

"You know why," James stresses simply.

She cuts her gaze from mine and looks back at him. Setting the mortar and pestle down, she leans back in her seat and waves a hand to the chair across from her. "Take a seat, Captain. You've come a long way, so I shall humor you."

James takes a seat, his giant body dwarfing hers. She looks at me. "And you, too."

But James raises his hand, stopping me. "She stays where she is, by Grimy's side."

Now Vanya smiles, and fuck me, but she has the most seductive sort of smile. Hebnor doesn't even see it from where he's standing, but he feels it. I can tell by the way he grips her shoulder that he's affected by her.

I'm starting to understand why.

"What's wrong, James?" she asks as she sets her elbows on the table and rests her chin in her hands. She studies him, amused. "Don't trust me?"

"Never trust a witch," he says simply.

"Then why are you here?"

"Because there's good in you. Because you're not fully poisoned by witch lust. I know this because of the man who stands behind you, guarding you even though it's truly you who's guarding him."

I look up at Hebnor. I see nothing but love in his eyes for the witch—such a strange duo.

Grimy shifts beside me, reminding me he's here, and that he's getting closer to me to emphasize the point that he is guarding me also.

Vanya tilts her head, studying James from across the table. I shift a little closer, aware that Grimy is following closely behind. I just want to look at James and see if he's okay.

This woman is raising all kinds of red flags.

"You know why I'm here," James repeats now in a steely voice.

Her expression softens. "The ruthless tyrant of the sea has fallen in love."

James taps the table with his index, saying nothing

for some time. She says nothing, either. She's waiting for him to crack. I sense frustration through the tether as he finally relents. "You're a very powerful witch."

Now her eyes dim, and she drops her hands, shaking her head quickly. "Don't do it, James."

"You have conjured up spells the Coven Academy could only dream of. You've helped King Wilheim—you're my only chance."

Vanya's eyes narrow, the distaste rolling off her in waves. "You've come a long way to be disappointed. I told you once already, James, that I couldn't help you."

"You told me I shouldn't be here, uniting with Wilheim when my purpose was out *there*, in the sea. You said Lona was a mistake, and that my true love was out there—"

"You were still being hunted by the last of the sirens," she cuts in sharply. "You would have driven Calla into the ground like your family line did to Goldspince with their lust for death. Your family encroached on the sea, and thus you were given your *reward*," she spits out the last word with disgust. "An eternity of misery on the ocean."

"Only bestowed upon me to keep the line going—"

"I cannot break the curse," she says, aggravated, even exhausted. "I was not the one who created it. The witch you seek has long perished. There is no way out, James. You must pay for the sins of your father."

My heart breaks as James buries his face into his hands. He drags his fingers through his short hair and then looks back at her. Wisps of black shoot out around him, like black fireworks. He's in emotional disarray, and

I can't stand the anguish I feel through the tether. I step forward, even as Grimy growls for me to stop. I don't. I make it to the chair and wrap my arms around James. I bury my face into his hair, kissing his head as I hold him tightly.

The room is silent.

I hear Hebnor whisper, "Vanya."

Vanya lets out a long sigh, appearing resigned. "I warned you the curse was cruel, James. The tether was created so that it would lead you to your love... so that you could not have her."

James looks up. "Except I have her."

Vanya gives him a long look. "You will lose her."

I'm standing right fucking here. I can't help but snap, "I'm not going anywhere."

She doesn't even acknowledge me. Her gaze remains fixed on James. "The curse is set so that danger will always find her. So long as she is with you, she is a magnet to it."

"That explains a lot," mutters Grimy, dryly. "Did the curse purposely make it so that it was a siren he would love?"

"That's not how a curse works," she retorts. "You can't make someone fall in love with you through magic. That's fate's job."

"But what are the chances she's a siren?"

Now Vanya shrugs weakly. "Poor luck, or the Goddess has a sick sense of humor."

"So I am to watch my love die," James states, his voice dead. "That's your answer?"

"Don't shoot the messenger," she returns swiftly.

"What will it take to make her immortal, then?" Grimy suddenly asks, a note of anger in his voice. He's had enough of Vanya's shit—we've all had enough of her shit. But his question makes my spine tingle, makes my heart blossom with hope for a brief flicker of a moment.

I'd do it.

I'd live an eternity by my captain's side.

Vanya slowly peels her gaze away from James to look at the old man. She shakes her head, a cruel smile forming. "James chose the two beings he'd take with him for eternity. You took the oath the second he put his bracelet on after you smuggled him off the ship that siren was attacking. He watched you and that dog starve, and thus he begged you to take the oath. He can't change it. Let me emphasize that, old man—*he* can't change that."

Just like that, my hope has been stomped out.

The room is uncomfortably quiet again. Holding James is like touching stone, hard and cold with no sense of warmth or comfort. He's gone quiet. The tether's gone numb. He's in shock.

His hope has been dashed—

"So my dream...my dream will come true?" he whispers, haunted.

What dream is he referring to?

Vanya seems to know.

Her face cracks with either sympathy...or pity. "Some variation of it."

"And I am to feel it through the tether?"

She takes a moment, swallowing hard as she composes herself. "Yes."

They're talking about my death.

I tremble, realizing he's had a dream of me dying.

I don't know what to say.

"But you can shelter her," Vanya assures him now, like she's trying to make him feel better. "What better person to be by your side than a siren? She will feel at home on the ocean." Her lips quiver as she looks down at the table. "A siren needs the water, James. Protect her vigorously, and she may live a full mortal life."

That's it.

Her way of dismissal.

"Make me immortal some other way," I sputter out desperately. "I'll do whatever you want."

She still doesn't look at me, and it bothers me more than I want it to. "A spell like that requires a powerful sacrifice. Something James' father had plenty in supply of given all the magical sea life he slaughtered in his quest for eternal power. Not only do I refuse to end the life of such a creature, but I don't believe any living being should have eternity."

"You wouldn't want to spend forever with Hebnor?" I question, voice as cold as hers. "Or forever enjoying the few days we get a year to be ourselves?"

Now her eyes shoot to mine, a flicker of surprise as she realizes I know exactly what she is. A siren. At least... some part of her is.

"No," she says resolutely. "There are places beyond death I'd rather be. Immortality is a sacrifice in its own right. You are denying yourself the natural way of things. You must understand the gravity of such a decision."

"I don't even get the opportunity to choose," I reply numbly.

Now she tilts her head to the side. "And if you did?"

"I'd choose him for eternity."

Vanya doesn't speak, but there's a current of emotion buried beneath her cold face. As a siren looking at another, I see the subtle glow in her eyes. A flicker of warm emotion; it's the only indication she's not happy about the situation.

"I cannot help you," she finally says, slamming that final nail of hope in the coffin. "Either you accept James for however brief a time you get, or let him go entirely. Good luck, Siren."

And that's it.

That's all the time we get with the witch.

CHAPTER 50

Aria

James is utterly silent when we step back out into the cool air.

Grimy is thoughtful as he glimpses at James with a heavy expression.

Surprisingly, Luca and Briggs say nothing to us, catching on quickly that something is very off. I'm still turned in James' direction, waiting for him to speak to me, but he's wandered off, away from the cottage and to a dark spot between the other residences. I can hardly see him. He practically blends into the darkness. Or maybe that's his magic at play.

The tether is mild. He's suppressing himself once more, and I feel a little fearful. I'm stuck between wanting to go to him and giving him space.

Grimy's voice breaks the silence. "Go to him, Aria, before he does something stupid."

"Like what?" I whisper.

"Like doubt himself."

I nod and begin to walk toward him. Behind me, I

hear Grimy call the fellas over. "We need to discuss what to do if things go sideways tonight."

"Is this, like, secret spy stuff?" Briggs wonders.

Grimy lets out a breath, saying dryly, "Sure, yes, Briggs, this is secret spy stuff."

Leaving them, I approach James slowly from behind him, testing the tether out by sending love down the line. I know the second he feels it, because he stops dead still and doesn't move. His arms hang limply at his sides as he peers down at the ground. I stop behind him, waiting for an acknowledgement.

He offers none.

"It doesn't change anything," I simply say, though an ache stings the back of my eyes. "I want you just the same. I just...I want to know you want me back, that...it doesn't change our trajectory."

He says nothing.

The tether is hollow.

But the darkness bleeds out of him, wisps of it shooting in all directions, the only intermittent giveaway that he is not alright.

"James..." I whisper desperately. "Don't shut me out! Talk to me."

"And say what?" he lets out, his tone as empty as his tether. "That this can work? That I can selfishly accept you into my fucking embrace while knowing I'm only leading you to your death?"

"James—"

"The right thing to do would be to let you go!"

My heart stops and panic floods me. "James—"

"But that's like asking me to cut my chest wide open

and drop my heart at your fucking feet." He turns to look at me, his chest moving fast as the tether sparks to life with his grief. It's so powerful, the pain of it, I'm knocked breathless as he watches me sadly. "I'd do it, though. I'd fucking do it if I knew you'd live a happy life elsewhere, with a man that can give you everything I can't—a warm home, a safe life, a child with your fighting spirit. Aria, I'll do that for you. Drop you straight back off at Norborne—"

"I'd just come right back to you," I cut in, shrugging in defeat. "If you left, I'd search for you, James, and the moment I shifted back into my siren form, I'd scale the entire ocean, waiting for our tether to spark." My smile is equally sad as I add, "There's no escaping me, Captain."

But he's not giving in.

The resistance in him is making him war with himself.

"You'll hate me, Aria," he says. "Even if I kept you safe, you'd grow old having lived only on the seas with a pillager, a smuggler with no title—"

"Are you trying to talk me out of wanting you?"

"I'm trying to make you see reason."

"I'm a big girl, James, you don't need to tell me what this means." I feel a surge of frustration now. "What do you think awaits me back at Norborne?"

"Your sisters for one!"

"My sisters lead their own lives. Honestly, there are so many of us, I doubt they even notice I've been gone. And anyway, they'd want me to be happy. They'd probably kill me for coming back and leaving you." Now, I'm tired as I come even closer to him. "You told me you were mine—"

"I am," he says heartily.

I press a hand to his cheek as I stare into his dark eyes. "And I'm yours, James, no matter what. I'll be yours for as long as I live, so long as you promise to take care of my heart, and to never leave the second something shakes your equilibrium. You can't speak for me, so let me speak for myself when I say that my life may be a blink of an eye compared to your eternity—"

"You'll be nothing short of the greatest period of my eternity," he cuts in, brokenly.

"Then don't push me away—"

"I'm not trying to—"

"Because if there's any part of you that isn't in this wholly, that can let me go, then do it—"

His lips capture mine, silencing me in one brutal kiss. His arms come around me, holding me tightly to him. He shakes around me, and I feel his horror mixed with need—a need to take me anyway he can.

He fears losing me.

He *can't* lose me.

I sense it through our connection, and it's devastatingly painful.

His hands roam my body, squeezing at me, gripping me around the hips, fingers digging into flesh as he pushes me back. I feel a stone wall at my back as he lifts me up. I wrap my legs around him instantly as he pushes my dress up. Our kiss is less intense now, lips brushing against lips as his eyes open slightly to look at me. I look back at him, aroused and equally needy, wanting every inch of him against me as many times in this lifetime I can get.

It's that realization that makes my arousal deepen.

That this is finite.

That every kiss, and fuck, and word matters.

So maybe the witch was right then—maybe this is just the natural way of things, and there's a beauty in that in itself.

Goddess, my heart is breaking.

We don't speak, but our breaths pick up as he undoes his trousers and plunges into me. It's not a desperate fuck. Nor is it rough. It's more in the middle. A scratch you have to itch. A fuck out of principle—to remind us it's the two of us, no matter what. That the world could fall apart around us and it wouldn't matter so long as our tether is strong and we have each other.

I groan, uncaring of how loud I'm being. I don't even care if we're seen, though I see the blackness around us and know he's used his magic to shroud us from view.

It doesn't even scare me anymore.

I look around him and into the abyss. It's just us, only us—

And what a beautiful thing this blackness is, after all.

To be obscured from an ugly world.

To know it's just two hearts beating in the void, gripping each other for dear life.

I feel him deep inside me, hitting that button that makes my legs quake around him. He's completely silent, his groans absent as he watches me carefully, reading my pleasure, running his tongue along my lips like he wants to taste it.

I feel so lost to the moment. The blood whooshes in my ears as my pleasure builds within me, hot and powerful. Every thrust is like a tiny pulse of pleasure, leading to an even bigger explosion.

He utters words.

Loving words.

Possessive words.

I could never let you go.

I'd kill any fucker you'd have chosen, Aria.

Ignore my insanity.

It's just me. I want it to just be me inside you, wanting you, caring for you.

I love you, Aria.

There was no one before you, there'll never be one after you.

I want you. That's all. I want you, Siren.

I come hard around him, swallowing his words with my mouth in one passionate kiss. He stills straight after, his cock jerking deep within me. His heart beats raucously against my chest as his head falls to my neck, buried there. I run my fingers through his hair as we ride through our emotions.

My lips tremble as the reality of our situation continues to sink in. The sadness of it. The heartbreak waiting for him upon my passing. Still, I swallow and push out into the quiet air, "If I live without you, it'll be half a life. I'd rather have a short, full life with you than an empty long one. Let's enjoy each other each day as it comes and make the most of this."

He stiffens a nod against me, but his emotions are blazing with grief and pain.

"I tried, Aria," he whispers against my skin. "And I'll keep trying. Maybe...maybe there's another way."

I nod, though full of doubt. "Maybe."

The idea ignites hope in him. He pulls away to look me in the eye. "I can find another witch. Maybe she'll be stronger. Maybe she'll know what to do."

On a deeper level, we both know it's a futile endeavor, but it's a purpose we're giving ourselves.

And without some form of purpose, what else would keep a hopeful flame burning?

Dropping his head, he captures my mouth and gives me a long, loving kiss before slowly pulling out of me and bringing me down to the ground.

And just like that, the black is gone and we're back to reality...and this fucking dinner with a king.

CHAPTER 51

James

The problem with Calla is it's so far off the beaten path, people despair at the notion of even paying a visit to it. No one wants to make a pit stop to Morda (for obvious fucking reasons), or endure weeks of Black Sea creatures, storms, and asshole marauders like myself.

The next problem with Calla is that it's filled to the brim with rich, high society snobs that don't want to leave Calla to have to visit Morda, to then endure weeks of Black Sea bullshit to get to the other side.

Combining the two, the biggest problem with Calla is that these rich, asshole snobs have nothing to do but get high off Gala Green and throw fuck parties where they talk about how great they are and swap fluids.

I imagine my visit is already stirring talk through the community, but given the state of my ship and the lack of men I bring along, I'm no threat. Therefore, the guards are at ease and bored. I wonder if they've ever broken up a fight. Calla may be high society shit, but in the world of danger, it's like facing off with kids with sticks than an actual fucking army.

And Wilheim, fat and bored and the biggest snob of them all, is the kid with the biggest stick. I think he's spent most of his time over the years decorating and renovating his fucking "castle" if you want to even call it that. It's like a stone mansion high off Gala Green.

We're led inside, Aria by my side, looking like a just fucked ragdoll. Even with the dull hair, she's radiant. I hope she can still feel my cum between her thighs. I hope it's everywhere and making a mess of that fucking dress I want to see her out of and back into my sweater.

We get led inside by bony guards and dressy maids. Aria is busy staring around in wonder, the extravagant rooms blazing by as we move from one rich dick room to the next.

Finally, we reach the great hall. It's even more pretentious than I remember, with more tapestries and paintings of Wilheim in ridiculous poses. My gaze lingers on a portrait of him in muscular form beneath his red, kingly attire. Behind him are swooning women—

I tear my gaze away, feeling a cringe come over.

This is hell personified.

Rich cunts flutter around the room, some greeting us in their prissy looking clothing. Meanwhile, I'm wearing a white tunic with the least amount of stains. I suddenly wish I didn't leave Grimy behind, but he stubbornly decided that we needed to have eyes and ears outside the castle, in case the Tempest got attacked and the last of our Gala Green robbed.

Aria mirrors my thoughts. "I don't like being here, away from the guys."

The amount of hungry eyes flitting her way is impossible to ignore. "In and out, Aria."

"That's what you said at Morda."

"When you ran?"

She lets out a sigh. "You'll never let that go, will you?"

"Never," I vow, but even that word sounds strained as I imagine a forever without her.

We stand there, watching as maids bustle about, setting up the large dining table. Aria's hands are clasped together as she stands beside me, pretending to be my submissive. Men edge a little closer as they eye her, one pretending to utter a friendly hello to me. I just stare hollowly at him, my cold stare causing him to flee.

"Silly me for thinking dinner with the King would have been a quiet affair," she says, eyes still glued to the bodies filling the space. Her eyes are large, watching with bewilderment at what she thinks is preparation for a large party.

I drift my hand across her lower back, settling my hand against her hip. "I'm sure the King has planned for a private dinner."

She quirks a brow, not understanding. This is all new to her—she has no understanding, no prior experience with the workings of royalty.

I can tell my siren wants to ask me questions, but she purses her pouty lips instead, watching a short man with a handlebar mustache reach beneath a maid's skirt. The maid jumps and he removes his hand quickly, crossing his arms over his chest as though he didn't just do what he did.

That was mild compared to what I've seen within castle walls.

We watch as a young man moves about the room, balancing a tray on his hand, offering guests a flute of a bubbling substance that has a tinge of fluorescent green. Champagne with a drop or two of Gala Green, I suspect. These fucks love getting high any chance they can. He stops before us, saying absolutely nothing, and Aria reaches for a glass.

A growl forms low in my chest, warning her, and she rips her hand back before it makes contact with the drink. Her eyes dart to mine. "Gala Green," I simply state and her eyes widen with horror as she realizes then exactly what makes the bubbly drink green.

Using my hand against her lower back to guide her, I turn us, directing our attention to a new group of castle-dwellers. Men flirt with women who aren't their wives—paid whores strategically placed by the King himself—their attention more on the women's breasts than whatever small-talk they're pretending to have, while the wives sulk against the large, picturesque window, acting as though they aren't aware their husbands are selecting which fresh piece of meat they'll be bedding tonight; they watch from the distance, but some will conspire to do the same. In royal culture, alliances are made and marriages arranged; love matches are rare and frowned upon.

Once darkness falls and we retreat back to the

Tempest, this very room will turn into a Gala Green induced fuck-fest.

"This would have been your scene had you remained a prince," she says now, thoughtfully, though I detect the teasing in her voice. "I don't see you charming everyone's pants off, James. You're being sort of scary, even in this form."

I pretend to look insulted. "You think I can't be that way again?"

"I guess I've never seen it."

"I can have the entire room surrounding me, eating out of my hand."

"That's a tall order from a filthy mouthed marauder."

It occurs to me then that maybe the quickest way out of this bullshit dinner is to play the fucking part.

I meet Aria's challenging stare. My tone is low and seductive when I murmur, "Stand back and allow me to prove you wrong."

My dark expression clears, my brows lift, the former arrogance of my royal status returning in full force as I step forward and charm everyone's fucking pants off.

Within ten minutes, there's a crowd around James as he talks aptly about his sailing voyages. The stuck-up men are enraptured, their ladies in fine gowns swooning as they stare at James with this look in their eye like they want him all to themselves. I sort of wish I didn't tease him because this version of James is unrecognizable.

Charming and funny, he talks with an ugly sort of arrogance. The kind that dismisses me like I'm just his whore on the side; the kind that flashes this pussy clenching smile to a lady or two, causing them to breathe a little faster. Holy shit, they'd fall to their feet for him, I'm certain of it. All he has to do is flash them that knee-wobbling smile—

Goddamn, he's doing it again!

I stand behind him, fake smile in place, but my insides are ablaze and I want to be away.

Back to the Tempest. To the smell of the ocean breeze. To Luca cracking jokes and Briggs' bickering over a non-issue. I'd be laying on the settee right this very second, reading with a lantern lit over my head while Rex napped in my lap. Grimy would be steering the ship and James would be sitting at the table before me, looking over the maps and planning the next route.

Suddenly, the crowd parts and the soft sound of heels on the marble floor brings my attention into focus. The air deflates from my lungs, and the air shifts. I distinctly realize I'm no longer on any man's radar.

The woman that appears in a tight pink gown before us is tall and slim, with raven black hair that is straight as a pin and ends at her chin. Her cheekbones are sharp, her dark eyes wide and almond-shaped. Her skin is bronze and perfect.

Instantly, I know this is Lona.

I feel foolish for envisioning an old lady.

If I'd done proper math, I'd have realized this woman was eighteen when she was engaged to James, and after a couple of decades, that puts her in her mid-thirties; still young, still gleaming with a youthful glow, and she is stunning. Drop-dead gorgeous, truthfully. My spine stiffens as I stand taller, heart beating fast as she comes to a stop before him. I want to look at James to see his reaction, but I can't stop looking at her.

"James," she purrs, and even her voice is soft and smooth.

"Lona," James says...*breathlessly.*

I quirk a brow as he steps forward, takes her hand into his own, and rests a kiss on her hand.

I can't help the jealousy I tear through the tether.

Immediately, he responds with a burst of love that

assures me it's just for play. But as he does this, he barely breaks out of character—his eyes solely focused on her as his heart thumps for me. The presence of the tether relaxes me, grateful in this moment that it exists between us. Had it not, I'd be going out of my mind with jealousy and doubts, resisting the urge to run *again*.

Instead, my shoulders relax as I remind myself quickly: this is in and out. It'll be over soon, and we'll be back on the Tempest, in the solace of our quarters. I'll make sure he takes extra care tonight fucking me after this shitshow.

"You haven't aged a day," she says, awed.

"Neither have you."

She lets out an infectious laugh. "Don't tickle my ear!"

I hover nearer, catching the panty-dropping grin he gives her. "I only speak the truth, Princess."

A throat clears nearby, and Lona slips her hand out of James' grasp and turns to an older man as he settles beside her. He smiles not-so-kindly at James. Lona immediately wraps a hand around his arm, saying, "James, this is my husband, Albert."

Now I feel totally relieved.

She's married.

Like James hoped she would be after the devastation he left her in. The happiness radiating out of Lona assures me she's moved on and is happy. They exchange pleasantries, the conversation and mood light, until Albert's gaze travels to mine. "Is that one yours?" he asks.

James doesn't turn to look at me. He simply responds with a slight twinge of dismissal, "She is mine."

His tone makes my heart sink, and I force myself to remember this is a ruse.

He's in character.

The character of a total fucking jerk, but it's fine, *I'm* fine, *everything* is fine.

"I wondered what you men do on the seas to fill your time," he continues, his eyes never leaving mine.

"Albert," Lona scolds lightly. "We don't speak of such things."

"It was a curiosity," he explains. "Now I can see that sailing has its perks, does it not?"

Lona looks at me sweetly. "You wouldn't want to touch a girl that's been used by so many, dear, would you?"

An arctic chill bursts through the tether as James says sternly, "This is Aria, and she is no whore. She is *mine.*"

Uh-oh.

How quickly he's shifted his demeanor.

I stare at him with wide eyes. That is so *not* part of the script, but the possessiveness he feels is too strong for him to ignore.

Turning to me, his eyes glow with pride, and he extends a hand out for me to take. My hand is swallowed up instantly as he tugs me to his side.

Albert sips on a flute, still staring at me like what James said has no bearing on his perviness.

Lona instantly apologizes, and I feel for her. "I'm so sorry, James! I had no idea."

"It's okay," I say, deciding to work my mouth in light of the awkwardness now. "Pretty dress."

Her cheeks flame as she smiles widely. "Thank you!"

Within minutes, the scent of food floods the air as a servant declares, "Dinner is served!"

Thank fucking Goddess.

IT'S ONLY when we're seated that King Wilheim's presence is announced. I have an idea of what to expect given the paintings of a burly, muscular, chiseled jaw man. Wilheim is fucking hot. One painting even had women swooning after him, and I have to say, I totally get why that would need to be added. A guy so glorious would realistically have a flock of women at his feet. Given how gorgeous Lona is, I anticipate this silver-haired fox to come waltzing into the room, all suave grace and shit.

James smirks at me from my peripheral, sensing my anticipation. "Tame those expectations," he whispers.

I'll tame nothing.

"Don't be jealous," I murmur back. "You men can't always be surrounded by only beautiful women. Us ladies need something to look forward to."

He just laughs, and in a matter of moments, I understand why.

The man that comes through with a crown that barely fits his gigantic head looks nothing like the paintings. My brows come together, confusion high as I wonder why anyone would grossly exaggerate themselves like this.

He's short and round, the red surcoat tight on his

frame. His tiny belt is studded with gems and gold. His sausage fingers sport a gold ring on every finger, too. In fact, there's gold everywhere. Bracelets, necklaces, even his ears have a gold stud in them. But that's not my problem with the man. It's that air of arrogance he walks in with. Like we're lucky to be breathing the same air as this royal cunt.

My eyes dart around the table, catching the stilted smiles directed his way. Yeah, there is no way in hell this man gets any voluntary pussy around here. Those paintings were a heartless lie, and shame on him.

James is seated in the guest seat next to the head of the table. The large, laborious breathing man takes his seat, his dark eyes latching immediately on James. I catch sight of some old food in his beard. *Ew.* "It's been quite a while, hasn't it, James?" he says, tone indecipherable. There's little warmth as he studies James.

"It has," acknowledges James.

"Still vying for your kingdom?"

"I've let the past go."

"Then Calamity Isle remains as is: a wretched wasteland."

"I'm sure a power will swoop in."

"And oppress your people?"

Whoa.

I glance around again, catching a few of the guests pretending to converse, though their eyes flit our way as they sneakily listen. Lona is across from me, with Albert by her side—Albert, who is still staring right at me.

"I was a child when we fled," James returns swiftly,

that charm still present. "And from memory, the people were already oppressed by our rigid ways."

King Wilheim grunts as he digs straight into the hot chicken leg he pulls from the still steaming bird on the tray. Lips smacking, he says, "I tried my hand at Calamity Isle many years ago. We braved the storms, made it with plentiful men to spare. Unfortunately, my men did not last long. They were run out by some huntsman and his clan. I've not thought twice of returning, not alone, anyhow."

"Best you stay on Calla."

"Perhaps." Wilheim shrugs. "But with all that Gala Green you delivered at my gate, I'm starting to think there are more devious ways to conquer." I don't ignore the way his gaze drifts my way. Neither does James. That same possessive tug pulls at the tether.

I don't look back at the King, pretending instead to eat. Albert's gaze is running along my see-through dress. I glance at Lona, worried she's noticed—

But Lona's looking at James, smiling sweetly as she listens intently to her father's words.

The king is being weird, casting glances my way more than normal. Red flags wave through my mind as I look down at the plate of food in front of me—my stomach twisted in knots as a horrible feeling slithers through my body like a snake.

King Wilheim is up to something, and I fear our attending this dinner has played right into whatever scheme he's concocted in his mind.

I t's fucking interesting how quickly the mood in the room can change.

The hall is too quiet.

Everyone's listening.

For a moment, the entire room becomes still, as though frozen in time.

Aria's tether goes a little wild with panic, but I keep my calm, though I'm distinctly aware that guests are standing and leaving. Either they know they're imposing on a private conversation, or they know something is about to happen.

I look evenly at Wilheim. "Are we to talk business? Is this why our guests are fleeing?"

"I have a proposition." Now Wilheim's gaze cuts to Lona. "Perhaps you can entertain James' woman for us, Lona. Give her a stroll around the castle—"

"She stays," I cut in.

But Wilheim's voice darkens. "You are my guest, James, and my daughter has been through an awful lot in your absence."

"Don't worry," Lona says, looking fearful of her father. "We'll just be in the hall, James."

Her husband, who's been frothing at my woman since the moment he's laid eyes on her, has the fucking cheek to look crestfallen.

"Aria," I start, my tone warning.

"It's okay," she reassures me quickly, and I can't help but feel like she wants to be away from the king and Lona's husband. I don't blame her. I knew the men would lust for my woman, but I didn't consider they'd brazenly eye-fuck her in front of me. Must have been the charming facade I played that gave them such entitlement. I should have remained a cunt.

I feel the pulse of her warmth and I relax a little.

The women stand, and Lona gives her a warm look, which further relaxes Aria. I think Wilheim's presence has more than rattled her.

"Just outside the door," I firmly tell Lona.

She nods, amiably. "Of course, James. We'll be right there from you should you need her."

They leave, and the tether stays strong as the doors close behind them, and Aria is removed completely from my sight.

I don't like it one fucking bit.

My palms are twitching, but I return my focus to Wilheim and say, "If you want to talk Gala Green, I can give you the rest I have onboard. We'll be leaving in the morning, so if you want it, I'll have to cut this dinner short and get my men unloading."

Mostly, I just want to get the fuck out of here.

There is no way in hell we're sticking around.

Wilheim smiles, and it's all wrong. "Gala Green is good when you reach shore, but it's when at sea I am most concerned about."

"I lost a lot in the storm," I tell him. "I have nothing to aid you—"

"You have a siren," he cuts in, that smile growing wicked now. "I have eyes and ears in the ocean. Vanya may not have warned me of your arrival, or what you're carrying, but my eyes and ears have detected a very strong presence on that ship. The presence of a full blooded siren."

I'm roaring on the inside, but I remain calm as I decide my next step. It would be futile to deny it. He's certain in his claims.

"How long have you had her?" he asks now, curious. "Is she the reason why you've not aged a day? I wondered why you'd rejected my daughter, but it makes sense now. To wield a siren, to have survived so long on the seas, ruthless and imperious. We may be far from the rest of the world, but your reputation precedes you. There is nowhere one can go without hearing of the ex-prince of Goldspince, now reaching for the title of King of the Underpass."

Albert is gaping at us from across the table, clearly not having been privy to any of this. I'm looking at him, my mind ticking on all the ways this can get ugly.

Because it *will* get ugly.

That's just what fucking happens.

Luckily, the tether remains strong, although it's a little more distant. I imagine the women are walking. I feel Aria's emotions. She's curious about something, and then sad. Why is she sad?

"This can go one of both ways," Wilheim continues, sounding cocky now as he gets comfortable in his chair. "I can give you a lot of trade. Gold, gems, anything you desire that you feel will be enough to let your siren go. Then we remain on good terms. It's more than you deserve, James, given the upheaval and anguish you had my daughter endure for years. Otherwise...I'll have to kill you right here and now and take your siren regardless."

I keep staring at Albert, and frankly, he's growing a bit fucking uncomfortable by it. I run my teeth along my bottom lip, counting the guards in the room. Eight of them, and they're growing a little closer. Albert's chair screeches back a bit, like he wants to get the fuck out of here.

I can use my darkness, I tell myself. Rattle them a bit as they find themselves obscured in it. It would buy me seconds—precious seconds to kill them.

"Well?" Wilheim presses, impatiently. "What will it be, James?"

Fucker can wait a minute while I decide how to do this.

"You want the crown, Albert?" I say aloud, voice deadly calm.

Albert freezes, staring at me in shock. "Wh—What?"

"I can give it to you. Just say the fucking word."

"I don't—"

But before he can finish, I grab the steak knife from the table and plunge it into the King's heart.

He screams, the pained voice causing his guards to come rushing at me.

Fuck.

Fuck.

"The crown is yours the second they're dead," I tell him. "Give me your fucking word!"

Albert shakes, jumping to his feet as he shuffles backwards, mortified of the blood pouring out of Wilheim's chest.

Before he responds, the guards descend on me, and before I can think to fight back, I realize the tether's grown distant.

Aria.

CHAPTER 54

Aria

Lona keeps talking in my ear, her voice soft and doting. But my eyes remain on the door, wondering if everything is okay with my captain.

"You'll have to excuse my father," Lona says now, sighing as she shakes her head. "He can come across rather heartless."

I force my eyes off the door to look at the beauty standing next to me, an apologetic smile on her face. "I can't imagine growing up around that."

She lets out a dry laugh. "You have no idea."

"You must have felt alone."

"Until eighteen I did."

I grow still, understanding what she means. "When James came."

She nods, looking down at her feet as a shadow of emotion flits across her features. "I grew very attached, very quickly. Probably more than I should have."

Sadness runs through me at the thought of her

heartbreak. I can't imagine living without James. "Does Albert make you happy?"

Lona's smile is wistful. "As happy as a woman can be when he eye-fucks your former flame's other half."

My cheeks heat. "I'm sorry, Lona—"

"How on earth is it your fault?"

True.

Still, I feel bad.

"Albert will make a fine king when my father dies," she tells me. "A bad husband, but a good ruler. I have a feeling Calla will change a lot by then. Whenever my father kicks the bucket that is. He just keeps going on."

A laugh bubbles up my throat as she giggles. At least she's got a sense of humor.

Staring at me warmly, she says, "You want to see where James and I used to go when we wanted to get away from all the castle drama?"

I hesitate. James would not approve if I left the door, but Lona looks like she wants to be far, far away from here. I have a feeling it's to do with the hurt of seeing Albert stare lustfully at me.

"Where?" I ask.

"Not far at all. There's a stairwell behind the kitchen quarter, and that's where we need to go."

I pretend to know where the kitchens are as I nod. "Okay."

We begin to walk down the marble hallway as I allow her to lead the way. "He came on that blasted black ship in the dead of night," she says. "Caused all sorts of chaos. I remember waking up to hysteria. Everyone thought we were about to be raided."

I look over my shoulder, memorizing the direction we're going as the tether remains strong. "He didn't anchor instead?" I ask.

"No."

"Funny, since he refuses to dock at night."

"Then he's come a long way."

I laugh. "Then what happened?"

"I wasn't there, but from what I hear, he was quite... demanding. You know how these royals are. I see he hasn't changed in that way."

She means the fake part he's playing. She thinks he's like this all the time. If only she knew I'd have kicked him in the balls if he so much as acted like a prissy, demanding royal.

No, I prefer my ruthless, savage captain.

"His reputation wasn't what it is now, but it was evident to my father that he wasn't...normal."

I'm cautious with what I say. "Normal?"

"Father instantly knew the Tempest, recognized the ship, knew this was the ex-prince who was beginning to raid and dabble in Green Gala. That he had some form of power."

Now I say nothing, offering only a smile as I pretend to be enraptured, though I worry they've found out about his immortality.

"To be able to travel in the Black Sea undetected— that's something any sailor or ruler would give up anything for. Most battles are fought at sea, so the alliance made sense."

I relax my shoulders. "It has helped him."

"Not only does he have the ocean at his feet, but he

looks completely preserved, while I...I'm just the forgotten love he probably never thinks of."

Now I shake my head, that sadness tugging on my heartstrings. "Not at all, Lona, he...he spoke of you, felt horrid about how things ended."

Lona's lips tremble as she stiffens a nod. She says nothing as emotions blaze through her eyes, her sadness and pain inescapable. We wind up going through the kitchens and then to a narrow corridor. Stopping at the end, she opens the door with a dark staircase leading up to the top where there is a lot of light. "This is where we would go," she says, voice thick with emotion. Grabbing handfuls of her dress, she begins to ascend the steps, her light cries echoing down at me.

I waver there.

Don't get me wrong. I'm sad for her and all, but this is fucking weird.

"You should see the view!" she calls down at me. "Oh, I remember it all now! The dances we had up here. The kisses! That man can kiss, am I right?"

My spine goes rigid, not liking that she speaks so candidly of kissing James. How heartbroken did he leave her? But she's got Albert now—the pervy soon-to-be-king.

Weakly, I call back, "He's pretty good at it."

The tether is very faint, and I wring my hands, unsure of what to do. On one hand I have a broken-hearted princess who is clearly still pining for my man and what could have been, and on the other, I should still be outside that fucking door.

I can't see Lona anymore, but I hear footsteps as she

roams the stairwell above. Her quiet sobs grow louder, and I sigh miserably, thinking back on my sisters and the countless nights I had to nurse their broken hearts.

This'll be quick, I tell myself. *Pat her back and come back down.* If she wants to still sob, that's her own prerogative. I need to get back to the door so I can feel James again. I'm worried something is going to happen to him. That this king will deceive him in some way. I'm anxious for him to be okay.

I climb up the steps slowly. When I reach the top, I'm awed by the moonlight streaming through the ceiling windows. Lona is, too, looking up, tears streaming down her eyes as she expresses her grief. "Things could have been different, you know?"

"I know," I say sympathetically.

"Do you ever wonder what could have been?"

"Uh, well, not really. My life's pretty good..."

"Well, you have James, so it would be." She lets out another cry. "I would have at least liked him to fuck me! Is he good at it, Aria?"

My lips gape open, and I have no words as I stare at her in my shock.

She's looking a bit desperate, still staring at the stars. "Instead, I have Albert, and he's just not the same, you know? For a while, I felt pretty special. But then I couldn't bear any kids and suddenly it was 'Lona, who?'"

Goddess, this woman's strife is out of control. "I'm so sorry, Lona—"

"And just when I think it can't get any worse, James' return is announced, and thus, my father schemes all over again! Prattling on and on how he's coming, how he's bringing another treasure with him."

I cringe, thinking of the Gala Green. At least this means the discussion in the dining room will go well. He'll get what he wants out of it—even more of the drug his people fawn over.

Hooray for Gala Green.

She comes to me. "Look at those stars, Aria! What do you feel when you look at them?"

I shrug, not in the mood for wistfulness, but I look up anyway. "I guess they're pretty—"

"He could have had a princess," she cuts in as her voice changes pitch, turning angry. "And instead, he chose a siren—a fucking fish! Disgusting. *Deplorable.* Even my father wants you!"

"What—"

A pressure suddenly slams into my stomach, twisting.

I gasp, a lightning bolt of shock tearing through me, along with horror as I look at her standing before me. It's not the face of a heartbroken woman that stares back.

It's of a scorned lover.

An angry, murderous lover.

Pain slowly radiates from my stomach as I look down, gasping at the handle of a knife sticking out of me. Blood pours out, and my legs go weak.

"What the fuck?" I let out.

Her teeth clench, the bitch looks like a crazed madwoman as she seethes, "*No one* can you have now."

Crazy.

So fucking crazy.

And fucking *ouch*, this hurts! Tears immediately stream down my face as I continue to look gobsmacked, realizing the amount of blood pouring out of me. It's running down my body. It's warm and dark red. I wrap a hand around the handle, my hand shaking as she steps back, like she's satisfied with herself.

Crazy. Crazy fucking bitch.

I'm going to die because I stupidly decided to pity this psychopath.

This is your fault, Aria. Not even the curse is responsible for this—you are.

Anger replaces my shock as I realize I'm probably minutes away from dying and that this bitch has taken away an entire lifetime with James.

With shocking calm, I lower my hand, too afraid to remove it from my body, not sure if it's something I should do. Instead my fingers slowly tug the fabric of my dress up and wrap around the handle of the switchblade secured to my thigh, pulling it out. With the flick of my wrist, it opens, and I'm pointing it at Lona.

My mind is on James and the thought of him having to grieve my death if I die in this stairwell tonight. My heart breaks in two as I reset my focus onto the woman who stabbed me.

If I'm going down, I'm taking this bitch with me.

Lona stares at me, growing still as her brows come together in surprise. Her gaze drifts between the knife in my chest and the one in my hand. "What are you—"

Screaming, I come at her with my hands outstretched, knocking her straight to the ground. Hovering over her, my breaths ragged, I take the switchblade and bring it down into her with the last of my strength. She screams, shocked, as I smile darkly at her.

The knife sinks into her chest, directly through her heart, and makes a bone crunching sound. Frankly, it makes me nauseous, but there's something a little poetic about the placement I've chosen.

The second it's in, I climb off her and barely make it a few feet before I drop to the ground limply, the burn in the center of my stomach unbearable.

Crazy bitch is still muttering under her breath as her lungs fill up with blood. "He could have had me. He could have had me..."

Despite it all, I feel pity. Her painful sounds make the tears run faster down my face.

Love is beautiful—

And ugly, too.

So ugly.

It was either her or me.

And now it's both of us.

She would have watched me die, maybe even finished me off...

"I'm sorry," I pant out, fighting to keep my eyes open.

I have to stay alive. I won't leave him, not when our time together has been so short.

I try to scream help, to push my pain down the tether, but it's barely felt.

Yanking the blade from my stomach, I wince at the pain and release my grip on it, letting it clatter to the floor. And before I can think of what to do next, my body betrays me and I'm pulled under.

My chest heaves and my fingers ache from the effort of strength it took to snap the final man's neck.

Eight men in all. Excluding the king, whose face is buried in the plate of food before him.

I killed three with my bare hands and five with the dull blade I ripped out of the hands of an imbecile who obviously was inapt at using it. I managed to use my darkness to disorient them, so it went off without a fucking hitch if I do say so myself.

I'm barely finished with my final kill, glancing fleetingly in Albert's direction. He's been crying in the corner, terrified I'm going to kill him, too.

"Congratulations," I growl. "You're next in line, cunt. Next time you see me, you better not stare at my woman again."

This is a fucking mess.

I've barely caught my breath, my focus back on the

tether. It'd been distant as I got attacked, and with all that was happening, I couldn't focus on it without getting stabbed a few times.

I hold my breath, shutting my eyes briefly to feel her.

Except, the tether's gone still—no emotion emulating from it other than my own.

Something suddenly feels very, very off.

Instantly, my darkness seeps again, surrounding me in a wispy cloud of rage. Bending, I pick up the knife that fell to the floor before my last fight, and grip it so tightly I'm positive either the handle or my fingers will snap from the pressure. I turn toward the direction of the doors and push through them, a knife held by my face in case of attack.

As the doors fly open, I'm met with silence. Looking from left to right, I see nothing but an empty walkway, the pristine flooring shimmering under the lights. No footprints, no trail. She could be anywhere.

Anxiety trickles through my body at the thought, and I push a wave of it through the tether, wanting to alert my siren, I'm on the move—and yes, I'm scared. Fearful of the dreams I've fought so hard to ignore or change the fate of coming true.

I will not lose Aria.

If even a single one of the disguised hairs on her head is harmed, this entire kingdom will burn to the ground.

"Please, Aria. Please," I beg to myself—to the Gods and Goddesses above who surely can hear me, who are watching me.

In a split decision, I veer left and head toward the copious amount of doors that line the never-ending wall.

I can't feel the tether at all, and I hope it's a sign of distance and not death.

It absolutely cannot be death.

I take off running, not caring how loud my footsteps are echoing off the vast stones and the high ceilings. I climb staircases, move past every door, turning corners and doubling back, checking every inch of the castle. I'm frustrated, my heart heavy in my chest.

"FUCK!" I roar, slamming my fists against the door I stand in front of. Nothing but hysteria fills me, and the sudden image of the Aria conjured from my dreams flashes before my very eyes—lifeless.

Dead.

Gone.

No.

Expelling a shaky breath, I close my eyes and think. I think about the castle, what I know about it, what I remember. The corridors and hidden passageways, the assignment of the rooms. I look around to get my bearings and realize I'm in the North wing—where the King himself resides. *Former* king.

Also, where his daughter used to reside.

Surely, Lona wouldn't have brought Aria to her old chambers—

A brief flicker ignites through the tether, so fleeting I almost miss it. *She's close.*

I begin throwing doors open, stepping inside with my blade raised, ready to strike at any attack. I've cleared the entirety of the wing, spooked half a dozen staff, before I realize she's not here. But I have no plans of giving up.

As I move down the long corridor, my eye catches on a portrait of the King that is slightly skewed. Instinct brings my hand to its frame, and I push it aside, revealing a divot in the wood, large enough for a hand.

The flicker through the tether returns—just a jolt—but it's enough to have me sliding my hand into the cleft of the wood and pulling.

The wall splits open, revealing a darkened staircase—the servants' stairwell—and at the base lies my siren. For a split second, I feel relief at finding her, but the moment my eyes scan her body that relief turns to pure, ice cold terror.

Aria is laying in the darkened passageway, a puddle of blood beneath her lifeless body. Next to her, Lona lies, her glazed, dead eyes wide open with my switchblade stabbed through her heart.

My body reacts and I'm moving, racing down the steps two at a time until I reach my siren. A glimmer of pain ricochets through the tether and another burst of relief hits me. If she can feel pain, it means she's alive. Though, the lack of potency has me feeling frantic.

Aria's on borrowed time.

Falling to my knees beside her, I immediately bring my fingers to her neck and feel for a pulse. It's weak, but there. My eyes drift lower to her body, the white dress I had her wear now stained red.

Stabbed.

My Aria has been stabbed in the abdomen as though someone was trying to gut her like a fish.

Lona.

In a daze, Grimy's incessant warnings on the nature of scorn run through me.

My gaze shifts to the woman I'd shortly been betrothed to and pure hatred swirls in my stomach. Reaching to her, I rip the switchblade from her chest before plunging it back into her heart. She's already dead, so the outcome won't change; zero satisfaction runs through me as the anguish sets in, heavy and hollow.

I remove the switchblade from her chest once more, wiping her blood onto her own gown, before pocketing the knife and turning my attention back to Aria. I waste no time and scoop her into my arms as I come to a stand.

"I'm here, my love," I whisper, bringing my lips to her temple. Her eyes remain shut, and her chest barely moves with breath.

Acting out of instinct, I follow the second staircase down, hoping it leads me somewhere to make a quick escape. Frankly, I'm surprised Wilheims' remaining men haven't found me yet, but I press on, ignoring the fact I could be caught at any moment. My priority is Aria and getting her somewhere safe, and figuring out how to save her life.

The staircase brings me to the kitchen and I then remember this is the exact staircase Lona and I would escape to for private moments.

She planned every detail of this. Lured my siren to her death.

No. I won't let her die.

The sound of water running and dishes clanking tell

me there are people in there working, but it's my best option. Using my body, I press against the wood until it gives away slightly, and peer around the corner.

Two men stand at a large basin filled with soapsuds, scrubbing cookware. Their backs are to me, and directly across from where I stand another door is propped open, revealing the darkened sky.

On silent feet, I strategically move across the space, keeping my back to the men. If they attack, it will be me who the attack hits, not Aria—but the duo is none the wiser of my presence.

The sound of water sloshing and a pot clattering to the floor, stops me in my tracks.

"Ah, shit," a squeaky voice complains. "Now I have to rewash the colander."

"How many times I gotta tell ya? Tighten your hands when ya clean. No one likes a slippery shithead creatin' more work."

I hold my breath, convinced I'm about to be discovered. How could I not? How do you miss a fucking pirate standing in the very same room, holding a woman who's bleeding profusely? And if discovered, I have no weapon of defense other than my hands, which will require me to set Aria down and—

I won't risk stealing away any more time I have to save her.

Not giving a fuck if these idiots hear me, I take off running and am through the open door before they can even think to turn around.

The darkness conceals us, and I move around the perimeter of the large, open area, taking in my surroundings and looking for any signs of ambush. I'm met with nothing but the sticky, humid air and night sky.

It takes several moments for me to gather my bearings, but when I do, I recognize I am on the west side of the castle and breathe out a sigh of relief. Calla may not be my home, but I know the land well enough to navigate even on the darkest of nights. And being on the west side of the castle is a gift from the Gods, because it means that just over the gates, is the ocean.

Sticking to the shadows, I creep my way along the wall that surrounds the castle and attempt to get as close to the gates as possible without being spotted.

Another slight flicker of pain illuminates the tether, causing me to stop and look down at the woman I cradle. Tilting my head to meet hers, I press my lips against her forehead and whisper, "Aria," hoping she'll wake up and her bright blue eyes will meet mine. But she doesn't, and the hope that lingers in my heart sputters.

Once again, I'm enraged, and the need to get Aria to safety drives me.

Ignoring the risk of being seen, I race to the edge of the kingdom's gates and squeeze through the opening. My large frame hardly fits and the gates produce a low groan, swaying slightly from the push of my body.

From the sliver of moonlight I have a straight view of the docks, the darkened silhouette of the Tempest looming in the far off background. Glancing up at the watchtowers above, I see one of the guards pacing around, moving from one end to the other, his strides swaying uneasily.

Strengthening my grip on Aria, I jog in the direction of the docks.

"Halt!" the guardsman slurs, sounding off. I ignore him and move faster. I'm unbothered by his demands for me to stop, his threats of shooting—he won't, not when I suspect he's hopped up on Gala Green. His shot would never reach me, anyway. I'm too far now and outside of the kingdom's gates and it's pitch black.

My boots finally make contact with the uneven planks, but as they do, my sight lands on another body. It lies in a heap, abandoned in the middle of the dock, halfway between me and the Tempest. As I approach, it becomes abundantly clear it's Grimy, laying lifeless with his legs bent in opposite directions, his neck looking bent and disfigured.

He won't be happy when he wakes up. Having his neck snapped is his least favorite way to die and an agonizing memory of the events that transpired on Morda.

Yes, Grimy will be furious when he comes to.

Crouching beside him, I lay Aria's body next to his and look down at the two most important people to me —both unmoving, both looking almost tranquil, while I feel anything but.

"Fuck," I mutter to myself, exasperated and at a loss of what to do. The heels of my hands dig into my eye sockets, and I press against them, digging my fingernails into my scalp to feel anything other than anguish.

Just then, Grimy inhales a sharp breath, coming back to life.

"Grimes," I breathe, watching the old man shake out

his broken legs one at a time, then roll his head to reposition his neck into place. He moves slowly, and with care, as he takes his time reconfiguring his body. "Grimes, I need you."

Still groaning, he rasps, "James?"

"Get up, old man."

Still lying down, he brings his frail hand to his neck, and rubs the tender skin. "Give me a moment to remember things. It takes a minute, doesn't it?" He works to regulate his breathing now as he runs through the events. "We parted from Vanya... I saw we were being followed by Wilheim's men...Then I tipped Briggs and Luca off about it, so we pretended to browse the market-place before luring them into an alley..." His eyes narrow in thought. "We left one breathing long enough to let us know of a planned attack and then...we plotted an escape. Yes, that's right."

"The guards—"

"Drugged."

"And Briggs and Luca?"

"They grabbed what they could from the chandlery."

This was a scheme then, right from the get go. I huff a breath, my eyes narrowing as I listen. Grimy takes another shallow breath of air, still recovering from his temporary death.

"When I returned to the docks to wait for you, I was attacked. The only thing I saw before all went dark was the shadows of two large men."

"The others?" I ask.

"Safe on board," Grimy tells me.

I barely react with the knowledge. I've lost most feeling. Body numb and broken, I let out a shuddering breath. "Grimes."

"What do you have next to me? My sight's still hazy."

One large, rage-induced tear rolls down my face, my heart twisting painfully as I emptily tell him, "Aria's been stabbed. She's lost too much blood, and the tether is fading. It's like the night of her shifting—when she nearly drowned. I can feel her imminent death. It's close, Grimy."

His body jolts from shock. Despite the pain of it, he turns his head to the face nearly pressed against his. His glazed, deep copper eyes widen in alarm. "Aria?"

My body shakes as I grab her cool hand. "There's nowhere to take her. This is it, Grimy. I feel her goodbye through the tether."

It's a light throb, a gentle goodbye. I feel a spark of love, and I crumble on the spot, bending over her. I wrap my arms around her slight frame and bring her closer to me.

I want to hold her.

I just want to hold her.

Her bloodied body is limp, and I feel her soul drifting. She's in my fucking arms and the tether isn't burning. Coolness begins to sweep through my chest, and I know this is it.

"I love you," I whisper through my anguish. "Don't go. Please stay, Aria. *Please.*"

"Put her down," Grimy says. "Listen to me, James. Put her down, son."

I shake my head, tightening my hold of her as his

large hand runs down my arm and to my hand to grip it. "Put her down," he repeats gravely. "Trust me."

Slowly, I detach from Aria and set her down flat on her back. I'm still over her, brushing her hair from her face, my tears landing on her lips. I brush them too.

"Did you listen to Vanya, my boy?"

"Yes," I whisper. "She said I'm to watch my love die."

"Do you remember what else?"

"The curse cannot be broken. I can't change it." My head drops to hers, and as it does, my eyes travel along her face. The glow of her skin has intensified, and I know instinctively her end is near—her siren nature is emanating once again. "No," I whisper to myself, fighting back the sense of hopelessness I feel.

"Look at me, James." Grimy's grip on my hand tightens, and he looks up at me with tears in his eyes—an emotion I haven't seen on Grimy since the day he and Rex almost starved to death. "James. My life has been dedicated to you, my boy. The son I never had. I would give up my own soul to protect yours. And I will. You cannot break the curse, but *I* can make it bearable."

He pulls his hand from mine and shifts his weakened body, turning onto his side to face Aria. He brushes the hair from her face, a muddled mix of brown and platinum as my masking retracts and the effects of her siren nature return. From her face, Grimy glides his fingers down her arm and picks up her limp hand in his.

I think I know what's happening, and it's like all time stops.

"Grimy—" I begin, but I'm lost for words.

No matter which direction this plays, I lose.

I either lose the love of my life, or the man who's stood by my side for decades.

As if he can read my thoughts, Grimy mutters, "We've lived a good life together, boy. It's time to let me go."

And with that he turns back to Aria, and with a firm voice he says, "Lives tied, immortality bestowed, eternal life unbound."

J*ames.*

He's the first thing—the *only* thing—I think of as I begin to open my eyes. Darkness surrounds me. Internally, I panic, wondering if I've left him. If I've *died*.

Fighting against the weight of my eyelids, I struggle to keep them open as the world becomes unblurred around me. Memories of what happened start to tear through my mind, making my head throb.

"James," I moan, his name practically unrecognizable through my lips.

It's dark out. The scent of sea air assaults my senses as my eyes come to focus. I'm on the ground and James kneels above me, my hand pressed between his.

I try to sit up, but he moves his hand to press me back, not allowing me to move. "Take it easy, Little Fish."

I shudder, the nickname now shrouded with negative memories.

"Mermaid," I croak through chapped lips, desperately needing water. "Call me Little Mermaid, but never fish. Not anymore."

He leans down and presses his lips to mine gently. A breathy tremor wracks through my body, the air expelling against his mouth. "I thought I lost you," he whispers, pressing his forehead against my own. "I almost lost you, Aria."

"But you didn't."

"And I never will."

I pull my head away from him and look up into his eyes. Reflected is a look of sorrow tinged with relief. "I wanted it to be your choice, Aria. Whether you live your days by my side as mortal or immortal, but watching you die...to see your body reuniting with your siren... Aria, your skin was glowing, and I knew your time was running out. *We* made a choice."

With his words, I turn my head and see Grimy sitting beside me. A silent tear escapes and rolls down his face as he watches for my reaction. Confused, I run a hand down my stomach. The wound in my abdomen is all gone. I barely feel any pain except for a dull ache. How is that—

My gaze shifts back to James, understanding dawning. "I'm immortal?" I ask, my voice small and timid, though my heart expands at the very thought of eternity with James.

James searches my eyes, words sitting heavy at the tip of his tongue, but it is Grimy who speaks.

"We watched the magic leave my body and enter yours. Saw your wounds heal before our eyes. You've taken my place as one of his chosen."

"But what will become of you?" I ask, emotion thick in my throat as I reach for Grimy's hand. He takes it and a small smile touches his lips.

"I'll live out whatever time I have left at sea on the Tempest. With my family."

Turning back to James, tears stream down my face. "And us?"

He leans down, taking both of his hands between my face, and coaxes my mouth to open with his tongue. He kisses me as though his life depends on it, taking his time to explore my mouth gently and lovingly. I kiss him back, never wanting to part from him.

Next to us, Grimy clears his throat, urging us to end our kiss. I smile against James' lips as he whispers so only I can hear, "You and I will sail across the seas for eternity, my love. We'll go wherever you desire, stop on any land you wish. We'll settle on sea or on land—whichever you choose to call home, we'll make it one. My heart and soul belong to you forever now, Little Mermaid."

Luca, Briggs, and even Rex look overjoyed to see the lot of us as we hobble our way up the ramp, James and I carrying the weight of Grimy's frail body between us. He's weak, both from age and the magic of immortality leaving him.

As we step on deck, I gasp at the array of men who stand before the small crew I'd grown accustomed to. Beyond them, the ship is lined with boxes and crates with what I can only imagine are supplies to fix the Tempest.

Luca makes quick work of overturning a semi-empty crate, scattering its contents across the deck and settling it upside down, before rushing over and lifting Grimy's arm over my head, scooting close to his body to take my place.

Together, James and Luca bring Grimy to sit on the crate, mindful of if he can sit without wobbling before they move away.

James straightens and takes in the sight of everything on deck—the new crew included. "You get everything?" he asks, directing the question at Briggs, who stands several feet away from everything.

Briggs pushes his hair over his shoulder and stands up straighter. "Everything we'll need to revive the Tempest back to pristine condition. And with the extra hands, it should take us no time at all. We just need to be a *clean* crew, not like the last one. I'll have the rules posted on the doors by morning."

"Even got us some new digs!" Luca exclaims triumphantly, reaching into a box and procuring a pair of black trousers that look entirely too small for any man on this ship. "Look at what I found for ya, Aria!"

I laugh, and a large, genuine smile overtakes my entire face as I watch Luca pull out a few more pairs of the small trousers, followed by some colorful tops.

"Thank you, Luca," I delight, so humbled that he took the time to think of me as he was ransacking clothing shops for the rest of the men.

James folds his arms over his chest and brings an

arm up to rest his pointer finger against his lips, still all business as he scrutinizes everything that's being presented to him. "We'll need time and a secure location to anchor for the repairs."

"Already planned, Captain," a man from the new crew speaks up, stepping forward. James and the man share a look, and James nods curtly, encouraging the man to continue. "While the sea is not my home, I know the islands throughout the Black Sea like the back of my hand. A few days' sailing from here is a small, desolate island. It's out of view of the kingdom, and if we sail around it slightly, we'll be hidden."

"Repairs should only take a few days 'round the clock with all of us helpin'," another crewmate adds.

"Very well. Let's prepare to disembark," James concludes in that imperious tone. He's trying to be calm and confident, but the tether is frantic. He needs us to leave *now*. In the dark. While the kingdom is about to discover their king is dead and the broken down ship at the marina is responsible for it.

The men scatter, already acting as though they've been prepped for their individual responsibilities on the Tempest. Briggs' doing, I have no doubt.

"What'll we do?" I whisper to him.

"I'll shroud the ship in blackness if need be and blend into the night," he whispers back. "They'll never see us on the water, and by first morning light, we'll be too far for them to catch up." He makes a humming sound, thinking. "Albert won't be grieving, but he'll play the mournful king for a little while, so he'll pretend to be searching for us."

"We'll come back in a hundred years?"

"Two hundred to be safe."

My chest swells with joy.

"After we get the ship all pretty, where should we sail to next, Cap?" Luca now asks, popping his neck and outstretching his hands like he's readying himself to steer for days. The sight makes me laugh—I'm fairly certain Luca has never steered the ship, at least not without Grimy's direct supervision.

James turns to me, encircling his arm around my shoulders and pulling me close. He buries his face in my hair, kissing the side of my head before he asks, "Where to, Little Mermaid?"

I tilt my head to him and smile widely. "To Norborne, Captain. Let's go home."

It's the dead of night, the cool ocean air trickles in through the open porthole. The bed next to me is empty. James is stationed in the pilothouse for night watch as we sail through the vast, wide-open ocean.

He could have assigned Briggs, but after the day we had, he felt he needed the time alone, steering his ship within the solace of the ocean.

Unable to fall back asleep, I slip into one of his sweaters and tiptoe my way out. I find him standing at the wheel, overlooking the Black Sea.

A single candle flickers nearby, casting a shadow as I enter the space, alerting James of my presence.

"I wondered if you'd find your way to me," he muses,

not turning around. His words hold a double meaning —he could be speaking of the present, or from his dreams.

"I'll always find you, James."

He turns then, outstretching his hand, and I move to him, ignoring his hand and instead crash into his chest. He wraps his strong arms around my waist and kisses the top of my head. The firmness of his body—the warmth of his skin—soothes me and fills the hole that's still resting in my chest, pulsating as fear continues to grip it.

I nearly died today, and if it wasn't for Grimy sacrificing his immortality, I would be dead.

"And I, you, Aria. Although I have a little less to worry about now that you're immortal," he chuckles softly as though the thought amuses him, and I guess it does, seeing as though now I can't die.

Tilting my head, I push up on my tiptoes and kiss him, pouring everything I have into the kiss, conveying what I long to tell him but struggle to find words for.

We kiss until we're breathless, our chests heaving. With our foreheads resting together, I tell him, "I need you," and hurry to move my hands down his body until I reach his belt buckle.

"Woman, I am steering a ship," he groans.

"Just a quickie, Captain."

"Fucking trouble, Aria, that's what you are."

I flash him a devilish grin. While I work his buckle, James glides his sweater up my body, forcing me to stop what I'm doing to lift my arms overhead so he can remove it completely. Once it's discarded on the floor, I rip his belt off and shove his pants down so forcefully, I hear the faint sound of seams bursting.

He catches my wrist, bringing it to his lips and kisses the inside.

He spins me around suddenly so my back is flush against his front. His hands glide up and down my body. "All mine, Aria?" he murmurs, nipping at my neck.

"All yours," I tell him just as his fingers skate along my core, his fingertips grazing along my folds. I shake, moaning needily. "Fuck me, James."

"What do you think I'm doing?"

"Playing, teasing..."

"Worshiping," he corrects.

"We have forever to do that."

But he doesn't listen.

Slowly, he drops behind me, commanding, "Take hold of the steering wheel, keep us straight. I'm going to shroud us just enough that none of the crew on deck can look in."

I take hold of the steering wheel, a little overwhelmed by how large it is. James kneads my ass, his fingers brushing along my pussy in light strokes. I grip the wheel tightly, moaning. I'm so wet, barely able to focus when he spreads my ass. I feel his hot tongue against my folds, lapping at me hungrily, his tongue prodding at my entrance—I might come on the spot.

"James, don't fuck with me," I tell him the second he pulls away.

"Just playing with you."

"I'm not having fun."

"You want to cut straight to the chase?"

"Yes, dammit."

He chuckles as he comes to a stand. "Turn to me."

The second I do, I'm pushing up the hem of his shirt with both hands, eager to see him. I dust my fingertips across his abdomen, which sends a chill through his body. His eyes darken as he gazes at me in that predatory way I love. I fucking love when the lightest of touches has the ability to weaken this man's knees.

He reaches behind him and grasps his shirt, pulling it over his head as he simultaneously steps out of his pants, leaving my eyes to worship every inch of his skin.

Will this ever get old?

Fuck no.

"You're beautiful, James. A creature designed by the Goddesses themselves. But I need the *real* you. Deliver him to me."

His kiss lands at the curve of my neck and he softly trails more up to my ear. Dusting his lips against it, he asks, "You want my scars? My gruesome truths?"

Turning my head, I catch his lips and thrust my tongue into his mouth. It's messy, raw, and so full of urgency. Our lips barely part as I breathe my demand through his greedy lips, "I want my ruthless captor. Give me the real Captain James Erickson."

A growl emits through his chest and he reaches both hands beneath my ass, gripping the skin tightly as he hoists me into his arms. My legs wrap around him and secure at the ankle. He holds me low on his hips, his cock standing erect and pushing against me, nudging my entrance as though it has a mind of its own and knows exactly where it belongs.

"Icht Nara A'benIff," James growls against my skin, and I pull back and watch with wonder.

James' skin begins to transform right before my eyes, every tattoo and scar rising from beneath his skin, his pristine hair growing longer, wilder. I run my hands through it, watching as the scar overtakes his face and his lip splits. I close the small distance between our faces and run my tongue along it, missing how it felt against my lips.

The moment the change is complete, he steps forward, pressing my back into the center of the helm and slams into me in one smooth stroke. Our mouths collide once more, his fingers circle around my wrists and he guides them up to each grab a spoke. My fingers wrap around the smooth wood and I grip them tightly, knowing exactly what's to come as he moves his hands to my waist, the bite of his fingernails digging into my skin while he repositions my body.

With every barbarous thrust, a strangled moan falls from my lips. My eyes roll back, and I lose myself to the pleasure—to the feeling of him inside me—our bodies moving together. James' grunts fill the air as he buries his face in the curve of my neck, sucking the soft skin so roughly, I know it'll leave a mark.

He doesn't stop there. He sucks more skin, grazing his teeth everywhere, up my neck, licking at my lips as he breathes harshly into my mouth, his groans leaving chills along my skin.

Pleasure builds within and blooms outwards, setting my body alight. Tingles ricochet throughout every cell in my body, and I know the slightest of touches to my clit will send me soaring.

James can read my body like his own, and as he slows his pace just slightly, he connects his gaze with mine and skates his hand down the entire length of my body until it reaches the apex of my thighs and meets my clit. His finger rests against it, unmoving, but every roll of his hip sends a small shockwave through it.

"Are you ready to come, Little Mermaid?" His eyes darken and he begins to move faster again, as though he's unable to physically restrain himself.

But I can read his body too. He's close.

"*Yes*," I moan and tighten my legs around his hips. "Please, James."

He swirls his finger, following the rhythm of his thrusts. He feels so fucking good, every part of him.

Heat scorches through me, setting every atom inside my body on fire, and I come with such force, tears escape my eyes.

James fucks me harder, chasing his own release. He slams into me repeatedly, bringing his own hand up to grab a spoke to stabilize himself.

"Forever," he pants. "We have this forever, Aria."

"Forever," I repeat.

His forehead falls to mine, the awe thick in him. "How fortunate I am…"

His movements are frenzied and when he finally finds his release, I can't help but wonder if the entire ship is now awake.

Collapsing against me, his heavy breaths mirror my own, our energy drained.

Lifting me by the backs of the thighs, my hands release the wheel-spokes. He guides us to the floor, laying us down—me on my back, him on his side, propped on his elbow.

A light sheen of sweat sits on top of our bodies and I shiver as a light sea breeze bustles through the pilothouse. James seems unbothered as he traces lazy circles against my skin, watching as goosebumps pebble beneath his touch.

"A siren could get used to this, James. Being loved by a cursed sea captain," I tell him, feeling its truth with every ounce of my soul.

His motions stop, and he brings his hand to my face, cupping it. His thumb skims soothingly against my cheekbone. The tether between us burns with a promise of forever, and love—so, so much love. It reflects through his gaze as he presses a chaste kiss to my lips and says, "We're just beginning, Aria, my love. We have the rest of eternity."

Just as I'm about to kiss him, I hear a man's horrified calls, "OFF COURSE! WE'RE OFF FUCKING COURSE!"

I burst out laughing as James jumps to his feet, spinning the wheel.

Bending to retrieve my sweater, I toss it over my head and begin to make my way back to our quarters as footsteps race up and down the deck, listening to the men screaming instructions as we deviate off course.

I press a hand to my mouth, trying to swallow down my laughter as one of them yells, "Who the fuck is this tattooed, naked fella and where the fuck's the captain?"

Oh, Goddess.

Norborne is in our rearview, and what a shitshow visit that was.

What's worse than one siren?

All fucking six of them together. I swear, they're just as wicked in human form as they are in siren form.

And don't get me started on their old man.

I hope I never have to see that old drunk again, but at least he didn't give me any shit. He took one look at me in my true form and looked like he'd swallowed his tongue whole. Part of me pities the old man. He seemed to have gone astray when their mother died, but it's no excuse to thrust six girls in two bedrooms and drink your soul away while they fought to bring themselves up.

No wonder Aria was a dreamer.

No wonder she flocked to the docks to escape.

My heart. I can't believe it's possible, but I've fallen even more in love with her just seeing where she's grown up.

Fucking hellhole Norborne is. If I have to see another person shoving the good word of the eternal Goddess down my throat, I might kidnap them just to watch them walk the plank.

Fuck that and hell no, and I don't plan on seeing this eternal Goddess when I have an eternity with my Siren by my side.

It took us nearly ten months to get there. We took our time going from port to port. The sail was all kinds of bullshit, but having so many hands on deck meant we got the ship up to scratch in record time. The Tempest gleams glossy and new. Sails are repaired, the holes gone, the bilges and engine room in tip-top shape.

As we leave port, that damned hellhole behind us, I walk up and down the deck, hands clasped behind my back, watching everyone come and go. Luca's roaring demands, giving men a hard time. That man's taken his promotion a little too far. Briggs is here somewhere, being absolutely fucking useless, but you know what? I wouldn't have him any other way.

I get to the bow of the ship where a wary Grimy stands, looking more withered than I've ever seen him before. Mortality has softened him up, made him appreciate every day as it comes, and I know he's content to go when it's time. To reunite with his soulmate, waiting patiently for his arrival. Rex sits at his side, tail wagging, as I approach.

"What are you doing, old man?"

He grunts, heaves a shrug. "Oh, you know, just looking out."

"Looking for anything in particular?"

"Not at all. It's a lovely day. Beautiful waters. No harm in looking, is there?"

The last two days, he's been fidgety and concerned. As we got ready to leave the port of Norborne, he spent most of that time staring out into the sea. Waiting, worrying, and fussing.

I grin, knowing what he's truly doing as I scope out the ocean before us. "She's alright, Grimy. She's done this before, you know."

Grimy heaves a sigh. "I don't like her being so far from us."

"But she's not," I assure him, wrapping an arm around his shoulders as I tug him close to me. His body relaxes in my hold. "She's closer than you think. Probably on her way back. In fact, I think the little shit-stirrer is going to be a problem. Her and her sisters are having too much fun."

He catches my meaning and stares into the horizon, at the dark clouds forming. "She wouldn't, would she?"

I grin just as thunder booms, and the sky crackles, the promise of a storm coming.

"She just fucking did." I pull out my pocket watch, my smile growing from ear to ear. "We have six more hours before the shift. Buckle up, Grimy, a storm is coming."

Acknowledgments

Thank you so much for reading Siren, the first book in the Twisted Heroes series by R.J. Lewis and A.R. Rose! We hope you loved this reimagined take on a beloved fairytale as much as we loved bringing it to life. Stay tuned for more fun from R.J. Lewis & A.R Rose!

We'd like to take a moment to say some very important 'thank you's' to our amazing teams standing behind us!

Thank you to our amazing editor for this project, Virginia, and to our two wonderful proofreaders Nicole and Amal. You three helped pull this book into tip-top shape and we could not be more appreciative!

Next, thank you to our families and friends who stood behind us and cheered us on throughout the many long days and nights writing Siren.

To the fabulous influencers who have helped spread the word about this book—we couldn't have done it without all of you amazing book lovers supporting us.

And to the readers, thank you so much for taking a chance on not only our first collaboration project, but our first book in the new-to-us Fantasy Romance genre.

We love you all so much!

OTHER TITLES BY R.J. LEWIS

The Ignite Series
Ignite
Burn
Ashes

Loving Lawson Duet
Loving Lawson
Saving Lawson

Borden Duet
Borden
Borden 2
Borden 3
Hawke (Spinoff)

Blackwater Boys
Conor Thames 1
Conor Thames 2
Locke Book 1

Captive Series
Captive Book 1
Stolen Book 2

Mister West Duet
Mister West

Sir

Unbroken Series
Unbroken Book 1
Unbroken Book 2

Standalones
Sex, Lies & Nikolai
Obsessed
Kiss a Stranger

OTHER TITLES BY A.R. ROSE

Ridgewood Series
Between the Flames
Wicked Games We Play
Marked By Cain

Standalones
Wreck Me
Only One Night

Twisted Heroes
Siren

With a Kiss Duet
Sins of Sorrow
The Sinners (Novella)
Sins of Bliss

New York Times and USA Today bestseller, R.J. Lewis, is the number one bestselling author of the Ignite series, the Loving Lawson series, the Borden series, and numerous other titles. At the age of 22, Lewis nervously fulfilled her year's resolution (a week before the year was out) and published her first title Ignite and has never stopped writing since.

She has been writing all her life and looks forward to sharing her stories with readers who are interested in character growth and romance of the unconventional kind.

A.R. Rose's greatest job in life is being a mom to her two boys. She is a born and raised California native who loves to hang out at home with her kids and her dog.

A.R. realized her passion for writing in the third grade, although it wasn't until early 2022 when she began to pursue it. Now, if she skips a day of writing, she feels as though her day is incomplete.

On any given day, you will find A.R. toting around her laptop and her Kindle, with a coffee in hand, daydreaming about the characters and worlds she's building. She is grateful to have the opportunity to bring her stories to life and is excited about her journey as a romance writer.